ABOUT THE AUTHOR

Stephen Goldenberg studied Law at Oxford University and, subsequently, enjoyed a career as an English and Media Studies teacher in London schools. He has previously published books and articles on English teaching and broadcast on educational issues on television and radio. He has published two previous novels – *Stony Ground* and *The Lying Game* (Matador). He is now living in London and the Aveyron in South-west France.

Visit Stephen at
www.stephengoldenbergauthor.com

CAR WHEELS ON A GRAVEL DRIVE

ACCUSATIONS
MURDERS
LIES...

STEPHEN GOLDENBERG

Matador
9 Priory Business Park,
Wistow Road, Kibworth Beauchamp,
Leicestershire. LE8 0RX
Tel: 0116 279 2299
Email: books@troubador.co.uk
Web: www.troubador.co.uk/matador
Twitter: @matadorbooks

ISBN 978 1785891 953

British Library Cataloguing in Publication Data.
A catalogue record for this book is available from the British Library.

Typeset in 11pt Stempel Garamond Roman by Troubador Publishing Ltd, Leicester, UK

Matador is an imprint of Troubador Publishing Ltd

To Sue for sharing many Aveyron adventures

1

It was the sound of car wheels crunching down his gravel driveway that woke him up that morning. He opened his eyes only to close them again to keep out the glare of sunlight flooding through his unshaded window. Who could be visiting them at this hour of the morning? He glanced over at the digital clock on the bedside table. Ten-thirty. Okay – not as early as he'd thought – but then, who would be paying them a visit at any hour of the morning – or for that matter, afternoon or evening?

Still half asleep, he stretched out and instinctively snaked his arm over to the other side of the bed only for his hand to paddle around in the empty space where Julia's warm comforting body should have been. It took a couple of seconds for him to register why she wasn't there before he turned away from the empty half of the bed and thumped his pillow in frustration. He knew he was being stupid. She'd only been gone for three days but how long should he expect this to continue? In a month's time, six months, a year, would he still be suffering this start-of-the-day amnesia?

He'd always been an early riser but, for the past few days, he'd found it hard to get out of bed much before midday. Maybe his problem was that he didn't have any reason to get himself out of bed first thing in the morning. No regular job to go to, no vital chores that needed doing round the house. He made a mental note – his first step on the road to recovery must be to establish a solid daily routine and then stick to it. Keep yourself occupied – wasn't that the advice that was always given to the bereaved to aid their recovery? Okay, Julia wasn't dead but, as far as their relationship was concerned, she may as well have been.

The sound of car wheels had stopped to be closely followed by the opening and closing of the doors and the crunch of footsteps approaching the house.

*

Gilles Montfort was nervous. This was the most serious investigation he had ever been assigned to. He had only been chosen for it the previous day because his superiors deemed him to be the most proficient English speaker in the department. For most of the slow drive down from Aurillac that morning, he had been running through in his head the English phrases he might need to use. He had had little opportunity to use his English in the past couple of years. The only professional occasion had been a year ago when he had acted as translator for two young English building workers who had stolen and crashed a motorcycle after a drinking binge.

The closer he got to his destination the less confident he felt. It was not only that he had to speak English but also the delicacy of what he had to talk about that concerned him. It could be embarrassing, not to say hurtful, if he were unwittingly to use inappropriate words or phrases. Elodie, the female officer who was accompanying him, was no help. She had some English but he had quickly ascertained that it was too limited for her to act as a guinea pig for him during the journey. She'd been sent along as a silent partner. His boss felt that a female presence would have a calming effect in such an awkward situation.

For the same reason, it was felt appropriate for them to

wear their own clothes rather than appear in uniform. Maybe it would have a calming effect on the Englishman, but it hadn't helped Gilles to relax. He liked his uniform. He liked not having to think about what to put on in the morning. He liked the fact that everybody knew automatically who and what he was whereas, this morning, the first thing he would have to do was wave his identity card and explain. It wasn't even as if he had been able to dress in the comfortable casual gear he usually wore when he was off duty. In the circumstances, he'd decided that his dark suit, white shirt and sober tie were more appropriate – clothes he hadn't worn since his cousin's wedding over a year ago.

He hadn't been to this part of the Aveyron before but he immediately recognised the old stone-built house with its pigeonnier, its powder blue shutters and its barn converted into additional accommodation, as typical of the kind of property bought up by the British, Dutch and Germans looking for rural French houses they could convert into smart holiday or retirement homes. He wasn't sure what to feel about this. Some of his colleagues were vociferous in their disapproval claiming that it put up property prices beyond the reach of young French couples and made it difficult for the older generation of Aveyronnais who had moved away to work in the cities to be able to afford to come back and spend their retirement in their patrimonial area. On the other hand, it was a boost to the local economy and had rescued many old village and rural houses that would otherwise be crumbling ruins.

He walked up the worn pitted stone steps to the front door, grasped hold of the identity card hanging from a lariat round his neck and turned his head to check that Elodie was ready before rapping on the frosted-glass panel.

✽

Jeremy studied the black Citroën in the driveway from the bedroom window and caught a glimpse of the two people walking up the steps to the house. He didn't recognise them. They were youngish, mid-thirties, and smartly dressed. His first thought was that they had seen one of the signs on the road into the village advertising the gîte, but the car had a French registration and it was very rare that they rented to anyone other than the English or Dutch and then it was almost always through the internet. His second thought was that they were trying to sell him something, although that was unlikely – in the few years they had lived there he couldn't remember them ever being visited by door-to-door salesmen. His third thought was that he would ignore them and go back to bed. Whoever they were, he was in no mood to speak to them. But he changed his mind. It was so unusual to have visitors that he was intrigued. If it turned out to be something trivial, he'd get rid of them. He slipped on his dressing-gown, descended the spiral staircase and crossed the open-plan living room to the front door.

"Monsieur Halliday?" The man held out a plastic card attached to a red lead round his neck. Jeremy didn't look at it but stared instead at the man's dark grey suit and short black hair, neatly combed and gelled. The woman was also conservatively dressed in a dark blue jacket, white blouse and black skirt. Their appearance triggered a memory from six months ago when they'd been visited by a family of Jehova's Witnesses. Before he could formulate in his head the French for "I'm sorry but I'm not interested", the young man started to speak in French-accented English.

"We are sorry to disturb you but we are police and we have a serious matter to speak about with you. May we come in?"

Jeremy continued to stare at them as if he didn't understand. He'd prepared himself for the fact that he might not understand as he'd expected them to speak in French. His French was improving but he was still far from fluent and found it especially difficult to tune in to a conversation when he wasn't sure of the likely subject-matter.

The policeman looked uncomfortable, still holding out his identity card, as he stood waiting for a response, thinking of what else to say.

Jeremy finally found his voice. "Of course. Come in."

He ushered them over to the far side of the room behind the open staircase where there was a sofa and two armchairs.

As they made themselves comfortable in the armchairs, he tried to guess what their visit might be about. Probably something to do with some element of the interminable French bureaucracy – some official form that he and Julia had forgotten to fill out or some local tax they had failed to pay. But as he sat on the sofa waiting for them to explain, he remembered that the young gendarme had referred to a 'serious matter'. Vendillac wasn't exactly a crime hotspot and he hadn't heard of anything happening in the village but then he had been closeted away for the past few days and hadn't seen or spoken to anybody.

"Can I get you something to drink? Coffee? Tea? Water?" He was gasping for a coffee.

"No. It's okay, thank you."

"Non, merci," the young woman muttered.

Jeremy adjusted his dressing-gown, draping the folds over his bare legs. He pictured how he must look to these scrubbed up, immaculately turned out young police officers. His bare grubby feet. His shabby blue towelling robe with the large yellow patch where he'd spilt bleach on it. His unwashed greasy hair sticking out at all angles. His stubbly face – it must have been four or five days since he'd shaved. A decidedly shifty person is what he must look like – a criminal – a rapist or a child-molester. That last thought sent a chill through him, bringing back uncomfortable memories of the last time he'd spoken to police.

"If what you want to talk to me about is going to take some time, maybe I could quickly get washed and dressed. I've only just woken up. I was working until very late last night," Jeremy lied.

"It won't take too long," Gilles said. He didn't want to sit round waiting for the Englishman to get dressed. It would only increase his nervousness and ratchet up his discomfort.

"It's about your wife, Madame Julia……Won…… Wonrit." He had difficulty pronouncing the surname. He kicked himself for not checking on it before they left the station. He paused. This was the difficult bit. He took a second to study Jeremy Halliday's face for any sign that he knew what was coming but it only registered curiosity.

"She's not actually my wife," Jeremy corrected him. "We are partners but we're not married."

"Yes, of course. I'm sorry." He paused. "I'm afraid it's bad news. It's not easy to say. Your…partner's…… Her body has been found in her car north of here. In the hills near Aurillac."

Jeremy's expression didn't change. It was as if he hadn't heard or didn't understand. Slowly, the policeman's use of the word 'body' registered in his brain.

"I'm sorry but I don't understand……" He was holding his breath as he waited for the officer to explain.

"Yes. I'm very sorry to have to tell you such news. She was found in her car yesterday afternoon. The car had been put on fire and it take us time to identify the body."

Jeremy shook his head vigorously. "A body? A dead body? There must be some mistake then. It must be somebody else. It can't be Julia."

"Why do you say that, Mr. Halliday? When did you last see your wife…partner?"

"Three days ago. She left here to travel back to England. She was going to stay with her sister. She'll be there by now." He spoke confidently as if his words would instantly clear up this misunderstanding.

"You know she is in England?" Gilles said. "You have talked to her?"

"Well, no. Not exactly." Jeremy thought about the number of occasions over the past few days when he'd been tempted to pick up the phone and dial her mobile but had decided it was best to wait.

"So you do not know she arrived in England." The gendarme's voice was slow and gentle. It was understandable that the man didn't want to believe that his partner was dead. It was his unpleasant task to make him realise the truth but he was trying to do it tactfully.

"Sorry. Where did you say the body was found?" Jeremy's head was clearing and he was starting to see evidence that the police must have got it wrong.

"Near Aurillac. You know where is Aurillac?"

"Yes, I know it. It's north-east of here. That's why it must be a mistake. That's not the road back to England. Not the route we take anyway."

Gilles realised with a growing sense of unease that there was a limit to how considerate he could be. In as gentle a way as possible he needed to make Monsieur Halliday come to terms with the reality of the situation.

"Mr. Halliday. Let me explain more what we have found. A French family walking in the hills near Aurillac found a burnt car at the side of the path. At first they just think how horrible that people dump a old car in beautiful countryside and they go to carry on walking but one of them see something in the car and go over to it. There is a body in the driver seat. They call the police. To make it short, the body and the car are not fully burnt. The car is a dark blue Volkswagen Golf, registration plate LTO 4ZYN. Is that Madame Julia's car?"

Jeremy stared at the gendarme as if he needed time to think about it.

"Yes, that's her car."

"Okay. The car was very full with cases and boxes. Of course, most of it was burnt in the fire but there were things in the back which were not much damaged. Some of them were documents......papers which identified a Miss Julia Wonrit."

"It's Wainwright...W-A-I-N-W-R-I-G-H-T......Julia Wain...wright." Jeremy corrected him as if enunciating Julia's name correctly would confirm her as a living breathing person rather than this other, dead Julia – this Miss Wonrit – who was clearly somebody else.

"Again, Mr. Halliday, I'm sorry to say it but our investigation team now confirms with medical records in England that the body is most certain to be Miss......Wainwright." He pronounced the name with exaggerated care. "Of course there are more tests to do on the body – to find the cause of death."

Jeremy stared uncomprehendingly at the gendarme and then shifted his gaze to the young woman. She stared back impassively.

"I'm sorry but I just don't understand. It doesn't make any sense. I mean why would she......where was she......?" His brain couldn't formulate the words he wanted to say. And then, whatever it was he had wanted to say, slipped away. He looked up at the ceiling focussing on a large cobweb hanging from one of the oak beams.

"I know how difficult this must be for you." As he was speaking, Gilles realised he had very little idea how difficult it was. "We need to ask you much more questions but it's not necessary to ask them all now. You need some time to recover yourself." He paused while Jeremy lowered his gaze and looked at the Frenchman. "But I would like to ask you one more question. What was the reason for Madame Wainwright's visit to England?"

"She was going to visit her sister mainly, but also on business. She's a designer – a fashion designer." Jeremy answered automatically without pausing to consider whether he should be telling this policeman the truth. After all, it wasn't entirely a lie – it just wasn't the full truth.

"Was it going to be a long visit? I ask this because her car was very full of things. A lot of clothes, books, papers."

This time he did pause and consider whether to tell the full truth but decided against it. He needed more time to think things through. Despite everything the gendarme was telling him, he knew this must be a mistake. A case of mistaken identity. Julia couldn't be dead.

"It was probably going to be quite a long stay. She had a lot of business to do. She sells her designer stuff to shops and stores. She'd be doing a lot of travelling around." Jeremy looked at the gendarme trying to ascertain whether he believed him. There was no sign one way or the other. "Anyway, Julia never travels light. I always complain to her when we go anywhere that she's packing far too much stuff. Unlike me. I'm the opposite. An overnight bag with some clean underwear and a toothbrush does me." He smiled at the gendarmes and they both squeezed out a faint smile in return.

"I won't ask you any more questions for now but I have to tell you what will happen next in the investigation," Gilles Montfort said.

Jeremy nodded. He was still feeling uncomfortable about not telling the whole truth but he decided to wait and hear what the gendarme had to say.

"The judge who is in charge of the investigation – Judge

Bouchon – need to ask you some more questions. If you feel okay to do it, he would like to interview you at three o'clock this afternoon at Villefranche gendarmerie. We can send a car to bring you if you wish."

"No. That's fine. I'm sure I'll be up to it. Might as well get it over with. I have shopping to do in Villefranche anyway. I can drive myself."

Gilles realised that the full import of what he had told the Englishman was still not registering. He was talking as if this was all part of a routine day's activity. A quick trip to the shops and then an interview with a judge about his partner's mysterious death.

"Bon. One more thing. In about half hour, our research team will arrive here to make a investigation of the house........."

Jeremy held up his hand as if directing traffic. "Sorry. It's taking me a while to get my head round this. I don't want to sound stupid but are you saying this is like...a murder investigation? You think Julia was murdered?"

Gilles took a deep breath. "We don't know for sure until we have full results of the examination of the body but, of course, it is a suspicious death. It is very likely there has been a crime."

Jeremy's mind was racing. He was struggling to take it all in. He was still half hanging on to the belief that it was all a mistake – the body must be somebody else. The only thing he felt certain about was that it was not the right time to tell them that Julia had left him.

"Does that mean I'm a suspect?" He forced the words out accompanied by a twisted grin.

"There are standard investigations that must be done with this kind of death, Monsieur Halliday. That is why the team will search the house. No-one is suspect until we know how Miss Wainwright died."

Gilles paused, while Jeremy stared blankly into space, looked across at Elodie and then started to rise from the sofa. Jeremy snapped out of his reverie and stood up with him.

"There is someone who can be with you – help you? A friend in the village?" It was Elodie's soft voice speaking. Both the men turned towards her as if surprised to find there was someone else in the room with them.

"Merci, Elodie," Gilles said. "Elodie is right. This is a very difficult time for you. Maybe there is someone near who can come to be with you? We could go and ask them for you."

"No. I'll be alright. Don't worry."

He had got to know some people in the village but there was no-one he was that close to. Anyway, he felt he needed time on his own to think things through. The last thing he wanted was to have to discuss it all with somebody and then the whole situation becoming gossip around the village. Of course, it would be that soon enough anyway.

As they crossed the room and reached the front door, Gilles turned back towards Jeremy.

"Je suis désolé. One last thing, Monsieur Halliday. You said Miss Wainwright was visiting her sister in England." He took a small black notebook out of his jacket pocket and flipped over a few pages. Is that Miss......" He paused taking care again to find the correct pronounciation. "Hattie Wainwright? Her address is in Brighton?"

"Yes, that's right. Hattie. That's Julia's sister."

"Bon. We will need to speak to Miss Hattie. Would you like that we contact her first and tell her about her sister's death or maybe you would like to tell her yourself?"

Jeremy stood still and took several seconds to think about what the gendarme was saying. Suddenly, there was a stampede of consequences from Julia's death crashing round in his brain. Having to tell people was one of them.

"It's okay. I'll phone her."

"I'm sorry to ask it. I know how difficult it will be but, if you could do it soon and let us know this afternoon because we do need to talk to her."

"Yes. I'll do it straight away." He tried to sound confident and in control. He knew that, once he phoned people and told them Julia was dead, it would mean he could no longer pretend to himself that the body in the car couldn't be her. It was tempting to leave it up to the police to phone Hattie but he knew he would have to do it. Hattie wasn't his biggest fan. Since the trouble he'd been in back in London, Hattie had tried to persuade Julia to leave him. She must have been delighted when Julia told her she was finally doing it.

"Does she have other family? Her parents?" The gendarme said.

"No. There's only her sister. Both her parents are dead."

"Okay, Monsieur Halliday. We must go. We are so sorry to bring you such bad news." He held out his hand and Jeremy stared down at it for a moment before limply shaking it. He went through the same ritual with Elodie and then the two gendarmes turned and walked down the steps.

2

Jeremy sat in the wicker chair by the window and watched the Citroën spray gravel down the driveway as it sped off on to the road.

Twenty minutes later he was still sat staring out the window when a dark blue police van pulled up outside the house. He had to check his watch before he realised how long he'd been sitting there trying to clear the miasma wafting around inside his head. He still hadn't washed or dressed.

Two men and two women introduced themselves and he showed them quickly round the house. The older of the men, tall and thin with a grey moustache and mostly light brown short hair flecked with grey, explained briefly, and in good English, what the team needed to do. Jeremy didn't take in much of what he was saying. When the policeman had finished, Jeremy said that, if they could manage without him, he would be in the bathroom taking a shower and getting dressed.

He stood under the scalding water for a long time hoping it would refresh his mind as well as his body, his tranquillity disturbed only by the occasional noises of cupboard doors and drawers being opened and closed in the nearby bedrooms.

Once he'd shaved and dried and brushed his hair, he studied his clean cut boyish face in the mirror. Could anyone think that this was the face of a murderer? He didn't think so. He put on a t-shirt and a pair of jeans and slipped into his moccasins. He felt much more human. He couldn't think what to do next. He didn't feel like eating anything and he couldn't face up to phoning Hattie. He made himself a cup of coffee and, while he sat at the kitchen table drinking it, he studied his French road atlas. It was as he remembered it when the gendarmes had mentioned Aurillac. It was on the edge of the Cantal region heading up towards the Massif Central. He tried to trace a route on the atlas from there through central France to the Channel Tunnel but, unless Julia had intended to make a very slow, meandering, picturesque journey back, it seemed a strange route to choose. Maybe she'd been having second thoughts about leaving him and was just driving around trying to make up her mind.

His thoughts were interrupted by the man with the grey moustache.

"Excusez moi, monsieur. The grange over there –" he pointed towards the window -"this is your property also?"

"Yes, but we don't live in it. It was converted into a gîte – for holiday rentals. There's nobody staying at the moment. The season hasn't got going yet."

"Is it closed? Do you have a key?"

"Yes – but, as I said, there's nothing in it. Well, there's obviously furniture and stuff but it's just for renting to holidaymakers."

"We would like to examine it," the officer persisted. "If you have the key?"

Jeremy scraped his chair back and crossed over to a drawer in the kitchen island unit which held all their house keys.

"Sorry to make more trouble for you," the officer said as Jeremy rummaged through the drawer, "but the silver Renault Estate outside. Is this your car because we need to examine that also?"

Jeremy retrieved the keys to the gîte, took his car keys out of his jean's pocket and handed them to the officer. Despite the assurances of the young gendarme earlier, the presence of these crime investigations officers sifting through his belongings with their white-plastic gloved hands made him feel every inch the murder suspect. Perhaps, in some strange way, he deserved their suspicions. That very morning he remembered thinking about Julia's loss as a bereavement. And then, if he tracked back to his angry feelings immediately after she'd driven away, hadn't he wished her dead, even if only for an instant? Even if he hadn't, he definitely remembered fantasising about her being in a car crash on the long drive back. Julia wasn't a very good driver. She drove too fast and he was always complaining to her that she tailgated other vehicles on the motorway. He usually drove on the long journeys to and from England. When she went back on her own, for business, she normally flew. This would have been her first time driving alone all that way.

He swallowed a final mouthful of coffee and then forced himself out of the chair and across the sitting room to the telephone. He couldn't delay any longer. He had to phone Hattie. He left the number ringing for about twenty seconds and just as he was about to put the phone down with relief, it was picked up. It wasn't Hattie, it was her partner, John.

"Hi, John. It's Jeremy – phoning from France."

"Jeremy. How're you doing? Whoops. Sorry. Silly question. Look mate, I was really sorry to hear about you and Julia. How are you bearing up?"

Jeremy was relieved to hear John's cheerful estuary accent. They had always got on well together forming a partners' defensive bond against two such close conspiratorial sisters.

"I'm fine, John." It was a stupid thing to say. Of course he wasn't fine. "Is Hattie there? I need to speak to her."

"No, she's not. She's at work. In fact, you're lucky to catch me. I've taken a day off. I'm working from home."

"Okay. I'll try her on her mobile. I think I've got the number."

"You can try but you won't get hold of her, mate. She's out on casework. She always keeps it switched off when she's on her calls." There was a pause. "Look, if it's about Julia, I think you might be wasting your time talking to Hattie. You know how she feels about you and Julia. I've tried to put in a good word for you but it doesn't do any good. I hate to say it but she thinks Julia's doing the right thing. Come to her senses at last."

Jeremy felt tears prickling in the corners of his eyes. It was a relief not to have to talk to Hattie and it was good to hear John's sympathetic and supportive voice. He needed to unburden himself – tell someone what had happened – and it would be so much better if that person was John.

"It is about Julia, but it's not what you think." He paused and took a deep breath. "There's no easy way to say this, John. Julia's dead."

There was silence on the other end of the line.

"Sorry Jeremy. Did I hear you right? Did you say that Julia's dead?"

Maybe this wasn't any easier than if it had been Hattie on the phone, Jeremy thought.

"Yes. She's dead." He knew he should say more but he waited for it to sink in.

"How? What happened?" John spluttered. "Was it a car accident? She was on her way here, wasn't she?"

"Yes. She set out on Monday morning. They found her body in the car yesterday."

"Oh my god! So what happened? A crash on the motorway?"

"No." He didn't want to go through it all with John.

He just wanted to end the phone call as quickly as possible. "They're still looking into the exact cause of death. The gendarmes told me the news this morning and I've got to go into town this afternoon to speak to a magistrate. I guess I'll find out more then."

"But – I don't understand." Jeremy could picture John's confused expression. "If it wasn't a car accident then what was it?"

"John, I can't really go into it all now. The important thing is that you get hold of Hattie as soon as you can and tell her what's happened. The police need to contact her to ask her some questions and I told them I'd let her know about Julia first. I thought it was better she didn't hear it from the police."

"Yes, I understand that. But she's going to be asking me the same questions I'm asking you. I'm going to feel a bit inadequate to say the least when I can't give her even basic details."

"I know, John. You're both going to be just as confused as I am. All that you can tell her is that I hope I'll know more by this evening so I can speak to her then. Also, when the police contact her I'm sure they'll be able to tell her more."

"Okay. If that's all you know." He sounded doubtful. "I'll ring her office and find out exactly where she is this afternoon and I'll leave messages for her to contact me urgently."

"Can I just ask you something?" Jeremy said. "When were you expecting Julia to arrive at your place?"

"I'm not a hundred per cent sure. Hattie made all the arrangements. I think it was sometime this weekend."

"Right. I'd better ring off now." The officer with the grey moustache had appeared in the doorway clutching a sheath of papers. Jeremy was about to tell John that he had to go because a forensic team were searching the house but he stopped himself, realising that, if he told him that, it would be difficult not to also have to explain all the other things he knew about Julia's death which he had so far avoided talking about.

"Alright. Christ! I started off this conversation saying I was sorry to hear about you and Julia but I'm even sorrier now mate. I don't know what else to say. This is awful. Hattie's going to be devastated. Anyway, you just try and keep your pecker up. I'll speak to you soon."

John had started out as a working class London lad running an East End market stall selling children's clothes before rapidly working his way up to where he was now – the owner of a chain of clothes stores married to the very middle class Hattie. And yet, he retained his old market stallholder's chirpiness.

The officer was still hovering by the door as Jeremy put the phone down.

"We are finished, Monsieur Halliday. We need to take some things away for more examination so I need you to sign papers for them."

He walked across to the table, put the papers down and removed a pen from his jacket pocket. Jeremy walked over and stared down at the printed forms. There were two of them with large boxes in the middle filled with handwritten scrawl. The French officer pointed to the hand-written section.

"We take some clothes we find in a basket near the wash machine." He beckoned across to a young blond-haired officer who had appeared in the doorway. He came across to the table carrying a blue plastic box, put it down and snapped off the lid. The older officer pulled out a pair of Jeremy's jeans, a t-shirt and two pairs of underpants. "Are these yours, Monsieur Halliday?"

"Yes." All three men stared at the soiled clothes as if they were antiquities discovered in an archaeological excavation.

"There are also these – which I guess are your wife's? We found them in a cupboard in the bedroom."

On cue, the young officer replaced Jeremy's clothes and held up in their place a pair of mud-spattered slacks and a faded pink sweat-shirt.

"Yes, they're Julia's gardening clothes."

"We also take the ordinateur – sorry, the computer, from the office downstairs."

"Oh no. That doesn't belong to Julia. That's my laptop. Julia had her own one. It must have been in the car with her."

"That's correct. We found Miss Julia's computer and we are examining it but we also need to examine this one."

"But why? Look, I don't mean to be difficult but I can't see what use all this is. I need my laptop. I run a business through the internet. I can't manage without it."

"I am sorry, Monsieur Halliday, but we need to take these things. We will return the computer to you as soon as possible – perhaps two days. If you could sign and put the date on both these papers. They are the same – one for you to keep, one for us." The friendly tone had gone. The officer was business-like and quick-fire, leaving no space for Jeremy to continue his protestations. He held out the pen. Jeremy stared at it and then at the box of clothes and then back at the tall thin officer. He took the pen and signed both sheets.

As he watched the police van crunch its way back up the driveway, he held on tightly to the windowsill as if it was the only thing preventing him from keeling over. After a couple of minutes staring at the empty driveway, he took a deep breath, walked across to the kitchen, opened the fridge and reached for the three-quarters full bottle of white wine in the door rack. He needed a drink. Several drinks. His life had been knocked sideways by Julia's departure and he'd been drifting in a kind of limbo for the past few days, but now he felt like he was in a car careening down a mountain road without brakes. He picked up the bottle of wine and then swiftly put it back and closed the fridge door. He had to keep his head clear. In a few hours, he would be sitting in front of a judge answering more questions. He needed to be fully compos mentis. He didn't want the judge smelling alcohol on his breath in the middle of the day. He found his thoughts going back to the investigation in London and all the mistakes he'd made then. The way he'd presented himself to the authorities. The search of their house and car. The police taking away clothes and their computers. It was all so horribly familiar. And now, just like back then, however hard he tried to rationalise what was happening as just normal police procedures, everything was pointing towards him as the chief suspect in a murder case.

3

Jeremy had lost track of what day of the week it was until he drove into Villefranche at lunchtime and saw that the restaurants were crammed full. Of course. Thursday. Market day. He zigzagged around the handful of stallholders in the Place Notre Dame, packing their produce into vans, skipping out of the way of the municipal dustcart hoovering up the fruit and vegetable detritus. He climbed the steps up to the terrace on the far side of the square and surveyed the café's outdoor seating area, firstly to check that there was no-one there that he knew and, when he was sure of that, to find an empty table. A young English couple in shorts and t-shirts had just got to their feet, shouldered their rucksacks and were sorting handfuls of change before depositing coins into a blue plastic tray with the bill clipped to it.

Jeremy took their place at the small corner table. He had plenty of time before he was due to meet the Judge. There was a hollow feeling in his stomach but he didn't feel hungry even though he'd had very little to eat that morning. He decided he'd just order a coffee. While he waited to be served, he glanced across the square until his eyes rested on two white-garbed nuns clearing away the charity produce they had been selling on their table in front of the church doors. At a time like this, he regretted that he didn't have any religious faith. How comforting it would be to enter the cool dark church and pray. Perhaps light a candle for Julia. Although John's friendly voice had offered a brief moment of comfort, now all he could think about, with growing apprehension, was the impassive face and legal formality of the Judge.

He moved to the other side of the table, under a sunshade, to get out of the early June sunshine which was causing beads of sweat to form on his forehead and damp patches under his arms. A sweaty appearance would make him look nervous and shifty in front of the Judge.

Once the coffee had arrived, he started to think about the upcoming interview. What kind of questions would he be asked? What answers should he come up with? He couldn't help thinking like an accused man trying to protest his innocence. That was stupid, he told himself. If that was the way he was thinking when he entered the interview room, then he was bound to look and sound suspicious. He had to think positive. Even if he was a suspect now, he soon wouldn't be. For a start, they didn't even know yet if Julia had been murdered and, even if she had, he had been over a hundred miles away when it happened. And anyway, why would he kill the woman he loved? Ay, there's the rub, as Hamlet had said. Best not to think about that.

*

Villefranche police station was an ugly brutalist 1960s concrete and glass building on the outskirts of the medieval town centre on one side of a large car park. The inside was equally depressing with light blue paint peeling off the walls, polystyrene ceiling tiles, some broken, others missing completely, and the dazzling glare of strip lighting. It had fallen into increasing disrepair as plans to build a new station in an out-of-town development had hit prolonged planning application problems.

Compared to the rest of the building, Judge Jules Bouchon's office was comfortable and stylish. In place of the melamine-topped tables, plastic chairs and grey metal storage units of the other offices, it had a large solid oak desk and the walls were lined with wooden bookshelves. On the far side, by the window, there was a seating area with a large red sofa, a glass-topped coffee table and an oak sideboard with a coffee machine on it.

Jules Bouchon had just finished studying the Julia Wainwright case folder laid out on the desk in front of him. He couldn't help but feel a sense of pleasurable anticipation. Mysterious deaths of this kind were rare in that part of the Aveyron. Almost all the murders he had investigated in his long career were simple 'conjugals'.Usually husband killing wife, sometimes wife killing husband, often followed by the perpetrator taking his or her own life. Very little investigating was called for.

He looked again at the photos of Julia Wainwright and Jeremy Halliday lying on top of the document pile. A good-looking couple. Both in their early forties – in their prime. A touch of the English rose look about her. Long straight blond hair curtaining a pretty face spoilt only by a slightly too large nose. His dark brown hair curling over his ears, his dark brown eyes, square jawline and swarthy skin giving him a more Mediterranean than English appearance. He could have been an actor or rock star. More than a coincidence that his name was so close to that of French pop star, Johnny Hallyday? He could picture both their faces splashed across the front page of *La Dépêche du Midi* in the next few days. Any local murder would be big news in an area so bereft of such dramas but one featuring such a photogenic English couple would have extra special interest. It would probably make the national press and television as well. Now that he was nearing retirement, maybe this case would provide his career with a final hurrah.

There was a knock at the office door and his secretary, Eva, poked her head around it.

"Monsieur Halliday is here," she announced.

"Show him in."

Jeremy entered purposefully, walking straight across to the Judge's desk and shaking hands with him.

"Good to meet you, Mr. Halliday. I am the juge d'instruction – sorry, the investigating judge, Jules Bouchon. Please take a seat." He continued to speak as Jeremy was settling himself into a chair. "I am very sorry for your tragic loss. I understand how difficult this must be for you and I thank you for coming to see me so quickly. In cases like this, we need to proceed as quickly as possible to be able to get to the truth. Can I get you a coffee or some water?"

"No, I'm fine thank you."

"Is it alright if we keep the interview in English?"

"Definitely. My French is improving but I'm far from fluent. Your English sounds much better."

"Thank you. I did live and work in London for two years when I was young. Near Camden Town. Do you know it?"

"A bit. I'm a South Londoner. There's quite a north south divide in London, as you probably know. I didn't often go too far north of the river."

The interview was not going the way Jeremy had imagined it. He had expected a more typical French formality and not this avuncular chubby grey-haired man chatting away genially. So determined had he been on entering the room to stay in control and give nothing away that he was immediately suspicious. Perhaps it was a tactic to soften him up, relax him, so that he would be less on his guard when it was time for the serious questioning.

He decided to take the initiative and cut short the social pleasantries. "Have you found out what the cause of Julia's death was?" He said.

"I'm afraid not. We are still waiting for results of tests on the body. Normally, we would ask you to identify the body for us but the top half was badly burnt so identification would be difficult as well as disturbing for you. As Gilles Montfort – the gendarme who spoke with you this morning – told you, we have identified it through the papers we found in the car and then the medical records in London. But, if you could look at a couple of things for us?" He reached down to a small cardboard box by the side of the desk and placed a shoe and a gold wrist bangle in front of Jeremy. Both were in good condition with no signs they had been in a fire.

Jeremy swallowed hard when he saw them. The shoe was a black leather slipper with a swirly silver band across the instep. The wrist bangle was an art nouveau style twist of snake-like loops. He recognised it immediately. He had bought it a couple of years ago for Julia's fortieth birthday. He reached out to touch them but withdrew his hand halfway. He shuddered at the thought of what Julia's body must look like, fighting to keep any image of the charred remains out of his head. Instead, he tried to picture her as she was when he last saw her but even that was difficult. She was already fading from his life like an out-of-focus photo.

"Yes, they're Julia's. She kept those shoes in the car. She found them comfortable to drive in."

"Thank you. That is helpful." Judge Bouchon replaced the items in the box. "You told Gilles Montfort that Madame Wainwright was returning to England to visit her sister and also for business purposes."

"Yes, that's correct."

"When did she leave your house?"

"She left on Monday morning at about nine."

"And did she say anything about how she was travelling back? Anywhere she might be visiting on the way?"

"No. As far as I knew she was heading straight back taking our usual route."

"And what route was that?"

"She would drive across towards Cahors and then take the motorway heading north through Brive and Orleans. She was probably crossing by Eurotunnel. She didn't much like the ferries – but I don't know that for sure."

"And would she go straight back in one day or would she make a stop for the night?"

"Normally we would make an overnight stop around Rouen and then get a Eurotunnel train at about midday the next day."

Judge Bouchon leaned back in his chair and touched the tips of his fingers together in a pyramid.

"So, why do you think she went to the Aurillac area? Did she have friends who live near there? Someone she might have visited? Stayed the night with?"

"No. We don't know anybody in that area."

The judge stared into space for several seconds as if in deep thought before continuing.

"You say *we* don't know anybody. Is it possible that Madame Wainwright might have friends that you don't know about?"

Jeremy paused to think about that. "It's possible, but I doubt it. We were a couple. We didn't keep secrets from each other. If she knew somebody in that area – I don't know – like, say, an old school friend, I'm sure she would have told me."

"You were a couple. You didn't keep secrets from each other." The judge pronounced the words slowly, as if trying to fathom their exact meaning. "So – do couples never keep secrets from each other, Monsieur Halliday? Surely, that's the very point of secrets – that the other person doesn't know about them?"

Jeremy stared at the judge trying to detect any sign that he was being sarcastic. Then he realised what the Judge was hinting. Maybe Julia had a lover who lived in the area. Before he could think of how to respond, the judge continued.

"That's okay, Monsieur Halliday. You don't have to reply to that. It was – how do you say – a rhetorical question."

The judge paused, shuffled the papers on his desk and picked up the sheet with Julia's photo and details on it.

"What was Madame Wainwright's mood when she left you on Monday? Was she happy, depressed, pleased to be going back to England?"

"She was her normal self. She was used to travelling backwards and forwards. She always looked forward to seeing her sister. They were very fond of each other." Jeremy answered without a moment's hesitation, instantly blocking out the image of a cold, silent, business-like Julia loading her things into the car while he sat disconsolately at the kitchen table staring at an uneaten slice of toast and drinking a cup of tea before she came back in to deliver a curt farewell and drove off.

"And her business. Was that going well?"

"Yes, very well. She was expanding all the time."

"So – there is no reason she might have taken her own life?"

"No, not at all."

Jeremy was taken aback by the suggestion. He tried to picture a distraught Julia, mentally unbalanced by their separation. He couldn't. He was the one who had felt suicidal. He waited for the next question – certain it would be about the state of his relationship with Julia – knowing that he wouldn't be able to prevaricate any longer. But it didn't come.

"Where were you during the daytime and evening on Tuesday?" The Judge continued.

"I was at home. In the house."

"And what were you doing?"

"Nothing much. Just pottering around. Some work on my computer. A spot of gardening. It was a nice afternoon as I remember. I might have sat in the garden reading. Watched a bit of television in the evening."

"Did you visit anybody? Did anybody come to the house to see you?

"No, I don't think so." He tried to stay calm. They found Julia's body on Wednesday. She must have died on Tuesday. With a sudden hollow feeling in his stomach, he realised that the Judge was checking to see if he had an alibi. He was a suspect.

"Maybe a neighbour walked past when you were in the garden. Maybe you just exchanged 'bonjours'?"

"It's possible but I don't remember anybody specifically."

"Did you make any phone calls? Receive any?"

"I don't remember. I don't think so." He paused, starting to feel angry. "Look, are you insinuating that I might have murdered Julia, because that's absurd."

"I am not insinuating anything, Monsieur Halliday. We do not know yet if Miss Julia was murdered. But, of course, it would be good for our investigation if we could establish exactly where you were for the past two days. Then we can......how do you say in English......écarte......put you out of the investigation?"

"Eliminate me."

"Eliminate. Yes, that's the word. So, once we have completed this interview, if you remember any other details – anyone who could confirm seeing or speaking to you on Tuesday – please let me know."

Jeremy put the key in the ignition, wound down the windows to relieve the stuffiness in the car and then sat staring across the car park at a group of people seated on wooden decking outside a café. He watched a tall blond woman in a pink jacket, a tight black mini-skirt and black stiletto-heeled shoes come out of the café and totter unsteadily towards him. She stopped by the side of a battered, mud-spattered jeep, opened the driver's door, climbed in and drove off. It was incongruous, he thought. It was the sort of car a farmer would drive and yet she didn't look like a farmer's wife. Unlike in London, in Villefranche he found it much harder to guess people's class or occupation by their appearance.

He continued to sit and stare out the window. There was nothing else he wanted to do in Villefranche and yet he was reluctant to go back to his empty house. Maybe he should go for a drive or for a walk along the banks of the Aveyron – give himself time to clear his head. The Judge had cut short the interview after he had failed to establish an alibi for Jeremy for the day of Julia's death. He told him he would need to question him further as the investigation proceeded but it would be best to wait until they could confirm the exact cause of death.

As Jeremy continued to gaze across at the people in the café, he tried to remember exactly what he had been doing during the few days since Julia left but his mind was a blank. That was probably because he'd been doing nothing in particular – just wallowing in his own misery. But it was a long time only to be doing that – three days. Maybe something more dramatic had happened but he had expunged it from his memory because it was too painful. He closed his eyes and pictured Julia's car on fire by the side of a sandy path, the flames scorching low hanging tree branches and scrub bushes. Flames were licking round Julia's body, slumped over the steering wheel. He snapped open his eyes to cut off the horrific scene and shuddered. It had been scarily vivid. Too real? It was as if he was remembering it, rather than imagining it.

He re-started the engine and drove out of the car park. There was nothing he could think of doing that might distract him from such thoughts so he drove back to the house.

An hour after he returned home, he received the expected phone call from Hattie. It was difficult to make out what she was saying through her sobs.

"When John phoned to tell me," she said, gulping for breath after every few words, "I couldn't take it in. I couldn't believe it was true. I thought…it must be a mistake…a misunderstanding……" she paused, struggling to catch her breath. "I was trying to phone you but you weren't home and there was no answer machine."

"Yes. I'm sorry. I was out." He decided it was best not to tell her that he was being questioned by the investigating judge. "Have the police spoken to you yet?"

Once again she sucked in a deep breath to steady herself. "Yes. About half an hour ago. They told me she'd been found in her car. It had been set on fire………" once again she was overcome with grief. "They said that's all they know at present. I don't understand. What on earth could have happened? Who would want to harm Julia?"

Jeremy considered several possible answers to her question before saying, "I don't know any more than you. They were asking me about her business – how it was going. I think they were trying to suggest that it might have been suicide."

"What?" The word 'suicide' appeared to halt the flow of tears. "That's absurd."

"I know. That's exactly what I told them. What questions did they ask you?"

"Not many. I was in even more of a state than I am now. I was barely able to speak. I just told them that the last time

I'd spoken to Julia on the phone was last weekend and she told me that she'd be arriving at our place sometime around midday tomorrow."

Jeremy waited a few seconds for her to continue. When she didn't, he said hesitantly, "Did she say anything about where else she might be going on her way back to England?"

Another pause. "Oh yes. They did ask me something about that. I told them I didn't know. As far as I knew, she was driving straight here."

What Jeremy most wanted to know was whether she'd told them the real reason Julia was returning – whether she'd told them about their break up. Since she hadn't mentioned it, he was tempted to ask her himself, but he resisted. She'd started crying again. He could hear John's voice mumbling in the background but couldn't make out what he was saying.

And then it was John's voice on the phone. "Hi Jeremy. Look, I think it's best to leave it for now. As you can imagine, Hattie's in a terrible state. I'm sure she'll phone you back when she's had time to calm down."

"No problem, John. I'm finding it difficult at the moment as well." He hoped John didn't think he sounded hypocritical. He was nowhere near as audibly upset as Hattie. In fact, now that he thought about it, he hadn't shed a single tear since hearing about Julia's death.

"Of course you are, mate. You look after yourself. Speak to you soon." John rang off.

Jeremy was relieved. He'd had no idea what to say to Hattie and he hadn't wanted to be the one to cut short the call. His biggest relief was that she had been so overcome with grief that there had been no hint of the hostility she felt towards him and no suggestion that he might have had anything to do with her sister's death.

Barely ten minutes after he'd put the phone down it rang again. He didn't want to pick it up. He couldn't imagine who it could be but he didn't want to speak to anybody. It kept ringing. He wished he'd left it on answer machine but, eventually, he decided to pick it up. It was Judge Bouchon. The autopsy results had come back. Julia had been dead before the car was set on fire. Strangled. It was now officially a murder inquiry.

4

As he strolled along the corridor on his way out of school, Jeremy was stopped in his tracks by what sounded like someone crying. He stood still for several seconds, straining to pick up the sound over the noise of music and laughter coming from the staffroom behind him. It was definitely the sound of a woman's choking sobs. He turned the corner in the direction it was coming from and stopped outside the female staff toilets.

Jeremy had left the end of term staff party early, depressed by the ritual jollity of it all: sitting with the rest of the English Department in their habitual corner of the staffroom watching the usual suspects getting steadily drunk. Despite having split up with his girlfriend a few weeks earlier, he was not in the mood for flirting. Not that he was ever in the mood for flirting – he'd never been any good at it. And anyway, the only candidate he halfway fancied was a petite dark-haired student teacher in the History Department who looked young enough to be a sixth former. Now that he was in his mid-thirties he found that the company of much younger women made him feel prematurely middle-aged.

He debated whether to knock on the door and ask if he could be of any help. He had no idea who it might be. He couldn't recall seeing any distressed-looking women in the staffroom earlier. The sobbing stopped and he was about to turn and go when the toilet door opened and Julia Wainwright came out blowing her nose into a fistful of scrunched up toilet tissues. He sashayed backwards as she almost bumped into him while she simultaneously gave a surprised jump when she saw him.

"Sorry Julia. I didn't mean to spy on you. It's just that I couldn't help hearing you and...... well, I just wondered if I could be of any help. Are you feeling unwell? Can I get you something?"

She leaned back against the wall and blew her nose vigorously into the soggy tissues.

"No, you're alright. I'll be okay."

"Can I get you a drink or something?"

"No thanks." She looked at him through red-rimmed eyes. "I could probably do with getting drunk but I'm not going back in there." She gestured down the corridor in the direction of the staffroom.

Jeremy hovered awkwardly next to her. He didn't know what else he could do but he didn't feel he could leave her like that.

"You haven't got a cigarette, have you?" She said.

"No, sorry. I don't smoke."

"Neither do I." She gave a rueful laugh. "I haven't smoked for about ten years but suddenly I really feel like a fag."

"I can go back to the staffroom and see if I can cadge one off of somebody."

"Thanks. It's kind of you, but don't bother. The way I feel I could easily smoke and drink myself to death right now but I'm not going to. I wouldn't want to give that bastard the satisfaction. He'd just love to see me all cut up and in pieces over him. It'd boost his ego – not that it needs any boosting."

As Julia continued to dab her nose with the wet tissues, the situation suddenly became clear to Jeremy. The 'he' she was talking about must be Pete Davies, a maths teacher with whom she'd been living for some time. Jeremy was not the most sociable of colleagues, usually spending his lunchtimes at his desk in the English office rather than chatting in the staffroom, but he did vaguely remember hearing some gossip about Pete and Julia breaking up. And then, earlier in the evening, one of his colleagues had made a disparaging comment of the 'he's at it again' variety while indicating Pete dancing energetically with Aysha Khan, a young science teacher. Jeremy had no time for Pete Davies. He was tall and thin with lank greasy blond hair and the kind of battered good-looks that women seemed to find attractive. His macho image was reinforced by his arrival at school every morning decked out in black leather on a powerful Honda motorbike. He was loud-mouthed and opinionated – invariably the first person to speak up at staff and union meetings in a semi-sneering, superior tone which suggested that no-one could possibly disagree with him. When Jeremy made disparaging remarks about Pete, his colleagues often accused him of jealousy. He and Pete were the male teachers who attracted the most flirtatious attention from some of the female students, especially sixth form girls. Jeremy hated to be categorised with Pete in that way as he prided himself on being professionally scrupulous in refusing to play along with such behaviour whereas Pete positively encouraged it.

A few minutes ago he'd been intent on going home and getting an early night but now, looking at Julia's tear-stained face, he changed his mind.

"Look. I was just leaving. I'm not in the mood for a party tonight. Would you like to come to the pub for a quiet drink? Then, if you want to talk about it......well, I'm a good listener."

She stuffed the tissues into her shoulder bag and smiled at him. "Okay, you're on. I need to get out of here...... and I need a drink."

Ten minutes later, they were seated at a corner table in *The Fox* with a vodka and tonic and a half of lager on the table in front of them. As it was a mid-week evening the pub was quiet. The only other customers were three middle-aged down-at-the-heel men propping up the bar chatting with the blond barmaid, like a South London version of a Toulouse Lautrec painting, and two young smartly dressed black women at a table over the far side.

Julia headed straight for the toilet when they arrived and re-applied her makeup to repair the damage to her tear-streaked face while Jeremy got the drinks. Now she was looking more her usual self – an attractive, pale-complexioned, blue-eyed blond looking smart in her black top, tight denim jeans and shocking pink jacket. She had been much fancied by the male members of staff, as well as the boys, when she first arrived at the school four years ago. But, as far as Jeremy was concerned, any attraction had worn off as soon as she succumbed to the blandishments of Pete Davies. As far as he was concerned, there had to be something wrong with any woman who could fancy that man.

For the next fifteen minutes, Jeremy fulfilled his self-appointed role, listening with genuine sympathy to Julia's account of her increasingly fraught life with Pete followed by a blow by blow account of her discovery of his betrayal with that bitch, Aysha. It was not difficult for Jeremy to be sympathetic. At times he found himself biting his tongue to stop himself from adding to her vituperative comments about the odious man.

When her account of their breakup was complete, Julia turned to berating herself.

"The trouble is that, no matter how angry I am with that bastard, I'm even angrier with myself. You see, I have this unerring ability to fall for the most unsuitable men. It's like déjà vu......here we go again. Utter shits – all of them. But then maybe I shouldn't beat myself up. Maybe it's not just me. I guess deep down all men are predatory beasts."

Jeremy must have looked aggrieved because she instantly reached over the table and patted his hand. "Present company excepted, of course."

She withdrew her hand and took another sip of her vodka. "I should have realised how it would end up before letting myself get involved with Pete. My very first boyfriend was just like him. He was called Aiden. We started going out when we were in the sixth form. He was all loving and romantic until he realised I wasn't going to let him go all the way with me." She grinned at Jeremy. "Then one Saturday we went shopping together in Knightsbridge. As we were heading back to the underground, I realised I'd left my sunglasses on the perfume counter in Harrods. I asked him to wait while I went back to get them. He told me to leave them – I could easily buy another pair, but I said they were expensive and it would only take me a minute. So I went and got them but, when I got back, he'd gone. When I had a go at him about it at school on the Monday morning, he ignored me and walked away with his friends, laughing. I'd been dumped."

"I think we're members of the same club," said Jeremy. "And to prove it, let me tell you about my first girlfriend." She waved her hand, gesturing for him to continue. "Her name was Ellie. We met at university and I fell head over heels for her. One weekend I had to come back home to London for my dad's birthday. When I got back to uni on the Monday, she suddenly announced that she'd met somebody else."

"Okay, you've matched me with that one but I think I can still trump you." She paused in thought as if going through a rollerdex of ex-boyfriends in her head.

"Oh, actually I've just remembered," Jeremy interrupted. "Ellie wasn't quite my first. I did have a girlfriend in school although we only went out on a few dates. You know – to the cinema and youth club discos. Then, one morning at break time, her best friend sidles up to me and says she's been sent to tell me that her friend doesn't want to go out with me anymore."

"Oh god." Julia put her hand over her mouth. "I've done that......been the go-between, I mean. Telling a boy my friend is dumping him. Mind you, we were only about twelve at the time. Actually, I take it back what I said about all men being shits. Pubescent girls are the worst."

As the evening wore on, their laughter swelled as they swapped ever more self-deprecating stories and vied for who was the biggest fuckup when it came to relationships with the opposite sex. Julia's growing good humour was lubricated by several more vodka and tonics while Jeremy carefully nursed his two half pints, conscious that he needed to drive home – or maybe even drive Julia home.

As it approached closing time, he offered to give her a lift. She leaned back and flashed an inebriated smile at him.

"Where do you live?" She slurred.

"Tooting."

"I'm Brixton. It's the opposite direction. It's alright. I'll get the bus."

"It's no trouble. It's not far out of my way. And, as you can witness, I haven't had much to drink so you'll be safe."

She continued to smile at him. "If only I could say the same. I am feeling rather squiffy. Maybe the bus wouldn't be such a good idea."

Jeremy stood up, taking that as a cue that it was time to leave but Julia stayed seated.

"Look, maybe it would be easier to go back to your

place. I don't really feel like going home to tell you the truth. Most of Pete's stuff is still in the flat."

Jeremy stared down at her trying to decode what she was suggesting. She was a very attractive woman and, now that it was all over between her and Pete Davies, maybe he could reconsider her as a potential girlfriend. He'd enjoyed their evening together and was surprised at how easy it had been to share intimate details about himself with a woman he barely knew. But was she attracted to him or was she simply maudlin drunk and looking for some token male company to take her mind off her unhappiness? Despite them spending the evening sharing intimate details of their romantic attachments, Jeremy felt it had been a flirtation-free zone. His role had been more of a friendly shoulder to cry on than a potential new lover. Would he be taking advantage of her drunken state if he took her back to his flat? For all of his adult life he'd been the perfect old-fashioned gentleman when it came to women. Perhaps now was the time to ditch that practice.

But, by the time they got back to his one-bedroomed flat, he couldn't entirely divest himself of his chivalrous nature and offered her his bed while he rummaged through the airing cupboard for a spare duvet and pillow for his night on the sitting room sofa. Before they went to bed they continued the earlier discussion over a, for Julia, sobering mug of black coffee. When the time came, Jeremy found himself being led gently but firmly into the bedroom by a slightly sobered up Julia. They spent that night cuddled up together, in their underwear, in his double bed – but there was no sex. Jeremy was relieved. It felt like a sensible compromise.

*

From that night on, their relationship developed rapidly. Within a month he had moved into Julia's two bedroomed flat. Everything fell neatly into place. They both liked going to the theatre, they enjoyed the same films, shared some favourite authors, loved going for long walks in the countryside. Having already discovered their shared propensity for choosing unsuitable partners, it slowly dawned on them that maybe, just maybe, they were made for each other. Jeremy was the exact opposite of Pete – caring, gentle, undomineering, cultured – while Julia was not at all shrewish or demanding like Jeremy's ex Mandy. And then they discovered their shared middle class childhoods in suburban South London and the added coincidence that both had experienced the death of a parent when they were young. The only major difference between them was that Julia had a sister who was two years older than her and whom she was very close to while Jeremy was an only child.

Much to Jeremy and Julia's relief, Pete Davies got another job and left the school at the end of the Summer term which helped dispel Jeremy's fear that he was merely an 'on the rebound' boyfriend who would soon be dropped if Pete decided he wanted Julia back. They also survived the initial staffroom gossip and the audible whispers and leering comments from students in corridors as well as the occasional obscene graffiti inscribed on their classroom desks.

As they drifted into their second year together, it became by some way Jeremy's longest relationship. He knew he was a good-looking man who was attractive to women and yet his relationships had always been short-lived. And not because, like her, he tended to pick unsuitable partners. It was more because he lacked confidence in his ability to sustain a relationship. Possibly something to do with him being an only child, he told himself – or maybe it was losing his mother when he was twelve. He didn't have a serious girlfriend until he was twenty-one and in his final year at university. And it wasn't until meeting Mandy two years ago that he had lived with a woman, albeit only for a messy three months. However established he and Julia had become as a couple he was always half-expecting the inevitable breakup – examining each newly arrived unattached male teacher as a potential rival. He could see the disadvantage of workplace romances – your partner's daily interactions with these men were constantly under your scrutiny. And so, when Julia announced that she was resigning her teaching post he was relieved. In her spare time, she'd been using her skills to design and manufacture a range of women's fashion accessories, mostly colourful bags, in their spare bedroom cum workshop. At first she gave them as presents to friends and family but, as her stock increased, she set up a weekend stall on Brixton Market. One Saturday, her wares attracted the interest of a woman who owned a shop on the Portobello Road and was about to open another on Upper Street, Islington. Soon the market stall was abandoned and she was spending all her weekends and holidays trying to keep up the supply to a growing chain of shops. Once she felt she had a viable business that she could expand, she had no hesitation in waving goodbye to the teaching profession.

With the growing success of Julia's business, their cramped flat was being colonised by mounds of her paperwork and manufacturing paraphernalia and so they purchased a three-bedroomed house in Tooting. They chose it chiefly for its large sunny loft-conversion room which made an ideal office cum design studio for Julia, although she no longer needed to fill it with piles of material, offcuts, cottons, zips, buttons and all the rest of her designer bits and pieces as the business had now grown big enough for her to outsource the manufacturing of her products.

For the first time in their relationship, Jeremy felt secure. Now they were a proper partnership.

5

Mary Groenwald stood in front of the full length windows of her ground floor office looking across at the gardeners putting the finishing touches to the new flower beds she'd requested to replace the grassy bank that the students had reduced to a mud slide. Two boys she didn't know, they looked like 8th years, walked along the path in front of the flower beds talking animatedly. Suddenly, the bigger of the two dropped his bag and put an arm-lock round the neck of the smaller boy. They both fell to the floor, the smaller one struggling to free himself. Mary rapped her knuckles on the window. The bigger boy looked round surprised to see her. She wagged an admonitory finger at him and shook her head. He reluctantly released his grip. The other boy twisted free and aimed a retaliatory punch before freezing in mid-action as he also caught sight of the head teacher. Both boys picked themselves up, dusted themselves down and, giving her looks of aggrieved innocence, walked off.

Since taking up the post of Head teacher of St. Saviour's Church of England School in Clapham, South London the previous September, everything had gone surprisingly smoothly for Mary. Despite, at the age of thirty-five, being one of the youngest head teachers of an inner London Comprehensive, most of her doubts about whether she might have over-reached herself by going for such a rapid promotion had been dispelled. The arrival of a full OFSTED inspection just two months into her new headship had panicked her, it was true. Would she be found out? Would they decide that her appointment had been a mistake – that she was too inexperienced to take on such a challenging school? Her friends and colleagues told her not to worry. It was a positive advantage to have OFSTED in so early. Any shortcomings or criticisms could be placed at the door of the previous regime. The inspectors were bound to give her the benefit of the doubt. They were right. She needn't have worried. The school was pronounced 'good' with 'some outstanding features' and their judgements on her leadership, with caveats about how little time she had had to stamp her authority, were very flattering. "...already showing herself to possess outstanding leadership skills"...... "excellent initial planning with a detailed and impressive overview of the school's future".........."quickly established good relationships with staff"...... "demanded and received high standards of teaching and general conduct."

For the last term and a half, she'd basked in that praise. And now, at the start of the summer term, she'd put in place a budget for the following year which had gained the stamp of approval from the governors and the local authority auditors. Her biggest challenge so far had been the awkward case of a student's assault on a teacher including the subsequent appeal by the parents against her and the governors' decision to permanently exclude their son.

Yes, everything that had been thrown at her (and there had been plenty) she had more than survived. In fact, she felt herself growing in strength and self-assurance. Despite her petite youthful appearance, when she patrolled the school corridors she exuded a natural authority and the children automatically did what she told them to, whether it was to remove a woolly hat or stop running: very different from the patrician authority of her predecessor, Mr. Scanlon – over six foot tall with a craggy face and stentorian voice striding the corridors Batman-like, his academic gown billowing behind him. And yet, she knew that what she was about to face would be easily her biggest test so far – and she was nervous. She returned to her desk, opened the buff folder in front of her and glanced once again at Jeremy Halliday's file. A good classroom English teacher – all the lesson observations were positive. Very good attendance record. Thirty-six years old. Second in the English Department. He'd been at the school for twelve years – his whole teaching career. Should she hold that against him? Did he lack ambition? Shouldn't he have moved on by now to a Head of Department post? Perhaps she should stop judging people by her own high flying, super-ambitious standards.

There was a knock on the door and Mike Harvey, her deputy head, poked his bald pate around it.

"Are you ready for me?" He said.

"Yes, Mike. Come in."

He entered, closed the door behind him and waited beside it. "Jeremy Halliday's waiting outside. Do you want me to call him in?"

"No, not yet. I need a brief chat with you before we talk to him. Take a seat."

Mike Harvey was the epitome of the affable Yorkshireman. He was short, tubby and on that day, as always, looked somewhat unkempt, as if he'd slept in his suit. His bald head was ringed by wisps of grey hair which curled over his ears and accentuated his permanently ruddy complexion – more an affable pub landlord than a senior teacher. He'd been a deputy head at the school for ten years and had applied for the headship but, at fifty-seven years old, Mary assumed it had been more out of a sense of duty than any feeling that he was likely to be appointed. He was the kind of solid, organised, strong disciplinarian who made a very good deputy but lacked the intellectual capacity for the top job. Nevertheless, Mary was sure he must have felt some resentment at being passed over for a young slip of a girl like her. Ever since she took up the appointment she had been wary of him – on the lookout for signs of that perceived resentment. And yet, so far, there'd been no sign. No overheard tittle-tattle from the office staff about him making denigrating comments about her. He'd been a model of loyalty and support. Even so, she was still constantly on her guard. Every time he spoke at leadership group, staff or governors' meetings she was alert to any hint of criticism, any indication that he might be belittling her. Sometimes she thought she detected something in his tone of voice and would go over in her mind exactly what he had said once the meeting was over. And then she would speedily dismiss it as uncomfortable evidence that she was still not as secure in the job as she had thought.

No, she had to admit that he'd been a very useful lieutenant – experienced, knew all the kids and staff and was well liked by most of them, and provided vital continuity. He had helped her through this first year. But, even so, early in the new school year she'd have to broach the subject of putting together an early retirement package for him. She would need a younger, more dynamic and imaginative second-in-command. She had it in mind to headhunt a couple of colleagues from her previous school.

"I just wanted to talk through a couple of things before we see Jeremy," she said, still flicking idly through the file. "This has all happened rather quickly and I haven't had much time to think or consult anybody about it. Obviously you know Jeremy much better than me. I know we have to carry out a proper investigation but, to put it bluntly, do you think there might be any truth in these accusations? I mean...... Is he the kind of man to do such things?"

"I'd like to be able to say 'no'," Mike said in his habitual blunt tone, "but, when it comes to this sort of thing, however much you think you know somebody they can always surprise you. It's hard to tell. Let's face it, if you could spot the type straight away, you'd never appoint them in the first place, would you? All I would say in his favour is that, to my knowledge, there's never been any hint of anything like this before."

His answer wasn't very helpful but she didn't expect anything else. "It says in his file that he's single. Has he got a girlfriend, do you know? Has he been in any long-term relationships? I know it's not necessarily strictly relevant but......" Earlier that morning she'd been trying to remember her previous conversations with Jeremy Halliday. She'd conducted brief informal interviews with all the members of staff during her first half-term but she'd been hard put to remember much of what Jeremy had said and she couldn't recall much more than a few words in passing with him since.

"He's been in a relationship for about three years if I remember rightly – with Julia Wainwright."

Mary looked blankly at him.

"Oh, of course. You won't know who she is. She was an Art and Design and Technology teacher here. She left last year – just before you arrived. I assume they're still together."

"Oh, right."

"They seemed very happy together – but I always feel these staffroom romances are a bit tricky. I'm always grateful that my good lady wife isn't a teacher – especially not one working in the same school. Not good to be on top of each other all the time......oops, sorry. Bit of an unfortunate phrase, but you know what I mean."

She nodded. "Was that the reason she left, do you think?"

"I'm not sure. It's always a bit awkward when two

teachers start up a relationship. The kids always get to know about it so they're bound to get some saucy comments from some of the more obstreperous ones. The kids are always quick to look for something to gossip about. You know how it is. A male teacher gives a female teacher a lift into school. They're seen getting out of the car together. Pretty soon it's round the school that something's going on even if one, or both of them, is already married – especially if one of them's already married."

"So you think there was a lot of interest in Jeremy's love life?"

"Certainly. At first. He's a good-looking bloke. Quite a few of the girls used to have a bit of a crush on him. They probably got a bit jealous when they saw he was teamed up with Miss Wainwright. We used to get occasional unpleasant graffiti about him in the girls' toilets. There was a whole chain of it in the sixth form block a couple of years ago."

"Thanks for that, Mike. It gives me a bit of background that I can't get from his file. I guess we better not keep him waiting any longer. If you could bring him in. Let's get this over with."

Mike left the room and returned thirty seconds later with a nervous looking Jeremy Halliday in tow.

"Take a seat, Jeremy. I'm sorry to interrupt your day like this," Mary said. "Were you in the middle of a lesson?"

"Yes. My GCSE English class."

"I assume Jenny has arranged someone to cover for you?"

Jeremy nodded.

She had been trying to think of a way of gently easing into the matter in hand but decided that it was better for both of them if she dived straight in.

"It's about Susie Meredith. I believe she's in your tutor group?"

Jeremy was sitting a few feet in front of her desk and she could see that he was staring down at his file still lying open in front of her. She swiftly closed it.

"Yes, she is."

"You're obviously aware she's been away from school for the past week?" She didn't wait for an answer but ploughed on. "Her mother phoned me yesterday evening. She was concerned that Susie had been feigning illness and, for some reason, just didn't want to go to school. Her first thought was that Susie might be being bullied."

"Yes, she was being bullied," Jeremy interrupted, looking more relaxed now that he thought he knew what the interview was about, "but I thought we'd sorted that out. I'm sorry if it's started up again. In fact, if it's the same girls, then I'm angry that it's still going on. The bullies were two other girls in the 11th year. If they're still at it then there'll obviously have to be some more serious action taken. Maybe they should see you..."

"No, Jeremy, it's not about bullying. Susie's mother sat down with her and spent a long time trying to get the truth out of her. Finally, Susie told her. It's because of you that she doesn't want to go to school."

"Me!"

"Yes. I have to tell you that she has made a serious allegation about inappropriate behaviour by you towards her."

Jeremy looked bemused as her words took time to sink in. "Inappropriate? Is that code for sexual behaviour?"

"I'm afraid so."

"Well I hope you realise that that's nonsense...... whatever she's said. What exactly has she said? I mean...... what's she accusing me of?"

"I'm sorry, Jeremy, but I'm not at liberty to go into the details of it now. I know it's difficult but you must understand that once we get an accusation of this kind we have to treat it seriously and there are set procedures that need to be followed......"

"For Christ's sake, I've been teaching here for twelve years. Why would I suddenly do something like.........well, like whatever it is she says I've done?"

He stared angrily at Mary, who looked back impassively, and then turned to the florid faced deputy head.

"Mike, you've known me most of that time. Surely you know I wouldn't do anything like this? Miss Groenwald's new. She doesn't know me, but you do. Tell her."

Mike Harvey was equally stoney-faced.

"I'm sorry, Jeremy. The Head is right. We can't rush to judgement one way or the other. We have to follow the procedures. You'll get a fair hearing."

Jeremy was now as red-faced as Mike and looked about to explode. Mary butted in, raising her voice to try and sound more authoritative.

"Mike is absolutely right. We can't have any more discussion about this now. We must follow strict procedures. This is as much to protect you, Jeremy, as for any other reason. I have arranged for a formal meeting to take place at ten thirty tomorrow morning at the local education authority offices. Myself and Mike will be there along with the chair of governors, someone from the local authority Human Resources Department and my p.a. Sally to take minutes. You will also need an adviser who can support and represent you. I believe you're a member of the National Union of Teachers?"

"Yes." His reply was barely audible.

"I would suggest we get someone from their regional office to support you. It's too serious a matter to rely on the school's union rep. If you like, I can get Sally to phone them at the end of this meeting and arrange for them to attend?"

"Yes. Thanks." Jeremy's brief balloon of anger was rapidly deflating.

"This meeting is just a first stage. Its purpose will be to outline the formal procedures and processes of an investigation. The Merediths won't be attending and there won't be any discussion or explanation of the actual charges laid against you." She paused to give Jeremy a chance to respond but he continued to look shell-shocked.

"While the investigation is going on," the Head continued, "you will be suspended on full pay. I must ask you – and I know this will be difficult – not to contact anybody in school during the period of the investigation. That includes members of staff, students, parents and governors. Again, that's to protect you against any accusation of trying to influence the proceedings. Of course, your union representative will be given access to anybody in school he or she wishes to talk to so that they can present your case."

"I'm suspended?" Jeremy pronounced the words as if they were in a foreign language. "That makes it seem like I've already been found guilty."

Mike intervened. "It's just the normal procedure, Jeremy. It's as much to protect you as for any other reason. I mean, think about it. You wouldn't want to be carrying on teaching with all this going on, would you?"

Mary didn't give him time to answer.

"You'll be notified in writing formally about the suspension although, of course, it starts from now so I'll have to ask you to leave the premises as soon as this meeting is over. If you want, we can get a taxi to take you home."

"No, it's alright. It was such a nice day I came on my bicycle. I'll cycle home. I suppose I can go back to the English office and get my bag and my cycle helmet?"

"If you tell Sally exactly where they are, maybe she can go and get them for you. It's just that, if you meet somebody on the way it might be hard not to start talking about what's happened."

Jeremy gave a barely perceptible nod. If all this was being done to protect him and look after his interests why did he feel like a criminal being banished in disgrace?

"Okay. Well, if you could arrange that with Sally, then we'll see you at the meeting tomorrow."

After a brief conversation with Sally about the exact location of his bag and helmet, Jeremy slumped down on one of the khaki-padded IKEA chairs in the waiting area outside Mary Groenwald's office. His mind had gone blank. He tried to think of what else he could, or should, have said. He felt he'd been too supine, too ready to accept the ridiculous accusation and his subsequent suspension. From the way that Mary Groenwald and Mike Harvey had been looking at him, he was sure they thought he was guilty. But guilty of what exactly? And how would his colleagues feel when they got to hear about it? It was probably going round the staffroom already. He could just imagine that old cliché being trotted out – there's no smoke without fire.

He stood up and walked out of the waiting area into the corridor, glancing up and down it. He hoped his bag was where he remembered leaving it and that Sally would return promptly with it. He wanted to get out of the building as quickly as possible and breath some fresh air.

"Are you Mr. Halliday?" The gruff cockney voice came from behind him as he went back towards his seat.

He turned to face a man of about his height and age wearing paint-stained jeans and a check shirt.

"Yes."

"You fucking pervert. Do you have any idea what state my daughter's in because of you?"

The man edged closer to him. Flecks of spittle hit

Jeremy's face as the man shouted at him. Jeremy didn't respond. All he could think about was that, if this was Susie's father, why didn't he recognise him. Then he remembered that her parents were divorced and it was Susie's mother who had always attended parents' evenings on her own.

"How the hell were you ever allowed to be a teacher? You're a fucking disgrace. She's a fifteen year old girl, for fuck's sake."

The door to the Head's office burst open and Mike Harvey rushed out followed closely by Mary Groenwald. They'd obviously heard the shouting.

"Mr. Meredith, you shouldn't be........." but before Mike Harvey could finish his sentence, the angry father swung a fist at Jeremy who, despite being stunned into silent immobility by Mr Meredith's unexpected appearance, managed to duck sufficiently to avoid the full force of the meaty fist but still caught a stinging blow to the ear. He overbalanced and fell backwards into the row of chairs as Mike Harvey dashed between them and pulled Mr Meredith away. Despite being four or five inches shorter and twenty years older than Meredith, he had the build of a rugby prop-forward gone to seed and managed to hold him back as he attempted to wrestle free and aim another punch at Jeremy. Within seconds Tom, one of the site care staff, appeared and helped Mike restrain the furious father and usher him away from the Head's office.

Jeremy sat down, embarrassed and disoriented, gingerly touching his stinging ear, examining his fingertips for signs of blood.

"Are you alright?" Mary Groenwald hovered over him, white-faced and visibly shaken. "Are you injured? I can get a first-aider to come and look at it for you. Can I get you a glass of water?"

Jeremy looked up as if he didn't recognise her or understand what she was saying.

"I'm alright," he eventually mumbled, just as Sally appeared clutching his blue rucksack and red and black cycle helmet. "I just need to get out of here."

It was only a fifteen minute cycle ride from the school to Jeremy's house in Tooting Bec Road but, after he'd gone half a mile, he dismounted and wheeled his bike along the pavement. He hadn't been concentrating and had veered out towards the middle of the road where a white van swerved around him hooting loudly, the driver screaming obscenities out of the window.

He hadn't been allowed to leave the school until Mike Harvey returned to the office to confirm that Mr Meredith had been escorted well away from the premises.

"Jeremy, I can't apologise enough about this. I had no idea that Susie's father was coming into the school. He didn't have an appointment." The head teacher was still very pale and appeared more disturbed than Jeremy.

His ear had started bleeding and Sally brought him a bowl of warm water and some cotton wool.

Mary Groenwald stared with dismay at the bloodied ear. "I think we ought to call the police, don't you?" She said to Mike Harvey, who was straightening his jacket and tie having returned from ejecting Susie Meredith's father from the building.

"No. I'd rather you didn't involve the police," said Jeremy before Mike could answer. "I'm perfectly okay. There's no need for any more fuss."

He wheeled his bike past the turn down Tooting Bec Road and headed for a café on Tooting Broadway. He locked his bike to a lamppost and went in for a cup of coffee. Suddenly he was in no hurry to go home. He needed to think. What was he going to tell Julia? Or, more importantly, how was he going to tell Julia? And what about their friends, his father, Julia's sister? And what if it got into the local paper? He tried to calm himself down. He was jumping the gun. Apart from Julia, maybe the others wouldn't need to know. Obviously it was all a ludicrous misunderstanding. There would be a simple explanation. It would probably be sorted out at tomorrow's meeting.

A vision of Susie Meredith's innocent, adoring face as she sat in the passenger seat of his car suddenly came to him. At the time he had felt a warm glow inside. But now?

He left the café without touching his coffee. His mind was in turmoil, going backwards and forwards like a tennis ball in mid-rally. One minute home was the last place he wanted to be, the next he was desperate to get back there. At first Julia had been the last person he wanted to know about what was happening to him, but now he needed someone to talk to and Julia was the only option.

As Jeremy opened the front door and wheeled his bike into the hallway, he didn't know whether Julia would be at home. She spent a lot of time visiting the shops she supplied and the homeworkers who manufactured her designs. He didn't know whether to feel pleased when he heard her calling downstairs from the loft room or disappointed because he'd wanted more time to think about how to tell her about what had happened. Probably better this way, he thought, as he heard her footsteps on the upstairs landing. He had a tendency to dither – to take too much time thinking things through. And then, when he couldn't delay any longer, all that thinking never seemed to make the final decision any better.

"What are you doing home at this time of day?" She

said as she clumped down the stairs. "The weather's too warm for the heating to have broken down again. Or has the sainted Miss Groenwald given you all a half-holiday as a reward for your hard work?"

She stopped on the bottom step and stared at Jeremy, her breezy manner replaced with a look of concern.

"Jeremy. Is something wrong? What's happened?"

He realised his face must be giving him away. "Come and sit down and I'll explain," he said.

She followed him down the corridor, into their spacious open plan living room, the sun streaming through the french windows at the far end.

"Sit down," he said. "Can I get you a cup of tea? I could do with one."

"No Jeremy. I don't want a cup of tea," she said tetchily. "I just want to know what the hell's going on."

He slumped down in the buttoned leather armchair and ran his fingers through his hair.

"The school hasn't been closed or anything like that." He paused. "The Head sent me home. I've been suspended."

It took a moment for his words to sink in. When they did, she looked at him with raised eyebrows, waiting for him to elucidate. When he didn't, she was forced to prompt him.

"Suspended? What do you mean? What have you done?"

He took a deep breath. "One of the students has made an accusation against me. They've suspended me from school while they carry out an investigation."

Julia was struggling to make sense of what he was saying and his reticence wasn't helping.

"An accusation? What sort of accusation? Who's made it?"

Jeremy gave her a forlorn look like a naughty child caught with his hand in his mother's purse.

"Jeremy, just tell me exactly what's happened. I'm not the police. You're turning this into an interrogation."

He took another deep breath. "It's a girl in my tutor set. She's accused me of molesting her......sexually molesting her."

"What?" Julia didn't know what she had been expecting but it certainly wasn't this. "Who's made this accusation? Do I know her?"

"Her name's Susie Meredith. She's in the tenth year...... in my tutor set."

"Susie Meredith." Julia pronounced the name slowly while trying to place her. "I think I taught her in the eighth year. A mousy-looking girl, reddish curly hair, very pale, thin, anaemic looking?"

"She's fifteen now. She's a bit more grown up." He was about to add that she'd filled out and developed into an attractive young woman but he stopped himself, knowing how wrong it would sound.

"What exactly has she accused you of?"

"I don't know...... for sure. She's been off school for over a week and she told her mum that it was because of me – because of what I'd done to her."

Julia waited for some further explanation. He knew he must look and sound pathetic but he couldn't summon up any of the feelings of anger he'd felt when the Head first told him he was suspended. He just felt demeaned and deflated.

"The Head couldn't give me any details of the accusations. There's a formal meeting at the education authority offices tomorrow. I should get more information then. I'll have a union representative in there with me."

"But this is ridiculous. If this is the girl I remember then she's a pathetic scrap of a thing. She's obviously developed an infatuation with you...... I don't know...... concocted a fantasy relationship and come up with some ridiculous accusations. It's not that uncommon. Most good-looking young male teachers get that kind of attention at some stage. Surely Mary Groenwald can see that that's what this is all about?"

"Unfortunately, they can't dismiss it so easily. They have to investigate. There are procedures laid down that they have to follow. Part of that is suspending me from school while the investigation proceeds. It's for my own protection." He hated himself for parroting almost word for word what he had been told by Mary Groenwald. He knew he must sound like the Head's lapdog, but he couldn't see how he could avoid it – he had to report back to Julia exactly what he had been told.

"Is that blood on your ear?" Julia had suddenly noticed it. "How did that happen?"

He told her about the incident with Susie's father.

"Bloody hell! What's the matter with that school? How could they allow that to happen?" Julia stood up and gesticulated as she spoke. "It's that bloody woman. She's far too young and inexperienced to be a head teacher. She's out of her depth." Julia had never met Mary Groenwald but she'd listened to numerous grumbles about her from her ex-colleagues when she met up with them and, even though Jeremy had always tried to give the new Head the benefit of the doubt when Julia repeated their complaints to him, she had retained her negative image of Mary Groenwald.

"Has this assault been reported to the police?"

"No. I told Mary not to. It's enough of a mess already. I didn't want to make it any worse. I'm not badly injured."

Julia stood in front of him, staring down disparagingly. "You're being far too reasonable about this. I think it's a mistake. If you don't press charges against this thug, it could look like you're admitting guilt."

Jeremy stared helplessly back at her. "He's the girl's father. It's only natural that he's going to believe his daughter and, if he thinks that she's been sexually assaulted by a teacher, then he's bound to be angry."

Julia looked hard at Jeremy as he slumped back in the chair. She had been about to pursue the issue further – harangue him for being too soft – but she saw how beaten down and exhausted he looked. He needed her support, not her badgering. And yet, the situation was so frustrating. She wanted to help him but, without more details, it was hard.

"I know this is difficult, Jeremy, but I just want to help you prepare for the meeting tomorrow." She perched herself on the edge of the armchair and slid her arm across his sagging shoulders. "Have you said anything to this girl that she might have misinterpreted? Paid her any special attention?"

Jeremy grasped her hand and shuffled awkwardly in the chair. "A few weeks ago she asked me if she could use my classroom after school to do her homework. She's got a small sister she shares a bedroom with at home and she said she finds it hard to concentrate there."

"So – she was alone in the classroom with you after school?" Julia couldn't prevent a feeling of irritation creeping into her voice.

"Yes. She just sat there doing her work and I got on with my marking. It happened for a few days running and then – on the Friday of that week – I told her I had to leave school early so she couldn't stay. That's when she told me the real reason she was staying behind at school. She was being bullied by two girls. Not just in school. They often lay in wait for her on her way home." He paused.

"So what happened then?"

"She was too scared to tell me at first but, when I persisted, she told me who the girls were. They were two other girls in the tenth year. She didn't want me to do anything. She said it would only make it worse for her – but I told her I couldn't ignore it. The school has an antibullying policy and I would make sure it was properly dealt with and she wouldn't have any more problems with them."

There was a long pause before Jeremy squeezed her hand and looked into her eyes.

"And that's it. It took a few days for me to track the girls down with the help of Brigid, the Head of Year. They're both pretty regular truants. Anyway, we sorted it all out and, as far as I know, the bullying stopped."

Julia let go of his hand. "Well, that would probably give her more than enough of a reason to be infatuated with you if she wasn't already, before this bullying business." Julia paused briefly to think things through. "The problem is – you've spent all that time in a room alone with her. I hate to say it, Jeremy, but that wasn't very sensible. Doesn't the school have rules or guidelines about things like that?"

"Not that I know of." For the first time since he started talking to Julia, he felt exasperated. "For fuck's sake, I'm a teacher. I was trying to help one of my students – so shoot me. It's not a crime, is it?" His anger was growing. All he had wanted was comforting words and support from Julia. Instead she was questioning his actions.

He sprang out of the chair brushing against Julia's shoulder, knocking her off balance so she had to steady herself to avoid falling.

"You think I'm guilty, don't you?" He said angrily.

"Of course I don't. I'm sorry but I'm just trying to help. To understand why she's making these accusations."

Julia perched herself back on the edge of the armchair. Jeremy had walked over to the french windows and had his back to her, staring out at the garden. The sunshine streaming in through the window created a halo effect round his dishevelled hair. Julia tried to think of something more supportive to say.

"At my first school – St. Augustine's in Newham – there was a teacher – Brian Caldwell – a girl accused him of molesting her. He wasn't like you. He was much older – nearing retirement. A bit of a loner. I didn't really know him but some of the staff suspected he might be guilty. He was suspended. And then it all just rumbled on for a long time. There wasn't much evidence against him and, in the end, they just settled it by offering him early retirement." She paused. Jeremy was still standing straight-backed in front of the window. "I'm just worried for you. I'm worried what this girl's been saying and how you can prove she's lying." She felt herself starting to burble with no idea why she was telling him this.

"I don't want to talk about it anymore – for now anyway. It's a nice afternoon. I need some fresh air. I'm going to do some gardening. I need something to take my mind off it."

The garden was long and narrow, walled on one side, west facing. Since they'd bought the house Jeremy had been the one to take an interest in it. His parents' house in Wimbledon had had a large garden and, after his mother died, he'd often helped his father look after it, learning a lot from him about the plants. It had been one of the only things they'd done together.

Once he'd changed into his gardening clothes, he went round the flower beds vigorously digging out the weeds. He emptied them into the incinerator at the bottom of the garden and then stood with hands on hips and admired his handiwork. When they moved in, the garden had been mostly scrubby lawn with the few flowerbeds filled with weeds and the odd rosebush. He'd redesigned and replanted it himself after studying various books and websites on small city garden design and maintenance. He was proud of his work and visitors were invariably impressed.

He felt the warm sun on his back. At least it was some compensation that it was not a bad time of the year to be stuck at home looking after the garden. He smiled to himself. Wasn't that the polite euphemism for being suspended from work – being on 'gardening leave'?

6

Tim Merriman stood with his arms folded watching Jeremy measuring the dimensions of a pegged out patch of earth at the end of his garden with a retractable steel tape measure. Jeremy pulled a notebook and pen out of the breast pocket of his hawaiian shirt and jotted down the measurements, adding some other rough calculations.

"Have you decided what sort of paving stones you want to use?" Jeremy asked.

"Yes. I've got the details written down in my diary," Tim said.

"And would you like me to lay a stepping stone path across the lawn? You wouldn't want it straight across. I could lay it in a nice curve."

"Yes, that'd be good. With the same paving stones if possible."

Jeremy took carefully measured steps from the pegged out patio area across the lawn, past the swimming pool, to the terrace at the back of the house and then scribbled more figures in his notebook.

"And what do you think of my idea of the raised rockery in that area behind the patio?" Jeremy said.

"We both like it. It looks very pretty – well, it does in your drawings at least. If you could give us a price for that as well, including the planting?"

His visit to the Merriman's was stage one in Jeremy's plan to get some semblance of a normal routine back into his life.

His and Julia's decision to move to France four years ago had been anchored financially by the success of Julia's business and her ability to run it just as easily from South-Western France as from London. Even though buying a property with an operational gîte attached provided an additional source of income, at forty years old Jeremy wasn't yet ready to drift into a very early retirement and live off Julia. And so, as the move was being finalised, he started looking for ways of occupying himself in France while making money at the same time.

When his father's dementia had got to the stage, a couple of years ago, where he could no longer continue to live on his own, Jeremy had found a care home for him and sold his flat to help pay the bills. It was while he was clearing out the flat that he found his father's stamp collection albums buried away in a cupboard. One of his happier memories of his father was the time they had occasionally spent together on dark winter evenings at the dining room table mounting the delicate stamps in albums, donning the white plastic gloves and delicately wielding the rubber-tipped tweezers and the double-sided sticky mounts. It was the only other thing, apart from gardening, that he could remember them doing together. During his teenage years, he would often take out the albums and leaf through them as a comforting memory of happier days. His father had given up stamp collecting, along with most other things in his life, after Jeremy's mother's death. The most valuable albums were collections from present and past British colonies and protectorates, places such as Aden and the Falkland Islands. For a brief period, he spent Saturday mornings trekking up to Portobello Road and Camden Passage to visit stamp dealers' stalls and trawl through their offerings to see if he could add to the collection but he rarely bought anything as the sorts of stamps that would have fitted in were well out of his price range. As he grew older, he forgot about the albums which remained wrapped in their plastic bags in the back of the cupboard under the stairs.

And so, it was a surprise to find them after so many years still intact and untouched in their plastic wrappings. No longer feeling the old sentimental attachment to them and knowing that many of the stamps were valuable, he decided to sell them. Since his youth, the world of philately had changed. Shops and antique market dealers were on the wane. Dealing was now done mostly over the internet. And so, he quickly established a site and linked himself to a range of collectors and dealers. Once he had successfully sold a large portion of the collection, he found himself captivated by the whole process – it had become a sort of addiction. Rather than waste all the knowledge he'd gained from his extensive research of the market and of his father's particular collection, as well as all the connections he'd established with the online philatelic community, he decided to set himself up as a dealer – buying as well as selling. Like Julia's, it was a business he could easily continue in France.

Those first few months in the French house, he'd divided his time between his stamp dealing on his laptop and decorating and renovating the house and re-planning the mostly unkempt and neglected garden.

Among the first people they met after moving in were the Carringtons, a retired couple with a holiday home on the other side of the village. Jeremy and Julia invited them over for drinks on Jeremy's newly constructed patio from where they admired the other work he was doing in the garden. They were so impressed that they asked if he'd be interested in doing some work for them. It was like a flashbulb going off inside Jeremy's head. After the house in Tooting, this had been his second garden project. He enjoyed it. He was good at it. Why not explore the possibility of doing it on a more professional basis? A second string to his bow, so to speak, in addition to his stamp dealing. And so, he took up the Carringtons' offer and, before long, as their friends and neighbours visited and were impressed with his handiwork, a steady trickle of new gardening projects materialised. Over the last couple of summers it had gradually become more of a business than a paying hobby and he had made enough money from it to invest in better tools and equipment and a battered second-hand van to ferry them around in.

The Merrimans had taken up residence two years earlier in an extensive old farm property of several stone buildings surrounding a courtyard a few kilometres from Vendillac, Jeremy and Julia's village. It had taken them four years to have the buildings renovated and, once that work was finished, they were ready to start on the garden. They were friends of the Carringtons and, having seen and admired Jeremy's work on their garden, the Merrimans had contacted him last summer and he did some work for them. They'd been pleased with it and now here he was drawing up plans and estimates for the next stage.

Tim Merriman was in his late fifties – a wealthy, upper class, go-getting businessman, every inch the typically buttoned up English gentleman – literally, as he always dressed in grey slacks, open-necked long-sleeved check shirts and a panama hat. Even on the hottest days, he would never be seen in shorts, polo-neck shirts or sandals. Felicity, his wife, was more relaxed. A consultant paediatrician, she was petite and stick-thin with a pretty freckled face surrounded by an afro-like frizz of black hair. Tim was her polar opposite – very tall, bent-backed, paunchy with a jowly florid face. Although they were the same age, she looked years younger than him.

Jeremy and Julia met up with the Merrimans occasionally for drinks and once went out for a meal with them but Jeremy felt he had very little in common with Tim. Although Tim was always a model of politeness and full of public school bonhomie, Jeremy complained to Julia that he treated him like the hired help. Julia was quick to dismiss such comments and assure him that he was imagining it. Not that she was over fond of Tim herself, but she did get on very well with Felicity. They found they had a lot in common. They came from similar backgrounds; neither of them had, or had wanted to have, children; and Felicity was a keen amateur craftswoman – mainly water colour painting and embroidery.

The two men returned to the shaded terrace overlooking the swimming pool. Felicity brought out a tray of coffees and slices of tarte aux noix – a local delicacy. She looked uneasy as she sat down on the other side of the patio table. Julia had paid her a visit over a week earlier and told her of her decision to leave Jeremy. She was unsure whether she should say anything about it and, if so, what exactly she could say. It was made more difficult because she'd been inside the house making the coffee while the two men had been talking so she didn't know whether Tim had already broached the subject.

Her tension was relieved by Jeremy opening the conversation while she was pouring the coffees.

"I guess you already know about me and Julia?"

"Yes. She told me last week – just before she left," Felicity said.

"I was very sorry to hear about it, old boy," Tim said. "If there's anything at all we can do."

"Thanks. I'm grateful for your support." He took a deep breath. "The thing is that Julia leaving me isn't the worst of it. I had a visit from the gendarmes a couple of days ago. They came to tell me that Julia's body had been found in her car near Aurillac. The car had been set on fire so it took them time to examine the body and determine the exact cause of death but they now know that she was murdered."

Felicity and Tim stared at him in stunned silence. Felicity's perma-tanned face grew ashen. Before either of them had had time to take in fully what he had told them and to respond with the obvious questions, Jeremy launched into a full account of everything the gendarme had told him – not the truncated version he'd given Hattie and John. Felicity looked as if she was about to throw up, shocked not only by the gruesome details but also by Jeremy's emotionless, quick-fire delivery.

"That's just awful. I don't know what to say," said Tim. "Of course, you have our sincerest condolences. I feel really bad about getting you to do the estimate for the garden. That must be the least of your worries now. Please – just forget about it. There's no hurry. Or we can get someone else."

"No. That's alright. I wanted to come over and talk to you about the work. I mean – I know it might sound bad – but life has to go on and I thought it might help if I could start to get back to normal. You know – keep myself occupied."

Felicity said nothing. She couldn't look at him. She reached for her coffee cup but left her hand hovering next to it while she concentrated on trying to stop it shaking before lifting it up and taking a gulp to further steady herself.

"I also had another reason to come and see you. It's connected with Julia's death." He paused. "I told you about the judge in Villefranche questioning me. Well, I have to go back and answer some more questions on Monday. I think I'm a suspect."

"You mean – they think you murdered Julia? Surely not," said Tim. Felicity remained tight-lipped.

"Well, it's not surprising. Julia was murdered and they

don't know who did it. In such cases, the husband or partner is always the chief suspect whether there's any evidence or not."

"Oh. So – they haven't got any evidence against you? No reason to think you did it – other than you being her partner?" Tim said nervously.

"No, but, nevertheless, I think I need some legal advice. Just to protect myself. And to help me understand the French legal system. It seems quite different from the English system." Felicity wondered suspiciously just how familiar Jeremy was with the English criminal justice system. "I mean, it's not unheard of for innocent people to get charged with murder. And then I remembered that you were involved in that legal case last year against that stone mason who did the work on your barn. I remember you saying you had this very good English lawyer, married to a French woman. I think you said he was based in Rodez? I wondered if you still had his contact details?"

"Yes I have," said Tim. "I don't know how hot he is on criminal stuff but, even if he isn't, he'll probably be able to recommend somebody who is. I'll just go and get his details."

Tim went inside the house. Felicity's discomfort was growing. She couldn't sit there with Jeremy. She had nothing to say to him.

"I'm sorry, Jeremy. This is a terrible shock. I'm going to have to go inside for a minute."

"Of course. I know how close you and Julia were."

She hurried into the house where she passed Tim on his way back out clutching his Filofax.

"Are you okay?" He said.

"No, of course I'm bloody not okay. Just get rid of him as quickly as you can." She didn't wait for a response but hurried past him towards the kitchen.

"Felicity. Where are you?" Tim shouted out when he came back into the house. He had endured a further ten minutes of awkward conversation before Jeremy announced he had to go.

He walked through the living room to the kitchen but there was no sign of his wife. He called out again before heading upstairs to the bedroom.

"Ah, there you are." She was lying on her back on the bed staring at the ceiling. "Are you alright? Bit of a shock, eh? Can I get you something? A brandy perhaps?"

"No. I'll be okay. Has he gone?" Felicity propped herself up on the pillows.

"Yes." Tim sat down on the edge of the bed and stroked her arm. "Well, there's a turn up for the book. Didn't expect that when I woke up this morning. Definitely not in sleepy old Vendillac. And we thought we'd come here for the quiet life."

Felicity sat motionless, still staring into space.

Tim said, "You don't seriously think he murdered her, do you? Jeremy Halliday – a murderer. He's such an unassuming, quiet chap."

"And aren't they exactly the sort who commit murders? The people you least suspect?" Felicity turned to look at him and put her hand on his. "Your trouble is you don't read crime fiction or you'd know."

"Maybe your trouble is you read too much of it." He chuckled trying to relieve her tension. "No. Sorry. I can't believe he'd do something like that."

"Oh just use your imagination, Tim," she said tetchily. "The woman he loves tells him she's leaving him. She packs up and goes. He's absolutely distraught – and angry. Is it any surprise he's the chief suspect?"

"Well, if you put it like that. But it's a big jump to go from that to murder."

"During our various tête à têtes over the last year or so, Julia told me quite a bit about their life together – and, also, about their finances. It was the money she inherited from her mother that paid for their house in London. And then, the money from that sale bought the house in France. And, if you add to that, the fact that it's her business that mainly supports their standard of living here......" She looked earnestly at Tim waiting for the penny to drop. "So, he's not only losing his lover – he's also lost his meal ticket and is possibly going to lose his home."

"Bloody hell. He's lucky you're not the prosecuting counsel. You've got him bang to rights. All you need to do now is put on the black cap."

"This is no laughing matter, Tim." She shoved his hand away. "Did you listen to the way he described what had happened to Julia? It was chilling. So cold. Like he was telling us about a story he'd read in the newspaper or describing some film he'd seen."

"Oh come on. It's a difficult thing to have to tell people. Everybody has their own way of dealing with that sort of thing." Tim was tempted to say that he was taking it like a man which is why Felicity didn't understand it, but he knew that wouldn't go down well with his wife. "I appreciate that there's grounds for the police to suspect him but you and I know him – and – well, I for one can't believe he'd do such a thing."

Felicity turned her back on him and curled into a foetal position on the bed.

"Well I'm not so sure." She twisted her head back round. "All I know is I don't want to see or speak to him at the moment. If he comes round or phones with the estimate, can you tell him we don't want him to do the work."

"Is that necessary? I mean I don't want him to think that we're ostracising him because we think he's guilty."

"For fuck's sake, Tim. Please do as I ask. I do think it's more than possible that he did it. I'm sure you'll be perfectly capable of explaining diplomatically to him why we don't want him doing the work at present. This has really shaken me up."

"Me too. I may not have been as close to Julia as you were but that doesn't mean I'm not just as shocked and upset as you are."

"Of course you are," said Felicity, making no attempt to hide her sarcasm.

7

Howard Stanton looked up at the clock in the Children's Services reception area of Wandsworth Town Hall. Jeremy Halliday was late. It was ten fifteen and he'd arranged to meet him at ten so they'd have time to get acquainted before the formal meeting started at ten thirty. Even though it was a preliminary hearing to set out the procedures, Howard was nervous.

Despite nearly twenty years as a regional officer for the National Union of Teachers, he'd only ever dealt with three cases where teachers had been accused of sexual misconduct with pupils. Two of those cases had been quickly and easily dismissed when it became clear that the accusations were unfounded and malicious. The most recent case had been much more difficult and personally uncomfortable for Howard. The accused had been a middle aged male teacher in a Battersea primary school. Several small girls had described how he had sat them down on his lap to read with them and touched them where he shouldn't. One said that he had tried to kiss her. It was also suspected from the children's evidence that he may have had an erection. In twenty-five years as a teacher, the man had an exemplary record and was respected and well-liked by his colleagues. However, as soon as Howard met and talked to him, he suspected that he might be guilty. The teacher vigorously denied the accusations but eventually admitted that he may have sat one of the girls on his lap although he claimed it was an entirely innocent action. The one mitigating circumstance that came out during Howard's questioning of him was that his own eight year old daughter had died of meningitis two years earlier. However, the man was adamant that he didn't want it to be mentioned in the hearing and Howard didn't argue with him since, while it may have elicited some sympathy, it was more likely to be seen as confirming his sudden aberrant behaviour.

Instead, Howard tried to persuade him to resign rather than face the disciplinary hearing and probable dismissal but the teacher wouldn't agree. The hearing went ahead, he was found guilty and dismissed. Again ignoring Howard's advice, he insisted on appealing but lost that as well. Unsurprisingly, the whole thing affected him very badly. His wife left him and his teaching career was over. It left him very bitter and he made a formal complaint to the Union about Howard's alleged incompetence in handling his case. The Union found no basis for the complaint but the man was still waging a campaign to clear his name by trying to get his local M. P. involved. Howard knew this because, despite the complaint made against him, he still received emails from the man informing him of his campaign's progress.

Howard didn't know Jeremy Halliday. He was not an active union member and never attended local association meetings. He'd had a brief telephone conversation the previous evening with the school's union rep. who told him that the whole staff were shocked at the allegations and could not believe that Jeremy would do such things.

The lift doors at the far end of the reception opened and a thin man in a dark grey suit and open neck shirt carrying a black shoulder bag and a cycle helmet walked out. He glanced anxiously round the reception area until he spotted Howard and rushed over to him. He was still wearing bright yellow cycle clips round his ankles. There was a rivulet of sweat down the side of his face and his light brown hair flopped over his forehead and was pasted to his brow.

"Howard Stanton?" He said.

"Yes." Howard stood up and they shook hands.

"Jeremy Halliday. I'm so sorry I'm late. A bad accident on the Broadway. The police closed the road and, even on the bike, it was difficult to manoeuvre my way around it."

"Don't worry," said Howard. "The hearing is only going to be a very short formal affair so there's not a lot I need to know from you at this stage. If you go over to the desk and sign yourself in, they'll give you an identity badge. There's a small interview room over there where we can go for a brief chat."

While Jeremy was at the reception desk, Howard sized him up. Mid-thirties but looked boyishly younger: a thin sculpted face with prominent cheekbones, like a male model in an aftershave advertisement: the sort of good looks that Howard would have liked to have had in his younger days rather than his round puffy cheeks, double chin and receding hairline. He couldn't decide whether the fact that Jeremy was good looking made him more or less likely to be guilty. It would certainly make it more likely that a teenage girl would have a crush on him.

Once they were seated in the cramped, box-like interview room, Howard got rapidly down to business. They had less than ten minutes.

"So – Jeremy. I know all the basic details of your career history so we don't need to waste any time on that. Obviously I'm not going to be able to do much for you this morning other than to be in the meeting to advise you if I think the proceedings are not being properly adhered to. But, maybe, it would help familiarise me with the situation if you could quickly tell me something about the girl who's making these accusations."

"Well – her name's Susie Meredith. She's in my tutor group and I also teach her English." Jeremy paused as if he was contemplating what else to say before looking up at Howard.

"Could you tell me a bit about her?" Howard prompted. "Any behavioural problems? Is she a bright student? Any special needs?"

"She's pretty average – certainly as far as English is concerned. Might scrape a C grade in her GCSE. She's not a problem in class. She used to be very timid and quiet." He paused once again trying to choose his words carefully. "She's one of those girls who are quite late developers. She always looked younger than the others in the class but, recently, she's had a growth spurt and she's......" He hesitated trying to avoid language that might sound inappropriate in the circumstances. "She's filled out, if you know what I mean. She's also become more outgoing, more sociable."

Howard scribbled some notes on an A4 pad and then looked back up at Jeremy trying not to appear as uncomfortable as he was feeling.

"Sorry to ask such a blunt question but it's best to get it out of the way. I know you don't know the exact details of what she's accusing you of, but is there likely to be any basis for her making accusations against you of sexual misconduct?"

"No, definitely not." Jeremy maintained firm eye contact with Howard. "Recently she was being bullied and, as her tutor, I helped to put a stop to it."

"So, do you think that this kindness and concern you showed for her might have led her to turn it into a fantasised, romantic......sexual relationship?"

"Yes......I guess so."

"And you haven't done anything else or maybe said

something to her that she might have misinterpreted in any way? For example, touched her reassuringly when she was telling you about the bullying?"

"No…I'm pretty sure I never touched her. Obviously she was upset……she did start crying……and I tried to comfort her……calm her down…… but I never touched her inappropriately."

"Yes, but did you touch her at all?" Howard was struggling to keep his voice gentle and supportive rather than overly interrogative.

"No, I don't think I did."

Howard would have liked a tad more certainty in Jeremy's response but he could deal with that later.

"Okay. We'd better go in now. We don't want to keep them waiting. We'll be able to go through things in more detail when we get to know exactly what she's accusing you of."

Howard and Jeremy sat on one side of an oblong boardroom table. On the other side, facing them, was Mary Groenwald and Mike Harvey, Mary's p.a. Sally Gallagher who was taking minutes, Reverend Timothy Jenkins, Chair of Governors at St. Saviour's, and Angela Ikole, a Wandsworth Council Child Protection Officer.

As the introductions were being made, Howard focussed his attention on Mary Groenwald. It was the first time he had met her and, like most people, he was taken aback by just how young and slight she was. Since she'd taken up the post at St. Saviour's, there had been no issues with union members that had required Howard's intervention. In his recent experience, this didn't signify that she was necessarily an accommodating liberal head teacher determined to deal fairly with staff and unions. She was still in her honeymoon period and, like most new young Heads, she would be establishing herself and treading carefully. Next year he fully expected his caseload at St. Saviour's to mount incrementally as Mary Groenwald started to edge out teachers she had decided were surplus to requirements – most likely the older, long-serving staff members. It was a pattern he'd seen increasingly over recent years with new head teachers often instituting a climate of low level harassment and bullying to force those unwanted teachers to leave of their own accord and find another job or to take early retirement. However, for the purposes of this meeting, she was all sotto voce concern.

"Just to get everybody up to speed," Mary said, "Mike Harvey and I had a meeting with Mr Halliday in my office yesterday morning to inform him that serious accusations had been made against him by one of our students, Susie Meredith, and, therefore, that we had no choice but to suspend him immediately on full pay while we carry out an investigation. This first step, as I'm sure Mr Stanton will verify," she glanced across at Howard, "is normal procedure taken to minimise any disruption to the smooth running of the school and to protect Mr Halliday from any fallout and unwelcome attention if, as seems inevitable however hard we try to prevent it, word gets out to students about Susie Meredith's accusations."

Howard nodded his agreement. "That's fine. Could I just ask, Ms. Groenwald, was Mr Halliday given any indication of exactly what he is being accused of?"

"No," said Mary. "We are naturally concerned that strict procedures should be followed. Mr Harvey and I have spoken to Susie's mother but not to Susie herself and we were satisfied, from what she told us, that there is a case here that needs to be taken seriously and properly investigated. Of course we are well aware of our responsibility to protect members of staff against unfounded and potentially very damaging allegations. However, our primary concern must be the protection of the children at St. Saviour's. A proper and rigorous investigation is the best way to achieve both of those goals. So, if that's alright, Mr Stanton, maybe I can go on to explain the procedures we will follow from now on?"

Howard nodded once again.

Mary waved her hand towards Angela Ikole. "Angela, in her role as a local authority Child Protection Officer, will carry out the investigation including interviewing everyone involved. I should just like to assure Mr Stanton and Mr Halliday that Angela, in the course of her normal professional duties, has had no connection whatsoever with the Meredith family up to now. Nevertheless, to ensure the absolute independence of the enquiry, we have asked Saira Begum, a Child Protection Consultant working for Pathway Education Services, to assist Angela with the investigation. Where they need to, they will liaise with Mike Harvey," she waved her hand towards the deputy head, "who is the senior teacher in the school responsible for child protection. I hope that's all clear and satisfactory."

Howard looked sideways at Jeremy who was staring inscrutably into space.

"That seems clear enough," Howard said. Jeremy nodded his agreement.

"Unfortunately," Mary continued, "there is a problem. I have to inform you all that, earlier this morning, I was informed that the Merediths have made a complaint to the police who have now begun their own investigation." Mary looked directly at Jeremy whose face reddened slightly but otherwise remained impassive. "What this means is that we will have to put the school's investigation on hold until the police have carried out their investigation. If the police decide to press charges then there will be no school investigation. However, I need it to be clearly understood that, if they decide not to press charges or they charge you, it goes to court and you are found not guilty, the school investigation may still proceed at that point. This is because the burden of proof for a criminal charge and/or conviction is not the same as for an internal disciplinary hearing. For example, we may find, in our own hearing, that you are not guilty of sexual misconduct but that, nevertheless, you acted in an inappropriate or unprofessional manner – not something obviously that the police or a court could rule on. I hope all that is clear."

Howard again turned to Jeremy who gave a robotic nod while a barely audible 'yes' issued from his lips.

"Once again, I apologise for this extra complication. I only heard about it a short while ago and I felt it was too late to postpone this meeting. And, anyway, it saves us having to reconvene it in the future. So, if it's okay with everybody, I would like to outline the procedures we will follow if the police decide not to press charges." Mary paused leaving space for a possible intervention. Howard kept his head down and scribbled on his notepad. "When Angela and Saira have completed their investigation, they will present the results to a Governors' Disciplinary Committee. Mr Halliday and his union representative will have had a copy of their report and will be able to present additional evidence refuting any accusations at that meeting. It is not a judicial hearing so no witnesses will be called. Evidence will be based on statements taken by Angela and Saira and Mr Halliday will be able to present written statements of his own, for example from character witnesses. The governors' committee will then reach a decision on what action to take, if any. In the worst case scenario – if the decision were to be dismissal, then Mr Halliday would have the right to appeal."

"How exactly will I be able to refute charges when I

have no idea what I'm accused of?" Jeremy's voice was thin and croaky.

"Angela, maybe you could briefly outline the process your investigation will take?" Mary said.

Angela Ikole gave Jeremy a reassuring smile. "We will start our investigation by getting a written statement from Susie Meredith. We do this because it's felt to be better to let her outline fully what she claims has taken place without feeling the pressure of an adult interrogation. Once we have the statement we will interview her about it. We will then seek written statements from anybody else who may have been a witness to anything described in the girl's statement or who may have some other material evidence. That could be other members of staff, school students, support staff or parents. Once we have all that, we will interview you, Mr. Halliday, and at that stage we will present those accusations to you and you will have your first opportunity to present your side of the case. Of course, you may have other witnesses to support your case who you might want us to take statements from." Angela leaned back and indicated to Mary Groenwald that she had finished.

"Right," said Mary. "The only thing I have left to do is to give you these." Mary passed across two buff coloured envelopes, one to Jeremy and one to Howard Stanton. "They just contain in writing the formal procedures that we've just gone through and the letter informing you of your suspension on full pay. Are there any further questions?"

Jeremy's head was in a whirl. He was sure there must be numerous questions he should be asking but he couldn't think of any. He tried to make eye contact with Mike Harvey and Sally Gallagher as possibly friendly supportive colleagues but Sally's eyes remained firmly on her laptop screen while Mike avoided making eye contact. He shifted his gaze to Timothy Jenkins who had struck him as very laid back and jolly for a priest when he'd previously met him at a couple of staff and governors' wine and cheese parties, but today he had his serious face on. With his shiny black hair, his black-rimmed glasses and his square jaw, he looked disconcertingly like the comic strip drawings of Clarke Kent, alias Superman. He imagined the reverend bursting out of his dog collar and grey suit, to reveal himself as the super hero righter of wrongs who would scoop Jeremy up and fly away with him to a place of sanity and safety before returning to vanquish the villainous Merediths and save the day.

8

Julia sat staring blankly at her laptop screen, her hand resting on the mouse, unable to concentrate on what she was supposed to be doing. Since leaving her teaching job and starting her own business, she'd made a conscious effort to be very self-disciplined: to get up with Jeremy every morning when the alarm clock went off and to be ready to start work as soon as he left for school. Each weekend, she would plan out the week ahead and stick to the plan as rigidly as if it was her old school timetable. That morning she had been due to meet Jamila, an outworker who manufactured some of her products, in Caffé Nero in Wimbledon to go through her latest handbag designs but she'd cancelled so she could be at home for Jeremy when he returned from the town hall meeting.

He looked drained and pale when he arrived back at the house, barely touching the salade nicoise she had prepared for lunch. He gave a brief stumbling account of his initial chat with Howard Stanton and the subsequent meeting to go through the procedures. Julia's disappointment and frustration was palpable when he told her there'd been no more information on the nature of Susie Meredith's accusations. He paused to drink some water before proceeding to tell her the worst part.

"However, the whole process – the school investigation, that is – is having to be put on hold because the Merediths have reported it to the police. It's now become a police investigation."

"You're joking. The bastards." Julia was dumbfounded and angry. "Mind you, it could be a good thing. The police will know what they're doing. I'm sure they'll be better, and quicker, at sorting this all out than the school. It won't take them long to see what nonsense this is."

Jeremy gave her a half-hearted nod and was about to explain what Mary Groenwald had said would happen if the police decided not to prosecute but he felt washed out and his head was starting to ache. He didn't want to talk about it anymore.

Julia could see he was in no mood for further discussion so she bit her tongue and allowed him to go upstairs, don his gardening clothes and retreat to his favourite therapeutic activity even though it had started raining.

Half an hour later the doorbell rang. It was two police officers in plain clothes, a youngish woman and a middle aged man, wanting to talk to Jeremy Halliday. She called the bedraggled Jeremy in from the garden and left him with officers in the sitting room after he had declined her offer to stay and support him through the interview. With his wet hair plastered across his forehead and a pale knee peeking through a rip in his faded muddy jeans, he looked like a nervous schoolboy called into the Head's office straight from the football field. Julia hated to leave him alone with the police but she did not want to risk starting an argument in front of them by insisting that she stay.

The homepage of her leather supplier's website remained stubbornly on the screen in front of her as it had been for the last fifteen minutes. She was supposed to be placing an order but she couldn't fix her mind on it. She stared out of the window at the garden where Jeremy's muddied spade and wheelbarrow full of uprooted weeds stood abandoned in the drizzling rain. She looked at her watch for about the tenth time since the police had arrived. The time seemed to be moving absurdly slowly. How long was this going to take? She felt anger still boiling up inside her. It was so unfair – that some disturbed adolescent girl could throw out wild accusations that could destroy a man's career, if not his whole life. But she told herself she mustn't think like that. It was just a matter of riding it out until everybody recognised how ridiculous these accusations were and Jeremy was exonerated. On the one hand, she felt it was good that it was all happening so quickly because the quicker it was over the better. On the other, she was worried that the police were interviewing Jeremy so soon after he had first been made aware of Susie Meredith's allegations. He was normally such a laid back character – able to take most things in his stride. It was what had first led her to fall in love with him. When she was falling apart over Pete Davies' betrayal, Jeremy had become her rock. Whereas Pete had been a macho control freak, Jeremy had also been in control but in a calm and caring way. It was the same when her mother had been going through the final stages of her terminal cancer and she had been shuttling backwards and forwards between Tooting and the hospice in Devon. Jeremy seemed to know intuitively how to pitch his support at the right level – solicitous and sympathetic without being mawkish and suffocating.

But now, over the past twenty-four hours, he'd become a different person. It was as if he was suffering the after effects of concussion. The initial allegation followed by his suspension was bad enough but now this police investigation – it was as if he'd been knocked to the floor and, before he could get back up, he was being given a good kicking. Maybe she should go downstairs and sit with him anyway. At least it would be better than sitting there staring out at the weeping grey clouds. Another look at the watch and then she gave herself a mental kick up the backside. This could go on for at least another hour. She had to have a distraction so she forced herself to click on the mouse and find the page with the materials she needed and start compiling her order.

Once she had completed the order, she resisted the urge to check her watch again or to get up and go to the door to listen out for any sign from downstairs of the police leaving and, instead, checked her emails. Then she logged on to her own company's website to make one or two minor alterations that she'd been intending to do for several weeks.

As she was navigating her way round the site, there was a gentle tapping at the door. She breathed a sigh of relief, thinking that the police must have left without her noticing and it was Jeremy coming upstairs to tell her what had happened. But, as she called out 'come in', she knew it couldn't be Jeremy. He wouldn't knock. The gaunt face of the male police officer appeared round the opening door.

"Sorry to disturb you, Mrs Halliday. Just to tell you that our interview with Mr Halliday is concluded and......"

"It's Wainwright. Ms Wainwright," Julia said tetchily. "I'm not Mrs. Halliday."

"Sorry Ms Wainwright. We have a search warrant which I have just shown to Mr Halliday – I can bring it up and show it to you if you like."

Julia responded with an impatient look. She just wanted him gone.

"Anyway," he continued, "as we've already explained to Mr Halliday, we need to take away your computers for further examination."

Julia stared at him, her anger beginning to mount.

"If you must," she said, "although I can't believe you're taking this girl's fantasies seriously. Jeremy's laptop isn't up here. It's probably in the front room downstairs."

"Yes, we know. We've already got Mr Halliday's computer. But we need to take yours as well."

"I'm sorry?" Julia was bemused. "Am I being accused of something as well?"

"No, Ms Wainwright. The warrant says that we need to remove all computing equipment from the house – for investigation."

"Look. This is MY computer. I run my own business from this office. Jeremy has his own computer. He never uses this one."

"Be that as it may, we have to take it as well, I'm afraid." The policeman had edged gradually round the open door and into the room. He was trying to sound as understanding and considerate as possible.

Julia's pent up anger and frustration over what was happening to Jeremy now had a focal point.

"I'll say it again." She enunciated the words slowly and clearly as if speaking to a small child or a foreigner. "This is my computer. I need it to run my business. It has no relevance whatsoever to this absurd investigation." Her voice was rising with every word. "Now I would be grateful if you would just leave us to try and get on with our lives."

"I'm afraid I can't do that." He was still trying to sound reasonable but there was now a slight edge to his voice. "I have to warn you that it's an arrestable offence to refuse to co-operate with a legal search warrant."

"What kind of fucking police state is this?" Julia exploded. "What's happened to my human rights......" She spluttered to a halt as Jeremy appeared in the doorway looking anxiously at her over the policeman's shoulder.

"Julia – just let them take the computer. I know it's ridiculous but they do have the right. We're going to have to co-operate." His voice was flat and expressionless.

"Oh fuck it. Take the bloody thing. Is there anything

else you'd like to do to fuck up our lives while you're here?" Julia sprang to her feet sending her swivel chair flying backwards into a metal filing cabinet. She glared at the policeman before turning her angry eyes on Jeremy and then stormed out of the room fighting to stop herself bursting into tears.

Jeremy stood on the front doorstep watching the police officers loading their computers into the car boot. He watched them drive away and then walked to the front gate and looked up and down the street to see if any of the neighbourhood busybodies had been watching the show from behind twitching curtains but there was no sign of anybody either on the street or peering out of windows. He dragged himself slowly back into the house. Gossiping neighbours were the least of his worries, he thought, as he stood at the foot of the stairs debating whether to go straight up and comfort Julia or go to the kitchen and make a pot of tea. He desperately needed a hot drink. It was a mild Spring day but he was shivering in his still slightly damp gardening clothes.

As he filled the teapot he listened out for any sign of Julia stirring upstairs but all was deadly quiet. He still had the image burnt on his brain of Julia's fierce disappointed face staring accusingly at him as she had brushed past him minutes earlier.

Ever since that first night at the staff party, he'd been proud of the way he'd been able to protect and support her. Not only in the fallout from her relationship with Pete, but also in her decision to leave teaching and start her own business and, more recently, during her mother's illness and subsequent death. For perhaps the first time in his life, he'd felt like a real man. But now, after that terrible look she'd given him, everything that had happened between them over the past few years suddenly seemed hollow. He wanted to be able to summon up the kind of anger that Julia was feeling but all he felt inside was a numb wooziness – as if he was coming round from an anaesthetic. And when he did try to summon up the anger, he couldn't decide who to direct it at. Susie Meredith? The police? Mary Groenwald? At that moment, as he carried the tea tray upstairs and prepared to confront Julia, he could only think of directing it at himself. He tried to tell himself that this was unfair – that it wasn't his fault that these nonsensical allegations were being levelled at him. And yet, as he approached the bedroom door with the cups rattling on the tray, his one overwhelming feeling was that he had failed Julia. Not only was he no longer able to protect her, but he was now putting her in harm's way; miring her in something that was none of her doing. Within the last twenty-four hours his feeling of masculine authority had vanished to be replaced by its antithesis. Now he was the one who desperately needed comfort and support – to lay his head against a matriarchal bosom and feel protective arms around him.

She was curled up on the bed with her back to him. He could sense that she'd been crying. He put the tea things down on the bedside table and perched himself on the edge of the bed. She didn't move – didn't acknowledge his presence. He reached out falteringly and put his hand on her shoulder.

"Julia, I'm so sorry about all this."

She didn't move. He was prepared for her to shrug off his hand but she didn't.

"I just wish there was some way I could keep you out of all this."

She put her hand on his and turned round to face him. Her eyes were red and weepy. "Don't be silly. Anything that happens to you involves me as well. We're a partnership."

He heaved a deep sigh of relief. "I've made some tea. I thought you might need a cup."

"Thanks." She let go of his hand as he turned and started to pour the tea. "Do you want to tell me what the police had to say or would you rather leave it till later?"

He was relieved that she was being so solicitous. He had half-expected her still to be bubbling with rage. In truth, he would have preferred to delay having to talk about it but that would be pointless. He had to tell her some time so it might as well be now. He swallowed a mouthful of too hot tea trying to steady himself.

"No, it's okay. I'll just give you the gist of it. They started off by asking me lots of questions about myself and my teaching career – stuff I'm sure they knew already. Anyway – then they asked some questions about Susie Meredith. Basic stuff about how long I'd been teaching her and about what sort of student she was." He paused and swallowed some more tea. "Then they told me they'd interviewed Susie Meredith and taken a written statement in which she had made allegations about several incidents in which I had behaved inappropriately towards her." Julia's eyes were fastened on him but Jeremy had his head bowed and was looking down at the carpet. "She told them about how she'd stayed after school in my classroom and she said that, on one of those occasions, I'd tried to kiss her and touch her but she'd resisted and it hadn't gone any further. Then she said I tried the same thing a couple of days later except this time she was in the car with me and she let me kiss and touch her. Finally, she said I had fuller sexual relations with her at her house.........although not sexual intercourse............... in her bedroom."

He glanced briefly up at Julia's face and, seeing her horrified, confused look, he hurriedly turned away again.

"Oh my god." Julia's mouth hung open as she struggled

to force out the words. "She must be mad. This is such obvious bollocks. The police must see that. She's gone completely over the top. Okay, you've admitted you were alone in the classroom with her so she might just be able to get away with that one but why would she be in your car? And how the hell would you be in her house?"

Jeremy shifted uneasily on the bed and bowed his head even lower towards his hands, which were resting on his knees, as if about to launch into prayer.

"Of course I haven't ever been in her house." He paused and swallowed hard. "But she has been in the car." He could feel Julia's eyes boring into the back of his head.

"What? She's been in the car? When? Why?"

"Twice. During that week. After school. It was because of the bullying – after she'd told me about it and I hadn't yet been able to track the girls down because they'd both been absent from school. She said they often lay in wait for her on the way home. She was scared.........so I said I'd give her a lift home."

Julia gave an exasperated sigh.

"I just dropped her at her house. I didn't go inside."

"Oh well that's alright then." Julia couldn't stop herself. She couldn't keep the irritation and sarcasm out of her voice. She quickly calmed herself down. "Was her mother home? Did you speak to her?"

"No. I just dropped her off. Her mother was at work."

"And this kissing and cuddling in the car. Did she say where it happened? Was it while you were parked outside her house?"

"No. She says I drove her to the Common and..........."

There was a prolonged silence while they both struggled to think of what to say next. Jeremy was searching for the words to justify his actions while Julia tried to control her growing feelings of dismay and disappointment at his behaviour.

"Is that it?" She finally said. "You gave her a lift home twice. You stopped outside her house. She got out of the car and went into the house and you drove off? You didn't get out and see her to her door? Might any of the neighbours have seen you?"

Jeremy swallowed the rest of his tea, still averting his eyes from Julia.

"On the second occasion I took her home......" he paused still not able to look her in the eye. "She'd left her door keys at home so she couldn't get in. I asked her if a neighbour had a key but she said they didn't. I felt bad about leaving her so I suggested I take her back to the high road...... to a café......for a drink. We sat in the café for a while. Had a chat about school, how her exam work was going. Then, when it got to the time her mum was due back from work, she left and walked round the corner to her house."

He looked even more beaten down than before but Julia was too exasperated to hold back any longer.

"For fuck's sake, Jeremy. Okay, it wasn't very sensible to be alone with her in the classroom but at least that's sort of understandable in the circumstances – but to give her lifts home? Take her out to a café? What were you thinking?"

"I was thinking that I was trying to do my best to help one of my students – a poor girl who was in trouble and needed my help." At last, Jeremy could express his anger. Deep down he knew Julia was right – his behaviour had been injudicious – but the last thing he needed now was to have her judging him. He held up his hands in mock supplication. "Okay, so I'm guilty of being a caring compassionate teacher. So lock me up and throw away the key."

Julia took a deep breath and fought to calm herself down.

"So, where does it go from here?" She said. "I'm sorry

to sound so critical. It's just that I'm really worried. These are serious accusations. It's her word against yours......and you've put yourself in a difficult position......"

"Yes, I know I've behaved stupidly but that doesn't mean I'm guilty of what she says I've done. It's only going to be her word. There's no other evidence against me. They've taken the computers to check for things like emails I might have sent her. There aren't any. And......I guess......for child pornography."

"And will they find any?"

Jeremy looked stunned, as if she'd slapped him across the face. "What do you think? Surely you know me well enough not to have to ask a stupid question like that?"

Julia knew she shouldn't have said it but she was glad that at last he was angry. It was preferable to the hangdog naughty boy expression. And it gave her the excuse to give vent to her own anger.

"I thought I knew you but now I'm beginning to think that maybe I don't after all."

Jeremy slammed his mug on the tea tray sending a teaspoon somersaulting on to the floor and stormed out of the room.

9

After the skirmishes an uneasy truce prevailed. Julia still couldn't believe how naïve and irresponsible Jeremy had been but, when she witnessed the turmoil he was going through during the following week awaiting further news from the police, she couldn't help but feel sorry for him and for the things she'd said to him. At least she had a business to run – to take her mind off it – but Jeremy was stuck at home all day with nothing other than his gardening to distract him and, even then, there was only so much weeding and planting he could do. The weather that week was cool with frequent heavy showers. Julia tried to get away from the house on business as frequently as possible, especially as she now had no computer at home to work on. Even sorting out her paper accounts at her desk upstairs was painful as she found herself intermittently glancing out the window at a dishevelled Jeremy pottering around outside.

The conversation during the meals they had together was desultory. Julia had apologised for the way she'd spoken to him and tried to maintain a sympathetic demeanour. However foolishly he'd behaved, deep down she couldn't believe that Jeremy had done any of the things the girl had accused him of. And yet, buried even deeper down, she couldn't prevent tiny doubts from occasionally rising to the surface. She kept remembering all those stories of the wives of serial killers and rapists who claimed never to have the slightest suspicion of what their partners had been up to.

Plus she could remember what it was like to be a teenage girl with a crush on a male teacher. And it was easy to imagine, after all those salacious 'Teacher in Sex Romp with Student' stories over the years in the gutter press, how difficult it could be for those teachers to resist the flattering attention of attractive teenage girls. But then, just how attractive was Susie Meredith? She had tried to summon up a picture of the girl but all that appeared was a fuzzy memory of an immature underdeveloped thirteen year old. She was almost tempted to drive past the Meredith's house to try and catch a glimpse of the fifteen year old Susie to see just how much she'd changed. Whether she was the kind of nubile nymphet under whose spell Jeremy might fall. But then she forced herself to cast such stupidity from her mind. Whatever she looked like, surely he couldn't have done it. Could he?

Obviously she couldn't talk to Jeremy about these doubts. What she really needed was somebody else to talk to. Most of her closest friends were teachers, several of them still working at St. Saviour's. It was tempting to pick up the phone and contact them if only to find out what was happening at the school. But there was no way she could openly discuss her feelings about Jeremy's actions – and certainly not any lingering doubts about his innocence. The only person she could talk to was her sister, Hattie, but she'd been reluctant to phone her. Hattie had never approved of Jeremy. She was the older, protective sister and, when Julia split up with Pete and immediately drifted into a relationship with Jeremy, she became a persistent warning voice. 'You need to give yourself time to recover from the way that bastard treated you – and that means steering clear of men for a while.' 'Bouncing straight into another relationship is the worst thing you can do.' 'On the rebound relationships rarely work'. The fact that it had worked cut no ice with Hattie. The way she always asked during their regular weekly phone conversations how things were going between her and Jeremy, sounded to Julia more sinister than the usual polite solicitations – it was as if she was just waiting for news of the inevitable break up. She took every opportunity to point out Jeremy's alleged shortcomings: to compare him unfavourably with some of Julia's previous boyfriends: to drift into amateur psychoanalysis (she'd studied Psychology and Sociology at university) by telling Julia that, having lost her father at such a young age, she was looking for a substitute – a dominant male figure – and Jeremy didn't fit the bill. Julia was easily able to dismiss her sister's comments, particularly when she considered Hattie's own relationship. Much as she liked Hattie's partner, John, if there was ever a mismatched couple it was Hattie and John not Julia and Jeremy. Hattie's disapproval of Jeremy was nothing compared to the surprise Julia had felt when her intelligent middle class university educated sister had teamed up with a comprehensive school dropout cum jumped up barrow boy. Despite these feelings, she'd always kept her criticisms of Hattie to a minimum, having settled into a habitual deference towards an older sister.

Finally, she put aside her concerns and picked up the phone. To her relief, Hattie was calm and measured in her responses as Julia told her the whole story in every grisly detail. Hattie didn't lay into Jeremy – there were no 'I told you sos' – but she did agree with Julia about how stupid and irresponsible he had been. When Julia confessed about her tiny seeds of doubt, she was quick to pronounce her confidence in Jeremy's innocence. As a senior social worker in East Sussex, Hattie had some experience of child abuse cases, although it wasn't her area of expertise, and was able to come up with several examples of troubled impressionable teenage girls making such false accusations. The conversation ended with Hattie suggesting that she come up to London to visit them. As well as supporting Julia, she felt she could use her professional experience to offer Jeremy some sage advice. Julia wasn't sure about it. Much as she would have loved to speak face to face with her sister, she very much doubted that Jeremy would be as welcoming. He was well aware of how Hattie felt about him and, as a result, their occasional get-togethers had always been tense with the cheery presence of John usually helping to smooth things over. Julia said she'd put it to Jeremy but she wasn't optimistic. Even though she felt that Jeremy needed to talk to somebody, and that Hattie's knowledge and experience might come in useful, she knew her sister was the last person he would want to talk to.

The following day, while she was still debating whether to tell Jeremy about Hattie's offer, there was a development. She was having a cup of coffee while skimming through the newspaper before setting off to visit a new supplier and Jeremy was, as usual, in the garden, when the doorbell rang.

It was the same two police officers from the previous week asking if they could talk to Jeremy. In the living room, it was almost a carbon copy of the scene from their previous meeting with the two officers seated on the sofa facing Jeremy in his grubby gardening clothes but, this time, they suggested Julia should stay as they were not there to question Jeremy but to update him on their investigation.

The young woman did all the talking.

"As you already know, we took a statement from Susie Meredith and then, subsequently, we interviewed you. Then we interviewed Susie's mother, your head teacher, Mary Groenwald, and some other members of staff at St. Saviour's." Jeremy would have liked to ask her exactly which teachers had been interviewed but he assumed that she probably wouldn't tell him. A couple of weeks ago, he would have said that he couldn't imagine that anybody in the school would have anything bad to say about him but now he couldn't be so sure. They must all know what was going on even if they didn't have the full story. And, of course, they wouldn't have the full story because none of them had heard his side of it. So, the rumour mill would be grinding away and, whatever his colleagues felt about him before, he could imagine that, by now, they would probably be thinking 'there's no smoke without fire'.

The police woman continued. "We then returned to do a follow up interview with Susie Meredith as we felt that parts of her statement needed clarification. During the second interview, Susie decided to change her statement. She now admits that she exaggerated exactly what happened between the two of you." Julia was sitting next to Jeremy squeezing his hand. "The part of the statement which she now says is untrue is where she said you went into the house with her and were intimate with her in her bedroom. She now admits that you have never been inside her house."

Jeremy listened as impassively as he had the previous week while trying to loosen Julia's grip, which was becoming painful.

"However, she still insists that the rest of her statement is true. That is to say, her account of you kissing and touching her in your classroom and in your car on the Common."

"Well, surely you're not going to believe anything she says now?" Julia said. "Doesn't this just go to prove that the whole thing is just an adolescent girl's sick fantasy? She's realised she's gone over the top so she's changing her story in a desperate effort to try and make it more believable."

"I can't comment on that," said the female officer, "but obviously her revised statement does change things. The good news for you, Mr Halliday, is that the Crown Prosecution Service, taking into account this new evidence, is not going to press charges. So, as far as we are concerned, the investigation is at an end. We'll return your computers to you this afternoon."

"Thank god for that," said Julia, clutching even tighter to Jeremy's hand. Jeremy looked shell-shocked.

"I'm afraid I must warn you not to celebrate yet," the young woman said.

Jeremy stared apprehensively at her. He feared that she was about to give voice to what was going through his mind.

"We're not prosecuting because we consider Susie Meredith to be an unreliable witness and, after this change to her statement, it's unlikely that we could secure a conviction based on the other things she is still accusing you of. When we leave here, we're going to St. Saviour's to report the results of our investigation to your head teacher. Of course, it will then be up to the school whether they proceed with their own internal disciplinary hearing."

"But surely they can't do anything now. It must be obvious to them as well that this proves what a liar the girl is." All of Julia's mixed up emotions showed in her face and her body language as she let go of Jeremy's hand and stood up abruptly. Jeremy put his hand on her arm.

"We can't comment further on that. It's the school's decision. If there's nothing else, we should be on our way."

After the police had gone, Julia was a bundle of hyperactive confusion, walking up and down the living room while Jeremy tried to calm her down. He went to his desk in the front room, retrieved the school's letter setting out the disciplinary procedures and gave it to Julia to read. He had been so convinced of the inevitability of this nightmare ending up in court that he'd not told Julia about the caveat in the letter concerning the different burdens of proof and that the school disciplinary investigation could still go ahead even if the police didn't press charges.

Once she had calmed down, Julia went from gesticulating outrage to sunny optimism. Whatever the letter said, she couldn't see how anybody could now take the girl's accusations seriously. She was confident that the school would have to drop the matter and reinstate Jeremy forthwith. Jeremy nodded along in apparent agreement but, inside, he was not so optimistic.

Later that afternoon, he received the expected phone call from Mary Groenwald. In her most formal voice, devoid of emotion, she told him that the police had informed her of their decision not to prosecute. But, as he had been informed at their initial meeting, the school would now be continuing with their own investigation.

10

The phone on his desk rang just as he was putting the finishing touches to his estimate for the work on the Merriman's garden. This time he had remembered to leave it on answerphone but he still ground to a halt in mid-calculation, his fingers hovering over the keyboard on his laptop which the police had returned to him earlier that morning. When the machine kicked in after the first five rings, he gave an involuntary shudder as Julia's cheery ethereal voice relayed their recorded message in French and English. It reminded him of those myriad of small tasks he still had to do to remove traces of Julia from his daily life. He held his breath in anticipation of who would be on the other end of the line – the gendarmerie, Judge Bouchon, Hattie – or anyone else in an endless list of people he didn't want to talk to.

"Oh…erm…hello. This is Ruth Gershon. I'm renting your gîte for two weeks starting on June 7th?" There was a pause while she considered what else to say to the machine. "When I made my original booking you said you'd send me more details nearer our time of arrival……… Such as directions on how to find you……"

Jeremy reached across the desk and picked up the receiver. "Hello. It's Jeremy Halliday. I'm really sorry about this."

"Oh that's alright. I'm just happy I've got hold of you." She sounded relieved to be talking to a real person.

"I'm afraid things are a bit chaotic here at the moment." Jeremy was beginning to regret picking up the phone. He was struggling to decide what to tell her. He'd forgotten all about the gîte bookings – Julia always organised them and looked after the website. He wished he hadn't used the word 'chaotic' – not good for customer relations – but it would be far worse if he told this woman that the reason for the 'chaos' was that his partner had recently been murdered. He didn't even want to tell her she'd died. But then he had second thoughts. Maybe it would be best to come clean and cancel the booking – or, at least, give her the option of cancelling. Did he really need the hassle of organising a gîte booking on his own what with everything else that was going on? Maybe he should tell her he was busy and would call her back. Give himself time to think. No – he decided against it. Like his preparations for the work on the Merriman's garden, he decided it best to see it as another opportunity to get back to a semblance of normal life; something else to distract him from the dreadful events unfolding around him.

"It's my partner, Julia, who usually organises the gîte bookings but unfortunately she's had to go away for a while – back to England. Her mother's been taken ill."

"Oh I'm sorry. Look, if you want to cancel and return our deposit, I'm sure we can easily find somewhere else at this time of year. It's so early in the season." She sounded nice. Jeremy tried to conjure up a face to go with her cheerful friendly voice.

"No, no. It'll be fine. I'm used to taking over the reins when Julia's not around. It's just that it all happened rather out of the blue and she rushed off without telling me about your booking. I can only apologise again for our disorganisation. As soon as we finish this call, I'll email you our introductory pack which includes full details of how to get here whether you're flying and hiring a car from the airport or driving all the way. And rest assured that, once you get here, you'll find everything in perfect order." Jeremy almost garbled his words he was speaking so fast in his eagerness to reassure her.

"Thank you. And please don't worry. I understand how difficult it can be when you get sudden bad news like that. How is her mother?"

Jeremy was momentarily thrown by the question, almost forgetting his own dissimulation.

"Oh…erm… she's fine. It's nothing life-threatening but it'll take a while for her to recover."

"That's good. Well, I guess we'll see you on the 7th June then."

"Yes. See you then. And if you have any more questions when you get the pack, please feel free to phone me back or email me."

"Will do. Thanks very much. Bye."

Jeremy put the phone down and stared at the almost completed estimate on his laptop screen. Damn. He realised he hadn't asked her for her email address. He saved the document and exited, nervously punching in their gîte website address praying that Julia had entered all of Ruth Gershon's booking details. While he was clicking on to the bookings page, there was a knock at the front door. He ignored it, found the page and scrolled down to Ruth Gershon's booking. Everything he needed was there. Whoever it was, knocked again, louder this time. He walked out of the office and across the hallway to his bedroom. From the window he could just see down to the front steps and the edge of the porch. At first he couldn't see who it was. They were standing too close to the door. But then they stepped back. It was a man in faded blue jeans and a black t-shirt with a Harley Davidson motorcycle motif printed on it. He looked up at the windows searching for a sign of life and his eyes met Jeremy's peering down at him. It was Guy Reynard, one of the few people in the village Jeremy knew well. Guy was a stonemason and, soon after Jeremy had become serious about setting up his gardening business, he'd been put in touch with Guy as a useful local contact. Since then they had worked together several times on gardening renovations that required the building of stone walls or the repairing of stone outbuildings alongside the landscaping that was Jeremy's area of expertise.

Jeremy swore out loud. He didn't want to speak to Guy or anybody else at present. It would be difficult, if not impossible, to enter into conversation with anybody he knew without telling them about Julia and he still didn't feel up to that. But now that Guy had seen he was in, he had to go down and answer the door. Guy had probably come to see him to check out whether Jeremy had any work for him so, hopefully, it would be a brief conversation and he could then get rid of him.

He opened the door to be confronted by Guy's hangdog face staring questioningly at him, his hands clutching the front page of *La Dépêche du Midi* in front of his chest as if he were an itinerant newsvendor. It took several seconds before Jeremy focused fully on the headline story covering the whole of the front page and, when he did, a lump came to his throat. The headline was in two inch high letters – *Une Femme Anglaise Est Découvert Assassiné à Aurillac*. Beneath it were two photos – one a head and shoulders picture of a very youthful Julia, the other of a gendarme standing between two trees, a red tape tied across them, the blackened bonnet of a car just visible, peeking out from some bushes in the background. Jeremy didn't attempt to read the story underneath – he was transfixed by the photos.

"C'est vrai? This is true?" Guy said.

Jeremy tore his eyes away from the newspaper to

confront Guy's worried face. "Yes, it's true." It was a relief that he didn't have to prevaricate. It had been a huge relief when he told the Merrimans but he had done that knowing that they had very little contact with anybody in the village so the story was unlikely to spread. But now it was in *La Dépêche* everybody would know so it was pointless to try and hide it.

"Come in, Guy. Let me get you a cup of coffee."

The Frenchman sat at the kitchen table while Jeremy put the kettle on and filled a cafetière with ground coffee.

"What does the story say?" Jeremy asked as he turned towards Guy carrying two mugs and a carton of milk to the table.

"It doesn't say much. Just that the body was found in the car which had been put on fire. It was very burnt but they have made tests which show she was murdered. It doesn't say your name but it says she lived in the Aveyron, near Villefranche, with her partner and that the police are questioning him. That's all."

Jeremy poured the boiling water into the cafetière, put it on the table and sat down opposite Guy. The newspaper story was hardly unexpected and yet it felt like he'd been punched in the solar plexus. He felt sick and dizzy. He lowered his head into his hands. Guy got up, walked round the table and stood behind Jeremy. He placed his hands on either side of Jeremy's head and then gently brushed his index fingers against Jeremy's temples barely touching his skin. Instantly, Jeremy felt a warm wave radiate across his forehead – followed by a feeling of relief and relaxation. The Frenchman's actions came as no surprise to him. A year ago, he'd arrived one morning at a gardening job he was doing with Guy and had responded to Guy's 'ca va' by complaining that he had a headache. Guy immediately walked behind him and placed his hands lightly around

Jeremy's head. There was that same warm relaxing feeling and, within seconds, the headache was gone. Guy casually explained that it was a gift he'd had for many years – healing hands. When Jeremy mentioned it in passing to others in the village, they confirmed that they often called on Guy to ease their aches and pains. He was especially effective with bad backs or stiff knee joints, they said. Jeremy asked him why he didn't set himself up in business full-time as a healer – he could make a fortune. He simply gave a gallic shrug. It was a god given gift which he felt he should share with anyone in need. He did not want any payment for it.

Guy's appearance went with both his gift and his relaxed attitude towards remuneration. He looked like a relic from the sixties with long grey hair pulled back in a ponytail, a drooping Viva Zapata moustache and a smudge of beard on the end of his pointed chin.

"Do you know anything more about what happened?" Guy said when he sat back down and Jeremy was pouring the coffees. "What have the gendarmes told you?"

Jeremy took his time to answer. He liked and trusted Guy mainly because, like Jeremy, he was an outsider in Vendillac having grown up in Normandy and only moved to the village five years ago when his then wife had wanted to return to the area she grew up in to be near her ageing parents. Soon after they made the move, the marriage broke up and, ironically, while his wife moved back to Northern France, Guy decided to stay. He liked the area and had started to find plenty of work – not least from the flood of English second home owners happy to employ him as he spoke such good English. But, in an enclosed society like Vendillac, it took more than five years to gain full acceptance, especially when you were a single, middle aged, decidedly eccentric man.

Finally Jeremy spoke, deciding to tell Guy the full story

starting with Julia's decision to leave him. When he reached the part where he had been called in to be questioned by Judge Bouchon, Guy's face registered surprise.

"Surely they do not think you have done this? Where is their evidence?"

"They don't need any evidence, Guy. You know how it goes. I'm her partner. She walks out on me. I'm angry and I want revenge so I chase after her and I kill her."

"But you were here all the time?"

"Yes."

"And you can prove this?"

"Ah – that's the problem. No, I can't. I was so upset after she left, I didn't leave the house. It was like I was in a daze. I didn't know what to do with myself."

"Mon dieu. This is a problem." The Frenchman stared at Jeremy with his pale liquid blue eyes and then looked down at the coffee mug clasped in his hands as if searching in it for an answer to his friend's problem. After a moment's contemplation, he looked up and spoke again in a hesitant, slightly embarrassed tone. "I could tell the Judge that I came round to see you on business. I could be your witness that you were here. How do you say – your aleebee? That you couldn't be in Aurillac."

"That's very good of you, Guy, but I couldn't let you do that." Jeremy struggled to keep the tears from his eyes. He hadn't ever had that many close friends in his life but, since moving to France, he had felt particularly isolated and so he was touched by the Frenchman's offer. "I've already told the Judge that I didn't see anybody during those few days. If you suddenly come forward he's bound to be suspicious."

"Of course. But you say you forget and it's only when you meet me again today that I remind you."

"No. It's very kind but I couldn't let you do that. I don't want you to lie for me. It could get you into trouble. And, if they were to find out that you had lied, it would definitely make me look guilty. And I'm innocent. They're bound to find the real culprit soon."

Guy snorted, almost choking on a mouthful of coffee. "Oh, mon ami. I wouldn't be too sure of that. This is the French gendarmerie you are talking about."

"You don't seem to have much faith in the French justice system?" Jeremy said, grinning at him. "Where's your patriotism?"

"Oh, I'm a very proud Frenchman but that doesn't mean I do not recognise how slow and inefficient most things are in France, especially out here in – how do you say in English? – the sticks? But then that's part of what I love about France. Also, I think, what makes English people like you come to live here. If France wasn't like this, it would be Germany."

*

Jules Bouchon scribbled a quick note to himself on the pad on the desk in front of him before looking up at the bird-like woman sitting opposite him. She looked nervous, her eyes scanning the room as if searching for something.

"Mrs. Merrigan. Thank you so much for coming to see me. I am very grateful for any help you can give with my enquiries."

"That's alright. When the police came round asking whether we knew Julia Wainwright and if we could help with any information, I knew I should come and see you – although I don't really know if I can be much help."

"If you just tell me everything you know, I'm sure I can decide on how helpful it is."

Felicity fidgeted in her seat trying to make herself more comfortable. She was confident she was doing the right thing in coming to see Judge Bouchon but it didn't mean that she could feel relaxed now that she was sat in front of him. When she told Tim what she was going to do, he had tried to discourage her as she knew he would. He'd given up reiterating his belief in Jeremy Halliday's innocence and, instead, rabbited on about how untrustworthy and corrupt the French police were rumoured to be. They would be looking for a quick conclusion to the case and Jeremy was the most convenient suspect to pin it on. And, of course, it was an added bonus for them that he was an Englishman. But his arguments were half-hearted. He knew that, once Felicity had made up her mind, there would be no dissuading her.

"If you could begin by telling me how long you have known Miss Wainwright and Mr Halliday and how you first came to know them?"

Jules Bouchon was an experienced and expert interrogator, calm and supportive with friendly witnesses like Felicity Merrigan, tough and incisive with suspects. Once she began to recount the brief history of their acquaintance with Julia and Jeremy, Felicity began to feel more at ease.

"So, you say that you became very close to Miss Wainwright. How often did you meet?"

"Well, Julia was very busy running her business and she did a lot of travelling around Southern France once she started to find outlets for her products in places like Toulouse and Albi so there were periods when I didn't see much of her. But when she was in Vendillac we used to meet up once a week for coffee and a chat."

"And when was the last time you spoke with her?"

"It was about ten days ago. She came round for a coffee."

The judge waited for her to continue but she seemed hesitant. He prompted her. "So what did you talk about?

Did she say anything unusual that......... I don't know...... might help to explain what has happened to her?"

Felicity swallowed. Her hesitancy had been partly because she didn't want to be the kind of neighbourhood gossip she had always despised. She quickly banished that thought from her mind. This was much more important than mere gossip. "Well, she told me straight away about the decision she'd taken to leave Jeremy. She said that she'd told him it was over and........."

"I'm sorry to interrupt, Mrs Merrigan." Judge Bouchon had stopped taking notes and was staring intently at her. "She told you she was ending her relationship with Mr Halliday?"

"Yes." It was Felicity's turn to stare intently back at the judge. "Didn't you know that? Did Jeremy not tell you that she'd left him for good and was going back to England?"

The judge returned to his note-taking. "I am not at liberty to tell you what was spoken about in my interview with Mr Halliday, Mrs Merrigan. If you could just tell me a bit more about what Miss Wainwright told you."

Felicity felt emboldened. She couldn't be certain but, from his reaction, he appeared not to know the real reason why Julia was returning to England. In which case, it was information that Jeremy had withheld from him. Any lingering reservations she may have felt about coming to see Judge Bouchon instantly evaporated.

"In our previous conversations we'd often talked about the difficulties of settling into life in rural France. You know – things like coping with the language and getting to know and be accepted by the locals. Julia felt that she was making good progress. Her French had improved dramatically, especially once she started to develop more business contacts in France. But she said that Jeremy was finding it more difficult. His French wasn't improving much and he wasn't keen on mixing socially with the locals although that did improve a bit when he started doing his gardening work. He'd teamed up with a local French artisan. They met in the village café and played chess together." Felicity paused for thought.

"And did she give any other reasons why she was leaving Mr Halliday?" The judge once again put his pen down and gave her his full attention.

"She said things had not been going well for them when they were living in London. Apparently, Jeremy had been in some kind of trouble – some sort of crisis – and, ever since then, things had been difficult. So, they decided to up sticks and start afresh in France, partly so Jeremy could get away from whatever it was that was hanging over him in London and partly because they felt it would help to refresh their relationship. From the way she talked about it, I think Julia regretted that decision."

The judge interrupted. "I'm sorry but you say Mr Halliday was in some kind of trouble in London? Did she explain what this trouble was?"

Felicity was trying hard to recall the nuanced details of their conversation. "Not really. I think it was something to do with his job as a school teacher but she wouldn't go into details. She said it wouldn't be fair to Jeremy to tell me about it."

The judge retrieved his pen and resumed scribbling on his notepad. "By the time of your last meeting with her, had she already told Mr Halliday she was going to leave him?"

"Yes she had."

"And did she say how he reacted to this news?"

"Well, naturally he was very upset – and then she said he was very angry with her."

"Was he violent?"

"I don't think so. She never mentioned anything like that. Just a lot of shouting. She said he accused her of having an affair."

"And was she?…… Having an affair, I mean?"

"Yes, she was. Well, at least, she had been. I think it was with a man in Toulouse who she was doing business with although she didn't go into detail about it."

"And did she tell Mr Halliday about this?"

"No. I don't think so." Felicity was hesitant.

Judge Bouchon's tone was becoming more abrupt and impatient. There was a motive forming and he was like a guided missile homing in on it. "Can you try to remember? It could be important. Did she admit to him she was having an affair when he told her of his suspicion? Did he have any evidence to support his accusation?"

While harbouring no wish to be helpful to Jeremy, Felicity was trying hard to be as scrupulously fair and accurate as she could in recalling her conversation with Julia. This time she took a long pause in an effort to scour her memory and be as forensically professional as she had always been in her medical career.

"I'm fairly sure she didn't tell him about the affair. I think she said she didn't want to admit to it because she had ended it a few months previously and she didn't want him to think that it was the reason she was leaving him."

The judge was disappointed with her response. He continued to probe her about the conversation with Julia but failed to get anything else of substance out of her. Instead, he moved his questions on to Jeremy Halliday and asked her to give her impressions of him. Her observations were very general and vague as she admitted that she had not had much contact with him other than the couple of occasions when they had met socially as couples. Any discussions about the gardening work he was doing for them were conducted with her husband.

"And did your husband have the kind of personal conversations with Mr Halliday that you had with Miss Wainwright?"

"I doubt it. They weren't very close. You know what men are like. They don't tend to talk much about their private emotional lives to each other."

"Perhaps so," said the judge, thinking that that was probably true of Englishmen, "but I will need to interview your husband just in case Mr Halliday may have spoken to him about his relationship with Miss Wainwright."

"Oh, I don't think he'll be very keen to speak to you," Felicity Merrigan said nervously. "He didn't approve of me coming to see you."

"It is not a matter of what he does or does not want to do, Mrs Merrigan. This is a murder inquiry. I will need to speak to your husband in case he has any relevant information. You can tell him that I will be in contact soon."

It was only after she reached the street and took several deep breaths that she realised how hot and sweaty it had been in the judge's office. She stood for a while in the cooling breeze, unpeeling her t-shirt from her damp back while observing the morning shoppers walking back to their cars with their purchases. She took several more deep breaths to calm herself before making her way back to her car. She was relieved the interview was over although it had left her with conflicting emotions. She felt she had done her duty. She may have made things worse for Jeremy Halliday but she felt no guilt about that. She had simply told the truth. But she could imagine what Tim's reaction would be when she got home and told him about it – especially when she told him the judge wanted to interview him. She wasn't looking forward to it but she was more than capable of standing up to her husband.

*

As soon as Felicity Merrigan had left the office, Jules Bouchon pressed his intercom button and called in his assistant, Eva.

"I want you to contact the police in London. You have the address where Mr Halliday and Miss Wainwright lived in the file. If you could speak to the local police in that area. You need to ask them if Jeremy Halliday had come to their attention for any reason. Also, could you contact the school where Mr Halliday worked. Try and find out why he left his job and what kind of teacher he was. Just any information they can give you about him." He waited while Eva, perched on the chair next to him, scribbled all the details down. "If you can, Eva, I need as much information as quickly as possible – preferably before I interview Mr Halliday tomorrow."

11

"You're not seriously asking me why I'm in such a bad mood? You know why. I can't believe you went ahead and invited your fucking sister to come and stay when you knew I didn't want to see or talk to her. As if I haven't got a stressful enough week ahead, I now have to put up with her as well." Jeremy spat out his words in an angry whisper.

Julia was bending down to take a casserole out of the oven and had her back to him. He had followed her into the kitchen and closed the door behind him to prevent Hattie and John from overhearing what he had to say as they sat at the dinner table awaiting Julia's return with the main course.

"I'm sorry but she is my sister and I needed to see her." She put the casserole dish on the hob and turned to face Jeremy. "This is very stressful for me as well and, even if *you* don't want to talk to my sister, *I do*. For Christ's sake, she's trying to be supportive."

"Well she's not trying very hard. It doesn't matter what she actually says – it's that patronising tone behind it. She treats me like a naughty schoolboy."

"Oh come off it, Jeremy. It doesn't matter what Hattie says or how she says it – you're convinced she doesn't like you and therefore she's bound to blame you for what's happened." Julia turned back to the hob and drained vegetables into a colander.

"Spot on. Isn't that exactly what she's doing? She's like a bloody vulture. She's just come to gloat."

Julia stopped what she was doing and took a deep breath. "I'm not going to have this argument now. She's here. Get over it."

Jeremy kicked the table leg like a petulant child. Julia put down the colander and turned to face him.

"Please Jeremy, calm down. Take a few deep breaths. Then can we please sit down and enjoy the rest of the meal in peace. Whatever Hattie says just bite your tongue. As soon as we've finished eating, why don't you take John to the pub. Then I can have a quiet girly chat with my sister and, by the time you get back, it'll be bedtime." He still looked exasperated but she could see that he was taking her advice and calming himself down. "Help me carry the food through."

Jeremy took that deep breath and released it slowly before going to the kitchen counter and picking up the dishes of vegetables.

"That smells fantastic," said John as Julia deposited the cast-iron casserole dish on a trivet in the middle of the dining table. Jeremy followed close behind with a bowl of couscous and the dish of vegetables.

"It's a lamb tagine," Julia announced as she removed the lid with a flourish.

"My favourite," said John turning to Hattie sitting next to him. "Remember the tagine we had last year in Marrakech?" Hattie nodded. "You two should go to Morocco...... when all this nonsense is over, of course. It's a really vibrant place. Great food. Bags of atmosphere."

"Is it alright if I serve everybody?" Julia started spooning couscous onto plates before they had a chance to answer. She passed the first plate of food across to Hattie.

"Thanks Jules. So, how long is the hearing likely to last?" She directed the question across the table to Jeremy who paused before replying, trying to follow Julia's advice and stay calm. His first impulse was to say that he'd rather not talk about the hearing but he changed his mind. He decided to let it run for as long as Hattie stuck to questions about basic facts. If she started bombarding him with advice, he vowed to cut her short.

"Probably only a day. It might go into a second day."

"And who's this guy who's defending you? Is he any good?" John asked as he helped himself to some vegetables.

"He's not *defending* me. It's not a court case. He's just a union official. He's there to advise and support me. I'm quite capable of defending myself."

"Of course you are." John was quick to reassure him. "It's just that......... Well, won't it be a bit uncomfortable for you if you've got to cross-examine the girl?"

Jeremy could feel his temperature rising. He'd expected this from Hattie and it didn't make it any easier that it was coming from John. He caught the look on Julia's face as she turned towards him – like a mother silently reminding her child to mind his manners and take his elbows off the table.

"As I said, John, it's not a judicial hearing. There are no witnesses. The girl gives her statement in writing. All the testimony is in writing – in an official report."

"Well, anyway, it's all going to be a formality, isn't it?" John paused to take a sip of wine. "If the police don't believe her then surely the school's not going to? I don't understand why they're even going ahead with this."

"Unfortunately, it doesn't work like that," Julia butted in, trying to take the focus off Jeremy and give him some breathing space. "It's not that the police don't believe her – it's just that they don't think the case will stand up in court."

"Yes, but you must be optimistic," Hattie said. "It'll be very hard for the school to come to a different conclusion from the police."

"Thank god it didn't go to court," John said. "Then it

would have been splashed all over the press – national as well as local probably."

Hattie said, "You're lucky the girl went over the top with her accusations and got caught out because…"

"Lucky," Jeremy blurted out, his fragile composure suddenly shattered. "What do you mean 'lucky'? I didn't do anything. I'm innocent. You make it sound like you think I'm getting away with something. Admit it, Hattie, you suspect there might be something in this girl's accusations?"

Hattie stopped eating and put her fork on the table, taken aback by Jeremy's rush of anger. Julia was about to intervene but Hattie held up her hand and responded first.

"Of course I don't think you did anything. You're misunderstanding what I said. What I meant was that you're lucky because if she hadn't made her story so unbelievable and had to withdraw that part of it, she could have got you in even more trouble. The fact that you didn't do any of it wouldn't matter. If it just became your word against hers, it could have dragged on and on. Being innocent wouldn't stop the mud sticking."

"Listen mate," John interrupted. "We're both a hundred per cent behind you. All Hattie's talked about for the past month is how helpless she feels and how she wishes she could do something more to support you."

Jeremy's anger evaporated as quickly as it had appeared and moroseness took its place. "Whatever the outcome is on Wednesday, some mud is going to stick. It'll be the end of my teaching career for sure."

"Nonsense," Hattie said, reaching her hand across the table towards Jeremy's but stopping inches short. "Once you're cleared of this you've got to get on with your life. Why should this girl drive you out of your job? You've not done anything wrong. If you quit, it'll look like you're admitting responsibility."

Jeremy was about to speak but Julia put a restraining hand on his arm.

"I think it would be best if we changed the subject," she said. "There's no point in talking about the future until this hearing is over. Let's just enjoy the meal and find something else to talk about."

There was a minute of awkward silence while they all turned their attention to eating their tagine.

John broke it. "So, how's business, Julia?"

"Oh, it's going really well. I've just designed a new range of shoulder bags. They're about to go into production."

"Have you ever thought of designing stuff for children?" John said. "Always good to diversify in business, you know. And you'd have the added bonus that you've got a ready-made outlet in my shops."

"No. I know you might think that my years of teaching might suggest an interest in children but you'd be wrong. You can probably tell that by the fact that I don't have any of my own."

"We don't have any either," said John. "It hasn't stopped me from setting up a children's clothes business. Let's face it, you don't have to be a vegetarian to cook and enjoy vegetarian meals, do you?"

Jeremy spent the rest of the meal in silence barely listening to the inconsequential conversation of the other three.

By the time the meal was over, Jeremy was feeling very lukewarm about going out to the pub for a quiet drink with John while Julia and Hattie were left alone to have their sisterly heart to heart. His only alternative would be to excuse himself and say he was feeling tired/had a headache and needed an early night. But, like a whole series of other decisions he should have made but didn't over recent months, he decided not to assert himself and go along with Julia's plan. John was usually good company, he reasoned. Maybe a couple of drinks and a dose of barrow-boy banter would cheer him up.

To his dismay, once they had ensconced themselves at a quiet corner table in the pub, John dominated the conversation with a stream of memories of his own schooldays and, in particular, of he and his mates lusting after female teachers while observing the male teachers flirting with the girls. In passing, he also threw out references to St. Trinian's films and all those erotic images of nubile teenage schoolgirls in gym slips, stockings and suspenders – "Apparently, most Japanese pornography features women dressed up as schoolgirls." All delivered in John's quick-fire comedic patter and intended to be supportive and sympathetic to Jeremy's dilemma. John was one of those people who believed that all life's adversities were best met with a hefty dose of humour. *Always Look on the Bright Side of Life* would have been one of his choices on *Desert Island Discs*. Jeremy let it all flow over him, paying scant attention while consuming far more alcohol than he'd intended.

When they returned to the house, the sisters were still sat where they'd left them on the sofa, both rosy cheeked and tipsy. Julia stared at Jeremy trying to gauge his mood but he was giving nothing away. This time, in his obviously drunken state, he had no difficulty in announcing his tiredness/headache and proceeding straight upstairs to bed.

*

Mary Groenwald stared at the thick wodge of paper on her desk. It was Angela Ikole and Saira Khan's report prepared for the Jeremy Halliday hearing. Next to it was a smaller pile of paper – character references for Jeremy from six senior members of staff at St. Saviour's. She'd already skim read the report and was gearing herself up to go through it again at a slower pace, taking notes.

It was a thorough report – maybe too thorough. Scrupulously professional – a detailed summary of the main points in the statements made by everyone involved with extensive lists of dates and times. There was not a hint of an opinion about the veracity of any of the statements. It was exactly what she would have expected and yet she knew she'd been hoping for at least a glimmer of evidence to support or disprove the girl's accusations. She'd have to go through it more carefully but her initial impression was that it changed nothing. Like most of these cases, it all boiled down to the simple fact that it was a fifteen year old girl's word against that of a teacher.

Mary was glad she didn't have to make the final decision on her own although she would be the person on the panel who would have the major say on the outcome. The problem was that she wasn't sure what the most beneficial outcome would be – either for herself or for the school. What she really wanted was for the whole affair to disappear – for Jeremy Halliday to disappear. She didn't want to see a man's career ruined but it would be so much simpler if he didn't return to the school. Perhaps the ideal solution would be for him to be exonerated but then decide to resign and find another teaching post, but she didn't know how likely that would be.

Whatever the outcome of the hearing, all the students now knew about it and, through them, most of the parents knew as well. Within days of Jeremy being suspended, there had been a stream of 'concerned' parents trooping into her office demanding to know how a pervert had been allowed to teach their daughters. How could they be sure their child hadn't been in danger – or even been abused by this man?

How many other girls had he had illicit relations with? She had had to try and calm them down and explain patiently that she could not discuss the case with them as it was sub judice although she endeavoured to reassure them that she had reacted promptly and firmly as soon as the accusations had come to her attention. The teacher concerned was suspended while the police and the school carried out their investigations. And, thus far, there had been no additional complaints made by other students. Had their daughters said anything to them about Mr Halliday that might have aroused their suspicions, she had asked. Well no, they all answered, but maybe their children had had a lucky escape. One or two of them said that their daughters had told them that they had always thought there was something a bit strange about him but they hadn't been more specific than that. One of the mothers said her daughter told her that he'd come into the classroom once with his flies undone.

As far as most of these parents were concerned, they were not interested in the notion of a proper investigation and a fair hearing. There was no 'innocent until proven guilty' for them. Mary could imagine them as peripheral members of the thirties' lynch mobs in the American South stringing up black men accused of having liaisons with white women. She shuddered to think how they would react if Jeremy Halliday was cleared and reinstated.

And then there was the way they looked at her when she tried to explain that she couldn't discuss it with them and then, in a flat tone of voice, outlined the formal procedures that had to be followed. She could read the thoughts going through their minds. Mere slip of a girl – should never have been given the job in the first place – always knew she wasn't up to it – and now here's the proof. And she doesn't even have any children of her own so how can she understand our feelings? Not for the first time it was coming home to her how difficult it was to be a head teacher who was younger than many of her staff and most of the parents.

She had to keep telling herself that this was the nature of the job. Was it any different from what she had expected when she took it on? Perhaps not, but then anticipating the demands of a job before you accept it was not the same as actually experiencing them. She'd always known she would have to take the rough with the smooth – the problem was that, at this point in time, it was beginning to look like rather too much rough and not enough smooth. For most of those parents who had walked into her office, she was to blame for what was happening. It had happened on her watch and the fact that she was too young and inexperienced for the job compounded her responsibility. She was the one who had allowed a paedophile to teach in her school. The fact that Jeremy Halliday had not been found guilty of anything yet and, anyway, he'd been appointed years before she'd taken up her head teacher's post, was irrelevant in their eyes.

With a heavy sigh, she picked up her yellow highlighter pen and began to read slowly through the report's preamble again.

*

As they waved John and Hattie off that Sunday afternoon, Jeremy's initial feeling was one of relief to see the back of his partner's sister – relief that he no longer had to endure the tense atmosphere between himself and Hattie. But, once he and Julia were left alone in the house, all the living room lights switched on to dispel the gloom of a grey London Winter Sunday afternoon, he wasn't sure that he wouldn't have preferred them to have stayed a little longer. A stressful weekend it may have been but, on the plus side, the couple's presence had been a not unwelcome change from what had become over the weeks leading up to the hearing, weekends spent alone together in a taciturn semi-silence. They'd discussed to death all the ins and outs of the case against Jeremy and the likely outcomes of the hearing until there was nothing left to say and any other conversation about themselves – their plans for the future – were inevitably in abeyance until this threat hanging over him was resolved. As for what was going on in the outside world, Jeremy watched the television news and occasionally flicked through a newspaper but hardly anything registered. It might as well have been happening on another planet or a hundred years ago.

Yes, he had to admit it, despite the awkwardness of their presence, Hattie and John had helped the weekend to speed by. Once they had gone, the clock once again slowed to a crawl. The more Jeremy longed for time to speed up – to race towards Wednesday so he could get this hearing over and done with – the slower it went. It didn't help that he couldn't concentrate on anything else. It was November. The weather was cold, grey and drizzly. His usual sanctuary, the garden, was unavailable. There was nothing left to do. He'd cleared the leaves and completed all the routine autumn tasks. He couldn't concentrate enough to read anything and spent a lot of time surfing the net for things he wasn't interested in or dozing in front of daytime television.

His only other distraction was his visits to his father in the care home in Wimbledon. He was in his mid-seventies and had developed the early signs of dementia five years earlier. As his mind deteriorated, Jeremy found it increasingly difficult to keep up a regular weekly visit. Once his father began to have difficulty recognising him, the gap between visits stretched out. And then there was the occasion a year ago when his father appeared to have a brief period of lucidity and dropped a bombshell on his son. Jeremy hadn't told anybody about it – not even Julia. Partly it was because he didn't want to believe it. In fact, he wasn't sure whether to believe it. Was his father as lucid as he sounded or was he giving voice to a false memory – a confusion of the events of twenty-five years ago issuing from his scrambled brain? Jeremy didn't want to believe it but, if it was true, it changed his already ambivalent feelings towards his father and made him feel even less like wanting to do his filial duty.

Just as he was falling asleep in front of the latest BBC costume drama that Sunday evening, he received a phone call from Roger Worth. Worthie, as he was affectionately known by the students, was one of the few colleagues that Jeremy felt close to at St. Saviour's. They'd started at the school as newly qualified teachers on the same day and had quickly become a mutual support service as they struggled through their first year, making a recprocal arrangement to send badly behaved students into each other's classrooms when they had a free lesson or a small sixth form group. Worthie was just the sort of volatile outgoing character that Jeremy needed to help him counteract his own more buttoned up approach to life. Worthie frequently stormed around the staffroom at break time after a particularly frustrating lesson announcing in stentorian tones that, if he thought his child (his wife was expecting a baby at the time) was going to turn out like some of those in 8D he'd strangle it at birth. He could have been modelled on one of the cartoon teachers in the *Beano* or *Dandy* – tall, thin and gangling with an expanse of pale hairy wrist and fair isle socks exposed by his too short jacket sleeves and trouser legs. He had a tuft of spiky black hair cut for him, as he freely admitted, by Alice, his long-suffering wife, a similarly bristly moustache and thick-lensed black-rimmed glasses. For a man whose own fashion sense was non-existent, he delighted in making disparaging comments about the attire of any young female teacher he came across in the staffroom. It was taken in good humour by all concerned, recognising the inherent absurdity of a man who looked like he'd been trapped in a tumble dryer setting himself up as a fashion pundit.

Like Jeremy, he cycled to work most days, although from a much greater distance and on a slick expensive racing bike with full lycra gear to match. As he freewheeled across the playground every morning, clusters of students would chase after him chanting 'Worthie, Worthie, Worthie'.

Once both of them had settled in and were more relaxed with the students, they took to playing little pranks on each other. While Jeremy was always more measured and careful with his, Roger often skated dangerously close to the unprofessional. Once he sent a small boy to Jeremy's class with a message. When Jeremy opened it up it read "don't you think this boy is the ugliest child you've ever seen?" During their first summer term at the school, Worthie, a Geography teacher, had accompanied an A level group on a week's field trip to Yorkshire. Jeremy's tutor set were unhappy to be without their favourite teacher for a week and asked him what had happened to Mr Worth. He pretended that he was reluctant to tell them but finally divulged that Mr Worth had been given leave of absence to take part in the Tour de France. The next morning some of the boys in the tutor set announced that they'd watched Channel Four's coverage of the latest stage of the race but they hadn't seen Mr Worth. Jeremy explained that there were a hundred and eighty riders taking part and Mr Worth was well down the field. The students' gullibility lasted long enough for them to bombard Worthie with questions about where he'd come in the race when he returned to school.

Roger Worth had been the only teacher to have phoned him after his suspension to offer support. Jeremy wasn't surprised. Once the staff had been warned not to have any contact with him while the investigation was ongoing, Worthie was just the kind of character to wilfully ignore it. This time he was calling because he had just heard that the hearing was on Wednesday and he wanted to offer Jeremy some last minute succour. They arranged to meet for a drink the following evening. Jeremy was doubly grateful, not only for Roger Worth's support but also because it would get him out of the house for an evening and help the time pass more quickly.

On his arrival at the pub, Worthie was his usual effusive self but, although he appreciated the support, Jeremy's spirits obstinately refused to be lifted.

"You've got absolutely nothing to worry about, mate," Worthie reassured him as soon as they were seated with their beers. "They're just going through the motions. It'll take them no time at all to dismiss that disturbed little girl's trumped up accusations."

"I hope so," said Jeremy. "I just wish I could be as confident as you. You don't know how demoralising it feels to sit in front of those people – even the ones you hope might be on your side or might at least feel some sympathy for you – like Mary Groenwald and Mike Harvey."

"Oh don't talk to me about those two hyenas." Worthie snarled out the words. "I know they have to do things by the book but they seem to revel in the authority it gives them. When they called the staff briefing to tell us what had happened and warn us not to talk to you, they were like the voices of doom. They could have at least said something to show they had some smidgeon of sympathy for the position you were in."

"Well, as you say, they have to watch their own backs." Jeremy gave a wan smile.

"Anyway, you've got the overwhelming support of the

rest of the staff. The English department are all rooting for you."

"Really? I have to admit, not being able to talk to anybody, I just assumed the worst. I thought they must be thinking I was probably guilty."

"Far from it, mate." Worthie sucked the foam from his moustache. "I could give you a whole list of people who've come up to me once they knew I was in contact with you to ask me to pass on their best wishes but it would take too long for me to mention them all – and waste valuable drinking time. Can I get you another pint?"

Jeremy forced a flicker of a smile, grateful for Roger Worth's efforts to cheer him up but suspecting that his encouraging words were overblown and that the alleged procession of sympathetic colleagues were either non-existant or, at best, a mere trickle.

On returning with the beers, Worthie continued his litany of encouragement by reporting back on all the students he'd overheard talking about how convinced they were of Mr Halliday's innocence and how eager they were to have him back teaching them. Jeremy believed this even less but, by the end of the evening, he felt a bit better, trying to put aside his scepticism and allow himself to feel pleased that, after such a long period of isolation, maybe there were some people out there who wished him well.

*

Although she had plenty to keep her occupied on the days leading up to the hearing, like Jeremy, Mary Groenwald felt that time was moving at a snail's pace. She felt herself delaying making important decisions and pushing things on to the backburner while her thoughts constantly strayed to Wednesday's hearing.

On the Monday morning she'd arranged a meeting with Mike Harvey, Angela Ikole and Saira Khan ostensibly to set out the procedures for the hearing. It wasn't scheduled to be a very long meeting as the procedures were mostly laid down in Department for Education guidelines. So, it only took fifteen minutes for the process and the timetable to be established. As Angela and Saira gathered their papers together and prepared to leave, Mary diffidently broached some questions about details in the report. She knew it wasn't strictly ethical but she was anxious to be as well prepared as possible. What was hanging heavily over her was the uncertainty. She was searching for any small clue as to how this mess might be resolved.

"I don't think there's anything else we can tell you, Mary." Angela was guardedly deferential to the head teacher, trying to avoid stating bluntly that they couldn't discuss it. "If you feel there are things we've missed out in the report..."

"No. You've been very thorough." Mary was quick to reassure her but continued anyway. "It's just that...... well, you've outlined all the facts but what's missing is some indication of your feelings about whether the girl is telling the truth. Of course, I wouldn't expect it to be in the report itself but I'm worried that we've got a major problem at the hearing. Since Susie has admitted to the police that she lied about one thing in her initial statement and, therefore, they've decided that the rest of her evidence is unreliable, it's going to be equally difficult for us to give credibility to the rest of her statement, isn't it?"

Saira Khan intervened. "Maybe it's best if we leave that to be sorted out at the hearing."

"Yes but it's not going to be able to be sorted out, is it?" Mary didn't want to let it go just yet. "It's not like a court of law. We can't question Susie and decide for ourselves whether she's telling the truth." She hesitated as if reluctant to probe further. "The point I'm trying to make is that you two are the only ones to have spoken to her. So, I guess I'm asking you how believable you found the rest of her story."

The two consultants looked at each other before Angela decided to answer. "All I can say, Mary, is that she stuck to her guns. Obviously we put it to her that she'd lied about Mr Halliday being in her bedroom and being intimate with her there and, therefore, how did we know she wasn't lying about the other incidents. Her response was that she'd been so confused and upset by what had happened that she'd started to confuse what had really happened with things she'd merely fantasised about. In other words, there was a kind of wishful thinking about Mr Halliday going up to her bedroom with her. I don't want to make any judgements on whether she's telling the truth but I will say – and I think Saira would agree with me…" She turned to Saira who gave a slight nod, "that she was very clear and articulate in her evidence. We weren't able to catch her out."

Mary took a deep breath. There was more she would have liked to ask but she could see that the two women had said more than they intended to and she wasn't likely to get anything else of value out of them.

"There is one more small thing before you go." Once again Mary halted the consultants in their tracks before they could resume putting documents back into bags. "When you outline in the report the amount of time Mr Halliday spent alone in his classroom with Susie Meredith, you state that there's no explicit school policy about teachers being left alone in a classroom with a student, although you do point out that there are general national guidelines for the conduct of teachers with students. Is it necessary to include that in the report? Surely rules for the professional conduct of teachers are implicit and every school shouldn't need to reinvent the wheel and issue their own rules?"

This time it was Saira who answered. "I'm sure you're right, Mary. We didn't intend it to be a criticism of you or the school. We were simply stating the facts. How they are used or interpreted will be up to the panel at the hearing."

After they'd gone, Mary asked Sally, her secretary, to bring her a coffee. She was feeling frustrated and needed to calm herself down before her next meeting with the chair of governors. She knew she should be hoping for an outcome to this hearing which would be in the best interests of Susie Meredith, Jeremy Halliday and the school as a whole but she couldn't help but focus on how the possible outcomes would reflect upon herself. As a result, she was angry with herself that she hadn't been more proactive in reviewing the school's policies since she'd been in post. Her plan had been to give herself time – most of her first year – to settle into the job; get to know the students and staff and the existing school ethos. She would wait until her second year to put the major changes in place. Even though it was a sensible plan, now that this unexpected situation had arisen, she knew it was a mistake not to have laid down some guidelines for teacher conduct once she'd realised that none existed. It was the one thing in the consultants' report that could rebound on her.

*

Howard Stanton had arranged a final meeting with Jeremy on the Tuesday morning to complete their preparations for the hearing the following day. Jeremy was glad of another opportunity to get out of the house and break up his mundane routine but, grateful as he was for Howard's advice and support, he couldn't say he looked forward to their meetings. After the police had decided that there'd be no charges brought against him, Jeremy had tried to be more upbeat than he actually felt about the school investigation but Howard's response had been to advise caution: to counter Jeremy's artificial optimism with a dash of reality. They couldn't rely on the school investigation dismissing the rest of the girl's accusations on the grounds that she'd lied about one aspect to the police, he said. Jeremy knew deep down that Howard was acting in his best interests – trying to keep his feet on the ground – but, after each meeting, he found himself going back over Howard's downbeat comments looking for signs that even the union man had his doubts about his innocence.

It had been several months since the start of his suspension and the longer the whole thing dragged on the harder Jeremy found it to maintain much confidence in the outcome. And so, when he received his copy of the consultants' investigative report, he left it unopened on the kitchen table for the rest of the morning, scared of what it might say. When he finally plucked up the courage to read it, it deepened his gloom. His initial feeling of pessimism led him to focus his reading on what were for him the most negative sections of the report – Susie Meredith's evidence and all the exhaustive details of when and where he'd been alone with the girl, whereas he skipped over his own rebuttal statement and not even the six glowing character references from his colleagues could raise his spirits.

Howard had grown used to facing a dispirited Jeremy Halliday in their meetings over the past few months. It was only to be expected of someone having to go through what Jeremy was going through. But now it was coming to the crunch he felt he had to do something about the despondent man sitting across the table from him in the NUT's Wandsworth office. He felt more confident than he'd previously let on to Jeremy about the outcome of the hearing but, if they were to ensure that Jeremy was completely exonerated, he needed him to come across as positive and confident in front of the panel and not the shifty looking character sitting in front of him now. Therefore, as he went through the report in detail, he endeavoured to sound as cheery as possible. At the same time, he was conscious of the need to keep it focused and brief. The report was long and, in his opinion, over-detailed so he skipped as much of it as he could, homing in on the most important sections.

Jeremy could feel his spirits lifting as Howard's more positive analysis of the report slowly eclipsed his own gloomy prognosis.

"I know I've asked you this before," Howard said once they had reached the report's summary pages, "but could you confirm again that, during those times you were alone with the girl in your classroom and she was distressed – you know, when she was telling you about the bullying – did you ever touch her at all – even just a hand on her arm, an arm round her shoulders – to comfort her? Of course, I'm not saying that, if you had, it would make you guilty of sexual abuse, but I'd rather you were open about it because they're bound to bring up the question of any physical contact between you and I wouldn't want you to be thrown by it."

Howard was right. He had asked him about it before and Jeremy had always been rather hesitant in his answers. The truth was he couldn't remember much of what happened in those after school sessions and the more time that had passed the less he remembered. However, this time he found himself thinking about it with a clearer mind. For many people, it would have been an automatic reaction when confronted with someone in distress to put a comforting arm around them or offer some similar form of tactile reassurance but, despite his poor memory of the events, he knew instinctively that that is not what he would have done. He was not a touchy feely person. Never had been. He assumed he'd inherited it from his parents. He had no clear memories of either of them cuddling him although he was sure his mother must have done. And when she died, while there was no shortage of reassuring words from his father, he could not remember any physical consolation. It was one of the reasons he'd been relieved that Julia had never brought up the subject of having children. He'd never been certain whether she wanted them or not. Since all his other relationships had been so short-lived, he had never before reached the stage where he'd had to give it any serious thought. He wasn't sure he knew how to be a parent. Having lost his mother so young, he knew there had always been something missing in his emotional make up, on top of which, his father had been a far from ideal role model. Considering what an enormous loss it had been to his father, Jeremy had been careful not to be too demanding – or demanding at all. It was as if he had taken on as much, or more, responsibility to nurse his father through those early single parent years as his father had to look after him. It was never made explicit but, somehow, his father's stoicism seeped into him. By osmosis, he knew he had to man up – take it on the chin. When he became even quieter and more isolated than usual at school, his head of year suggested that the school should provide some counselling. His father was not keen on the idea but, under pressure from the school, reluctantly agreed. However, he grilled Jeremy after each of the first two sessions with the counsellor and Jeremy told him what he wanted to hear –that he didn't think he wasn't getting any benefit from them – and so his father brought them to an end.

At University, he considered making use of the student therapeutic support service and even got as far as turning up outside the psychotherapist's office to make an appointment but the reception desk was busy, he had a lecture to get to, so he decided not to wait. Soon after, he started to make friends and acquired his first girlfriend. Any need for counselling melted away as his social life coughed and spluttered into motion. He had never considered psychotherapy or counselling since although, as he sat answering Howard Stanton's questions, it occurred to him rather late in the day that the past few months might have been the ideal time to take it up.

"No. I can say with absolute confidence that I never touched her – never had any physical contact with her. It's just not me. I'm not a very physical person – even with my own family – or my partner for that matter."

Howard felt like punching the air but restrained himself. It was the most unequivocal, forceful statement he'd elicited from Jeremy since taking up his case. If this new, self-assured Jeremy was the one that appeared in front of the hearing tomorrow, he felt confident they would be home and dry.

*

Julia's mobile call was instantly transferred to Jeremy's voicemail. She paused, debating whether to leave a message. She didn't want to convey the impression that she was being over-anxious although she had every reason to be. She'd never have said it to him because it sounded sacrilegious but, when she saw him off on his way to the hearing that morning and wished him well, she suspected the day ahead might be worse for her than for him. He would be in the thick of it, fighting to save his career, whereas she would have to try and carry on with her normal work routine – starting with a mid-morning meeting in a coffee bar in Wimbledon village with the owner of a fashion accessories' shop who was considering stocking some of her designs. As she had feared, her mind had only been half on the conversation with the shop owner and she'd been surprised, and relieved, when the meeting ended with the woman agreeing to sell her new range of bags. After the woman left, Julia decided to stay and have another coffee and a Panini rather than make her way back home to spend the afternoon sitting in her office pretending to work but with her mind focused on what was happening two miles away. She assumed that the hearing must have broken up for lunch and pictured Jeremy and Howard Stanton perched on stools in a Prêt A Manger eating their sandwiches and discussing how the morning had gone.

"Hi Jeremy. It's me. I just felt I had to ring you. I assumed you might have broken up for lunch. I just wanted to see how the morning had gone. If you get this message and have time, call me back. If not, don't worry." She paused, wishing she hadn't sounded so anxious. "Good luck," she added.

He wouldn't need luck – she was sure of it. Her nervousness wasn't so much about the outcome of the hearing – it was concern at the effect it would have on Jeremy. This whole saga had hit him hard and her worry was that, even if he was exonerated, their life would never return to what it had been before. As the months had passed, the disparity between her busy, increasingly successful business life and his existence, stuck in a hellish limbo, pootling around in the garden or dozing in front of the television, grew ever more apparent. Conversation between them was difficult. He didn't want to talk any more about the 'case' and she didn't feel it would be appropriate to prattle on about her latest expansion to her business. They'd stopped having sex. They had an unchanging bedtime routine. She would go up first and read in bed. Just as she put down her book and switched off the bedside light, he would come into the bedroom, slide gingerly under the duvet and curl up with his back to her. She was clinging to the hope that, once this was all over, she would get back the old Jeremy. The problem was that the whole experience had left her unsure whether there was an 'old Jeremy' to get back to or whether this was now the real Jeremy who had sunk back into the shell he'd briefly burst out of since getting together with her.

Having dismissed Hattie's doubts about him for so long, she was now beginning to think that her sister might have been right all along. Maybe she had jumped into the relationship too soon, seduced by the contrast between Jeremy and Pete. One evening, when she'd been feeling particularly low, she had made a list of all the boyfriends she had had since her schooldays. Ten of them. Was that too many over twenty years? Did it make her seem like a flibbertigibbet? Anyway, she had attempted a forensic analysis, dividing them into different columns according to their personality traits – extrovert/introvert, macho/effeminate, sporty/arty. As she could have predicted, the results formed a simple matrix – she had consistently bounced from one extreme to the other. Okay, but what did that tell her about her relationship with Jeremy? She thought about it for several days but kept drawing a blank. Then she rearranged the list into two columns – the ones she felt she might have been in love with and the ones who were just passing fancies or who she had been physically attracted to. That didn't tell her much either. The one incontrovertible fact was that Jeremy now represented the longest relationship she'd had. And if you added to that the fact that it was a relationship started by her mature thirtysomething self rather than the gauche teenager or the callow twentysomething maybe that showed that he was indeed the right man for her. The right man. Did any woman ever know who the right man was? None of her friends who she'd discussed the subject with over the years seemed to know. Her sister was convinced she'd found the right man and Julia, while being pleased for her, couldn't see how she'd come to that decision. No, the whole thing was a myth perpetuated by the media and the romantic fiction industry.

Her only solution to the problem was to try and expunge it from her thoughts for the time being. Every time she met up with her female friends she'd want desperately to discuss it but she resisted, feeling that she had to maintain an outward dogged loyalty to Jeremy. To give any hint to someone else that she was having doubts about their relationship smacked of treachery. She was conscious that Jeremy still harboured resentment for her critical comments when he told her the full story of his involvement with Susie Meredith and, since then, she'd bent over backwards to be the loyal supportive partner.

As she drained the last of her coffee while watching a brace of young attractive Wimbledon village mothers chatting animatedly to each other while their offspring ran up and down between the crowded tables yelping and laughing, she knew deep down that, however important today's decision might be for Jeremy, she was going to have to make an equally important decision for both of them over the coming weeks.

*

Despite the late November gloom and the spitting rain, Jeremy decided to walk the two miles from Wandsworth Town Hall to Tooting Bec. Having been incarcerated all day in an overheated meeting room he needed to breathe as much fresh air as possible. Even the drizzle felt refreshing. The Christmas lights were up on Tooting Broadway but not yet switched on. A few seasonal makeshift log cabins selling a range of Christmas gift tat lined the pavements with well-wrapped up assistants sitting inside looking distinctly uncheery.

Jeremy stopped to look in several shop windows in a vain attempt to deflect his attention away from that day's proceedings. It was all over. There was nothing more he could say or do. And yet, he couldn't stop himself from re-running extracts in his head from the statements he'd made and then agonising over the things he hadn't said but now wished he had. He kept telling himself to snap out of it. Forget it. Instead, he stared at the window displays and tried to concentrate on what he could buy Julia and his father for Christmas. It didn't work. He'd never done his Christmas shopping until the last minute and he wasn't in the mood to change that habit now. He turned away from the plastic reindeer with glitzy scarves and hats hanging from their antlers in *Monsoon's* window and trudged home through the puddles.

Julia put her book down and rose apprehensively from the armchair as Jeremy closed the front door behind him and entered the sitting room. Her stomach tightened and she held her breath as she stared at the sodden figure in front of her. She didn't know what she'd been expecting but it wasn't this bedraggled Jeremy – the one she'd become so accustomed to over the past few months. What she'd been hoping for was a glowing, beaming Jeremy, punching the air in victory. Seeing the worried look on her face, he smiled weakly at her, like a torch low on battery power trying to penetrate a thick fog.

"Well. Aren't you going to tell me what happened?

Don't keep me in suspense." Julia could barely get the words out.

Jeremy sighed. "I'm afraid there's nothing to tell. The hearing's over but it finished so late that they decided to hold over making the final decision till tomorrow morning."

Julia poured them both a large glass of red wine and then started to probe him gently on how he thought it had gone. His responses were as taciturn as they had been over the previous weeks although he did say that Howard Stanton thought it had gone well and was very confident of the outcome. There was no way that she was going to get a blow by blow account out of him so, after he'd provided a few desultory comments about the general demeanour and appearance of the panel, she went to the kitchen to finish preparing a meal while he went upstairs to shower and change his clothes.

*

As he and Howard seated themselves in their accustomed place in the meeting room, Jeremy surveyed the faces in front of him for any tell-tale clues as to their decision. Most of them didn't make eye contact. Their faces were as near expressionless as possible as they fidgeted with papers on the table in front of them or sipped their coffees. The only exceptions were the Reverend Jenkins, who had a slightly pained expression on his face as if he had just swallowed a mouthful of bitter cold coffee, and Mike Harvey who, when he finally looked up at Jeremy, had the faintest of smiles playing across his lips. Jeremy speculated on whether it was the facial equivalent of a thumbs up.

Mary Groenwald cleared her throat, shuffled in her chair and looked along the table at the rest of the panel checking to see if everyone was ready.

"I don't think we need to waste any time on formalities this morning as we've all been introduced and we know why we're here." She concentrated her gaze on Jeremy. "I can only apologise again to Mr Halliday for having to make him wait overnight for our final decision. It can't have been easy but I'm sure he'd prefer us to take our time and get this right rather than rush to a conclusion. So, I don't intend to keep him in suspense any longer." She coughed nervously and took a sip of water. "We've decided that there is no convincing evidence that Mr Halliday indulged in any sexually inappropriate behaviour with Susie Meredith. We have considered Susie's evidence at great length and do not think that it is reliable. Therefore, as from today, Mr Halliday's suspension is lifted and he is free to return to his teaching post at St. Saviour's."

Howard Stanton smiled broadly and put his hand on Jeremy's shoulder. Jeremy remained impassive, feeling as dazed as if he had been pulled out of a car wreck amazed to find himself unscathed.

"But...... there is an important caveat that we have to add to that decision," Mary Groenwald continued. "Although the panel have found Mr Halliday not guilty of these accusations, they have decided that, in his general behaviour towards Susie Meredith, he has not maintained the proper professional standards. Furthermore, because of his inappropriate conduct towards this student, he must accept some responsibility for, albeit inadvertently, encouraging Susie to develop fantasies about having a sexual relationship with him. The panel feel that, whilst he had a pastoral responsibility for Susie as her form tutor, once he realised the depth of the bullying problem and of her resulting distress, he should not have taken the situation completely into his own hands. He should have liaised far more with Susie's head of year who would have been responsible for making more formal arrangements for Susie's safety and well-being." Mary Groenwald paused and stared hard at Jeremy. "As a result of this decision, you will receive a formal letter from the governors' warning you about your conduct and you will be put on probation for a year to ensure there is no repeat of this kind of conduct. That's all I have to say." She was still looking directly at Jeremy. "Are there any comments you would like to make to the panel – anything you would like to say?"

Jeremy stayed silent, his mind a blank. He considered thanking the panel but decided it wouldn't be appropriate.

"If I could just ask something?" It was Howard Stanton. "Could I ask on what basis Mr Halliday's behaviour has been deemed unprofessional and why it's necessary to warn him formally about his conduct? I ask this because I'm rather concerned that, as these accusations against Mr Halliday were very serious, the panel may have understandably felt uncomfortable about exonerating him completely and looked for some way to sugar the pill for the girl's family and any other people who might be unhappy about this outcome. To be precise, have Mr Halliday's actions broken any school rules or policies in relation to the conduct of teachers toward their students?"

Mary Groenwald bridled in her chair and gave Howard Stanton a disdainful look. Before she could reply, Reverend Jenkins put a restraining hand on her arm and started to speak.

"I think it might be more appropriate if I answer that question, Miss Groenwald." Mary Groenwald turned towards him and nodded. "Firstly, Mr Stanton, I resent your implication that this panel has been influenced in any way in coming to its decision by outside influences. We have taken expert advice throughout these unfortunately lengthy and regrettable procedures. The reason we took our time in coming to a decision was to ensure it was a correct one in keeping with the principles of natural justice."

He paused and stared pointedly at Howard Stanton who, unabashed by the reverend's reprimand, waited for him to continue.

"In answer to your actual question, the panel were disappointed to discover that there was no explicit school policy on the relationship between teachers and pupils but we felt that this was partly excused by Miss Groenwald having been in post for such a short time. This will be rectified in the near future. However, we decided to reprimand Mr Halliday for a lack of professional standards on the basis of the 'Standards of Professional Conduct' guidelines instituted recently by the General Teaching Council, which I'm sure you're aware of. If the panel will bear with me, I'll read out the relevant passages from the document."

There was a long pause while he rifled through his papers before finding the page he needed. He then removed his reading glasses from their case and perched them on the end of his nose.

"These, I think, are the relevant sentences." He read out the extracts from the document in the kind of exclamatory tone that Howard imagined he used for his sermons. "You (the teacher that is) must maintain appropriate professional boundaries, avoid improper contact or relationships with pupils and respect your unique position of trust as a teacher. You must take care to avoid becoming personally involved in a pupil's personal affairs. You should be aware of the potential dangers of being alone with a pupil in a private or isolated situation, using common sense and professional judgement to avoid circumstances which are, or could be perceived to be, of an inappropriate nature. At all times, observe proper boundaries appropriate to a teacher's professional position." He concluded by removing his glasses with a theatrical sweep of his hand. "Would anyone else like to add anything?" He looked up and down the table. No-one else spoke.

"Do you have anything else you would like to say, Mr Stanton?" Mary Groenwald said.

Howard glanced sideways at Jeremy who continued to stare straight ahead.

"No." He briefly considered pointing out that the GTC guidelines for teacher conduct had been instituted without any consultation with the teaching unions but knew it would be pointless.

"Okay then," the head teacher continued. "That's the end of the formal procedures but, if I could ask everybody to bear with me for another minute, I'd like to finish by running through a few details of where we go from here. Jeremy – " He snapped his body upright, the sudden sound of his name re-focussing his attention, and made eye contact with Mary Groenwald. "While you've been reinstated with immediate effect, as it's Thursday today, I am requesting that you don't return to school until Monday. Partly, this is because you probably won't receive a copy of the warning letter before Monday, but also because, as you can imagine, we have arrangements we need to make to smooth the way for your return. Firstly, as soon as this meeting is over, I will have to inform Susie Meredith and her family of the result of these proceedings. Although Susie's attendance at school has been very poor this term, we will have to make arrangements on the assumption that she will be in school on Monday. Obviously she will have to be moved to a different tutor set and a different English teaching group. We'll make these changes straight away but, Jeremy, I'd like you to report to me in my office when you arrive in school on Monday morning so that I can update you on the arrangements we have made."

Jeremy nodded, still saying nothing. Not for the first time in recent months, he was desperate to get out of the room, out of the building, and breathe in the heavily polluted Wandsworth High Street air. For the time being, the last thing he wanted to think about was having to walk back into school on Monday morning.

12

The front page of La Dépêche stared up at him accusingly from where he had left it on the kitchen table. It was a reminder that everyone in the village must by now have either read the news themselves or had the story reported to them by others. Jeremy was trapped inside the house. He didn't want to risk going into the village or even outside into the garden for fear that he would meet somebody or be spotted by a passer-by who might try to talk to him about the newspaper story, even if it was only to express their condolences. Once again he left the answer machine on all day. He was behaving as if he was under siege and pretty soon he was. Calls started stacking up from most of the English daily newspapers.

He shouldn't have been surprised that the news had reached England and yet he found it disheartening to imagine the shock that would be felt by all his and Julia's friends, acquaintances and ex-colleagues when they saw the reports. Later in the day, he summoned up the courage to check out various English newspaper websites and, as expected, there was the story copied almost word for word from *La Dépêche* together with the photos.

There was only one knock at the door that day. An attractive young woman in a beige trouser suit. He didn't recognise her. He thought she might have been another police officer come to ask him more questions so, against his better judgement, he opened the door. She was a reporter from *Le Figaro* and he dismissed her with a brusque 'no comment'.

The following morning, as he walked across the driveway to his car, a man wielding a camera with a phallic telephoto lens appeared over the top of the wall separating his garden from the road and audibly clicked off a batch of photos while Jeremy tried to shield his face. As he got in the car and drove off towards Villefranche, he hoped they would use one of the first on the reel rather than one of him with his raised arm covering his face in that classic pose of the murder suspect being led into court by police.

Miles Joseph sat next to Jeremy on an orange plastic chair in the narrow striplit corridor outside Judge Bouchon's office. He was the English lawyer who lived and practised in Rodez recommended to Jeremy by Tim Merrigan. It was stuffy and uncomfortable and they both had to tuck in their long legs every time a gendarmerie official needed to squeeze past. Miles was reading through the latest update on Julia's murder in that morning's La Dépêche. The story added no new facts, merely embellishing the previous week's news with quotes from the police and comments from Vendillac residents who claimed to have known Jeremy and Julia and expressed the usual shock that such a thing could have happened to someone from their peaceful village.

When they had met for the first time an hour earlier in a café near the gendarmerie, Jeremy had been surprised at how young the lawyer was – he guessed in his late twenties. He was mixed race with a shiny shaved head and a long thin face with a neatly trimmed moustache and a goatee beard. He started by telling Jeremy about his background. He had studied for his law degree at Bristol University where he met and married Marie, a young French woman and, once he had completed his Law Society exams, they had come to live in France. Most of the clients for his legal practice were English ex-pats but, as he had become a more fluent French speaker, his native clientele had expanded. Jeremy then brought him up to speed on the investigation and Miles briefly outlined the French criminal justice procedures including where Judge Bouchon, as the investigating magistrate, fitted in.

They had been waiting in the corridor for twenty minutes when Eva, the judge's assistant, ushered them into his office. Jeremy was sure the wait had been deliberate – to make him as uncomfortable as possible. If so, it had succeeded.

Once they were all seated and Miles had introduced himself, the judge ramped up the tension by slowly shuffling through and re-arranging the piles of paper on the desk in front of him before looking up and fixing Jeremy for several seconds with a penetrating stare.

"I am sorry to have kept you waiting, gentlemen, but we have been receiving new information all the time and I wanted to be as up to date as possible before we started this interview." He scooped up a sheet of paper from the top of his pile as if it contained some vital new evidence hot off the presses. "Mr Halliday, I would like to start by asking you why you and Miss Wainwright decided to leave London and come to live in the Aveyron."

Jeremy had wanted to sound as confident and in control as he felt he had been in the first interview with the judge but any such feeling evaporated with the first question. He hesitated, struggling to think of the best way to respond to what should have been straightforward.

"Well...... we both felt we needed a change. I guess it was just the usual things that make people decide to up sticks and move. Wanting to get out of the rat race.........that sort of thing. We were both fed up with London. We'd lived there more or less all our lives. We were looking for a less stressful lifestyle. You know – get out of the city and into the countryside. And then, we thought back to the holidays we'd had in France. We particularly liked this area – the food, the culture, the scenery, the more laidback lifestyle – and so we booked another trip here and spent most of the time going round estate agents and looking at properties."

His answer had been rambling and hesitant and Judge Bouchon allowed a lengthy pause once Jeremy had ground to a halt as if giving him time to add something important he may have missed out.

"You were a teacher of English in London?" He said, looking at the piece of paper he was holding.

"Yes, that's correct."

"And you already told me that your French wasn't very fluent. So, did you expect to get work as a teacher here?"

"No. I think I already explained that Julia had a very successful business that she could easily run from France and we deliberately chose to buy a house with an attached gîte as an added source of income. And then, of course, since moving here, I've started up my gardening business."

The judge looked down at his piece of paper and then back up at Jeremy. There was a pained look on his face as if some old injury was bothering him.

"Mr Halliday. During our first interview, you told me that Miss Wainwright was going back to England on business and to visit her sister. This was not the truth, was it?"

"I'm sorry. I don't understand what you mean." Jeremy's discomfort grew as he felt the eyes of the three people in the room focus on him.

"She was going back to England for good. She was leaving you. At least, that's what her sister and some of her friends have told us. This would of course explain why the car was so full of her things. Is this not true?"

Jeremy swallowed and turned his head slightly to look at Miles who was staring at him with raised eyebrows. "We had fallen out...that's true......and, yes, we were separating..."

"So, Mr Halliday, why did you not tell me the truth when I asked you the reason Miss Wainwright was returning to England?" The judge's tone of voice was now abrasive – far removed from his sympathetic affability during their first interview.

Jeremy glanced across at Miles as if for support. "I did tell you the truth. She was going back to the UK on business and to see her sister. The trip had been organised before we decided to separate."

"Mr Halliday." The judge's voice was now that of a parent chiding a recalcitrant child. "I specifically asked you why she had so many things packed into the car. That was surely your chance to tell me the truth. But no. You tell me – oh she always packs too much, you know what women are like." He pronounced the last sentence in a wheedling high-pitched approximation of Jeremy's voice. "Is it not true that you didn't want to tell me that Miss Wainwright was leaving you because you knew it would make me suspicious? Because it would mean that you have a motive for murdering her?"

"No, that's not true." Jeremy was struggling to keep his head above water. But, most of all, he was angry with himself. How could he have been so stupid? Surely, he should have realised that all this would come out sooner or later? "I was upset. I was confused. I......"

"If I could just say something on behalf of my client, Monsieur le juge?" Miles interrupted much to Jeremy's relief and the judge's irritation. "I think what Mr Halliday is trying to say is that he was still in a state of shock. He was finding it hard to come to terms with the fact that he and his partner had split up and then, on top of that, he gets the terrible news of her death. It's hardly surprising that he should be confused, upset, disorientated."

"Yes. Thanks Miles. That's what I was trying to say." Jeremy was grateful for Miles' intervention because it had given him a few vital moments to think of what else he could say to explain. He took a deep breath and steadied himself. "I was in denial. I didn't want to believe that Julia was leaving permanently. I was trying to persuade myself that it would just be a temporary separation – that she needed a bit of space and time and then we could sort it all out."

"Fine, Mr Halliday. But, even if I accept what you say – and I cannot say I'm convinced – then you have now had several days to get used to the situation and calm yourself down. Why haven't you come back to me to explain the truth?"

"Well – I'm still finding it very hard. I guess I didn't think it was relevant. Once I knew Julia had been murdered, then I didn't see how her splitting up with me could have anything to do with it."

Judge Bouchon again raised his eyebrows and pursed his lips in a mini pantomime of disbelief. "You are not convincing me, Mr Halliday. Let me remind you of our first interview before we had the medical reports confirming the cause of Miss Wainwright's death." He took a few seconds to shuffle his papers and retrieve a sheet lower down the pile. "I asked you about her state of mind before she left for England. Whether she was worried about her business, for example. Whether she might have any reason for taking her own life. And when I asked you these things, you expect me to believe that you did not think it was relevant to tell me that she had just decided to end your relationship? One of the most stressful things that can happen in someone's life?" The judge gave an exaggerated Gallic shrug as he finished speaking.

Jeremy sat in silence looking down at his knees.

"I don't know," he eventually mumbled. "Of course, I should have told you but I......"

"Okay. Let me ask you something else." The judge paused, waiting until Jeremy lifted his head and made eye contact. "When you were in London there had been an investigation by the police and by the school where you were teaching into allegations that you sexually abused one of your students."

Jeremy's face reddened as Miles swivelled his head to stare at him.

The judge continued. "Did this not have something to do with you choosing to leave London? Was it also the reason Miss Wainwright decided to leave you?"

Jeremy felt like he had caught a sucker punch to the kidneys. It momentarily knocked the wind out of him but he quickly recovered as his anger surfaced.

"That's got absolutely nothing to do with it. It happened years ago. In fact, it happened a couple of years before we decided to move to France. And anyway, if you know about it, you know full well that I was completely exonerated by the school and the police brought no charges."

"I simply ask you about this because..."

"In fact, how the hell do you even know about it? It shouldn't be anywhere on my record. I was innocent. The original complaint to the police should have been removed from the records as should any reference in my school file." For the first time in the interview Jeremy felt he was on the front foot. He searched for other things to say to stoke up his anger and hit back at the judge.

"I cannot discuss with you how I get this information. That is something you can take up with the English authorities, if you wish." The judge showed no sign of being unnerved by Jeremy's attack. "I mention it here because it is relevant to the questions I am asking you about your relationship with Miss Wainwright."

Miles again took the opportunity to interrupt. "I'm sorry but Mr Halliday is right to object. Complaints made against him which were subsequently dismissed as unfounded should not be brought up as part of this investigation. That's certainly the case in English law and I'm sure similar principles apply in France."

Judge Bouchon looked at Miles, a pained expression on his face. "Mr Joseph, it's a pity you don't understand French law better. This is not a court hearing. I am a juge d'instruction and I am conducting an investigation into a murder. My job is to gather together all the facts in the case. Whether or not Mr Halliday's past experiences in London will be admissible evidence in any future trial will not be decided here. For me, for now, I try to discover as much as possible about your client's relationship with the murdered woman."

"Look, I'm really sorry that I was not more open with you in our initial interview." Jeremy was determined to assert himself – to try and avoid appearing to be the cowering suspect. "Of course I should have told you the full reason for Julia leaving, but none of that could have possibly led me to murder her. For Christ's sake, I loved her. I wanted her back. I certainly didn't want her dead. If you're trying to suggest that I killed her then......well, it's absurd."

"May I ask, Monsieur le Juge, if you have any firm evidence linking Mr Halliday to Miss Wainwright's murder? Are you thinking of charging him?" Miles said, trying to put aside his annoyance that Jeremy hadn't been open with him about the state of his relationship with his partner. Despite Jeremy withholding vital information from him, he still needed to support his client as forcefully as possible against an investigating judge who he could see was scenting blood.

Judge Bouchon scratched the bald patch on the top of his head, looking across at Miles and then at Jeremy.

"There will be no charges at present but I must warn you, Mr Halliday, that there is some serious evidence building up against you. As well as these facts about your relationship with Miss Wainwright that you deliberately kept hidden, we also have the fact that you have no alibi for where you were at the time of her death. And also, your fingerprints are all over what remains of Miss Wainwright's car."

"Oh please, Judge Bouchon." Miles was quick to seize an opportunity to leap to his client's defence. "With the greatest respect, you can't consider it important evidence that Mr Halliday's fingerprints were found in Miss Wainwright's car." He turned to face Jeremy. "I assume that you were sometimes a passenger in her car?"

"Yes, of course I was. I even drove it sometimes if mine was out of action."

"Okay. I think that concludes my questioning for this morning," the judge said. "In the meanwhile, I must instruct you that you are not permitted to leave the country for any reason. To ensure this, I must ask you to surrender your passport to the Villefranche gendarmerie. I don't suppose you have it with you today?"

"No, I don't."

"Okay. Then could you bring it in as soon as possible. I will of course keep you informed of any developments in my investigation and will need to call you in at some stage for further questioning. Thank you both for coming today."

Jeremy was taken aback by the judge's abrupt conclusion to the interview, taking a while to follow Miles Joseph's lead and rise from his chair and head for the door. The judge followed behind them and shook hands as they stood in front of the open door.

"Oh, there is one more thing, Mr Halliday. Could you

tell me who owns your house in Vendillac? Did you take out a loan to buy it?"

Jeremy answered instantly. "No. We paid for it with the proceeds from the sale of our house in London."

"So you owned the house in equal shares?" Judge Bouchon smiled as if he already knew the answer.

Jeremy hesitated. "No. Julia put most of the money into buying the London house. She inherited the money after her mother died." He paused as if doing the sums in his head for the first time. "Officially I owned a quarter and she owned three-quarters."

The judge's smile broadened. "Thank you, Mr Halliday. That is......interesting. That's all for now. Au revoir."

"I haven't got much time now. I'm due back in the office this afternoon. I have an appointment." Miles and Jeremy were sitting on a bench in front of the Villefranche war memorial. "But we obviously need to talk further and go through what happened this morning. So, if you phone me tomorrow, I'll have my diary and we can arrange a meeting."

"It wasn't good, was it?" Jeremy said. "Do you think he's going to charge me with Julia's murder?"

"I wouldn't think so. Not at present, anyway." They were interrupted as a chain of hand-holding schoolchildren singing at the top of their voices trailed past their bench led by two scruffy-looking young teachers.

"But..." Miles continued when they were out of earshot, "you haven't helped yourself. I can just about understand you not being completely honest with Judge Bouchon but, if I'm to be able to represent and advise you fully and professionally, then you do need to tell me everything."

"I know. I'm sorry about that. It won't happen again." Jeremy had been thinking about whether he should tell Miles about Guy Reynard's offer to provide him with an alibi but decided against it, although the way things had gone that morning it had become very tempting to take it up.

"What do you make of his question about the ownership of the house? Presumably he's trying to suggest that I murdered Julia because I was afraid I'd lose the house?"

"It would seem that he was flying that kite. It's something we will need to talk about in more detail but, just to be clear, you weren't married?"

"No."

"Had either of you made wills?"

"I certainly haven't and I'm not aware that Julia had."

"So, when Julia told you she was leaving you, did you discuss what was going to happen to the house?"

"No." Jeremy stared into the distance across at the busy traffic on the ring road. "As I told the judge, I hadn't given up on us. I was hoping that Julia just needed a break away from me and we'd eventually be able to talk things through and get back together."

"Have you thought about what will happen to the house now that Julia is dead?"

"No, of course not. I'm not that mercenary. Do you really think I would murder my partner just because I wanted to secure ownership of a house?"

"Well if you did think that, you'd be stupid. Under French inheritance law, since Julia was not married to you, her share in the property would go to her next of kin. She doesn't have any children, I assume?" Jeremy shook his head. "Are her parents still alive?"

"No." Jeremy frowned. "I guess her next of kin would be her sister, Hattie."

After Miles had gone, Jeremy remained seated on the bench for some time. The conversation about the ownership of the house had left him reluctantly thinking about his future. But his thoughts went nowhere. However hard he tried, he couldn't picture in what direction his life would go. It would have to go somewhere because, after what Miles had said, it was unlikely that he would be able to continue living in the house in Vendillac.

Jeremy ran his hands through his hair and stared at a pair of mangy pigeons on the pavement in front of the bench pecking at the remains of a croissant.

13

Jeremy walked across the sparsely populated playground early on that Monday morning, relieved that it was too early for him to be likely to encounter any students, and made for the head teacher's office .

When he left the meeting with Mary Groenwald twenty minutes later he felt considerably less stressed. The first thing she had told him was that Susie Meredith's mother had decided to find a new school for her daughter and would not be sending her back to St. Saviour's.

"Jeremy. Welcome back, mate." Roger Worth smothered him in a bear hug. "The prodigal son has returned. Slaughter the fatted calf," he trumpeted to the eight other colleagues dotted around the staffroom.

"Good to have you back," said Sunil Singh, patting Jeremy on the shoulder as he walked past him towards the door.

He was the first of numerous colleagues that day to express variations of 'good to have you back' although none of them were as effusive as Roger Worth. Jeremy doubted their sincerity. He suspected they were going through the motions of polite society. No one mentioned Susie Meredith or her accusations. He might as well have been returning from a sabbatical or extended sickness leave. The students were even more guarded. Only one girl in his tutor set expressed pleasure at having him back. Others either appeared indifferent or muttered a 'hallo sir' as if he'd never been away let alone suspended after an accusation of serious misconduct.

Walking along the corridors, he felt students' eyes focussing on him, followed by snatches of whispered conversations. His lessons in the following weeks were lacklustre, overshadowed by a feeling of wariness as if waiting for the first student to make an inappropriate jokey remark. Even though none had been forthcoming, he couldn't shake off that nervous feeling. Ostensibly, his relationships with his colleagues returned to what they had been before his suspension and yet, as with the students, he was constantly on the lookout for a cold shoulder or a veiled critical comment.

"Has anybody actually made any snide comments?" Said Julia after he'd expressed his concerns to her one evening. "Do you have any evidence of anybody being standoffish or unfriendly?"

"No. That's what I've been trying to tell you. They're being polite. But I can sense it's there – bubbling away beneath the surface."

Julia sighed and reached out to stroke his arm. "It's understandable that you're apprehensive about returning to school after everything you've been through. But it sounds to me like this is more your problem than anyone else's. I'm sure they've all consigned Susie Meredith to the past and just want to return to normal. It's only you who can't put it behind you. You're like somebody trying and failing to get back on their motorbike after surviving a terrible crash."

He somehow staggered through the three weeks until the end of the Christmas term. He managed to relax for most of the holiday and keep thoughts of school at bay. He even survived a weekend in Brighton with Hattie and John unscathed.

Things were better for the first week back but then small signs started to appear – evidence that the past was not so easily shaken off. In a tenth year English lesson, as he was walking round the room helping students write a poetry essay he'd set them, he stopped next to a Slovakian girl, Elena, who was not fully fluent in written English, and leaned over her to read what she had written so far. She instantly jerked her head and upper body away from him as if he was about to attack her. From that moment on, he became ultra-sensitive about the way he interacted with female students. It got so bad that, in the days following the incident with Elena, he realised he was avoiding helping any of the girls in the class with their work. Even his marking was affected. After writing a gushing comment at the bottom of an essay by one of the brightest girls in his GCSE class, he immediately obliterated it with correction fluid fearing that it sounded flirtatious and replaced it with something bland.

On the Friday of that week, when he was tidying up his classroom at the end of the day, he came across several comments scrawled in felt-tip across a table at the back of the room; all variations on the statement that 'Mr Halliday is a paedo'. He scrubbed them off.

He'd been so upbeat to Julia about the start of the new term that he couldn't bring himself to mention either of these incidents. It wasn't just his working life that he'd hoped would return to normal; he was also desperate for his life with Julia to get back to what it had been before. It seemed like all they had talked about for the past nine months had been the sex abuse case and now all they could talk about was its aftermath. It was beginning to feel like a shadow that might hang over him for the rest of his life.

*

On the following Monday morning things got much worse. He was walking along the corridor to the staffroom when he saw two boys, in the middle of a line of students waiting outside a classroom, wrestling with each other.

"You two. Let go of each other and line up sensibly," he ordered.

Reluctantly, they let go of each other and moved back into line glowering at him. As he turned his back on them to walk away, one of them muttered 'paedo' in a voice just loud enough for Jeremy to hear.

He spun round.

"What did you say?" He didn't know either of the boys but directed his question at the mixed race one, even though he couldn't be sure who had said it. The boy smirked at his friend.

"Didn't say nothing," the boy said in a tone of outraged innocence which, in Jeremy's experience, guilty schoolboys were masters at.

"Yes you did. Come on. What did you say? What did you call me?"

"Nothing. I didn't call you nothing." One moment the boy was all feigned innocence, the next he turned towards his friend screwing his finger in the side of his head. His friend started giggling.

Jeremy had already been in danger of losing control but this sent him over the top. He grabbed the boy by his blazer lapels and pushed him against the wall.

"Hey. What the fuck you doing, man? Let go of me."

The boy was much smaller than Jeremy, probably in the 8th or 9th year. He tried unsuccessfully to wriggle free, disconcerted by the teacher's unexpected burst of aggression.

"I want you to tell me what you called me." The boy continued to try and free himself from Jeremy's grip. "You called me a 'paedo', didn't you?"

"Hey, let go of him. You can't grab him up like that. That's assault." It was his friend coming to his aid: an equally

160

small boy but white with straggly fair hair and freckles. A noisy crowd had gathered round by now blocking the corridor.

Jeremy let go of his jacket but still stood close enough to keep him pinned against the wall. "Are you going to have the courage to admit what you said or are you the kind of skulking coward who whispers behind people's backs?"

The boy tugged at his clothes trying to straighten his jacket and tie and scowled at Jeremy. "I already told you I didn't say nothing. Whatever you think you heard, it weren't me."

"Leave him alone, weirdo." The voice came from somewhere in the crowd behind Jeremy, now pushing and shoving each other to get a better view. The ones at the front were pushing back to prevent themselves from being propelled into Jeremy.

He tried to calm himself down. It was getting out of control.

"Alright, if we can't sort this out here, you'll have to come with me," he said.

"Where do you think you're taking me?" The boy was still tugging at his tie which had slipped over the top of his shirt collar.

"We're going to see the deputy head – to Mr. Harvey's office. You can talk to him about what you said."

"I'm not going nowhere with you." The boy was emboldened by the crowd of students surrounding them. He tried to push past Jeremy who grabbed his jacket sleeve to keep him pressed against the wall.

"What's going on here? Clear the way – all of you." It was the booming voice of John White. The crowd parted in front of the six foot five, track-suited teacher. As he emerged through the crowd, he spotted Jeremy for the first time.

"Oh, sorry Mr Halliday. Is there a problem here?"

"Yeh. He's just assaulted Shaka. He's not allowed to do that." It was Shaka's mate, the straggly haired boy.

John White bent down until he was face to face with the boy. "Is your name Mr Halliday?"

"No sir." The boy shrank back against the wall. With his shaved head and ginger stubble sprouting from a craggy face, it wasn't only his height that made John White an intimidating presence.

"Then I wasn't speaking to you. Keep your mouth shut." He stood up and turned to face the crowd. "Right. All the rest of you. You've got lessons to go to. I want this corridor cleared in the next five seconds. Anybody who doesn't move now will have me to deal with."

With much muttering under their breaths, the students began to disperse along the corridor in both directions. Jeremy let go of Shaka's sleeve. The P.E. teacher's intervention had given him the breathing space he needed to calm himself down.

"What are you lot hanging around for?" John White bellowed at Shaka's classmates still lined up along the wall.

"Please sir. We've got a lesson here," said a girl in a purple headscarf pointing at the classroom.

"Who's your teacher?" He asked her.

"Miss Evans, sir."

"Okay. She's in school today. I'm sure she'll be here any second." He walked over to the classroom door, sorting through the bunch of keys hanging from a lariat round his neck, until he located the classroom master key and opened the door. "Right. In you go and sit down – in silence – and wait for Miss Evans. If there's any noise or misbehaviour, the whole class will be in detention with me after school."

They filed meekly into the room.

"Not you son," Mr White said to Shaka as he started to

follow the others. Once the rest were inside he turned to Jeremy. "So, what's this all about, Mr Halliday?"

"This young man called me a paedophile as I was walking past him. I was about to take him to Mr Harvey's office."

"But I didn't......" Shaka started to protest but the P.E. teacher cut him short.

"Shut it."

"But sir. It wasn't him. He didn't say nothing." It was Shaka's straggly-haired mate who'd been hovering unnoticed behind the P.E. teacher.

"What are you doing still here? I already told you to keep your mouth shut. Now get in that classroom."

"But sir. I'm a witness. I can come with you and tell Mr Harvey what happened." The boy had found the courage from somewhere to face up to the scary P.E. teacher. He was determined to play the loyal sidekick and stick by his friend.

John White was having none of it. "If you're not in that classroom in the next three seconds, you'll be tidying up my equipment room in the gym for an hour after school every day next week."

The boy opened his mouth to protest further but, seeing the look on Mr White's face, he thought better of it, sucked his teeth and turned and walked as slowly as he could manage through the classroom door.

"Now." John White turned round to face Shaka. "It's Shaka O'Neill, isn't it?"

"Yes sir."

"Why do I know who you are, Shaka?"

The boy didn't answer. It was obviously a rhetorical question. John White knew the names of almost all the students.

"It's probably because wherever there's trouble in this school you are never far away. Isn't that so?"

Shaka lowered his head, stared at his shoes and said nothing.

"Okay Mr Halliday. Let's take this young reprobate to see Mr Harvey."

Jeremy was still angry but in control of his anger when they entered Mike Harvey's office. John White excused himself as he had a lesson to go to.

"Aha, it's young Mr O'Neill. I presume you haven't brought him here to ask me to reward him with some house points for some helpful act?" Mike Harvey said to Jeremy.

"No, I'm afraid not."

"I didn't do nothing, sir." Shaka's denial was now more of a muted platitude than a cry of outraged innocence.

"Of course you didn't, Shaka. Every time you're brought to this office – and that's far too often – it's always a mistake. The teachers are always picking on you. So let's hear what Mr Halliday has to say about it." Mike Harvey spoke in his bored 'I've heard it all before' voice.

Jeremy explained what had happened in a calm and measured tone. Shaka repeated his plea of innocence but Mike Harvey gave him short shrift. It was to Jeremy's advantage that Shaka was such a notorious character. The boy had been so determined to express his innocence that he failed to mention anything about Jeremy grabbing hold of him and pushing him against the wall – something Jeremy had judiciously left out of his own account. Mike Harvey suspended Shaka from school for three days and told him to wait outside while he phoned his mother to tell her what had happened and check that it was alright to send him home immediately.

As Jeremy walked away from Mike Harvey's office towards the staffroom, he felt a palpable sense of relief that all the tensions bubbling away inside him had at last reached the surface. The pressure had been building up and now a valve had been turned and the trapped fetid air could rush out. He knew he'd handled the situation poorly but he didn't regret it. That valve had also released all his pent up frustration. He felt much better – the way you feel just after you've vomited, he thought – although he wasn't sure that was the most appropriate analogy.

Jeremy stayed in his classroom at lunchtime, ostensibly to catch up on his marking, but mainly to avoid talking to any of his colleagues about the incident with Shaka which he assumed they would now know about if only through having picked up garbled versions from students who had witnessed it.

His first lesson after lunch was with his favourite 8th year class. Despite the turbulent events of the morning, he felt more relaxed than he had for some time. They were studying Chaucer's *The Pardoner's Tale*, reading aloud a dramatized modern version with students taking parts when Jeremy was distracted by a face pressed up against the glass panel in the classroom door. It was a young woman with a pasty complexion and a mound of thick black hair pulled into a tight pony tail on top of her head. Jeremy brought the play reading to a halt, asked the class to wait quietly for a minute and went over to the classroom door.

Outside in the corridor, he saw that the pasty faced woman had a companion – a slightly older woman with long straight red hair and a roll of fat tumbling over her jeans. Lurking behind the two women were Shaka O'Neill and his freckled friend.

"It's Mr Halliday, isn't it?" The pale woman said half to Jeremy while half-turning for confirmation to Shaka who nodded his head.

Jeremy spoke calmly. "I'm sorry but you shouldn't be here. I can't talk to you now. I'm in the middle of......"

"I'm Miss O'Neill, Shaka's mother." She had a tinge of an Irish accent. The other woman did not introduce herself but the resemblance suggested she was the other boy's mother. "I wanted to have a word with you about what happened with Shaka this morning." She spoke in a calm and controlled voice.

"Mrs O'Neill, it's........."

"It's MISS O'Neill."

"Sorry. Miss O'Neill. It's really not appropriate to have this conversation now. If you could......"

She interrupted, determined not to be fobbed off. "Shaka and his friend Terry here," she turned to indicate the other boy, "came home at lunchtime very upset about what happened this morning. Shaka says you picked on him. You accused him of calling you a name which he didn't do."

"Miss O'Neill, Shaka did call me a name and Mr Harvey, the deputy head, dealt with it and punished him. I think, if you wish to complain, you should go and see him."

"I don't want to see him. I've come to see you." Now her volume was rising. Jeremy pulled the classroom door closed behind him, aware that some of the class were out of their seats edging forwards for a better view. "I've never seen Shaka so upset about something that happened in school." Shaka didn't look upset now. He seemed to be enjoying himself. "I know he's no angel but just because he's been in trouble once or twice he gets blamed for everything."

Miss O'Neill's voice was getting louder. She was building up for a confrontation. Jeremy glanced up and down the corridor in the hope that help would arrive but there was no sign of anybody. His brain was spinning trying to think of a way of extricating himself from the situation.

He turned to the smirking boy. "Shaka, could you

please take your mother to the school office and ask them to contact Mr Harvey?" The boy looked at him blankly. Jeremy realised that it was a waste of time asking the little miscreant for help.

"Did you lay your hands on my son? Did you grab hold of him and push him against a wall?" The woman's pale face was reddening, her volume ratcheting up another notch.

"Miss O'Neill, I must insist......"

"How dare you put your hands on my son? I know all about you. We live across the street from the Merediths. It's not enough for you to lay your filthy hands on Susie but now you're putting them on my son."

To Jeremy's relief, classroom doors were opening further down the corridor with teachers' heads peering round to see what all the noise was about. And then Roger Worth appeared from behind Jeremy looking puzzled. Like her son earlier that day, Miss O'Neill seemed encouraged by having an audience.

"You're not going to get away with this. I'm going to make a complaint about you to the Council. You may have got away with what you did to Susie Meredith but you're not going to get away with this. You shouldn't be allowed to be a teacher." She was jabbing her finger at Jeremy's face.

Roger Worth edged between the two of them and touched Jeremy's arm. "Mr Halliday, I think you need to get back to teaching your class. You can leave me to deal with this."

Jeremy stood still for a moment, transfixed. Roger Worth pushed open the classroom door and gently steered him through it, at the same time keeping his own body between Jeremy and Shaka's irate mother. As the door closed behind him, Jeremy faced his shocked and bemused class – half of them out of their seats.

"Right. I'm sorry about that unfortunate interruption. If

you could all sit back down, we can carry on with the play where we left off. If I remember correctly, we were with you, Nabil, reading the part of the pub landlord."

Angry voices could still be heard from the corridor. More people had arrived including Mike Harvey. Fortunately for Jeremy, 8C were a docile well-behaved class stunned into silence rather than over-excited as many St. Saviour's classes would have been. They meekly returned to their seats and Nabil continued with the reading.

*

At the end of the school day, Mary Groenwald sat at her desk awaiting the arrival of Mike Harvey and Jeremy Halliday. She was using the brief interval to give herself a mental kicking. Despite her initial worries, up till now she'd been relieved that Jeremy Halliday's return to school had gone so smoothly, helped enormously by Mrs Meredith's decision to find another school for Susie. Unsurprisingly, the Merediths had been outraged by the school's decision and had threatened to take legal action against both the school and Jeremy. To date those threats had not been carried out. Mary had also feared a reaction from other parents when they heard the news and had been prepared for some to follow the Merediths in removing their children but that hadn't materialised either. And so, Jeremy had returned, Mike Harvey had been assigned the task of managing his reintegration and, until today, she'd had no reports of any problems.

But now, she was kicking herself. She'd been naïve not to expect some repercussions, especially from the students, and, in retrospect, she should have done more to avoid the present situation. She should have had Jeremy more closely monitored; set up regular meetings with him herself. As it was, this meeting would be the first time she had spoken to him since the briefing on his first morning back at school.

Jeremy sat down on the other side of the desk opposite Mary Groenwald and Mike Harvey. It was uncomfortably redolent of that morning last May when he'd been called to the head's office, only this time he knew what it was about.

Mary Groenwald looked solemnly at him. "Obviously you know why we're here. Let me start by apologising to you for what happened this afternoon. It must have been very awkward and distressing for you. You shouldn't have been faced with a situation like that when you were in the middle of a lesson and I have instructed Mike, together with the site manager, to review our security arrangements. Parents – or anybody else for that matter – shouldn't be able to walk into the school unannounced." She paused and took a deep breath. "Anyway, Mike and I eventually calmed Miss O'Neill down, asked her to moderate her language and then we listened to what she had to say about the incident with Shaka this morning. I can reassure you that we told her in no uncertain terms that you had our full backing over the incident and we were convinced that Shaka had called you an insulting name and Mike had punished him accordingly. It goes without saying that she wasn't very happy about it and wanted to know what action we were going to take against you for assaulting her son. She said that if we were unwilling to do anything about it, she would be forced to take further action herself. Namely, she would report the incident to the police." She paused again to let what she had said so far sink in while scrutinising Jeremy. The colour had drained from his face and he shuffled uncomfortably on his chair.

"You'll be relieved to hear that Mike and I talked her out of taking any such action, mainly by warning her that we would take counter-action against her for trespassing on school premises."

Jeremy still showed no reaction except to shift into a more upright position on his chair. There was a short awkward silence broken when Jeremy realised that she was waiting for a response from him.

"Thanks for your support. I appreciate it. I'm really sorry I lost control. I've had a difficult few days. Things had been going so well.........but then I found some nasty graffiti about me on a classroom desk and there were one or two other minor incidents."

"I suppose we could have predicted that things like this would happen," Mary said, "but I did make it clear to you on your first day back that Mike was going to be supporting you. You should have gone to him as soon as these problems arose."

"Yes. I'm sorry. I know." Jeremy looked suitably recalcitrant.

Mary Groenwald paused and then leaned forward on her desk as if to add emphasis to her next point.

"Despite the fact that we have given you our fullest support over Shaka, we all know that your reaction in grabbing hold of him and pushing him was unprofessional and, in most circumstances, should lead to a formal reprimand. However, I've discussed the situation with Mike and, assuming that Miss O'Neill is true to her word and doesn't pursue a further complaint, we will not be taking any action ourselves." Jeremy was about to express his gratitude once again but the head continued before he had the chance. "Of course, it goes without saying that we can't risk......you can't risk......this sort of thing happening again. And, let's face it, it might well happen again. There were a lot of students who witnessed the incident with Shaka and inevitably it will have spread round the school.

Unfortunately, we know that Shaka is not the only awkward character we have in this school so there may well be others who'll decide that it's a fun idea to provoke Mr Halliday. If they do, you cannot react in the way you did today."

"Of course not. I understand. As Mike can tell you, that kind of behaviour is not typical of me. It was a one off. It won't happen again."

"Let's hope not." She didn't sound convinced. She turned her head and nodded towards Mike Harvey as she continued. "Mike and I have discussed where we should go from here. We both take some responsibility for what's happened. We feel we should have been more pro-active in supporting you. So, we have a couple of suggestions to make to you. Firstly, Mike will continue to monitor and support you but we will make it more formal by timetabling a regular weekly meeting between the two of you."

"Fine." Jeremy nodded his head in agreement.

"Secondly, we feel that we haven't paid enough attention to how damaging this whole situation has been to you – the effect that the last nine months must have had on you emotionally. So, we feel that you would benefit from some counselling. The borough employs a psychotherapist on a part-time basis. Her name's Beatrice Varley. Her job is to offer counselling help to staff suffering from various kinds of stress at work. It seems ideal for a situation like the one you find yourself in. It's a free service but, of course, it has to be voluntary. We can't insist that you take it up but we are strongly advising you to do so.........unless, of course, you are already involved in some form of therapy......not that that's our business." She had not felt comfortable about suggesting counselling to him and now she was tying herself in hesitant knots.

Jeremy remained silent for a while unsure how to respond. "No, I'm not involved in any therapy," he finally replied and immediately regretted saying it. He wasn't sure what he felt about the suggestion but, if he was minded to refuse the offer, then she had given him an easy way out which he had now closed off. Although, if he didn't want to take up the offer, he could still tell her that he had been considering going to a therapist and would prefer to make his own arrangement.

"Could you give me a bit of time to think about it? I'll come back to you with a decision tomorrow."

"Of course," Mary said. "Take your time."

"So, you decided not to broach the subject of whether he should think about moving to another school?" Mike Harvey said as soon as Jeremy had left the room.

Mary stared at him, trying to detect whether he was having a dig at her. It was true. She had told him that she thought the best solution for Jeremy, as well as for the school, would be for him to look for another job.

"I thought about it but, on balance, I decided that now wasn't the best time to broach the subject. Even if he were to look for another job, and find one, he's unlikely to leave before the summer so we'd still have to deal with things in the meantime. Plus there won't be that many jobs being advertised until after Easter. My feeling is that we see how things go for the next month or so and then I make the suggestion to him nearer the end of term." Mike nodded his head sagely. "Anyway," she continued, "you never know. The counsellor might suggest it to him."

Mike nodded again. For all the outward support he'd given her over the previous months, he still wasn't convinced that the governors had made the right decision in appointing her. He felt his initial doubts were now being confirmed. She didn't have the stomach to take difficult decisions.

14

"Échec. Pardon – I mean check."

Guy Reynard leaned across the chessboard and waved his hand in front of Jeremy's face to attract his attention. As the weather outside had turned cool, grey and showery, they had abandoned their usual table under the arches on the terrace of the village café and were installed inside at a drab white melamine-topped table next to the window.

Guy had knocked on Jeremy's door earlier that morning ostensibly to find out whether there was any more news of the murder enquiry. When Jeremy invited him in, he declined and instead suggested Jeremy come with him to the café up the road. Jeremy was reluctant. He hadn't seen or spoken to anyone in the village, apart from Guy, since the news of Julia's death had appeared in *La Dépêche*. Guy then admitted that the real reason he'd come round that morning was to lure Jeremy out of the house. It couldn't be good for him to keep himself locked up like a prisoner. Finally, Jeremy agreed to accompany him.

"Mon ami." He poked Jeremy's arm to get his attention. "I said check."

Jeremy eyes were fixed on two elderly Frenchmen he vaguely knew who had just entered the café.

"Oh, I'm sorry, Guy. I'm finding it hard to concentrate. I'm a bit on edge."

"I can see that, my friend. That's why I'm going easy on you. I could have had you échec et mat several moves ago."

Jeremy's hand was hovering over his black chess pieces switching between his king and a bishop.

"I'm finding it difficult to concentrate with everybody looking at me."

"Don't be stupid. No-one is looking at you. It's your imagination."

"Well they're not coming over to talk to me – or you, for that matter. I've even managed to make a pariah of you." His hand stopped wavering and settled on his bishop which he moved in front of his king, holding on to it for a few seconds before making up his mind.

"Of course they are talking. Some have nodded at us. Some have said 'bonjour'. How many of these people do you normally stop and have a conversation with?"

"Well, they're certainly not going to talk to someone they think might be a murderer."

"Oh pfff." Guy blew through his lips dismissively. "I doubt that that is what they are thinking. They are more likely to think it if you hide away in your house. Because you are here, in the outside, not afraid, they are less likely to think you did it. And then, of course, there is the fact that you are English."

"What's that got to do with it?"

"Around here, they think Englishmen don't do such things. It is a crime passionel. That is what the French do. The English are too – how do you say? – stiff upper lip. Cold-blooded."

"And where do they get this idea from? I suppose it's what they read in the papers and see in the movies and on television," Jeremy said. "Although, don't they all watch *Midsomer Murders* in France? Surely that would change their view that Englishmen don't murder their wives and girlfriends?"

"I don't know about television. I don't watch it."

"Well, they can't have much experience of real-life murders round here. It's a virtual crime-free zone, isn't it?"

Guy raised his eyebrows. "You'd be surprised, mon ami. You know Cransac – the little village about twelve kilometres from here?"

"Not sure. I might have driven through it."

"It's very small. About fifteen houses. A few years ago a carpenter who lives in the village – I used to work with him sometimes – he thinks his wife is having an affair. So, what does he do? Does he try to find evidence to prove it? Does he ask her about it – demand to know the truth? No. He waits till she is upstairs one evening in the bath and he sets fire to the house burning her to death. That's a typical French murder."

"And had she been having an affair?"

"Nobody knew about it. And, if she was, in a tiny village like that, everyone would know. And then, if you had seen her, I don't think you would believe someone else was having sex with her."

They both lapsed into silence while they studied the chess board.

"So, you have heard nothing from Monsieur le Juge?" Guy said.

"No. Not a sound. I don't know if that's a good or bad sign. It's been over a week since I had the last meeting with him. What do you think?"

"Oh mon ami. I would like to say it's a good sign to make you feel better but I don't lie to you. The problem with the French police is that they are lazy." He emphasised the final word by elongating the vowels – laaazeee. "They will always do what is the easiest. Most people are murdered by one of their relatives. Husbands kill wives, wives kill husbands, children kill parents, lovers murder each other because of jealousy. You are the partner so they think it's you. They have no evidence but then you have no alibi. It's too much trouble for them to carry out a full investigation especially...how you say in English...out here in the sticks. And Aurillac is even more in the sticks than here. So, if Madame Julia was murdered by some madman who she accidently meets somewhere, it will be too much trouble for them to try and find him. No – you are easier to find."

"Thanks Guy. I thought you brought me here to cheer me up because, if so, you're not doing a very good job."

"I'm sorry but you know me – I like to be always honest. Another coffee?"

"No thanks. I'm alright." Jeremy turned his attention back to the chessboard.

The café door opened and a gust of wind blew Guy's newspaper off the table. Madame Gomez stood in the doorway shaking out her umbrella. She was the wife of Serge, an electrician who had rewired Jeremy and Julia's house when they bought it. When she saw Jeremy she gave a small involuntary jump as if she had seen a ghost and then quickly regained her equilibrium.

"Bonjour Messieurs. Ca va?"

"Ca va bien," Jeremy said as she offered him a weak smile before turning away and proceeding to the bar.

Jeremy gave an 'I told you so' raise of the eyebrows to Guy before moving his queen to a position where she was sure to be taken.

*

Apart from a follow-up meeting with Miles Joseph in Rodez, what he had told Guy was true – it had been a very quiet week during which he had been on tenterhooks waiting for a phone call from Judge Bouchon or another visit from the gendarmes. The weather had been fine and he'd driven out to the surrounding countryside several times and gone on lengthy walks with the idea that fresh air and exercise would clear his head. It hadn't. The spectacular scenery made little impression as the same thoughts carouselled around in his head. Still, at least it got him out of the house and occupied his time, he reasoned. For the rest of the time, he tried to relax and resist the lassitude he was feeling after too many sleepless nights.

At least the phone calls from journalists had dried up. Apart from the usual cold callers, the only call of any importance came from Hattie. He was surprised and embarrassed to hear her voice and she sounded equally awkward on the other end of the line. She dispensed with any pleasantries – not bothering to ask him how he was bearing up or such like. She got straight to the point.

"I'm phoning because the French police have just informed me that they're releasing Julia's body. But I guess you already know that."

"No, I haven't heard anything about it." He told her the truth without stopping to think and immediately wished he hadn't. It was strange that they'd told Hattie and not him. She was Julia's sister but he was her partner. He could only interpret it as further evidence that they thought he'd killed her.

"Anyway, you know now," she said in what Jeremy felt was a disdainful tone of voice. "I've arranged to have her body flown back here for cremation."

Jeremy shuddered at the word 'cremation'. Wasn't the body already mostly cremated? He remembered Judge Bouchon telling him that there would be no need for him to identify the body as it was so badly burnt.

"I've made preliminary arrangements for the ceremony. It's on Friday week at St. Cuthbert's church in Hove and she'll be cremated at Brighton crematorium straight afterwards." Her tone was now formal, matter-of-fact, more like a funeral director than the deceased's sister. Just like the gendarmerie, not bothering to tell him that his partner's body was being released, Hattie was treating him like some distant relative or semi-detached acquaintance. He should have been angry that she had had the presumption to arrange the funeral without consulting him but he didn't have the heart to get into an argument with her.

After a brief pause during which Jeremy thought she had put the phone down, she continued.

"You're welcome to come, of course."

He felt the 'of course' was tinged with a touch of irony. He gave the offer a moment's thought before realising he couldn't attend if he wanted to. The French police had his passport and he was forbidden to leave the country. Maybe they would relent and let him go on compassionate grounds if he asked. His mind was spinning. He guessed that if he told Hattie he didn't want to come, she would assume it was because he didn't want to have to face all of Julia's family and friends – that he would be consumed by feelings of guilt. He tried to conjure up another excuse but couldn't. He'd have to tell her the truth about the confiscation of his passport.

Once he had told her he waited for some sort of response but there was nothing. "Hattie. You have to believe me. Despite what the French police think, I had absolutely nothing to do with Julia's death." He was tempted to elaborate on why the police always suspected the nearest and dearest first but knew it would sound feeble to someone as inclined as Hattie probably was to suspect that he was the culprit.

"It's only a matter of time before they find the real murderer and I'll be in the clear."

"Yes," Hattie intoned like a softly hissing snake.

He waited for her to say more – maybe something positive or supportive – but he wasn't surprised when she didn't. He considered whether he should push her by asking directly "you don't think I could have had anything to do with Julia's death, do you?" but he didn't, afraid of what her answer would be. Knowing what her answer would be.

He clicked on the delete button to remove the usual pile of crap that had accumulated in his inbox over the past week, only saving the ones from his fellow stamp dealers. Just as he was consigning the rest to trash, one of the titles triggered a vague memory flash. He immediately summoned up his delete box and scrolled through the fifty plus messages until he came upon one headed 'Gîte Rental'. It was from Ruth Gershon. It took a few seconds for the name to register. Of course – the woman who phoned him the other week about her gîte rental. He'd forgotten all about it what with everything else that had been happening in his life. The email was to confirm that she would be arriving on Saturday afternoon but she'd be on her own because her partner had unexpected commitments at work and so would not be flying out to join her until the following week.

Jeremy had lost track of time – he had to check the date and day of the week in the space bar on his laptop. It was Thursday so she was arriving in two days. He had a moment's panic. It had been Julia's responsibility to organise the gîte bookings and prepare the house for the new arrivals although he'd done it once when she'd had to go away on business. His first reaction was to curse out loud. He didn't need this. He had enough on his mind without having to spend time preparing the gîte, trying to remember all the procedures Julia had put in place. Why hadn't he just cancelled the booking when she phoned?

But, after that initial reaction, he paused to think about it and slowly changed his mind. Perhaps it would be a good thing to have some useful, if mindless, activity to keep him busy for a couple of days and take his mind off the investigation.

His first move was to go on to Julia's gîte rental website. He scrolled through it quickly until he came across the details of arrival and departure dates and, more specifically, the couple of sentences stating that there would be a 'welcome pack' of provisions in the gîte on the client's arrival. Apart from some basics – milk, washing up liquid – there were no further details. He tried to remember what Julia used to include in the wicker basket on the gîte's kitchen table. He'd have to check the locked store cupboard. She kept a supply of small catering packs of things like tea, coffee and jam in there but, since it was a good nine months since the last rental, she might not have restocked it. Where the hell did she get those things from? He'd have to see if he could find any paper accounts in her desk drawer. Apart from the basics, he remembered her including a few items of local produce – a half bottle of rosé, some wild boar saucisson, a jar of duck rillettes. And then he calmed down and told himself to stop worrying. Ruth Gershon wouldn't be expecting anything in particular. She'd be grateful for whatever he provided. He grabbed a sheet of paper and a pen and started making a list. He could go shopping in Villefranche tomorrow morning.

Meanwhile, he grabbed the keys and headed out the front door and across the driveway to inspect it. It would need a thorough clean and an airing. He'd have to get the linen out of the store cupboards and make the bed. Damn. He doubled back to the house and skipped upstairs to Julia's office. He needed to dig out the gîte inventory to check that all the equipment was still in there, especially the itemised kitchen stuff. If there had been any breakages at the end of last summer, Julia might not have bothered to buy replacements. Normally he hated cleaning – hated any kind of housework – although he'd always done his fair share. But now he was looking forward to some boring, time-devouring activity.

15

Beatrice Varley scribbled a few final notes on her previous patient before getting up from her chair and pouring two glasses of fresh water for herself and her next client from the jug on the chest of drawers on one side of her cramped consulting room. Despite the clip-framed Renoir and Matisse prints she'd brought from home to cheer the room up, it was still not very welcoming with its institutional pale green walls, mud-coloured carpet and cheap IKEA furniture. So unlike her own consulting room at home – a light airy conservatory extension to her Victorian semi-detached Surbiton house looking out on to her pretty walled garden. Here, the one tiny window looked out over a goods delivery yard. Still, she enjoyed the change of scene for one day a week – the opportunity to journey into London, even if it was only Wandsworth High Street.

And then there were the clients. Although they were referred to her by Wandsworth Council and were coming to see her about work-related problems, normally stress, they weren't that different from her private patients. Usually they were less problematic as very few of them suffered from the kind of borderline mental illnesses and suicidal tendencies of some of the people she saw at home. Her previous patient was typical. He was a senior engineer working for the council's road maintenance department. He was becoming increasingly stressed both at work and at home. Within minutes of their first session, Beatrice could tell that he was suffering from a form of obsessive compulsive disorder. He was getting so worked up and frustrated by minor details and problems during his working day that he was failing to complete the tasks he'd been given. His department head had sent him to see Beatrice as a last resort – he was on the verge of dismissal. By the end of their first session, it became clear that things were no better at home. His constant complaints and irritations about the most minor things around the house were driving his wife to despair and alienating his teenage daughter.

He was a challenge. They'd had four sessions together and progress had been slow. Beatrice suspected that, even before this OCD had crept up on him over the past couple of years, he'd been able to bore for England. He could spend ten or fifteen minutes talking about the ring of grime his daughter left round the bath and then failed to clean despite his constant admonitions. And then, the following week, having at last got her to clean the bath, the problem now was that she didn't do it properly.

She had a few minutes before her next client was due so she speedily re-read the notes she'd been given about him. In the two years she'd been working for the council, the sector of employees she'd seen most were schoolteachers. If anyone doubted teaching was a stressful profession, she had plenty of evidence to prove them wrong. Jeremy Halliday appeared to be an interesting case. There was far more information in the notes than she was normally given, nearly all of it detailing the sexual impropriety case brought against him by Susie Meredith. She'd had plenty of patients who had experienced sexual assault or abuse in their childhoods, either at school or in their home, but this was the first time that she would have to deal with it from the angle of an adult who had been wrongly accused.

*

Jeremy lowered himself on to the Scandinavian armchair, shifting around to get comfortable, resting his elbows awkwardly on the leather straps that functioned as armrests. Once he was settled, he studied the woman sitting opposite. On the short cycle journey from school that afternoon, he'd formed an image in his mind of a typical psychotherapist. She was a middle aged woman in glasses, her long greying hair tied up in a bun, wearing sensible shoes, a hand-knitted chunky jumper and knee length skirt. Or, if it was a man, he would be of similar age with a bald head, half-framed spectacles perched on the end of his nose, wearing a dark suit and bowtie and, if he was to take the stereotype to the extreme, speaking in a thick mid-European accent. Beatrice Varley did not fit the image. Jeremy guessed that she was about the same age as him. Her light brown hair was immaculately cut and shaped to frame an attractive, lipsticked and powdered face. She was expensively dressed with a pastel-coloured chiffon scarf draped round a long slender neck above a crisp white blouse, the top buttons undone to reveal a smidgen of cleavage. The ensemble was completed by a tapered black skirt, dark stockings and red and black high-heeled shoes. She looked like the kind of prosperous middle class woman who'd never suffered a moment's tribulation in her life.

Sprawled uncomfortably opposite this elegant woman, he was conscious of his own dishevelled dowdiness. He still had his cycle clips on, his favourite brown cycling shoes were scuffed and muddy, there was an oil stain on his trouser bottoms, his hair had been swept into untidy peaks and troughs and his eyes were still watering from the effects of cycling into a strong wind. His crumpled red cagoule and shabby shoulder bag were deposited on the floor next to his chair. Nobody entering the room could be in any doubt, he thought, about who was the therapist and who the schoolteacher.

After Mary Groenwald had made the suggestion that he use the council's psychotherapy service for employees, he'd taken more than the twenty-four hours he'd promised to consider the offer. He wanted to say 'no thanks' but he was afraid that, although she had emphasised that it was voluntary, the subtext was that she expected him to take it up. He felt under pressure. He was already on a warning after the conduct committee's decision on the Susie Meredith case. And now, he'd been fortunate not to face an unprofessional conduct charge after the way he'd, literally, handled Shaka O'Neill.

He had vague memories of being sent to see a counsellor after his mother died. He remembered it was a woman but he couldn't remember anything else about her or what was said during the only two meetings he had had with her. Maybe his 'hair in a bun and glasses' image came from that experience? He couldn't say. His only memory of it was feeling uncomfortable and embarrassed and being relieved when his father told the school he didn't want him to attend any more sessions. Even though, this time, the purpose was to help him overcome the trauma of the Susie Meredith case and resume normal service in his job, he knew that therapy sessions were bound also to focus on his childhood, his mother's death, his subsequent relationship with his father and the state of his present relationship with Julia – all things he didn't want to talk about.

It wasn't until two days after the meeting with Mary Groenwald and Mike Harvey that he had finally summoned up the courage to discuss what had happened with Julia. Up to that point, he hadn't told her anything about the previous week's incidents in school, including his contretemps with Shaka O'Neill. He felt his relationship with Julia had mirrored the situation at school. Since he'd been exonerated and had returned to work, outwardly it appeared that things at home were also returning to normal. There was more intimacy between them – they even occasionally had sex – and yet, as at school, Jeremy feared it was an illusion; that, at any moment, something could happen – a wrong word, a sudden rebuff – that would shatter their fragile reconnection. And now that his 'phoney' peaceful return to school had fallen apart, he feared that the same thing might be about to happen at home. It would spread like an infection.

When he finally communicated the full details of his awful week to her, she was far more understanding and supportive than he had expected. Not a hint of disappointment in him or admonition for the way he had handled the incident with Shaka or the follow up altercation with the mother.

"Thank God that stupid woman is showing some sense at last," she pronounced disdainfully. "It would have been disgraceful if she'd disciplined you for pushing that little shit. You should have given him a good slap. That's the least he deserved."

It was a typical Julia comment. She'd been a good teacher – a strict disciplinarian – but, in her final year, she had started to show signs of growing less tolerant and more impatient with students. Jeremy often felt uneasy about the unprofessional and extreme comments she made about some of the less well-behaved ones. He felt that her decision to leave teaching had come at the right time.

Hesitantly, he filled in the final details of the meeting in the Head's office. "Mary did add a couple of caveats at the end about my future conduct."

"Oh here we go," Julia interrupted, frowning at him. "I knew there'd be some sort of 'but' coming."

"No, it wasn't anything like that. She just wanted to offer me some extra support to help me avoid incidents like that in the future. She suggested regular weekly meetings between me and Mike and a periodic review meeting with her." He paused before adding the final detail. "She also suggested that I should see a counsellor. Apparently, Wandsworth have a free counselling service for employees. She didn't insist on me going. She left it up to me but, reading between the lines, I think there's an expectation that I take up the offer. Anyway, I said I'd think about it and let her know tomorrow."

"I think you should take it up," Julia said without a moment's hesitation. "As much as I hate to agree with Mary Groenwald, I think it's a good idea. You've been through a lot and it was bound to take time to get back to normal. Talking it all through with an expert – someone who doesn't know you – might help."

Her enthusiasm took Jeremy by surprise. He had been half-expecting, maybe even hoping, she'd be against it and would back him in rejecting the offer.

"I was going to suggest that you see a therapist months ago," she continued, "when you were in the midst of it all and obviously depressed. The only reason I didn't was because I was worried about how you'd react. Things weren't going particularly well between us at the time and I decided that my suggesting counselling might only make things worse. But, now that the worst is over, I think you should go for it. Even if it turns out to be unhelpful, what have you got to lose? It's free. If you went privately to a psychotherapist, it would cost you at least £50 an hour."

*

Beatrice Varley's voice matched her appearance – a softly spoken, received pronounciation, Home Counties' accent. Their first session together raced by. He started by giving her a brief history of his teaching career up to his involvement with Susie Meredith. Then, for the rest of the session, he recounted the events leading up to her accusation, his subsequent suspension and the build up to the final hearing. It was strangely calming and reassuring to relive that traumatic period with someone who knew nothing about it and was such a patient empathetic listener. There was none of the tension he had felt when explaining it to Julia and none of the acerbic comments that she had expressed at the time. If only he'd had someone like Beatrice to talk to then rather than Julia. He was so at ease with the therapist that he was even able to tell her about those hurtful comments of Julia's and give vent to all the anger and betrayal he had felt back then – including his suspicion that Julia had harboured doubts about his innocence.

On his way home after the session, he felt that a weight had been lifted from his shoulders. He had been able to express his anger. He had felt the same about the incident with Shaka. He may have handled it unprofessionally but at least it had provided him with an outlet for his pent up frustration. Just what he hadn't been able to show when he had sat in Mary Groenwald's office listening to those accusations for the first time – or when the police had questioned him and taken away their computers.

*

The following weeks passed uneventfully, punctuated by his two weekly after school meetings – the counselling with Beatrice Varley and the mentoring session with Mike Harvey. For the rest of the time, everything else in school continued in much the same way it had before the Shaka incident. Thus far, Mary Groenwald's fears had proved unfounded. There was no repeat of the corridor incident, although Jeremy could still feel students' eyes turned on him as he walked by and he could guess that the muttered conversations that followed were about him and his alleged paedophilia. There might have been the odd name mumbled behind his back but they were too indistinct for him to hear them. Shaka was back in school but he either turned away when he saw Jeremy approaching or looked aggrieved daggers at him as he passed.

As he had predicted, the sessions with Beatrice gradually switched from questions about the trauma he'd been through in the past nine months to subtle probing about his childhood, his mother's death etc. The more she prodded him the more he tried to resist by giving away as little as possible or changing the subject. Although it was exactly what he had expected, he couldn't help resenting that this woman who he'd earlier seen as so warm and nurturing – a cross between the mother he'd lost and the perfect girlfriend that Julia had failed to be when he'd needed her most – had metamorphosed into a challenging inquisitor. It was a battle he couldn't win. Whether he opened up to her and talked about all those things or resisted, he was exposing more of himself and his feelings than he wanted to. There was only one thing he was tempted to talk about – the only thing he'd never talked about to anybody else: his father's shocking, dementia raddled account of his mother's death. But, when it came to it, he couldn't bring himself to do so.

During his periods of silence, he spent the time appraising his psychotherapist. She wore different clothes for every session, all as stylish, smartly co-ordinated and expensive as those she'd been wearing at their first meeting. Julia was into fashion and owned a lot of clothes – their bedroom wardrobe and cupboard space was seventy-five per cent hers – but he imagined Beatrice living in a suburban mansion containing walk-in wardrobes with rack upon rack of designer clothes and row upon row of fancy shoes. On his cycle home after these more difficult sessions, he found himself starting to resent her. How dare she, in her silver-lined, sugar-coated, perfect world claim to have any insight into his shambles of a life? He pictured himself leaping from his wood and canvas Scandinavian chair and reaching across the coffee table to muss up her perfect coiffure and rumple her neatly laundered clothes. The image of Catherine Deneuve in the film *Belle de Jour*, in her white nightdress, tied to a tree, having mud thrown at her, came to mind.

For the first few weeks, Julia restrained herself from asking him much about the counselling sessions, meekly accepting his minimalist responses such as 'it's going well' and not pressing him for any more details. It was only once his feelings about Beatrice had begun to sour that he became more responsive to her polite enquiries. He started to find it cathartic to talk to Julia – to share with her some selective extracts from what he had talked about in that day's session. It was as if the roles of these two women in his life were being switched around. Now he found it easier to talk to Julia because she was happy to just sit and listen. Unlike Beatrice, she didn't seem to be judging him or digging deeper by firing questions at him that he didn't want to answer.

For her part, Julia was relieved. The therapy appeared to be working. What had first attracted her to Jeremy was how unlike Pete Davies he was. None of that macho posturing or the determination to dominate. He was caring – more in touch with his feminine side – and happy to listen, unlike Pete who only ever wanted to talk about himself. But, once she got to know him better and they started living together, and especially since the sexual abuse allegations, she'd realised that he was not as open and in touch with his emotions as he had seemed. However different he may have been from Pete, he was still an archetypal man in the way he bottled up his emotions. During the past year, it had been impossible to get him to talk about his feelings. Every time she had tried to get him to open up, he would disappear into the garden, just as other men retreated to their workshops or sheds. But now here he was talking about his mother's death and his subsequent strained relationship with his father in a way he'd never done before. In fact, now that he was sharing with her the things he had been telling his therapist, she realised how much he'd been conning her in those early years together – appearing to share his childhood traumas with her but, in truth, not telling her very much at all.

*

Beatrice glanced over her previous week's notes and sat back, pen in hand, wondering where to go from here. Today would be their sixth session. She felt that she had broken through some of his barriers and he was now more in touch with his emotions and more aware of the problems facing him but he still needed to face up to what he wanted for the future. He had reached a crisis point in his life and yet all he could think to do was to carry on exactly as he had before as if nothing had changed. Even if he came to terms with, and recovered from, what had happened with Susie Meredith, it had soured teaching for him. But he was in denial.

She kept him waiting outside for a couple of minutes while she planned her strategy and then ushered him in to the consulting room.

"So, how's your week been?" She said, starting things off gently, giving him time to put down his bag and settle in his chair.

"Pas grande chose, as the French say."

"Oh. How come the sudden burst of French?"

"I've been trying to brush up on it. We've just booked a cottage in South-West France for Easter."

"That sounds nice. I guess you're looking forward to it?"

"Very much. We didn't have a holiday last summer what with the abuse case hanging over me. Actually, we haven't been away together for nearly two years – except for occasional trips to Julia's sister in Brighton."

"Any particular reason for choosing that part of France?"

"Yes. It's an area we've been to before. In fact, it was where we went on our first holiday together. We really liked it. I guess it was a kind of honeymoon just after we'd decided to move in together."

Beatrice paused and seemed to be thinking about what he'd said, as if there was something more to it than sociable chat about his week. "So, this is going to be a second honeymoon? A chance to turn back the clock? Refresh your relationship with Julia?"

"I don't know about that." He paused for thought. "I suppose so. Yes. Trying to return to happier times, I guess. Get back to what life was like before the trauma of the past year."

"Is that how you see your future? Moving on by going back?"

"I'm not sure what you're getting at. Of course I want to return to a normal life."

"Yes, I can see that. But often, what was normal in the past isn't anymore. Things have changed. We can't stop time – or turn the clock back – however much we would all like to at times."

"I think you're making too much of this. You always want to overcomplicate things. It's simple. We need a holiday – a break – and we're going back to a place we've been to before which holds good memories for us." Jeremy often felt irritated by Beatrice but he rarely expressed it. This time he couldn't help himself. He wasn't going to allow her to put a damper on something he felt so good about.

"Okay, let's leave it at that and get back to what we were

talking about last week. You've talked quite a bit about your relationship with your parents before your mother died. How did it feel to be an only child? Did you miss not having any brothers or sisters?"

"No, I don't think so. It was what I was used to. You can't miss what you've never had."

"Can't you?"

Jeremy treated her question as rhetorical.

"Did you have friends or relatives who were in large families? Perhaps you felt jealous of them?"

"I told you before that I didn't have many friends and the ones I did have............well, I can't say I was bothered one way or the other about them having brothers and sisters. The impression I got was that they were either older than them and bullied them all the time or they were much younger and were nuisances. I think it made me feel glad that I didn't have any. I've always been good at amusing myself. I liked my own company. And anyway, by the time I was a teenager, I wasn't just an only child, I was the only child of a single parent – and a single dad at that. I didn't know anybody else with the same home life as me."

Beatrice allowed a pause for his response to sink in – a space to give him the opportunity to elaborate. When he didn't, she changed the subject. "You've never said much about why you chose teaching as a career."

"I guess it was the same reason as most people. I left university with an English degree and couldn't think of much else I wanted to do." Jeremy answered instantly, relieved to be off the subject of his family. "I kind of drifted into it. I have to admit it wasn't a very positive decision."

"And yet, you said you really enjoyed it. You thought you were a very good teacher."

"Yes. Once I got into it and got through the first year I was never in any doubt that I'd made the right decision."

"And was that because you particularly like working with children? Being an only child, perhaps it was a way of making up for your solitary childhood?"

"I don't know about that. Again, I think you're reading too much into it. Sure I enjoy working with children. They're challenging. And it's rewarding to see them growing up and developing as human beings and feeling that you've been a part of that."

"And how about having children of your own? Are you and Julia planning to have children?"

There was a pause as Jeremy took time to consider his response. This was another subject he wasn't very comfortable with.

"I don't know. I guess it's getting a bit late now that we're both heading towards forty."

"Forty's not too old these days. More and more women are putting off having children until well into their forties after they've established themselves in their careers. Do you want to have children?"

Another long pause. He found himself thinking about whether she had children. He suspected she didn't. They'd mess up her pristine life.

"I don't know. To be honest, I've never given it a lot of thought. I guess – with my history of pretty short term relationships, I didn't think it was ever likely to happen."

"Yes, but now you're in a long, fairly established relationship. Does Julia want children?

"I don't think so."

Beatrice waited, hoping Jeremy would go into more detail. He stayed silent so she continued. "You don't think so? Have you discussed it?"

"No, I can't say we have. There's been the occasional conversation – sometimes when we've been out with friends or with Julia's sister, when she's hinted that she's not particularly interested in having children. Plus, we're not that established as a couple. We've only been together for three years. We only moved in together a couple of years ago. I guess we still need more time together before making that sort of commitment."

"Yes. I understand that you don't want to have a child at this point in time. What I find harder to understand is that you haven't discussed the possibility."

She was putting him on the defensive again. He thought she was supposed to be helping him so why did he feel under attack most of the time? "I'm sorry if I'm beginning to sound like a broken record but I think this is another of those things you're trying to make too much of. We've had a lot on our plates over the last year or so what with Julia leaving teaching to set up her own business and me having to go through all that shit at school. Whether or not to have children was the last thing we were thinking about."

"I'm sorry if the question embarrasses you......"

"No – it doesn't embarrass me at all."

"It's just that we've spent almost all of our time during the last five weeks talking about the past so, this week, I wanted to talk more about how you see your future and my question about children seemed a natural starting point."

"I was under the impression that I came here to sort out my feelings about the stress I'd been through recently and how I could come to terms with it. Until I do that, I don't see the point of thinking about the future."

"What I would say to that is that you can only put all that trauma behind you by moving on. You seem to have been trapped by those events. You're in a kind of stasis and you're only going to free yourself from it by moving forward."

Jeremy stared blankly at her as she waited to see what he had to say.

"How do you feel now about teaching?" She continued. "Has what's happened to you during the past year changed the way you feel?"

"I'm not sure. I guess it must have done. Obviously I've found it a lot more difficult since I returned to work. As I've said, I've been a bit on edge. I used to be confident in my relationships with the students – and with my colleagues. But now......well, I guess I'm suspicious......worried all the time about how people see me...........what they're thinking about me."

"And has that made you change your mind about teaching?"

"I don't know. I don't think so. I feel it's just a stage I've got to get through. I've just got to wait for it to pass and for everything to return to normal." It was beginning to feel like a very long hour. He was tempted to check his watch but resisted.

"We're back to where we were at the start of this session – your need to return to normal. Have you considered the possibility of leaving teaching? Is there another career you might consider?"

"No. I haven't given it any thought. To be honest, I've no idea what else I could do."

＊

Once again, on his journey home from the session, he felt frustrated and dispirited. If it was making him feel like this, he couldn't see how the therapy was helping him. He needed to think seriously about whether to continue with it. Having previously been so open with Julia about what he and Beatrice had been talking about, he knew he'd be uncomfortable about discussing that afternoon's session with her. But then he rewound in his head what they had discussed and had second thoughts. Maybe Beatrice was right to be surprised that they hadn't ever talked about having children. And maybe, going through with Julia what he and Beatrice had discussed would give them the perfect opportunity to have that conversation. On third thoughts, maybe not. He found it hard to own up to, but it was the kind of conversation he was too scared to have with her. Even after being together for three years and having bought a house, he couldn't feel confident about their relationship. In the early days, after they first started living together, he was constantly expecting things to go wrong. He studied other couples who appeared to be happy to try and fathom the secret of their success – to compare their life with his and Julia's. Did they talk together enough? Did they share things? Or did they share too much? Were they trying to do too much together? Did they need to give each other more space, more independence – or less? He imagined most people's models for a good partnership were their own parents but his had had their marriage abruptly severed when he was twelve and his memory of what they were like together before that was vague.

And so, with Julia he was constantly holding his breath in anticipation, waiting for the inevitable car crash. And then Susie Meredith came along. He had fully expected them not to survive that debacle but, now that they had, he still wasn't satisfied. Just waiting for the next bump in the road. And bringing up the subject of children and, thereby, the whole question of their future together, seemed like tempting fate.

✳

It was Julia who started talking about the future when they were on holiday in France. As they sat on a restaurant terrace in the warm evening sunshine sampling the local cuisine, their conversation turned to comparisons between their life in London and the rural existence of the locals in the tiny Aveyron villages and medieval market towns that they had visited. The dramatically different pace of life.

While they didn't want to cast themselves into premature middle age, their approaching fortieth birthdays inevitably represented a milestone in their lives. Perhaps it was time to think about making a radical change to their lifestyle, Julia suggested. London was for the young and in a hurry. Okay, they weren't old but neither were they that young anymore. Once Julia had expressed her doubts, Jeremy felt confident in giving voice to his own. He had to admit that he'd been finding that life in London was starting to sap his energy. Everything moved so fast. Whereas, in the Aveyron, life seemed to be in permanent slow motion. You never saw anyone hurrying anywhere. No car horns blared out impatiently. You didn't get woken up at night by wailing police sirens. Everything took time; queueing to fill the car with petrol; paying for groceries at the supermarket checkout; waiting to be served behind old women in the market as they chatted endlessly to the stall holder; having two hour lunches in restaurants. It was a mystery how *MacDonald's* did so well in France – fast food seemed an anathema to the French way of life.

And then, during the final few days of the holiday, they gravitated as if by accident from gazing in estate agents' windows to going inside and arranging to view some properties. They treated it as a bit of fun – indulging a fantasy – although they couldn't help but be impressed by how far the money they could get for their house in Tooting would go in the Aveyron. They viewed several honey-coloured stone built houses with oak beams and wood-burning stoves. They didn't know exactly what they were looking for but some of the ones they saw were very tempting.

*

The Northern line train was crowded and stuffy in the May sunshine. Jeremy was heading into central London for an English A Level standardisation meeting. The train was moving at a crawl. The driver explained that there were delays due to an earlier signal failure at Kennington. Jeremy was going to be late. He hated being late. There was a young woman with long black hair sitting opposite him putting on her makeup. He tried not to stare at her. What was the matter with people these days? It was bad enough that so many of them seemed to think it was acceptable to consume smelly burgers and cartons of chips and stink out the whole carriage but this was embarrassing. He regretted he'd forgotten to bring a book or pick up a free newspaper that he could hide behind. But then, to his horror, she delved deeper into her makeup bag, withdrew a small razor and a tube of gel and proceeded to shave her legs.

Over the following weeks, that incident became a catalyst for his feelings about London life. Everywhere he went he encountered things that annoyed him; to be followed instantly by the observation – it wasn't like this in the Aveyron. In the past, people walking along the streets talking to themselves were obviously mentally disturbed but now everybody did it – except they were on their mobile phones, needing to let someone know where they were and what they were doing every minute of the day. On the top deck of the 94 bus, he was sitting minding his own business when a young woman behind him started yelling into her phone – 'you bastard! You get me pregnant and then you start treating me like shit......'. It goes on and on until he comes to his stop. Is there now no aspect of peoples' lives that can't be performed in public in London? How long before people will be fucking and shitting on the trains and buses? And then there were the people who dropped litter in the street when they were only yards from a litter bin.

But it wasn't just that he hated seeing it. It was the moments after that he spent agonising, wrestling with his conscience, over whether to catch up with them and ask them to pick it up. Of course, he never did – which made him feel a coward. If it was a child or a woman, he was more tempted but that made him feel even worse about himself because he knew he'd never even consider it if it was a young man with tattoos.

And then, there were the endless chains of identical coffee shops selling barely drinkable coffee in bladder-bursting sizes, enticing you in with wifi and leather sofas, full of people in suits holding business meetings or interviewing prospective employees: a far remove from the cafes in Villefranche or the *Café de Flore* or *Les Deux Magots* in Paris where intellectuals sat around all day discussing literature and the meaning of life – where Sartre met up with Albert Camus and Simone de Beauvoir and wrote *Being and Nothingness.*

And what was all that tension doing to his health and well-being? He was in no doubt – living in a city like London must shorten your life. Too much daily stress, too many petty annoyances and the constant wrestling with his conscience. And you couldn't even escape sitting quietly of an evening in your own home. One night, he was interrupted while watching the television news by a young couple on the pavement outside having a noisy argument. It got louder, more violent and impossible to ignore. He peered through a slit in the blinds and watched the man shrieking vitriol at the woman, backing her up against his garden wall, the young man's snarling face inches from hers. He was so out of control, it could only be a matter of time before he hit her. Yet again, Jeremy moved into conscience wrestling mode. Should he go out and intervene before it got even more out of control? Should he phone the police? Would the police be interested in a domestic argument in the street or might he be deemed to be wasting their time? While he vacillated between these options, the couple disappeared up the street but, by then, it was too late: his evening had been ruined. All he could do was sit on the sofa while the television flickered in front of him, his mind occupied by pictures of the young woman being beaten to a bloodied pulp – possibly even murdered – all because he had been too weak to intervene.

Was he becoming a prematurely grumpy old man? Was all this just because he was approaching forty? When he shared these moans with Julia, it was a relief when she admitted feeling the same way before firing off her own list of whinges. Pregnant women wearing 'baby on board' badges. Being pushed off the pavement by mothers wheeling buggies as big as tanks. Heaters on poles outside cafes and restaurants. Plastic signs on lampposts inviting you to stick your used chewing gum on them. Parks and green spaces covered in dog mess.

As the end of the summer term approached, it was Julia who, once again, brought up the idea of moving to France. Although Jeremy's life at school had settled back into a calm uneventful routine, he was not enjoying teaching as he had done in the past. The sessions with Beatrice had come to an end and he was no longer having regular meetings with Mike Harvey but he could now see that the therapist had been right in trying to get him to think about his future. After the Easter holiday, he had briefly considered whether a change of school might be the solution – even going as far as browsing through the jobs section of the Times Educational Supplement and emailing for an application form for a Head of English post at a school in Peckham but, when he started to fill it out, a feeling of listlessness came over him and he knew that, even if he got as far as an interview, he would find it impossible to disguise his palpable lack of enthusiasm which would kibosh any hopes of him being offered the job.

It was while he was once again pouring out his frustrations to Julia one evening, voicing his dissatisfaction with his job at St. Saviour's and his failure to drum up any enthusiasm for applying for other teaching posts, that she asked him how he would feel about buying a property and moving to South-West France. He was struck dumb at first. He'd assumed that their brief flirtation with house hunting at Easter had been a playful indulgence. When he did find his voice, his initial reaction was to pour cold water on the idea.

"I'm not sure. It's alright as a fantasy – an imaginary dream life – but we have to forget about that and concentrate on the reality. Okay, we could easily afford to buy one of those beautiful old stone farmhouses and still have enough money left over from the sale of this house to live on for a while, but how would we make a living once the money ran out?"

She flashed him an indulgent smile. "That's your problem, Jeremy. You're too cautious. No sense of adventure. Sometimes you've just got to go for it and live the dream."

"And your problem is that you're not cautious enough. I'm just trying to be practical."

"Okay. Let's be practical." She uncrossed her legs and sat upright on the sofa as if to emphasise she was now in serious mode. "My business is now so well established that I can just as easily run it from Southern France as from here. In fact, moving to France would open up new markets for me. Of course, you'd want to find some work too but there'd be no hurry. I could support us both while you searched round. I'm sure you could find work teaching English – either a post in a school or college or giving private lessons

– you know, extra after school tuition for French children."

Jeremy was lost for words. This was obviously no sudden whim of Julia's; she'd planned it all out. As he thought about it, he started to find himself infected by her enthusiasm.

" I could carry on with my stamp dealing," he said. "Not that it brings in a lot of money but it would help. Mind you, we'd have to buy a property in an area that had broadband access."

"I checked that out with the estate agent in Saint Antonin. Almost all of the Aveyron has it now as long as you don't go for very isolated areas," Julia said.

She'd done her homework. Jeremy was impressed. He didn't stop to think about it then but, later, he realised that what excited him about the whole thing was not so much the idea of living and working in Southern France but more the fact that Julia's enthusiasm for it was all the evidence he needed that she was committing herself to their future together. The question about having children no longer needed to be asked.

"But how would you feel about being so far away from Hattie?" He was trying to keep his growing excitement under control by searching for other flies in the ointment.

Again, Julia had an instant response. "Let's face it, we only see each other occasionally at present. Southern France isn't that far away from Brighton. Plus I'd have to make frequent trips back to England on business and I'm sure Hattie and John would love to come and spend holidays with us in France. We'd probably end up seeing more of each other than we do now."

Jeremy could feel his enthusiasm growing to match hers even though he didn't want to dwell too much on the thought of spending stretches of time with Hattie in rural France.

"But what about all your friends in London. Would you

really want to leave them to go and live somewhere where you don't know anybody?" He didn't feel the need to talk about his own friends because he had so few he felt close to. "And then there's the language. Neither of us have much beyond O level French."

"That's part of the excitement and the challenge. Becoming fluent in another language. Making a whole set of new friends." Julia's enthusiasm was coming to a boil. "And, like Hattie, I'm sure my friends would jump at the chance to have a place to come and stay in Southern France." Julia paused, furrowing her brow, and looked with concern at Jeremy. "Oh, but I'm being rather self-centred. I'm forgetting about your father. It would be difficult for you to visit him. You'd hardly ever see him."

Jeremy responded with instant reassurance. "I don't see that much of him now. And, when I do, he doesn't recognise me anymore, as you know. And he's only going to get worse."

"Even so, he's still your father. You can't abandon him."

Jeremy paused before responding, considering whether it was time that he told her the truth.

"You know I never got on with him even before he started to get ill. And now I have to force myself to visit him."

"Yes, but…"

"There's something I haven't told you. It's difficult to explain it. I can't fully make sense of it myself." He paused and took a deep breath. "It was one time when I visited him about a year ago, just before all the business with Susie Meredith blew up. He wasn't as dozy as he normally is. He still wasn't sure who I was but he was a bit more alert than usual. He started talking but what he was saying didn't make much sense. He didn't seem to be talking to me – it was more like he was talking to himself. It was a kind of stream of consciousness. I let him carry on and then it gradually dawned on me that he was talking to Mary – his wife – my mother."

Jeremy stopped and stared into space, struggling to find the words to explain what his father had said. He decided to backtrack and prepare the ground first.

"You remember what I told you about my mum's illness and death. That it all happened very quickly and both my mother and father did a very good job of keeping it hidden from me?"

"Yes. I remember how surprised you were when you found her death certificate when you were clearing out your father's flat."

"That's right. It was a bit of a shock because I realised that I'd never really known what caused my mum's death. I assumed it was some kind of cancer – probably pancreatic. So, when I saw on the death certificate that it was Creutzfeldt-Jacob disease, I was taken aback. I researched the symptoms of the disease to see if I could think back and remember what she was like just before she died. I thought I could remember some examples of her losing her memory but then everybody has those sort of interludes from time to time, especially when they're ill. And then I remembered the problems she had speaking clearly just before she died and the occasional violent jerky movements. What I don't remember was her being in any pain but that may have been the medication or because they both kept the amount of time I spent with her down to a minimum, I guess so she could keep up a brave front – keep her true condition hidden from me."

He ground to a halt and sat in silence as if he'd run out of things to say.

"You were telling me about what your father was saying when you visited him......"Julia reminded him.

"Yes. Sorry. I just wanted to remind you of exactly what she was supposed to have died from. What was I saying about my dad?"

"You said he was talking but you couldn't work out what he was saying or who he was talking to and then you realised he was talking to your mum."

"Oh yes. At first it was like he was comforting her and he was trying to persuade her to do something. He was telling her that he didn't want to see her getting any worse and having to endure more pain. Then he said something about how she'd never wanted to be a burden on anybody and he was finding it very difficult coping with her illness. He seemed to be asking her to forgive him. He rambled on for a bit longer and then he stopped talking and closed his eyes. All that long burst of talking must have worn him out because he drifted off to sleep. I stayed sitting there for a while trying to take in what he'd been saying. I've made it sound a lot clearer than it was at the time. I've kind of sieved out all the more rambling stuff and left in just the coherent bits – the bits that made some sort of sense. Once I'd given it some thought and pieced it all together, I thought I understood what he was saying. What he'd been doing was re-living the moment when he decided to end my mother's life. He must have put a pillow over her face and killed her."

Julia edged closer to him and put her hand on his while Jeremy stared into space. Finally, he turned his mournful eyes towards her.

"You can see how that must have affected the way I feel about him. I looked up lots of stuff about the disease. Sure, death can occur fairly quickly – within six months of diagnosis – but she could have lived another couple of years."

"Jeremy – from the way you've described him rambling on – he's suffering from dementia, don't forget – you can't be sure that he ended your mother's life." Julia leaned closer, stroking his arm.

"I've given it a lot of thought. I'm almost certain he did. It would explain a lot about his behaviour afterwards."

"But – even if he did do it, it would have been a mercy killing. He would have done it to save her from unnecessary suffering. He........."

"No, I don't think that's why he did it. He's always been a selfish man. He's never shown much concern for anybody else. I often used to think that, if I'd been younger when my mum died, he would have had me taken into care. The only reason he didn't was because I was getting to an age when I could look after myself and he could get away with doing the minimum amount of parenting."

"I know I've never really known him that well – what he was like before he started getting ill – but I think you're being harsh......"

"No. He did it because he couldn't cope with having to look after her. It was more about his suffering than hers. So you can see why I'm not that bothered about moving away from him."

Julia searched for some words of comfort but she couldn't think of anything else to say in defence of his father so she let go of his arm and stood up. "I'll go and make us both a cup of tea."

*

"If you want my honest opinion, I think you're making a mistake. My advice would be, don't do it. Or, at least, give yourself more time to think about it."

"Yes. You do seem to be rushing into it. It's all happening very quickly."

Julia was sitting at a window table in *Chez Bruce* in

Wandsworth having lunch with two of her oldest friends, Jane and Celia, who'd been colleagues in the Art department in her first school. It was late August and she'd just returned from another trip to the Aveyron with Jeremy, this time to take a more serious look at prospective properties. At the very end of the visit, they'd seen what they both felt was the perfect house and made an offer which had been accepted. So, Celia was right about them rushing into it. It was all happening far more quickly than they had envisaged. But they were excited and they couldn't see any reason to delay when they'd found a house that they both loved, in the perfect location, and any pussyfooting around might only lead to somebody else getting in first.

"If you're not feeling secure in your relationship with Jeremy, then moving yourselves to a foreign country hundreds of miles away from all your family and friends doesn't seem to me to be the most sensible thing to do. You need to give yourself time – wait till you feel more confident about you and Jeremy – before you take a gamble like that."

Julia regarded Jane as the most adult and level-headed of her friends. She was the only one who had a seemingly happy marriage and children. Whenever Jane talked about her settled, middle class suburban life, she made Julia feel like a 1960s hippy. Although Jane was being the responsible adult and Julia could see the logic in her advice (indeed, the same thoughts had been going through her mind for the past couple of months), like a rebellious teenaged daughter, she was determined to ignore her.

"I understand what you're saying," Julia said, "but it's like I'm in a catch-22. The problems that we've had have been because of all the stress and disturbance that Jeremy's been through. And now that it's all over, he's been left in a kind of limbo. He just can't seem to put it all behind him and move on. If we stay as we are, nothing's going to change. In fact, I'd go as far as to say that we'll definitely split up. But, if we make this move – have a fresh start – I'm pretty confident it will save the relationship. I've given it a lot of thought over the past year and, as you two know only too well because I've bored you to death with talking about it, I had my doubts about staying with him but, in the end, I felt I was duty-bound to stick by him while he was going through all that shit. And then, when it was finally all over and yet nothing seemed to have changed between us, I began to feel it might be time to call it a day. But, in the last few months, since we started talking about the possibility of this move to France, it's revitalised Jeremy. It's like he's rediscovered his old self and I'm rediscovering him too."

After this long burst of passion, Julia slumped back in her chair as if she had used up all her energy. She picked up her spoon and scraped at the remnants of her crème brulée.

"I don't know what else to say," said Jane. "I should probably just shut up. I hate to sound like a harbinger of doom. To be honest, although I don't know anybody who's made such a radical move as you're making, I can think of examples of couples I know who've made big changes in their lives to save their relationships, including moving house. In my experience, it never works."

"Look, I know about the dangers." Julia waved her hand dismissively in Jane's direction. "And maybe I'm giving the impression that the only reason we're moving to France is a negative one – we're not very happy so let's go somewhere where the sun will always shine, the wine will flow, the air will be pollution free – where we'll be happy. But we don't see it like that. We both see it as a positive move. We're pissed off with life in London and we've fallen in love with the Aveyron. It's a positive life choice."

"If that's the way you feel, I guess you better go for it," said Celia, always the sunnier of her two friends. "Maybe a part of why we're against it, which we're not admitting to, is for purely selfish reasons. We're going to miss you. That's why we don't want you to go." She spoke in a mock whiney, tearful voice and reached across the table to clutch Julia's hand. Julia frowned at her.

"Stop thinking about it as us losing contact with each other," said Julia. "Instead, start thinking about all those sun-soaked summer weeks you can spend relaxing in our garden, quaffing vin rosé and stuffing yourself with saucisson, rocquefort cheese and confit de canard."

Celia squeezed out a smile.

"Oh, before I forget – let me show you some photos we took of the house. They're not very good but they give you a general impression of the place." Julia took out her phone and scrolled through her photos until she found the ones of the house. As Celia and Jane flicked through them, Julia gushed about the delights of the local markets, the stunning hilltop villages, the dramatic Aveyron gorge and the delightful family farm restaurants, like a demented travel agent.

As Julia ran out of steam, the discussion reverted to the safer concerns of the middle classes of Wimbledon village, like which primary school Jane should send her daughter to next year. They'd started attending the local church six months ago but she feared it might be too late to guarantee her a place at the local, highly rated by OFSTED, Church of England primary school. And, she opined, if you didn't get a place in the primary, you were unlikely to get one in Saint Augustine's Academy when the time came for secondary transfer.

Julia was only half-listening to her two friends droning on and on, their discussion confirming for her that she was making the right move. Theirs was the life she wanted to escape from.

16

Felicity Merrigan's stomach tightened and her heart fluttered when she opened the door to be confronted by Jeremy Halliday clutching a white envelope.

"Hi Felicity. Sorry to disturb you. I thought I'd deliver the estimate for the gardening work personally." He held the envelope out towards her. She stared at it apprehensively as if it might contain ricin or some other deadly poison.

"Oh, hasn't Tim spoken to you?"

"No, not since last week – you know – when I came to do the measuring up."

Felicity tried not to let her irritation show. Typical of Tim. She should have known not to leave it up to him to phone Jeremy to tell him they were cancelling the work.

"It's just that we've decided to delay doing the work on the garden. Bit of a cash flow problem at present. I'm sorry. I thought Tim had told you."

"Oh, that's okay. Look, you may as well have the estimate anyway now that it's done. Then, if you want to go ahead with it later – well, I'm sure my prices won't change much, if at all." He continued to hold the envelope out until she took it from him.

"Is it alright if I come in for a minute?" He held up his hands in mock surrender. "I confess I do have an ulterior motive for coming round. It wasn't just to deliver the estimate. I need to ask you something."

"Well…" Felicity hesitated, racking her brain to think of

a way of getting rid of him. "Tim's not here. He's had to go to......"

"That's okay. It's actually you I wanted to talk to."

The sinking feeling in Felicity's stomach grew worse. Had he somehow got to hear about her interview with Judge Bouchon?

"Actually, I was just about to go out myself. I've got some things I need to do in Villefranche," she lied.

"I'll be quick, I promise. I'll only keep you a few minutes."

"Well alright. As long as it's brief. Come through to the kitchen." She stood aside allowing him a wide berth as he crossed the threshold and walked down the corridor. As she closed the front door, the disturbing thought flashed through her mind that she was shutting herself in her house alone with a suspected murderer. Maybe it would be safer to invite him to sit outside on the patio? Her mind was in a whirl. She wasn't thinking straight. In the end, her autopilot hospitality overrode her fears.

"Would you like a tea or coffee?"

"No thanks. As I promised, I won't keep you long."

She was relieved to see that he looked more presentable than he had on his visit the previous week. His hair still needed cutting but it had been washed and brushed flat and his chinos and short-sleeved shirt were clean and uncrumpled. She invited him to sit down on one of the kitchen chairs at the far end of the open plan kitchen/diner.

"It's about Julia," he said.

There was that hollow feeling in her stomach again. She shouldn't have been surprised. If he hadn't come to talk about the garden what else was she expecting he would want to discuss – the upcoming French elections? The state of the euro?

"Have you heard anything more from the police?"

She asked, trying to sound concerned, aware that he might think it strange that she hadn't asked him earlier about the investigation.

"No. At least there's nothing else they've told me."

Felicity thought she detected a slight emphasis on the word 'me'. Was he hinting that they may have told someone else something – namely, her? She perched on the edge of the creaking chair waiting to hear what he had to say – hoping it would be over as quickly as he had promised.

"I suddenly remembered that, last week, when I told you what had happened to Julia, you said you'd talked to her the week before she left and she told you then that she was intending to leave me." Felicity gave an apprehensive nod. "Did she tell you any more about why she was leaving?"

Felicity stared at him, not sure what to say. All she could think about was how to get rid of him. She glanced at the clock over the stone fireplace. Tim wouldn't be back from his trip to Montauban for at least another couple of hours so there was no hope of rescue there.

"She didn't say much at all. Just that things hadn't been going well between the two of you and she'd decided to pack up and go back to England. Other than that, she didn't really say much. Of course, I said how sorry I was to hear it and that I hoped things might be able to be sorted out between you but I didn't grill her for any more details. It was none of my business."

Jeremy put the tips of his fingers together as if in prayer and lowered his eyes. "Did she tell you she'd been having an affair?"

Felicity squirmed in the chair and then sat rigidly still as the creaking echoed round the tall-ceilinged room.

"I don't think I should be talking to you about things that Julia told me in confidence," she said.

"Oh for fuck's sake, Felicity. Julia's been murdered. The

police think I did it. The partner's always the chief suspect – you know that. So, if she was involved with somebody else, I want to know about it. It would mean there's another suspect."

If she was feeling uncomfortable before, this outburst ratcheted up the tightness inside her as if her intestines were being compressed in a vice. "I'd rather you didn't talk to me in that tone of voice, Jeremy." She croaked out the words from a dry mouth.

"I'm sorry. I didn't mean to raise my voice. I'm sure you can understand how wound up I am about all this."

"Of course I can. It's just that I don't think it's me you should be getting angry at. I think it would be better if you talked to the investigating judge about this. He's the one who should have all the information."

Jeremy leaned forward and looked straight at her. "I presume the police have interviewed you?"

Felicity didn't reply. She realised, too late, that it had been a mistake to mention the judge. She should have stuck to referring to the police. Now he would put two and two together and guess that she had been questioned by Judge Bouchon. She didn't respond but knew that her silence and her awkward demeanour had given him his answer.

Jeremy didn't wait for her to reply. "I'm almost certain that Julia was having an affair. I just want to know if she told you about it and, if so, whether you then told the gendarmes because they're still treating me as the chief suspect and, if they knew she was involved with somebody else, that would change everything."

Felicity wanted to get up and ask him to leave but she couldn't summon up the courage. It would have been easier if he'd kept up his angry badgering tone, then she would have had no compunction about kicking him out, but he had sunk back into his gauche little boy lost manner. Although she had little sympathy for him and was more than ever inclined to believe him guilty of murder after what she had discovered during her interview with the judge, she was reluctant to give him that impression. Maybe the quickest way to get rid of him was to tell him what she knew which, when it came down to it, wasn't very much. So that's what she did.

*

Gilles Montfort could feel the damp patches under the arms of his blue uniform shirt spreading as he sat impatiently in the narrow stuffy corridor outside Judge Bouchon's office. His fingers were sticky with sweat from clutching the plastic evidence folder. But it was not only the heat and the wait that was causing him discomfort. It was the contents of that plastic folder – or, rather, the lack of contents. The judge was always a hard taskmaster but this case, being so high profile and therefore stirring up so much media interest, made him even more impatient than usual for a speedy resolution. The judge had not been happy with the pace of the investigation so far and Gilles had little to show him that would lighten his mood. The fact that it was proving to be a very difficult case with minimal evidence and very few leads would cut no ice with Judge Bouchon. He would see it as slack work by his underlings and, for now, the foremost slack underling was Gilles Montfort.

The office door opened and a middle aged couple stepped out into the corridor, the woman in tears blowing her nose into a crumpled white handkerchief, the man with his arm round her shoulders comforting her. Jules Bouchon appeared in the doorway behind them.

"Thank you so much for coming to see me. I'm sorry not to have better news for you but I promise we will do everything in our power to secure a positive outcome. I will keep you fully informed."

The man nodded at the judge while the woman continued to dab at her eyes.

"Come in," he said to Gilles as the couple headed off down the corridor, his tone instantly changing from obsequious to abrupt.

"So, what have you got for me? I hope there's some good news," Jules Bouchon said once they were both seated on either side of his desk.

Gilles opened his folder and withdrew a sheath of papers hoping that the volume of the material might hide the fact that it contained little significant new information. He decided to start with his trump card, although it was more a jack of hearts than an ace of spades.

"We are still in the process of tracking down and interviewing all of Miss Wainwright's business contacts but, yesterday, we interviewed Marc Dessailly, the owner of two women's fashion shops in Toulouse and one in Montpellier. He admitted that he had had an affair with Julia Wainwright." Jules Bouchon leaned forward in anticipation. "He first met her nearly two years ago when he started buying some of her designs for his shops. About six months later they started the affair. He is a married man with two children. His family home is just outside Montpellier and he keeps a small apartment in the centre of Toulouse where he stays when he's working in the city and doesn't want to travel home late at night. It was in that apartment that he carried on the affair with Miss Wainwright. However, last September he ended the relationship and also all contact with Julia Wainwright, including no longer buying her products. This was because his wife found out about them."

Jules Bouchon's brief spark of animation was replaced with his habitual sullen expression.

"And how do you know he's telling the truth? If he knows she has been murdered – which I presume he must do – then it is in his best interest to pretend that he was no longer having sex with her." Jules Bouchon frequently questioned gendarmes as if they were imbeciles whom he expected would fail to follow the most basic investigative procedures.

"We've checked his business records and his mobile phone history. No orders have been placed with Miss Wainwright's company since last September and he was making and receiving calls regularly from her until then but there have been none since."

"Yes, but maybe......"

Gilles interrupted the judge to short-circuit any more questions designed to expose his inefficiency. "He also has an alibi for the day of the murder. His staff verify that he was in his shop in Montpellier all day and he went home and spent the evening with his family."

"So, is that it?" Judge Bouchon looked at him disparagingly. "Any other useful information from her other business associates?"

"None so far. Monsieur Dessailly is the only one that we know of who has had a sexual relationship with her. The others only met her on a strictly business basis as far as we can ascertain. Virtually all the rest of them are women anyway." He paused. "There is one person we haven't been able to interview yet. A Madame Hafeez who owns a shop in Decazeville. She could be important as our check on Miss Wainwright's phone records shows that she was the last person to contact her on the morning of the day she died."

"Yes – I can see how that might make her important." Sarcasm was second nature to the judge. "So why hasn't she been interviewed?"

"She's in Morocco at present visiting her husband's family but she'll be back the day after tomorrow."

"Fantastic." Judge Bouchon slouched down in his chair,

tilted his head back and stared at the ceiling in exasperation.

Gilles shuffled his papers nervously. Now that he had played his trump card to little or no effect, he was left to flip through the rest of his even less inspiring information.

"We are still in the process of checking CCTV footage in filling stations and shopping precincts on the route between Villefranche and Aurillac but, so far, we have no sightings of Miss Wainwright or Mr Halliday or their cars."

"And how much longer will this process take? This is a murder investigation, Montfort. We can't afford to hang around. This needs to be done speedily. If necessary, I can request that more gendarmes be put to work on it."

"We have covered all the cameras on the main route to Aurillac and found nothing. So now we've started on the more peripheral roads but that covers quite a wide area."

"And how well are these routes covered by cameras?"

"Not very," said Gilles. "And, of course, we are finding that some of them were not working and others weren't switched on."

Judge Bouchon shrugged his shoulders and waved his arms in the air. "That's the trouble with working in a backwater like this. We are twenty years behind the times. If this was Paris or Toulouse it would be so much easier. There would be mountains of evidence. The judiciary have it so much easier in the big cities. But try telling that to my superiors. They're not interested in excuses. They only want results."

So they put pressure on you and then you transfer the pressure to me, thought Gilles. Still, unlike the judge, he couldn't feel too sorry for himself. For all their extra resources and profusion of surveillance cameras, he would much rather be a gendarme in sleepy Villefranche than in Paris.

*

When he was disturbed at his laptop by the sound of car tyres crunching down the gravel driveway, Jeremy's first reaction was to breathe a heavy sigh and assume that it was another visit from the gendarmes with yet more questions. So he was relieved to see from the window that it was a silver VW Golf with English number plates. Of course – Ruth Gershon. As so often since Julia's departure, he had lost track of what day of the week it was. It was Saturday – the day she was due to arrive.

"Hi. I'm Jeremy Halliday. Welcome to Vendillac. So, you found us okay?" Jeremy greeted the petite woman in blue jeans and a green and white stripy t-shirt as she stood by the side of the car surveying the house and garden through her dark glasses. She turned to face him and removed the sunglasses to reveal large dark brown eyes and a pretty elfin face topped with thick shiny black hair held in a ponytail by a green scrunchie. From a distance he had been surprised at how young she looked but, as he got closer, he could see from the tell-tale lines round her eyes that she was probably in her mid to late thirties.

"Ruth Gershon." They shook hands, hers as thin and delicate as the rest of her. "Your directions were very clear and easy to follow although I did get a bit lost when I came off the motorway. I went round in circles for a bit but I found the right road eventually. You know how difficult it is when you're the driver and the navigator? I keep meaning to invest in a satnav but I'm not very good with technology."

"Me neither. You should see my mobile phone. It's steam-driven. Julia, my partner, laughs at me every time I get it out." She laughed. The high trilling sound was like a refreshing cool breeze. A woman laughing at his jokes – how long had it been since that happened? "Let me help you with your bags and then I'll show you round – give you the guided tour of the estate and show you how everything works."

"That's very kind of you. How's your partner's mother, by the way?"

Jeremy was momentarily thrown until he remembered the excuse he'd made over the phone for Julia's absence.

"Oh much better but it's a slow process. Julia's still looking after her."

"What was wrong?"

Jeremy paused trying to remember whether he'd mentioned an actual ailment during their initial phone conversation. "She had a stroke. Not a very serious one, fortunately. She should make a full recovery. Julia's probably going to need to stay and look after her for another few weeks. She hasn't got any other family around for support." He decided it was safe to keep up the pretence. She was unlikely to find out for herself about Julia's death. He knew it had been reported in the English media but obviously she hadn't heard about it or, if she had, she hadn't connected it with Jeremy and her holiday in Vendillac. And he couldn't see that she was likely to talk to any of the locals or read the local newspapers.

He helped her unload her bags and carry them into the gîte. He was surprised at how much stuff she had with her. As well as a large suitcase and a laptop computer, the heaviest item was an oblong cardboard box full of books and papers.

"Sorry to be nosey but that's a lot of paperwork for a fortnight's stay. Have you had to bring your work on holiday with you?" Jeremy put the box down on the sturdy oak coffee table in the living room.

"Yes, I have as a matter of fact. I'm a writer." She pointed at the box. "That's the research I've been doing for my latest book. I've completed a first draft. I brought it with so I can make some revisions and do some redrafting."

"What sort of stuff do you write? Should I have heard of you?"

"It's a crime novel – set in the Victorian era – the third in a series. I write under a pen name – M.J.Kellis."

"Sounds interesting. I'll have to look you up on Amazon"

"Are you a reader then?"

"Oh yes. Not as much as I used to be. I was an English teacher back in London – before we moved here."

"Oh right. Maybe I could get you to check my grammar and spelling. It's not my strong point." They both laughed.

"Well, then you probably won't need to make use of our extensive library." Jeremy gestured at the bookshelves in the alcove next to the fireplace containing a handful of dog-eared paperbacks. "Although there are also some maps of the area and a book of local walks – in French, of course. How is your French?"

"Far from fluent but enough for me to get by. I can just about ask for directions when I get lost which I'm bound to do as I have no sense of direction. Whether I understand the answers is another matter." It was Jeremy's turn to laugh.

"Do you know this area at all?"

"No. It's new to me. I've had several holidays in France ever since I first went camping as a child with my parents. They always went to Brittany. I've been to Provence. Who hasn't? In fact, I'm pretty boring and unadventurous. I tend to go to all the popular tourist areas for Brits – the Dordogne, the Loire valley, the Cotes d'Azure. So I thought I'd branch out this time – try something new."

"Well, I'm sure you won't be sorry. It's a beautiful area and not overrun with tourists, especially this early in the season."

Jeremy walked back across the driveway to the house as if he was floating a couple of inches off the ground. It felt so good to have a normal conversation about everyday matters with no worries about having to discuss the events of the past two weeks – and, as a bonus, with an attractive woman.

17

"Nathalie, could you hurry up please. How can it be taking you this long to clean your teeth and brush your hair. You're going to be late for school."

Mireille Hafeez was feeling flustered and disorganised. They'd only returned from Morocco the previous evening and she'd not finished unpacking let alone re-adjusting herself to the daily routine and her six year old daughter's petulant behaviour wasn't helping. But it was difficult to get too angry with her. She wasn't normally so obstreperous. Mireille knew it was because she was still tired after their long hot journey home. Maybe it would have been better to keep her off school for one more day – give her time to recover – but Mireille already felt guilty for taking her out of school for a whole week. As for herself, she could have done without the trip to Rabat. Not only had it disrupted her daughter's schooling but it was also very ill-timed for her, coming just two weeks before her shop was due to open. She was still angry with Mohammed. He'd made the arrangements and booked the flights without discussing it with her because he knew she would have objected. And then, when she had tried to protest, he had been adamant that they attend his grandmother's eightieth birthday celebrations, while slipping in an additional justification that it was also for her benefit as she had been getting more and more stressed in the build up to the shop opening and a week away from it would help her relax.

In the end, the only reason she didn't make a bigger fuss or even refuse to go, which she had considered doing, was because of the shocking news she had received two days earlier. Struggling to cope with her grief and distress, she decided that it might not be such a bad idea after all for her to be out of the country for a week. It might help her recover – take her mind off what had happened as she struggled to come to terms with it. But once they were in Mohammed's family's sprawling courtyard house in Rabat surrounded by his extended family, she was not so sure it was a good idea. Despite all the bustle and noise of the preparations for the family celebration, she couldn't keep thoughts or images of Julia Wainwright out of her head and frequently had to rush off to the bathroom, or anywhere else she could grab a moment's privacy, before bursting into tears.

Mohammed had been born in France and, despite his Moroccan Muslim heritage, Mireille was relieved, when she first started going out with him, that he didn't practice his religion and, in every other way, appeared to be a typical Frenchman. It was only after they were married that he started to show signs that he had not entirely escaped his upbringing. When it came to the more important decisions, he expected, as the man of the house, to make them with little or no reference to his wife. As time wore on, Mireille was finding it harder to accommodate herself to this. Tensions were rising and her worry was that, as their daughter grew older, those tensions would multiply – maybe to breaking point.

She was just about to shout up the stairs to Nathalie again when the doorbell rang.

"Madame Hafeez?" A young gendarme in full uniform with a solemn-looking face stood on her doorstep.

"Yes that's me," Mireille said.

"My name is Gilles Montfort. I'm very sorry to disturb you at this time of the morning but I have some questions I need to ask you concerning one of our investigations."

Mireille's already frazzled brain went into a tailspin. She could feel her cheeks growing hot. She was lost for words.

The gendarme stared querulously at her. "Can I come in for a minute?"

"What's this about?" She finally asked, although she knew full well why he was there. "It's just that I am rather busy at the moment. I'm just about to take my daughter to school and we're already late."

"I'm really sorry about this. Unfortunately, we couldn't talk to you earlier because you were away on holiday so it is urgent that we talk to you now. Is there somebody else who could take your daughter to school for you?"

Once again she was speechless, staring at him as if he was speaking in a foreign language. "I don't know...... I could see if my husband will do it. You'd better come in."

Gilles Montfort took off his cap and walked through to a large open plan living room overlooking an immaculately manicured garden. He could hear the sound of running footsteps upstairs and a radio was playing loud pop music in another room.

"Take a seat. I'll be with you in a minute."

Gilles sat down on a white leather sofa and surveyed the room. It was expensively furnished in what most people would regard as very good taste but it was too ordered and anti-septic for Gilles – like a show flat in a luxury block. There was little that gave a clue to the type of people who lived there: no books or racks of CDs or DVDs and nothing to show that there was a child in the house. He could hear voices upstairs but couldn't make out what they were saying.

A couple of minutes later, Mireille Hafeez reappeared.

"It's okay. My husband will take her to school. He wasn't going to go into work till later but he's decided he will drop her off and go in now."

She looked uneasy. Her shoulder-length blond hair was dishevelled and she wasn't wearing any makeup. She was dressed in a pale blue track suit and trainers. There were dark circles under her eyes as if she'd not been sleeping well.

The clatter of tiny footsteps on the stairs preceded the entry of a small dark-haired girl skipping into the room. She held a shiny pink satchel with a white rabbit appliqued on the front.

"Maman, I can't find my reading book."

"Never mind about that, frou frou. We haven't got time to look for it. We have to go." The man speaking stood in the doorway, tall and strikingly handsome in his light grey suit, his swarthy symmetrical face topped with a stubble of black hair.

"But I'll get in trouble with Madame Marin." The little girl stamped her foot and screwed her face into an exaggerated mope.

"Don't worry. I'll explain it to her. Now go outside and wait by the car." Despite his Arabic appearance, Gilles noted that he spoke with an uninflected Southern French accent.

"Bye Maman." Nathalie ran and hugged her mother's legs. Her mother in turn bent down and kissed the top of her head.

"Have a good day, cherie."

"Do you need me to answer any questions, officer? I can come back, if you like," Mohammed Hafeez said as he was turning to leave the room.

"No, that won't be necessary, Monsieur Hafeez."

"Is this about the English woman who was murdered?" He added.

"Yes, it is. I just need to ask your wife a few routine questions about her contact with Miss Wainwright."

Mohamed Hafeez stood hesitantly by the doorway, as if deliberating about something else he wanted to say. Instead he walked over to his wife and kissed her on the cheek.

"I'll phone you once I get into work." He turned to face the gendarme. "My wife was very upset when she heard about the English woman's death." He paused momentarily, his eyes firmly fixed on the gendarme, before turning and leaving the room without saying anymore. Gilles was left in no doubt that there was a subtext in his parting words, a veiled unspoken warning – 'so treat her gently'.

When they were alone, seated opposite each other, Gilles Montfort took out a notebook and pen.

"Madame Hafeez, could you start by telling me how you first came to know Miss Wainwright?"

"She was recommended to me by a friend of mine, Adèle Gironde. She works as a buyer for a chain of fashion shops – *Les Vêtements Blancs*. I was planning to open my own shop in Decazeville and Adèle told me that Julia Wainwright was a very good designer of women's accessories who was looking for more outlets for her products in France."

"So you arranged a meeting with Miss Wainwright, I presume?"

"Yes."

"And how long ago would that have been?"

"We first met about nine months ago."

"And are you buying her products?"

"Yes, I am. My shop is due to open the week after next."

"And would you say you became friendly with her? How often have you met?" The gendarme looked up from his notepad. Mireille felt his eyes scanning her face like radar, searching for any sign of discomfort. She still felt nervous inside but felt confident that it wasn't showing. Making the arrangements for Mohamed to take Nathalie to school had given her time and space to calm down and think about how she was going to answer the predictable questions from the gendarme – and, so far, it was going as she had predicted.

"We met in Decazeville for coffee a couple of times……… had lunch together once. She came to see me here at the house once as well to show me some of her designs." She reeled off the details in an assured voice. She felt confident she was showing no signs of incriminating agitation. After all, she was telling the truth – it just wasn't the whole truth.

"Did Miss Wainwright talk to you about her personal life at all? For example, about her partner?"

Mireille steeled herself before answering. Now she would have to veer away from the truth. "A little bit. She told me she had a partner. She told me where they live. Somewhere near Villefranche if I remember correctly. She spoke a bit about moving from London to France, but not much. Just the usual small talk."

"You phoned Miss Wainwright from your mobile on the morning of Tuesday 21st May – the day she died." He had abandoned the notebook and pen and was staring intently at her. "What was the phone call about?"

Mireille was thrown by the question but, in her determination not to show it, she answered immediately. "I'm sorry but I think you must be mistaken. I don't think I contacted Miss Wainwright that morning. I may have spoken to her a few days earlier. We were in frequent contact because, I have to admit, I was starting to panic about the opening of the shop. You know – worrying that everything wasn't going to be ready. It's my first business venture."

The gendarme picked up his pen and tapped it impatiently on his notepad while raising his eyebrows. "Madame Hafeez. We have Miss Wainwright's phone records and, although you may not remember it, I can assure you that you did contact her that morning." He flipped over a few pages of the notepad. "At 9.37 to be exact. Oh, I'm sorry. You didn't speak to her, you sent her a text message. 0680039143. Is that your mobile number?"

"Yes." Now it was impossible to hide her discomfort. Her brain was reeling. She was certain she couldn't have contacted Julia that morning as she tried to wind back the clock inside her head and recall exactly when she had last spoken to Julia. "If I did contact her, and I don't remember doing so, then it could only have been about my order for her handbags. That was definitely what we talked about the last time I spoke to her. There'd been some delays on the delivery date and I was trying to get confirmation."

He flipped over a page and studied his notepad again. "According to Miss Wainwright's phone records for those few days since she left home, you phoned her three times and she phoned you twelve times. That's a lot of calls to make just about a delivery of handbags. You say you phoned her because you were worried but it sounds more like she might have been worried to phone you twelve times in three days. Are you sure you didn't discuss other things?"

"No. Look, I was very anxious about the bags arriving before the shop was due to open. They are very striking designs and I was planning to use them in my window display to attract customers in."

"Were you aware that she was returning to the United Kingdom that week?"

"Yes. She told me that. She said it wouldn't be a problem as all her manufacturers were in London and she would be going back to see them."

"So, did she tell you she was phoning her suppliers in London to find out about your delivery?"

"Yes, I'm sure that's what she was doing. I think she was

having difficulty getting through to them and she was trying to keep me up to date."

"The problem is, Madame Hafeez, that there is no record of her having made any phone calls to London from her mobile during those three days." There was that forensic stare again.

"I'm not sure what you want me to say. I can't account for Miss Wainwright's phone calls." The anger in Mireille's voice was aimed as much at herself as at the gendarme.

"Did she tell you that she was going back for good? That she had left her partner?"

Mireille tried to summon up a look of surprise but she had never been a very good actor. "No. She didn't say anything about that to me. I'm sorry. It's been very rude of me. Can I offer you a coffee?" She was desperate to buy herself some thinking time. She needed to calm down and clear her head before the gendarme fired any more questions at her.

He gave her an impatient look. "No thank you. I'm fine, Madame. I need you to think back to that morning and try to remember that message. It is quite possible that, apart from the person who killed her, you were the last person to have any contact with her. Did you know where she was at the time?"

"I'm sorry, Monsieur......"

"Montfort."

"I'm sorry, Monsieur Montfort, but I truly can't remember texting her. If I did, it would only have been about business."

"I'm sorry to be so persistent about this but we have been trying to trace Miss Wainwright's movements after she left her house on the morning of Monday May 20th. As her partner has pointed out to us, if she was driving straight back to England, she would not normally have taken the route up to Aurillac which is where her body was found. So, if she went that way, she must have had a reason. Perhaps she was visiting somebody in the area. The only person we have traced among her associates who live anywhere in that direction is you, Madame Hafeez."

Gilles Montfort's earlier convivial tone had hardened. Mireille was trying to stay calm but she could see that he sensed her underlying agitation and probably suspected she was hiding something. She couldn't think of what else to say. She wanted to put an end to the interview but she wasn't in control of it – she was fighting to stay in control of herself.

"I'm sorry but I can't add anything to what I have already told you," she finally said. "I knew Julia was going back to England but I didn't know which way she was travelling. I didn't even know how she was travelling. For all I knew, she might have been flying. I must have spoken to her on the phone that week but I definitely didn't meet up with her." Lying was now coming much easier to her. Once she'd started, there was no going back. The one thing she regretted was that she had started to refer to her as 'Julia' rather than 'Miss Wainwright'. Would the gendarme pick up on it – spot it as a tell-tale sign that their relationship was more than the formal business one that Mireille had described?

"Can you tell me where you were and what you were doing on Tuesday 21st May?" The gendarme's eyes were still boring into her. She could feel her cheeks reddening and knew that she was losing the battle to present herself as calm and collected.

"As far as I can remember, it would have been a normal day for me. I would have driven my daughter to school in the morning and then, that morning.........ah yes, I remember. That morning I went to the shop to talk to the fitters. They were due to lay the flooring and I wanted to check that it was all going to plan. Then I came home at lunchtime and, after lunch, I went to collect my daughter from school."

"And was your husband at home at all that day?"

"No. He would have left for work at about the same time that my daughter and I left for school. We have two cars."

"What does your husband do?"

"He's a doctor. His practice is in the centre of Decazeville."

"Do you have anybody who could verify your whereabouts during that day?" His pen hovered over his notepad.

"Is this necessary?" Although Mireille was starting to feel angry, her voice was pleading. "Surely you don't suspect me of having anything to do with this?"

"Madame Hafeez, these are standard questions and investigative procedures in this type of case. There's nothing more to it than that. So – if you could give me that information, please. Oh – it will also be necessary to take your phone away for analysis since you don't remember your calls or messages. Again, it's just routine."

Mireille was now struggling harder than ever to keep calm. She was fighting back tears. "Okay. If you insist," she said as she stood up and walked across to retrieve her handbag from the dining table. She took out her wallet and returned with it to the sofa. She opened it and took out a printed business card. "Those are the details of my shop fitters. They should be able to confirm that I was at the shop that morning. I can't think of anybody else I would have met or spoken to that day......" She paused. "Probably some of the mothers at the school gate. I could give you some names."

"That won't be necessary." He took the card from her. "And the phone?"

She swallowed hard. "I'm sorry. I don't have it."

"You don't have it?" He said, raising his eyebrows.

"I seem to have misplaced it somewhere. I couldn't find it this morning. I think I may have left it in Morocco. We only got back late last night and I haven't had time to check with my husband's family."

Somehow she was managing to keep her mounting panic under wraps despite the look of incredulity on the gendarme's face. He directed his disbelieving stare at her for several seconds as if waiting for her to break down and admit she was lying.

"That is a pity, Madame," he said with a hint of sarcasm, "but it doesn't matter. I can get a court order from the juge d'instruction to access the phone company's records and retrieve your call log and messages." He paused, studying her face for a reaction. "Anyway, thank you for your assistance this morning," he said with a further hint of sarcasm as he slid his notebook into his briefcase.

"I'm sorry I haven't been able to be more helpful. I'm still very tired. We had a long hot journey home yesterday and I didn't get much sleep last night. That's why I may seem to be a bit confused."

"That's okay. I understand. I'm sure I will be back soon with some further questions. Hopefully, then you will be more rested and your memory will have improved. In the meantime, here's my card." He reached into the top pocket of his jacket and handed it to her. "If you remember anything at all about those phone calls, or anything else, please don't wait for my return – call me straight away."

*

It was typical of Guy Reynard to live in such a quirky building, Jeremy thought as he sat on the terrace outside the circular converted pigeonnier on the outskirts of Vendillac. Guy squeezed through the narrow doorway carrying a tray with their coffees and two slices of tarte aux noisettes.

"You look tired, mon ami," Guy said as he sat down on one of the metal patio chairs. "Still not sleeping well?"

"Not too bad. Better than last week." Jeremy stood up and dragged his chair round the other side of the table to get out of the sun. "Mind you, I'll tell you what one of my problems is – I'm finding it hard getting used to sleeping in a double bed on my own. I try and sleep in the middle but I find that, when I wake up, I've edged right over to my usual side. Sometimes I'm so close to the edge, I'm almost falling out."

"I know how you feel. I was the same after my wife left. Do you still turn round to talk to her sometimes before you remember she's not there anymore?"

"No, I can't say I do that."

They sat in silence for a while sipping their coffees and eating their slices of tart. Guy was the first to break the silence. "Have you heard any more from the Judge or the gendarmes?"

"No. It's all gone very quiet."

"Well, that's good news, isn't it?"

"I don't know about that. I'd like some definite news one way or the other." Jeremy paused, considering whether to be more open. It wasn't a difficult decision. He needed to talk to somebody and Guy was the only friend he had. "I've found out that Julia was having an affair, just as I suspected. I think it was some man she was doing business with in Toulouse."

"I'm sorry to hear that. Does the Judge know about it?"

"Yes, he does."

"So, maybe this man is the killer. Perhaps he is now the number one suspect instead of you?"

"I don't know about that. I mean why........."

The spluttering engine of an ancient orange tractor drowned out the rest of his sentence as it trundled past the house sending up a cloud of dust. Jeremy waited for it to go past before continuing.

"Why would he want to kill her?"

"For the same reason that most murders in France happen. Perhaps it's different in England," said Guy. "It's a crime passionel. She tells him she wants to end the affair. He's heartbroken, angry. If he can't have her, then nobody else will. Or maybe he's a married man and he won't leave his wife so she threatens to tell the wife..." Guy put a stop to his musings when he saw the pained expression on Jeremy's face. "I'm sorry, mon ami. I don't think this conversation is very helpful. Would you like a game of chess?"

"No. You're alright. It's just that I'm confused. I don't know whether it makes it better or worse that she'd been having an affair. I suppose it's better if it means there's another suspect apart from me but, on the other hand, it's painful to find out that she was cheating on me." Jeremy pointed at a copy of La Dépêche lying on the patio tiles under the table. "Is there anything more in the paper about it?"

"No. There's been no more news. I suppose they have nothing to report because the gendarmes are making no progress with their investigations."

Another uneasy silence followed before Guy changed the subject. "I see you have someone staying in the gîte. I saw a woman sunbathing in the garden when I drove past yesterday. Is it a family? I didn't see anybody else."

"Spying on me again, Guy?" Jeremy raised his eyebrows in mock outrage.

"No, I was just passing and it's easy to see into your garden from the road, especially when there is a pretty woman there sunbathing in a bikini."

"It's okay, Guy. I'm only kidding."

"So, is there a family?"

"No. She's on her own at the moment. I think her husband's joining her next week."

"Quel dommage. I only got a brief look but she is pretty, n'est-ce pas? If she was on her own, I was wondering if she might be interested in meeting a handsome available Frenchman for some company."

"And which handsome Frenchman do you have in mind?"

Guy smiled. "Touchez mon ami."

*

As Jeremy finished browsing his stamp dealer websites and was logging off, he saw Ruth Gershon come on to the terrace outside the gîte wearing a white halter-neck top and skimpy black shorts. She sat on a lounger and began to apply sun cream on her face, arms and legs. Although she'd only been there a couple of days, she was already developing a rich even tan. She was fortunate to have the kind of skin that tanned easily rather than turning a garish pink. Once again, he found himself admiring her trim figure and wondered whether to invite her over to the house for an early evening drink, trying to persuade himself that it was nothing to do with sexual attraction – just politeness – and it would be good for him to have some company, help take his mind off things.

He went downstairs and headed for the front door before pausing on the threshold. He wouldn't want her to misconstrue his invitation – to think he was taking advantage of her being alone. Maybe it wasn't such a good idea. She was a married woman and her husband was due to join her in a few days' time. And, as far as she knew, he was a man with a temporarily absent partner. No, he wouldn't want to appear creepy, which he was sure he would do if he invited her over. She was renting his gîte – best to keep the relationship on a purely business footing.

But the decision was taken out of his hands later that afternoon when there was a knock on the door. It was Ruth Gershon.

"Sorry to disturb you but there's something I wanted to ask you." It was a warm evening and she was still wearing the halter top and shorts.

"Why don't you come in? Can I get you a glass of wine? I'm just having one myself and it would be nice not to have to drink alone."

"Oh, okay. That would be nice." She stepped into the open plan living room and he closed the door behind her.

"What would you like? Red, white, rosé? I might even be able to stretch to a glass of sparkling."

"Oh I'll just have what you're drinking." She looked across at the half full glass on the coffee table. "Looks like rosé. Very refreshing on a hot day like today."

He went into the kitchen and returned with a glass in one hand and the bottle in the other.

"What I wanted to ask you," she said once they were both seated and Jeremy had poured her wine, "is whether you have anybody else renting the gîte after I'm due to leave at the end of next week because, if not, I'd like to rent it for another couple of weeks."

"I'm pretty sure it's free although, as I told you on the phone, it's my partner, Julia, who normally organises the rentals. I'd have to check it on the website to be absolutely certain but, if I remember right, the last time I looked there were no other bookings till the end of July. Of course, it's just possible that she didn't update it, what with all the worry about her mother."

"Could you phone her to check?" She asked delicately.

"Yes, of course. I'll do that." Not for the first time, he wished he could drop the pretence and just tell her the truth. "Meanwhile, I'm confident it'll be fine. You must really like it here."

"Yes. It's great. Ideal. Very quiet and relaxing. A good opportunity for me to get on with redrafting the novel. I must admit I wasn't very hopeful that it would be available. I would have thought you would have been fully booked. It's such a beautiful area."

"As I said before, the area's not very well known to the Brits. We get most of our business through repeat customers and word of mouth. The main drawback is that there's no swimming pool so it doesn't attract families with children. We've been considering putting one in. Still, it didn't put you off."

"No." She sipped her wine and looked sheepish. "I'm ashamed to admit it but I can't swim. In fact, I hate water. So, for me, not having a pool was a plus. And this place is a double plus because you're so far from the sea. I never go on beach holidays. Hate them. I don't even take baths – only showers." There was that infectious laugh again. He joined in.

"And will your husband be staying for the extra weeks? When are you expecting him?"

She lowered her head and stared at the glass of wine in her hand. Jeremy waited out the uncomfortable silence wondering what else he could say. He could only see the top of her head but her shoulders heaved as she sucked in a deep breath. When she finally raised her head, he could see there were tears at the corner of her eyes.

"I'm sorry. I shouldn't be bothering you with my problems. I should go."

"No,no. It's alright," he said.

She took another deep breath, fighting to pull herself together. She took a gulp of wine. "He's not coming. I'll be here on my own."

Jeremy couldn't think of anything else to say. He wanted to know more but he didn't want her to think he was prying. She wiped a tear from her eye with the back of her hand and smiled at him. "I'm sorry to be so stupid and emotional." Jeremy was about to speak but she held up her hand to stop him before continuing. "He told me he wasn't coming to join me in France a couple of days before I was due to leave." She paused, deciding how much to tell him. "Things haven't been right between us for some time. He's a musician and he's away from home a lot – you know, gigging around the country. We've been married for five years and it's been the kind of marriage where we've both had our own space – kept our independence."

"It's been a bit like that with me and Julia – although we're not actually married." As he spoke, he thought how easy it was to talk about Julia as if she was still alive.

"Anyway, he didn't just tell me he wasn't coming to France. He told me it was over between us............ he was leaving me. It was all very matter-of-fact and business-like. He thought it was a good time to do it because he could be all packed up and gone while I was away which would make it less painful for me. He's very thoughtful like that," she said with heavy sarcasm. "And then, he gave me the full monty of a confession. He told me he'd been having affairs with other people ever since we'd been married. Affairs with both men and women." She sighed and wiped her eyes again. Jeremy felt the urge to reach out and touch her hand but, instead, he got up and went into the kitchen, returning with an open box of tissues.

"Thanks." She pulled one out, wiped her eyes and blew her nose. "I'm sorry to be pouring this all out to you. It seems all wrong. I mean – we hardly know each other. I shouldn't be unloading all my troubles on you. It's just that it's been hard to bear on my own and it does feel good to have someone else to talk to."

"Don't worry about it. I'm happy to listen. No, sorry – that sounds wrong. Of course I'm not 'happy'. What I mean is......if it's helpful to you then I don't mind......" He tailed off awkwardly. It was a Freudian slip, he thought. He had felt a tinge of happiness at her announcement.

She seemed not to notice his discomfort. "But that wasn't the worst. If I'm honest, it was no surprise that he was having affairs. He's ten years younger than me. And he'd admitted that he was bisexual when we first met. He told me he'd had sex with men although he said they were always only one night stands and didn't mean anything. But now it was different. He'd met a woman who he'd fallen in love with......" She paused and swallowed hard as if removing a constriction in her throat. "And she was pregnant. So, he was leaving me to be with her and their child." She swallowed the rest of her wine and poured herself another glass. "You don't mind..." She said, glancing up at Jeremy as she was pouring.

"No, go ahead. I can open another bottle."

"My first thought after he'd made his confession was to abandon the trip to France, but then I changed my mind. I decided it would be good to escape – have time on my own to think things through. And he was right – I wouldn't have wanted to watch him packing up all his stuff and moving out. Plus, I didn't want to have to tell my parents. They'd never approved of me marrying Ruari. That's his name by the way – Ruari. They never liked him – thought he was too young for me. And I'm Jewish and he's not so that didn't help matters. I couldn't face up to them saying 'we told you so'. But then, as soon as I got here, I thought it was a mistake. I needed someone to talk to and I thought I might go straight back but I've since spoken to a couple of friends on the phone...... and now I'm talking to you...... so I'm feeling much better...... and I've been able to get back to revising the novel which helps to take my mind off it."

There was another uneasy silence while Jeremy racked his brain for something empathetic he could say to her.

"What kind of musician is he?" It just came out. As soon as he'd said it he wanted to kick himself. "Sorry. You don't need to answer that. Stupid thing to ask. It's irrelevant."

"No, it's okay. He's a jazz saxophonist. Are you interested in modern jazz?"

"No, I can't say I am."

"Oh well, then there's no point in mentioning his band because you won't have heard of them. He made a living mostly as a session musician. You know, a backing musician on lots of top ten hits. I should have steered clear of him when I first met him – taken Marilyn Munroe's advice in *Some Like It Hot*. Have you seen *Some Like It Hot*?"

"Yes. One of my favourite films."

"Do you remember the bit where she tells Jack Lemon, when he's pretending to be a woman, that she always falls for saxophone players and they always end up doing the dirty on her?"

"Yes, I do. It sounds very apt. I guess it's always difficult with creative types. They often seem to have a tendency to be irresponsible. Sexually, I mean. But then, of course, you're a creative type yourself – with your novel writing." He wished he could stop burbling. The situation had thrown him and he couldn't think of anything helpful to say. He was relieved that she seemed so wrapped up in her misery that she was barely listening to him.

"The pregnancy was the part that really hurt," she continued. "My biological clock is ticking away fast. I'd wanted to have a child before it was too late but he kept putting me off. He said his lifestyle was too peripatetic for him to be a good father but he was going to cut down on the touring soon and just do the recording studio work and the London jazz club venues. And then, once he had this more settled life, we could consider having a child."

"He sounds like a complete bastard."

"No. He wasn't at all." She sighed. "It's mostly my fault. I tried to tie him down – to trap him. I should have realised he was too much of a free spirit."

"If you don't mind me saying so, it sounds to me like you're letting him off lightly and being far too hard on yourself. You might feel better if you let your anger out. You're probably bottling it all up inside you which isn't going to do you any good." For the first time in the conversation, Jeremy felt in control of himself – at least, he was no longer talking bollocks. He felt a powerful urge to tell her all about what had happened to Julia – to explain how their relationship had ended. To show her that it was easy for him to understand how she was feeling and to empathise with her. To thank her for sharing her pain because it was an enormous help to him. Like her, he had had no-one he could talk to about it so he was grateful that she was giving him the opportunity to share similar experiences with her.

As he uncorked the second bottle and she continued to fill in details of her fractious relationship with Ruari, he was reminded of that night in the pub in Clapham sitting opposite Julia as she poured her heart out after her break up with Pete Davies. So much in his life was going round in circles. What was it they used to say – it's déjà vu all over again.

When her painful reminiscences had come to an end there was a lengthy silence. Jeremy felt himself standing on the edge of a swimming pool, summoning up the courage to dive head first into the cold water.

He decided to take the plunge. "I have a confession to

make. I haven't been honest with you. It's not true that Julia's gone back to England to look after her sick mother. Her mother died a few years ago. I made that up. She's left me. She's gone back for good."

Now he had dived in, the water felt fine – like a warm comforting bath. For the next twenty minutes, he filled in the complete history of their relationship from that night in the pub in Clapham to her departure ten days ago. Then he paused, deciding whether to submerge his whole body – dive to the bottom of the pool: tell her about Julia's death and the police investigation. Before he could make up his mind, she turned and glanced out the window.

"God, it's getting dark. We've been talking for ages. I only came in for a minute to ask about the gîte. I feel terrible."

"Don't be silly. I'm really glad we've talked like this. It's been a great help to me. I hope it has for you as well?"

"Oh yes. Definitely. Thanks for listening. But I really must go. I feel exhausted. All this baring of the soul is tiring stuff." She laughed. "Look, I hope I don't sound too presumptuous," she continued, "but, if you're not doing anything tomorrow evening why don't you come across to the gîte and I'll cook you a meal?"

"That would be very nice. I'd love to."

"But I must warn you, there'll be a strict rule. No more talking about our partners or our break ups. We can find something more cheerful to talk about." Jeremy stared at her. Was she flirting with him? He'd never been any good at detecting the signs. He'd been close to telling her the full story of what had happened to Julia but now he was glad he hadn't. Perhaps he would tomorrow evening. He needed to give it more thought. He was sure he would have her full sympathy; that she wouldn't think for one minute that he could be the killer – but, even so, he wasn't sure he wanted to risk it.

18

Half an hour after Gilles Montfort had departed, Mireille was still on the sofa, her mind a swirl of confusion. She was so bound up in thought that she jumped when the phone rang.

"Mireille. Has the gendarme gone? How did it go?" Mohammed sounded anxious.

"He left a half hour ago." She hesitated. Part of what had been going through her mind since the gendarme's departure was a whole series of questions she needed to put to her husband, but now wasn't the time, and especially not over the phone. She had a lot more thinking to do. "It was okay. I don't think I was able to be much help to him. He just wanted to know how I knew Julia Wainwright: how often I'd met her: whether she told me anything about herself: when I had last spoken to her."

"And did he say anything about who they suspect killed her? Are they anywhere near finding the killer?"

"No. He didn't say anything about any of that and I didn't ask him, so I don't know."

"Are you alright? You sound a bit upset."

"I'm fine. It's just that it brought it all back. You know – that horrible feeling that someone you know has been murdered."

"Yes. Well, let's hope they find who did it and it can all be over and forgotten about. Try to put it out of your mind. I should be home normal time this evening. See you later. Love you."

"Love you too." He rang off. All over and forgotten about. Put it out of your mind. If only, she thought.

While Officer Montfort had been questioning her, she hadn't had time to think but, as soon as he left, she sat down with a cup of coffee and thought about those phone calls she'd made to Julia and the calls that Julia had made to her that week. That Tuesday morning – the day Julia had died – she knew why she couldn't possibly have sent a text message. She had lied to the officer about leaving her phone in Morocco, but it wasn't a complete lie. She had lost her phone, but it had been on that Tuesday morning that she'd first realised it was missing, not last night when they got back from Morocco. She checked that week in her diary to make sure she wasn't mistaken. It had definitely been that Tuesday morning. She had been looking for it before she left the house to go and see the fitters at the shop. She remembered searching the house from top to bottom, rummaging under the sofa cushions, searching her car and then phoning Mohammed from the house phone to check that he hadn't taken it by mistake. She even got him to search his car, although she knew she hadn't been in it for at least a week.

Why hadn't she told the gendarme the truth about the lost phone? It was a question she didn't need to ask herself. She knew why. She just didn't want to admit it to herself. She was a hundred per cent certain she hadn't left the phone anywhere the previous day. She knew she'd had it with her when she'd returned home that Monday evening. It had been in the house. Which meant there were only two people who could have taken it. She had grilled Nathalie when she collected her from school that afternoon. Had she taken maman's phone to play games on it and then put it somewhere? Maybe in her bag and then she had taken it to school by mistake? She remembered being so persistent

244

in her questioning, not trusting her mischievous daughter's answers, that she had reduced Nathalie to tears. No, it couldn't have been her daughter. That left only one person. She grilled Mohammed again when he got home that evening until he grew almost as petulant as his daughter.

She wished she could persuade herself that she was being paranoid: that her memory was playing tricks on her: that she must have left it somewhere on her travels the day before. But now she had further evidence. It hadn't just gone missing. Someone had it and they had used it to send a text message to Julia on that fateful day. How likely was it that it was some random stranger who had found her phone, picked Julia's number from her contacts list and sent her a message? Not very. She was trying her hardest not to believe it but there was only one suspect. It had to be Mohammed. She didn't want to ask herself the next question but there was no avoiding it. Why would Mohammed have sent a text to Julia Wainwright and why from her phone? The second part of the question was easy to answer – he could only have got Julia's number from her phone. She could feel her pulse racing and her cheeks growing hot as she forced herself to acknowledge the only possible answer to the first part of her question.

He must have found out about her relationship with Julia.

But if he knew, why hadn't he confronted her? Why go to the trouble of taking her phone and contacting Julia? She tried running a possible scenario through her head. Mohammed texts Julia and arranges to meet her. Julia would think it was a text from Mireille so she'd be happy to arrange the meeting. But why would he want to meet her? Presumably to confront her with his discovery that she was having sex with his wife? So, Julia's sitting at some meeting place waiting for Mireille to arrive and, instead, it's some strange man. Does he introduce himself immediately as Mireille's husband? And, if so, wouldn't Julia beat a hasty exit? Why would she want to stay and speak to him? But then, maybe he had been more cunning and not said anything about his suspicions. He could have thought up some subterfuge. Something to do with her business? Perhaps he'd texted her to say his wife was ill but had needed to sort out an urgent business matter so he'd agreed to stand in for her? No, she couldn't see how that would have made much sense to Julia.

She beat the side of her head with clenched fists trying to rid it of this chain of thoughts. It was what was lying in wait at the end of those thoughts that she didn't want to face up to.

If Mohammed had arranged a meeting with Julia that morning and Julia had been murdered later that day, then Mohammed becomes the number one suspect.

This was madness. How could she possibly think that her husband of seven years, the father of her child, could be a murderer? To think that, she needed to speculate on how Mohammed would react to finding out about their affair. It wasn't a new speculation. She'd thought about it with mounting fear ever since she first went to bed with Julia. If he found out, it would destroy her life. He'd divorce her and he'd probably get custody of Nathalie once the court heard about her irresponsible and immoral behaviour. She had to end the relationship. But she couldn't. She continued to meet up with Julia, persuading herself that this time she'd make it clear that the madness had to stop – that, from now on, it would be a purely business arrangement. And then, they'd end up in bed together – once even in Mireille and Mohammed's own bed. Mireille was scared to death and yet, that very fear made the sex even more exciting. It must be like being addicted to heroin, she thought. You know it's going to destroy you and yet it feels too good to stop. And then, as soon as Julia left, she would once again imagine what would happen if he found out. But none of the possible consequences she had come up with had involved Mohammed killing Julia. She had once considered whether Mohammed might kill *her* but she'd immediately expunged the thought. He was a doctor for god's sake – an educated man. He wasn't one of these antediluvian Muslim men from Somalia or Pakistan who would kill their wives or daughters at the drop of a hat if he found out they were dishonouring the family. No. There had to be another explanation for the disappearance of her phone and the text message to Julia. Maybe it was some weirdo who had found the phone. Or, if it was Mohammed, perhaps he had sent a message to warn her off. Amidst all this speculation, there was one incontrovertible fact – Julia had been murdered. And no matter how many theories she came up with, she couldn't duck the possibility of Mohammed's involvement and the need to ask him some serious questions.

*

For the first time he could remember, Gilles Montfort entered Judge Bouchon's office with a bounce in his step and not one iota of trepidation. With a smug look on his face, he waved the sheath of papers he was carrying in front of him as if it was a telegram announcing he'd won the lottery.

"Take a seat, Gilles," said the judge, his only reaction to the gendarme's buoyant mood being his usual downbeat expression. "You look like you might be the bearer of good news for a change."

"Yes, I think you could say that," said Gilles, taking a seat and sliding the papers across the desk towards Jules Bouchon. "We have the full phone records for Mireille

Hafeez and Julia Wainwright. Plus we have Madame Wainwright's credit card details."

"Good." The word was tinged with suspicion. "So, I presume they give us some useful information. You're obviously bursting to show me. Sum up the important facts for me. I'll study them in detail later."

"Okay. I'll start with the credit card." Gilles had planned out the order in which to present the information for the maximum dramatic effect. "The most interesting entry is in April of this year when she paid for a double room in a *Campanile Hotel* in Aurillac. The bill includes two breakfasts so she must have been staying with someone else."

"And you know who this other person was?" The judge posed the question as if he already knew the answer.

"Not yet......"

"So it could have been Monsieur Halliday?"

"I'll visit the hotel later today and see if any of the staff recognise her and remember who she was with." The judge looked sceptically at him. Gilles knew it was a longshot which is why he'd presented it first. He was anxious to move on. "As for the phone records, they show an increasing number of calls and messages between Madame Hafeez and Julia Wainwright from last January up to the day she died. The texts are all short and simple – mostly to arrange meetings or answer queries about her products."

"So, nothing of great interest?" The judge's impatience was growing.

Gilles played the first of his trump cards. "Except for the message I have circled in red." He pointed across the desk to the papers he had given the judge.

Jules Bouchon found it and read it out loud. "Hotel booked. Meet u there 18.30." He looked up at Jean.

"The message was sent to Mireille Hafeez the day before the Campanile booking."

Jules Bouchon's face remained impassive but Gilles detected a flicker of interest in his eyes.

"So you think the person she spent the night with in the hotel was Madame Hafeez?"

"That's what it points to." Gilles Montfort leaned back with a self-satisfied look on his face.

"How do you know they weren't just using it as a meeting place to discuss business?"

"Why book a hotel room for a meeting? And don't forget the breakfasts the next morning."

"So you think this married woman – with a child – was having an affair with Miss Wainwright?" The judge once again adopted his equivocal expression. "Do you know whether either of these women has a history of lesbian relationships?"

"No – but I will obviously look into it."

Before the judge could express any further doubts, Giles played his final card. "If you look on the other sheet of paper." He paused while Jules Bouchon shuffled the papers. "Those are Mireille Hafeez's phone records. Again, I have circled the relevant message in red."

It was longer than the previous one. The judge studied it before reading it out. "Need 2 see u. Urgent. Meet me in Café L'Abside next to l'église de Saint-Joseph, Aurillac at 12.00."

"And then, if you look at Miss Wainwright's reply." Gilles signalled for him to swap the sheets back over.

The only other message circled in red, dated the same day, read, "O.K. – see u at 12.00."

The judge leaned back and stared into space. Gilles waited expectantly for his response.

"Very good, Montfort," he finally said. "Now we're getting somewhere at last. We need to gather as much information as quickly as possible. See what you can find out, if anything, about these two women's sexual histories. See if any of the staff in the hotel and the café in Aurillac remember the two women being there on those days. Then we will have to bring in Madame Hafeez so that I can question her."

The smile he'd had when he entered the office was still glued on Gilles Montfort's face as he left. It was rare for him to receive any praise from Bouchon and he was basking in it.

*

"Jeremy? It's me – Hattie. I know you probably won't want to talk to me but I've got a small problem I'd like your help with so – if you're in – I'd be grateful if you'd pick up – or, if not, could you call me back as soon as possible?"

She was right. He didn't want to talk to her but, if he was going to have to eventually, he might as well get it over with.

"Hi Hattie. How are you?"

A moment's silence. Presumably, she hadn't expected him to answer. "Thanks for picking up." She ignored his asking after her health and, eschewing all other social niceties, got straight to the point. "I'm phoning you because I've been getting a bit snowed under here what with having had to organise the return of Julia's body and the funeral and everything." Jeremy was about to interrupt to ask how the funeral had gone but he stopped himself. He didn't want to know. And anyway, what could she say? It was a funeral for her murdered sister. It went well? Everyone had a good time? "On top of that, I'm starting to get enquiries about Julia's business and a number of other issues about Julia's estate which need sorting out."

Jeremy felt his chest tightening. He remembered his discussions with Miles Joseph about the ownership of the house and French inheritance laws. Was this Hattie's first salvo to warn him that she intended to claim her share of the inheritance?

"Do you know Clive Shraeger, Julia's accountant?" Hattie continued.

"I've heard the name but I've never met him. I never had anything to do with Julia's business affairs."

"Well, neither did I," Hattie said waspishly. "It's just that he's been in contact with me for some reason. I don't know how he got my number. Anyway, some of Julia's business associates – shop owners and manufacturers of her designs – have been contacting him to find out what's happening to the business. Some of them are owed money, some have goods they need to deliver. He can't deal with it so he's passed it on to me even though I told him I can't deal with it either. I've had no connection with Julia's business whatsoever. And, what's more, I feel I'm having to deal with more than my fair share of the fallout from Julia's death. I'm finding it all rather distressing, as I'm sure you can imagine."

"So, you feel I should take control of it because I wouldn't find it upsetting as I'm obviously a heartless murdering bastard?" It was her supercilious tone of voice that triggered his angry response. He was sure he wasn't imagining it. There was a clear assumption in her tone of voice that she was a lot more upset by Julia's death than he was.

It took her a moment to respond as if she was taking a deep breath and composing herself. "Look Jeremy, I don't want any unpleasantness. I'm just asking you for help. If you don't want to, then I guess I'll just have to try my best to sort it out myself."

She was being surprisingly conciliatory. He knew why she was doing it. She wanted something from him and she realised she wasn't going to get it by antagonising him.

Nevertheless, he calmed himself down and decided to offer her an olive branch. "I'm sorry, Hattie. I guess we're both rather het up about Julia's death. I didn't mean to be awkward. It's just that I don't know any more than you do about Julia's business affairs."

"I'm afraid I've already taken the liberty of giving your email address to Clive Schraeger so that he can forward any future enquiries to you. My reasoning was that you have access to Julia's office at the house."

Jeremy stayed calm. There was no point in getting angry. "Most of her stuff would have been on her laptop and, as I understood from the gendarmes, it was destroyed in the fire. I suppose I can look through her desk just in case she's left any paper records."

"If you could, Jeremy. What the accountant said he'd do is email you a list of the shops and manufacturers that Julia dealt with – at least, all the ones he has in his account records. He thought that you could send them all a gently worded message to inform them of Julia's death because it's possible that some of them won't know about it. You could also ask them to be patient as it may take time to sort out Julia's business affairs. Do you think you could do that?" Hattie's patronising tone resurfaced.

Jeremy was minded to say no but took a deep breath and bit the bullet. "Okay. I'll see what I can do."

"Thanks. I'll speak to you again soon." Hattie rang off. He assumed she'd got what she wanted from him and wasn't going to give him any opportunity to change his mind. For his part, he was happy to end the call, relieved that she hadn't asked him about the investigation; not that he had anything new to tell her. He doubted he'd be speaking to her again soon. In fact, he doubted he'd ever speak to her again. It was a door in his life that was closing. The only thing they would have to talk about was the dividing up of the house and his and Julia's remaining possessions and that would be best done through solicitors.

⁎

He woke up bathed in sweat in the stifling box-like hotel room. The plain black crucifix on the white wall opposite the bed was intermittently illuminated by blinding flashes coming through the flimsy white window blind. At first, he assumed it was the irritating neon restaurant sign on the opposite side of the road flashing off and on but then there was a cacophonous clap of thunder. It was sheet lightning. He was frightened.

When Jeremy jerked awake and realised he was in his own bedroom in Vendillac, he expected to see lightning flashes and waited for the next crash of thunder, but there was no storm outside. It was a still, humid night. The sky was clear and the light from a full moon caste deep threatening shadows across the walls and ceiling. He tried to turn over and check the time on the digital clock but his duvet was wrapped tightly round him like a shroud and he had to wriggle and twist his body to free himself. It was 2.30 a.m. The dream he had been having was a familiar one – often recurring when he was anxious or stressed. Unlike most dreams, where the surroundings are vaguely familiar but not immediately recognisable, he knew exactly where and when this was. It was the last holiday he and his parents had been on before his mother became ill. He must have been twelve. They'd driven to a seaside resort on the Adriatic coast but the only thing he remembered about the holiday was the night they spent in a cheerless low budget backstreet hotel in Milan where he was deemed grown up enough to have his own room. It was in that tiny room that he'd been woken up by that terrifying storm and wished he could return to being a small child so he could crawl into the safe haven of his parents' double bed.

He switched on the light and headed for the bathroom to splash his face with water and towel himself down. There was a portable air-conditioner in the bedroom but he rarely used it as it was a tossup whether he would be kept awake more by its rumbling growling noise or by the heat. Climbing back into bed, he knew it wouldn't be the heat or the noise of the air-conditioner that would keep him awake; it would be the bewildering thoughts rattling around inside his head – the result of the discoveries he'd made on his laptop that afternoon. He couldn't get them out of his head. He must have spent at least an hour sat staring at the computer screen that afternoon, reading and re-reading the emails to be sure that he wasn't misinterpreting them.

He'd only come to his senses when Ruth Gershon knocked at his front door. He stared at her, bemused.

"I thought I'd better come over and remind you." She indicated the watch on her wrist. "It's just that I wouldn't want the dinner to spoil."

It took several seconds for the word 'dinner' to register. "Oh God. I'm sorry. How stupid. How could I forget something we only arranged yesterday? I've been so engrossed in work on the laptop."

"It's alright. I'm a writer. I know how easy it is to get so involved in what you're doing that you forget about everything else."

"If you could just give me another fifteen minutes to shower and get changed?"

"No problem. See you in fifteen minutes."

As he showered and dressed, he was wishing he could find some way to back out of the meal – maybe tell her he was feeling unwell or come up with some other excuse. But it was too late. He regretted now that he'd been in such a hurry that afternoon to follow up Hattie's phone request and start researching Julia's business contacts. He'd been so looking forward to spending the evening with Ruth Gershon. That frisson of anticipation of an evening of mild flirtation – the possibility of an inkling of the start of a romance. Instead, it had now become an inconvenient duty he'd have to get through with as much goodwill as he could muster, straining to keep his mind on the conversation rather than on that afternoon's perplexing revelations.

In the end, it wasn't as difficult as he thought it would be. She was good company and the food was delicious despite his lack of appetite. She asked him what work he had been doing earlier that had so occupied his mind that he'd forgotten about their dinner arrangement and he stumbled through a garbled explanation about his online stamp dealing and his gardening work. After what he'd discovered earlier that afternoon, any lingering thoughts of telling her about Julia's murder were definitely off the agenda. Instead, he went on to talk about his career as an English teacher and his gradual disillusionment with the job and life in London, leading to his and Julia's decision to move to the Aveyron. He assiduously avoided mentioning anything about the Susie Meredith incident. Then they discussed their favourite books and authors before Ruth reciprocated with her own back story. After she left university, her first job had been as a trainee journalist with the *Hampstead and Highgate Express*. From there, through a friend of her father's, she'd got a job with the dreaded Rupert Murdoch Empire, mostly writing a sexual advice column for the *News of the World*. Apart from being an interesting icebreaker at dinner parties, it was much more tedious than it sounded as well as being deeply unfulfilling. She turned for relief to her love of History (she'd studied it at Warwick University) and signed up to do a part-time M.A. in Victorian Studies which led her to trying her hand at writing detective fiction set in the Victorian era and the rest, to coin a phrase, is history. He loved listening to her – loved the way she listened to him, her head tilted to the side, concentrating. He revelled in the attention. It reminded him of the early days when he and Julia were first getting to know each other. How long ago that now seemed and how he wished he could erase the last few years and return to those halcyon days.

As they'd agreed the day before, they steered clear of any further discussion of their failed relationships. Jeremy accepted her offer of coffee when the meal was over but, soon after, he made his excuses – he had to get up early to go and check out a possible gardening job – and departed for an early night.

Although there had been no hint of flirtation from either of them during the evening, Jeremy tried to get back to sleep by dreaming up scenarios for how he could initiate a romance with Ruth during the next week. But, however hard he tried, even summoning up images of her naked body sprawled across his bed, he couldn't prevent them being pushed aside by the discoveries he'd made that afternoon.

As soon as Hattie had put the phone down, he had decided to check his emails for want of anything better to do. Sure enough, as Hattie had warned him, there was one from Clive Schraeger, Julia's accountant, with an attachment listing all of Julia's suppliers and retail outlets. He went to her office and checked the drawers in her desk but, as he suspected, there was only some stationery and old sketchpads containing embryonic designs. He should have left it at that but a light drizzle was starting to fall so he abandoned any thoughts of gardening and sat back down in front of his laptop and considered how best to gain access to Julia's business affairs. He tried her designer website but all that came up was a home page with a large distressing photo of Julia's smiling face beaming out at him and numerous photos of her products. He thought about trying to access her business bank account. He knew it was with Natwest but he didn't know where to start in trying to guess her login code number let alone her password.

Instead, he went to her email account. That might be easier. All he had to do was come up with the password. It would probably be futile but he'd spend a few minutes on it. He remembered discussions they'd had about how difficult it was these days to come up with different passwords for the numerous accounts and websites you needed access to. They both agreed that they never followed internet security advice and often used the same or similar passwords for most of their accounts. One that he knew she often used was hattie, her sister's name. He tried it with and without an upper case h and with a variety of numbers after it; their house number in London, her birth year, Hattie's birth year. None of them worked. He was about to give up when he remembered her telling him, probably in that same conversation, that she often used the name of her favourite childhood pet – her dog Bruno. Again, he tried numerous variations until he combined lower case with the year of her birth – and bingo.

He clicked on her contacts list and was pleased to see that she'd divided it into two folders – one for her business and the other for friends. In the early days of their relationship, the one thing that had irritated him about Julia was her disorganisation and general untidiness. A frequent morning ritual before he could leave the house for work was to help her search for whatever it was she had misplaced – mobile phone, keys, purse, gloves. Jeremy found this especially annoying as he was meticulous when it came to his own possessions; his books and CD collections alphabetised, his desk drawers organised into labelled files, his clothes neatly folded in their organised sections in his cupboard drawers. He had worried that maybe he was too fastidious and, once they moved in together, she would find it off-putting. She would label him a nerd. But that hadn't happened and, when she started up her own business, it propelled her into becoming more organised.

He entered the business section, which was further subdivided, and began by accessing the retail outlet list, copying them on to a notepad. Once his list was completed and he was about to logout, he hesitated – the cursor hovering over her inbox. Jeremy had always prided himself on being morally scrupulous. It was what had most upset him over Susie Meredith's accusations. He regarded himself as the consummate professional. When female students had flirted with him, he had resisted any temptation to play along – the polar opposite to the way his nemesis, Pete Davies, behaved. And, when it came to his relationship with Julia, he had always respected her privacy. Even when he had feared she might be having an affair, he'd never been tempted to search her bag or examine her private correspondence for evidence. But now that she was dead? Could you invade the privacy of a dead person? It was often argued that you could, especially if the person was famous and the purpose was to write a warts-and-all biography. In the circumstances though, if he needed a reason to justify an invasion, then he was simply continuing the task he'd been given by Hattie to sort out Julia's affairs. He would check through her recent messages for enquiries from her business associates. Anyway, Judge Bouchon had probably already gained access to her account and had trawled through it for evidence so there was no reason why he, as her ex-partner and the chief suspect in her murder, shouldn't do the same.

It was a tedious task. The tide of unopened messages was vast – inevitably almost all junk. He scrolled through them at speed, only opening a handful that he recognised as business addresses. He added some names and email addresses to the list on his notepad with brief details of their enquiries. There were a few messages from Julia's friends in London which he read, but they contained nothing of interest.

He was about to close his laptop down when he decided on a brief scrutiny of her sent box. He only got as far as opening the most recent message, sent a few days before she died. It had been sent to mireille.h@googlemail.com. He read through it several times to be sure that he fully understood it. It was written in French. Julia's written and spoken French had been much better than his but the language used in the message was not complicated and he got the gist without having to go to the bookshelves downstairs for a dictionary. The first paragraph was straightforward; Julia explaining that she was leaving on Monday morning, driving back to England to stay for a while with her sister while she sorted out what she was going to do with her life. It was the second paragraph that was puzzling – and not because of any difficulties he was having with the French expressions. There was no doubting the meaning – but doubt it, he did. She was telling this woman, whoever she was, that her, Julia's, future depended upon this 'Mireille'. She understood how difficult Mireille's situation was and didn't expect her to make an immediate decision. They both needed time. But maybe, given that time, there would be some way they could be together because that's what Julia wanted more than anything. She finished by asking whether there was any possibility they could meet up somewhere next week when she was on her way back to the UK. She signed off "Je t'embrasse, Julia."

He was still puzzling over it when he had been interrupted by Ruth Gershon knocking on his door. Was it what it seemed – a love letter? Was Julia having an affair with this Mireille? Or was he misreading it? Was it merely a reflection on the difficulty of saying goodbye to a close friend – someone you feared you might never see again? No. There could be no ambiguity. Surely, you didn't tell somebody that your whole future depended upon them if it was only a matter of losing a friend? He wasn't surprised at finding proof that Julia had been having an affair. He had been expecting it for some time. Perversely, he felt he'd been willing it to happen from the day they moved in together. Put it down to his lack of self-esteem; his scepticism that any woman as beautiful and talented as Julia could be in love with someone like him. But a lesbian affair? Julia had been open with him about her sexual history. He was sure that, if she'd experienced lesbian relationships in her youth – even a passing passion for an older woman or teenage schoolgirl fumblings during a sleepover – she would have told him. Was it more painful if she'd been having an affair with a woman than if it had been a man? It was harder for him to understand but the thought didn't disgust him. He'd always been liberal in his views on same sex relationships. No. What disturbed him about it was that it was more difficult for him to fit it into the scenario he'd been building up of Julia's murder – a rejected male lover seeking retribution. Or was he being sexist to discount the possibility that a thwarted lesbian lover could be a murderer? Maybe this Mireille wasn't a woman at all? It could be a name her lover used to disguise himself just in case Jeremy intercepted their messages.

It was as these thoughts were still whizzing around inside his head as he struggled to get to sleep that he had a sudden memory flash. He climbed out of bed and padded barefoot across the corridor to his office where he picked up the scribbled list of Julia's business contacts and ran his finger down them until he came to the name of a women's fashion accessory shop in Decazeville, *Joli Printemps*. Underneath was an email address – mireille.h@googlemail.com. There was also an address and phone number for the shop. He turned on his laptop, logged in to Julia's email account and scrolled slowly down the recent messages in her inbox searching for a reply from Mireille. Had she agreed to meet Julia somewhere on her way back? It would explain why Julia had taken that unusual route. There was nothing. Of course it didn't mean they hadn't arranged a meeting. Julia might have deleted any reply or they could have arranged it over the phone or by text message.

He copied down the shop details on a separate sheet before switching off the laptop and returning to bed to spend the rest of the night tossing and turning.

19

Nathalie sat at the dining room table hunched over her mathematics workbook carefully colouring in sections of a circle while her mother sat by her side supervising. Maths had never been Mireille's favourite subject at school and teaching methods had changed so much since then she usually found she wasn't much help and would leave Nathalie to get on with it on her own while she prepared dinner. This evening, however, she was looking for distractions.

An hour earlier, she'd received a call from Judge Bouchon's secretary asking her to come to the gendarmerie in Villefranche de Rouergue for an interview the following day. Mireille tried to put her off – her shop was due to open in three days' time and she still had so much to do – couldn't it wait a week? The woman was unswerving – insistent. This was a murder investigation. The judge would not accept any delay.

It had been two days since her interview with Gilles Montfort and she still hadn't summoned up the courage to have a conversation with Mohammed about her suspicions regarding her missing phone. It had been easy to put it off. She'd been busy with the final preparations at the shop and Mohammed had had a series of evening consultations at his surgery so they'd seen very little of each other. But this evening she was expecting him home at his normal time, which meant he would arrive in the next half hour and, once dinner was over and Nathalie was tucked up in bed, they would have the rest of the evening together. There would be no excuse.

It wasn't just that she was scared to confront Mohammed with her suspicions, it was more that she couldn't decide tactically how best to broach the subject. What if her suspicions were unfounded and Mohammed knew nothing about her affair with Julia Wainwright? Was there some way that she could subtly probe him while not giving away the truth about her and Julia in case he didn't know about it?

She was distracted from these thoughts by the sound of the front door. Nathalie abandoned her crayons, jumped down from her chair and raced across to the doorway where she wrapped her arms round her father's legs.

"Papa."

Mohammed dropped his briefcase, knelt down and hoisted her up. She wrapped her legs round his waist and her arms round his neck and kissed him on the nose.

"Have you had a good day at school, ma cherie?"

"It was alright, but Madame Peyral was horrible to me at lunchtime. She made me eat my carrots and I didn't want too because they were all floppy."

"Oh you must always eat your carrots, cherie. If you eat lots of carrots you will be able to see in the dark."

"Don't be silly, Papa. How can you see in the dark? It's dark."

Mohammed laughed as he lowered her back to the floor. He turned to Mireille. "She's getting much too grown up and smart to believe my stories anymore," he said.

Mireille felt herself growing tearful as she watched the show of affection between her husband and daughter. Perhaps it would be best if she waited until after her interview tomorrow before saying anything to Mohammed.

She wasn't optimistic but maybe the judge would have some new information which would render any further enquiries about her missing phone unnecessary.

*

The weather had broken after the previous night's thunderstorm. It was cooler and cloudier outside and so, Mireille's fifteen minute wait in the narrow corridor outside Judge Bouchon's office was not as stuffily uncomfortable as it would have been a few days' earlier – physically, at least. Mentally, it was a different matter. She couldn't remember a time in her life when she'd felt more nervous. The panicky drive to the hospital when her contractions started; the preparations on the morning of her wedding; perching on the edge of a diving board at nine years old with her swimming instructor encouraging her to take the plunge. None of them was as bad as this excruciating wait.

Last night, once Nathalie was asleep, she knew that, even if she said nothing else to him, she had to tell Mohammed about the impending interview with Judge Bouchon. He was surprised and concerned, firing off a series of questions about what she thought he could possibly want to ask her. She kept telling him she had no idea but he persisted, getting her to go through again the questions that Gilles Montfort had already asked. Originally, she had given him the gist of the interview but left out the bit about the text message sent from her missing phone. This time she was tempted to tell him all just to see his reaction but she resisted, sticking to her initial plan of waiting to see what the judge had to say. Finally, he dropped the subject and they sat in silence watching the evening news roundup on television.

Once they had switched it off and she was heading out

of the sitting room on her way upstairs to bed, Mohammed halted her in her tracks.

"Look, why don't I come with you to Villefranche tomorrow? I can phone in sick to the surgery. It'll be no problem for them to rearrange my appointments."

She stood still by the door, taking a deep breath to calm herself before turning to face him.

"Don't be silly. That's not necessary. I'm sure there won't be any problem. It'll just be routine. Anyway, I don't know how long it might last. It'll be very boring for you if you have a long wait."

"I didn't mean coming with you just to wait outside. I meant so I could be in the interview with you – so I could offer support." He sounded agitated, insistent.

"Why would I need support? It's just some questions about a woman I hardly knew. And anyway, I don't think the judge will want you to be present." She was tempted to raise her voice and tell him to stop treating her like a child – that she did not want him there – but she held her tongue.

"I don't understand why they want to talk to you again. Surely, you've told them everything you know. I can't see why they should have, but if they do have any suspicions about you, then I can support you. I can back you up."

She couldn't keep the lid on her irritation any longer. "Mon dieu, Mohammed. I'm a grown woman. I'm not helpless. I don't need you around me all the time to hold my hand. I'm not..."She was about to say "I'm not your property" but she swallowed the words. It could open up a whole new area for recriminations about their relationship – one which she had wanted to broach with him for some time. But now was not the right moment. "I'm sure they just have some further routine questions to ask. I can't see how you could be of any help in answering questions about a woman you never met." She stared at him with flashing angry eyes, scrutinising his face for any incriminating sign. He opened his mouth to reply but thought better of it.

Mireille lay on her back in bed staring at the moonlit reflections on the ceiling. She was not surprised she couldn't sleep. A jumble of thoughts were whirling round in her head like clothes in a tumble drier. It was partly the looming interview that was keeping her awake but it was also her disquiet at Mohammed's reaction earlier that evening. It was so much more than the natural solicitude of a husband for his wife having to endure yet another cross-examination. Unlike Mohammed, she had been expecting to be questioned further by the gendarmes because she knew about the text message from the missing phone. He must have thought it was all over after that initial visit. Now that he knew it wasn't, she was sure she detected a hint of panic. Perhaps he feared these new enquiries would uncover things he had hoped to keep hidden?

Every now and then, she pressed the pause button on her thoughts and listened for the familiar sound of heavy adenoidal breathing that would signal that Mohammed was asleep. She was praying that she would hear it but he lay with his back to her and there was no sound coming from him. If he had fallen straight to sleep, she would have welcomed it as a sign that he was not as conscience-stricken and concerned about the interview as she thought. But he was finding it as difficult to get to sleep as she was – not a good sign.

*

She was a fraction less nervous once she was in the office sitting opposite Jules Bouchon. He was much less scary than she'd imagined. With his round jowly face , ruddy cheeks and ring of fluffy grey curls surrounding a shiny bald head, he reminded her of her favourite uncle, Ferdinand, who used to bring her little presents and entertain her with magic tricks when he visited her parents' house. This initial avuncular impression was confirmed when he started to speak. He was the epitome of old world charm.

"Madame Hafeez. I am so sorry to have to call you in for this interview at such short notice and I must thank you for coming. I do appreciate how busy you must be preparing for the opening of your shop." Mireille smiled pleasantly at him while inwardly seeing through his charm. She was only there because he had insisted. "And, by the way, how are your preparations going?"

"Oh you know – the usual ups and downs. Trouble with the lighting, not helped by an electrician who keeps going off to do other jobs. And then, of course, there's been the inevitable delays with some of my stock orders. It's good of you to ask but I'm sure you don't want to hear all the boring details." Despite her wariness, she could feel her tension easing while, at the back of her mind, a suspicious voice was telling her to be on guard – this was most likely a wily old interrogator's technique to soften her up.

She was right to be suspicious. His cuddly uncle demeanour did not last long. There was a pause as Judge Bouchon picked up a sheet of paper from his desk, perused it as if seeing it for the first time and then shifted his focus back to Mireille.

"Madame Hafeez. I've called you in to see me because we have now received your mobile phone records. That is the records from the phone that has…disappeared." He pronounced that final word with slow sceptical deliberation. He paused again, keeping his eyes focused on her. She returned his stare, determined to appear unflustered. "Do you know any more about where the phone might be? I understand from Gilles Montfort that you thought you might have left it in Morocco."

"No. I've checked with my mother-in-law and nobody's found it there. I don't know what could have happened to it."

The judge's lips tightened as he glanced back down at the paper. "There was a message sent from your phone to Julia Wainwright on the morning of the day she died." He paused again and looked up at her. He was playing on her nerves. She could feel her heart thumping. It was so strong she could almost hear it. "The message said, 'need to see u. Urgent. Meet me in café L'Abside next to l'église de Notre-Dame-aux-Neiges in Aurillac at 12.00.'" Yet another pause as he waited to let it sink in. Mireille sat frozen, trying to keep the expression on her face as impassive as the rest of her body. "You received a reply seventeen minutes later from Julia Wainwright confirming that she would see you there at 12.00. Can you tell me what happened at that meeting? Why did you need to see her so urgently?"

Mireille was relieved to be given the chance to talk. Her mouth was dry and she would have liked to ask for a glass of water, but she held back, fearing it would signal her nervousness. She tried to steady her voice, hoping she would sound more confident than she was feeling.

"I didn't meet her in Aurillac. In fact, I didn't send that message to Julia. Since the interview with the gendarme, I have tried to remember exactly when I last had my mobile phone. Then I realised I was mistaken in thinking I had taken it to Morocco. I remembered that I had actually first noticed it missing on that Tuesday morning – the morning you say I sent that text message. I don't know who could have sent it or why, but it couldn't have been me."

The judge took a deep breath and leaned forward, his

arms resting on the desk. Any trace of the kindly uncle was long gone. "And when did you realise this? You didn't think to inform us straight away?"

"No......I.........I was confused. I've been under a lot of pressure and......"

"Madame Hafeez." His voice was stern, like a school principal about to berate a naughty student. "We are conducting a murder enquiry. I believe Gilles Montfort gave you his card with his contact number. As soon as you had any new information, you should have informed him immediately. I must warn you that you could be in danger of being charged with obstructing the course of justice."

"I'm sorry." What little sang-froid she had managed to hold onto was gone. She was now fighting to hold back tears.

"If you didn't send this message, then who else do you think could have done so?"

"I don't know......I have no idea."

"Madame, you are trying my patience. Why on earth would somebody steal your phone and then send a message to a business associate of yours to arrange a meeting? How would they even know where she was?"

"I......I......"

He didn't wait for her to translate her stumbling response into a coherent answer. "The truth is that Julia Wainwright was much more than a business associate, wasn't she Madame Hafeez? You were having an affair with her, were you not?"

Mireille's mouth was now so dry that, even if she could think of anything to say, she doubted she would be able to get the words out. It was spinning out of control. She had lain awake last night imagining how the interview might go but the reality was beyond her worst imaginings. Her earlier composure had evaporated. Her shoulders slumped and she could no longer hold back the tears. Judge Bouchon pushed a box of tissues across the desk towards her. She took a couple, wiped her eyes and blew her nose.

"Do you think I could have a glass of water?" She croaked.

The judge reached over and pressed the intercom button on his phone. "Eva, could you please bring some water for Madame Hafeez?" He turned his attention back to Mireille. He had no intention of letting her tears further delay his interrogation.

"Looking through your and Madame Wainwright's phone records, we know that you met up regularly over the past few months. In particular, we know you spent the night together in a hotel room in Aurillac and you had breakfast together there the following morning. Not something a shop owner and one of her suppliers would normally do, don't you agree?"

Mireille was still smothering her face with tissues in an unsuccessful attempt to stem the flow of tears. She flinched when Judge Bouchon's secretary appeared surreptitiously at her side with a glass of water.

"Thank you, Eva," the judge said. Mireille nodded her thanks and swallowed a mouthful before pulling another tissue from the box.

"So, Madame," Bouchon continued. "Let me put to you what I think happened that Tuesday. Julia Wainwright had already told you that she was leaving her partner. However, she was not leaving him so that she could be with you. She was leaving to go back to England and restart her life there. She tells you that your affair is over. You are distraught. You send a message to arrange the meeting so you can get her to change her mind but she tells you her mind is made up and there can be no future for the two of you together. You are angry. You have been willing to sacrifice your marriage –

indeed, your family – for her. So, you drive off with her and you kill her."

Mireille dropped her hands from her face and let the screwed up bunch of tissues fall to the floor. She stared at him in disbelief. It was as if he had thrown the glass of water over her and then slapped her in the face. The tears stopped and she found her voice.

"That's ridiculous. Of course I didn't kill her. I couldn't possibly have done that."

Judge Bouchon observed the stunned look on her face. She was a petite, attractive, expensively dressed, middle class mother. He doubted that she could, or would, have murdered Julia Wainwright. At a moment like this, he regretted that, despite his long career, he had such limited experience of investigating serious crimes, especially murders as mysterious as this one. His image of the person most likely to have strangled Julia Wainwright came as much from crime films and detective fiction as from his own cases. And yet, what that told him was that he should put his doubts on hold and remember that the most unlikely people could turn into murderers given the right circumstances.

Her shock at the judge's accusation had forced Mireille to regain possession of herself, like a drunk being plied with strong black coffee.

"I can only repeat the truth. I did not send that message to Julia because I did not have my phone. I did not meet Julia in Aurillac and I certainly did not kill her." She spoke slowly and deliberately, before adding, almost as an afterthought, "and, anyway, I already told your officer where I was on that day. I was at my shop and then, in the afternoon, I went to collect my daughter from school. I was nowhere near Aurillac."

"Yes. That is what you told us." The judge paused while he shuffled another piece of paper to the top of his pile and again took his time to examine it. "We have checked out your whereabouts on that Tuesday. Your assistant confirms that you were at the shop until midday. We also spoke to a Madame Joubert. I believe she is the mother of one of your daughter's school friends?" Mireille nodded. The judge continued. "Madame Joubert says that she collected your daughter from school that afternoon because you had asked her to. You phoned to tell her you were delayed at the shop. So – where exactly were you that afternoon?"

Mireille took her time before she answered. She was getting back her equilibrium. This time she would not let his question throw her into turmoil. She was a strong intelligent woman, she told herself. She must not allow herself to be intimidated by this man, even if he is a Judge. She stared back at his austere face and superimposed an image of her smiling affable Uncle Ferdinand over it. Slowly, her memory of the events of that Tuesday swam into focus.

"I'm sorry," she said. "I remember now. I told you about the trouble I was having with the electrical fittings in the shop? Well, I spoke to the electrician on the phone that morning. There had been a mix up over ordering some of the display lights so I arranged to meet him at an electrical supply store at the Zone Industrielle du Combal on the Route de Rodez outside Decazeville. When I got there, I waited for a while but he didn't turn up so I phoned him. He apologised and said he'd had an emergency job he'd had to go to and it was taking longer than he thought so he wouldn't be able to meet me. We would have to reschedule. So I returned home and collected Nathalie from the Jouberts early that evening."

The judge tightened his lips and narrowed his eyes. "So – what you are telling me is that you have no alibi for that afternoon. Did you go into the electrical store? Did anyone see you there?"

"No. But I can give you the contact details for my electrician. He's not very efficient but he should be able to confirm that I arranged that meeting with him and that I phoned him that afternoon from the shop."

"I thought you said that you had lost your phone. How did you phone the electrician?" He was determined not to loosen his grip on her but Mireille was now much more composed.

"We keep a mobile phone for general use in the shop. I took that with me."

Judge Bouchon re-established his tight-lipped sceptical expression. "Why didn't you say all this to Gilles Montfort when he questioned you? It seems rather convenient, if not desperate, for you to come up with this now. Is the mobile phone still at the shop or has that one disappeared as well?"

"I don't appreciate your sarcastic comments." Mireille's anger was genuine. She resented this pompous little man implying that she was a liar. Within a space of a few minutes, she had gone from being distraught and beaten down to feeling indignant and self-assured. She must stop behaving as if she were blameworthy. She'd done nothing wrong. "Of course the phone isn't lost. You are welcome to have it or I can give you the number if you'd prefer and you can check the call log and see that I'm telling the truth."

"Rest assured, we will do that."

To emphasise her innocence, Mireille unhooked her bag from the back of the chair and rummaged through it, searching for her diary.

The judge resumed his questioning. "Does your husband know about your affair with Julia Wainwright?"

She stopped rummaging and removed her hand from the bag. Her stomach tightened. "No, he doesn't."

"Are you certain about that?"

"Yes. Julia and I were very careful. And, if he had

known about it, he wouldn't have kept quiet. He would have confronted me."

"Yes, I imagine he would. He'd be very angry – violent even?"

"Mohammed isn't a violent man."

"Even the gentlest of men might turn violent if they discover their wife is having a lesbian affair."

The Judge stared at her, waiting for a response, but Mireille remained impassive.

He clasped his hands together on the desk. "I say that because I feel I should warn you that it will be necessary for us to question Monsieur Hafeez."

Mireille's rollercoaster of emotions took another sharp dive. "Why? I can't see why that should be necessary. Or are you just trying to punish me because I'm a wicked sinful woman who was not only cheating on her husband but doing it with a woman?"

"Oh please, Madame Hafeez." Judge Bouchon raised his hands and shrugged his shoulders. "There is nothing vindictive in this. You admit you were having an affair with Julia Wainwright. That makes you a suspect in her murder. But, of course, it also makes your husband a suspect. Although you say he knows nothing about it……"

"I swear to you he doesn't." Julia's voice was loud and desperate.

"I would like to be able to take your word for it but I have to do my job. I know you may not think so, but I am being considerate in warning you. I will be contacting him to arrange an interview tomorrow. Normally, I would not want you to have a chance to talk to him about it but, considering the situation you are in, I'm giving you that opportunity."

If Mireille could have sunk any lower, she would have disappeared through the floor.

20

As Jeremy ate the final piece of his ham and cheese baguette, he watched the young woman crouching in the window of Joli Printemps on the other side of the street, balancing colourful cloche hats on black mannequin heads. He had been sitting at the table outside the café for the past hour slowly drinking his coffee and eating the sandwich he'd bought from the bakery down the street.

On his arrival in Decazeville, he'd driven straight to the shop, parked nearby and then walked up and down past it summoning up the courage to knock on the locked door to attract the attention of one of the two female assistants he'd seen working inside. The one who came to the door informed him that Madame Hafeez wasn't there but they were expecting her to arrive soon. And so, he sat patiently outside the café worrying that anybody observing him might think he was a stalker or peeping tom as he stared at the pretty young woman in a short skirt and skinny t-shirt, illuminated in the shop window by the glaring midday sun, like a living mannequin.

After a sleepless night, he'd risen early determined that he was not going to spend the rest of the day mooching around, brooding over yesterday's revelations. He'd wasted too many hours of his life agonising over events, weighing up the pros and cons of how to react, only to end up paralysed by indecision, doing nothing. He couldn't carry on like that. The predicament he was in was too serious. However many times he sat in front of his laptop reading and re-reading Julia's emails, their meaning wasn't going to change. So, he decided to print them off and go into Villefranche to present them to Judge Bouchon. Of course, the Judge would probably know about them already but at least it would give him the opportunity to squeeze some up-to-date information out of Bouchon.

The Judge's secretary was perfunctory when he arrived in her office and told her he had some important information and needed to see the Judge urgently.

"The Judge is busy. You can't see him without an appointment." As she spoke, she flipped through a large leather-bound desk diary. "I could squeeze you in after lunch tomorrow."

"I don't think you understand. I have important new evidence in the Julia Wainwright case. I need to see him now."

"I don't think you understand, Monsieur Halliday. The Judge has just started an interview. I should think it will last at least another hour. If you want, you can wait until he's finished. He has another appointment immediately after but, if you have important new evidence, he might be able to squeeze you in. Alternatively, you could leave details of the information you have with me and, when he's looked at it, he could call you." She peered up at him over her half-rimmed reading glasses. She was obviously well-practiced in dealing with disgruntled visitors.

Jeremy was exasperated. Just as he was attempting to change the habits of a lifetime and had finally forced himself to be pro-active, obstacles were being put in his way. The last thing he wanted to do was sit outside Judge Bouchon's office churning everything around in his head for the next hour, especially when he knew that his 'new' evidence probably wasn't going to be new at all.

"Okay. I'll come back later. If you could tell him that I was here and I need to see him urgently." Before she could reply, he turned and walked out of the office.

He was resolute that he was not going to let go of his new-found dynamism. If he couldn't get to see the Judge, he would put plan B into action. He recalled his conversation with Guy about the laziness of the French police – the fact that, having settled on him as the most likely suspect, they wouldn't waste their efforts looking any further. If Guy was right, then maybe he should take things into his own hands. As he headed back to his car, he felt in his jacket pocket to check that it contained the slip of paper on which he'd written the address of Mireille Hafeez's shop. He'd always fancied himself as a private detective – a watered down Philip Marlowe – even though the mean streets of Decazeville were a long way from Los Angeles, in atmosphere as well as distance. He hadn't paused to consider what he would do if she wasn't at the shop. He certainly couldn't have imagined that, as he was talking to his secretary, Mireille Hafeez was metres away from him being grilled by Judge Bouchon.

As he was about to order another coffee, a silver Peugeot estate pulled up on the other side of the road and a young woman in sunglasses, wearing a flouncy white summer dress, her blond hair tied back in a ponytail, got out, walked towards Joli Printemps and unlocked the door with a key she'd taken from her handbag. Jeremy's stomach tightened. He checked the bill on the table in front of him and counted out a handful of change. When he knocked on the shop door, the same assistant he'd spoken to earlier appeared. She looked him up and down suspiciously through the glass before opening the door.

"Hi. My name's Jeremy Halliday. I came earlier to see Madame Hafeez. Is she here now?"

The young woman had only opened the door a sliver. "What is it you want to see her about?" She said.

"It's a personal matter."

"What did you say your name was again?"

"Halliday. Jeremy Halliday."

"Just a minute." She closed and locked the door on him and he watched her through the glass panel as she walked across the shop, past the counter and through a door at the back. The wait started to play on Jeremy's nerves but now he'd come this far, he wasn't going to allow himself to get cold feet.

The shop assistant returned and opened the door wider this time. "Go through to the office," she said, indicating the door at the back of the shop.

Jeremy walked between the display tables containing handbags, hats and scarves. The girl in the mini-skirt had stepped out of the window and was staring at him warily. He wondered if she'd noticed him watching her from the café.

As he entered the office, Mireille Hafeez stood up from behind her desk, her expression as full of suspicion as those of her two assistants.

"Hello. I'm Mireille Hafeez. How can I help you?"

Jeremy shook her hand across the desk. It was obvious she hadn't recognised his name and had no idea who he was. There were dark shadows under her eyes and her pretty elfin face looked pale and drawn.

"Jeremy Halliday," he repeated as if it might jog her memory, but there was still no sign of recognition. "I'm...... er, that is to say I *was* Julia Wainwright's partner."

She stood still for a moment, staring blankly at him. He wondered if she hadn't understood his faltering French. Before he could reformulate what he had said, she abruptly sank into her chair as if her legs wouldn't hold her up. He waited but she didn't say anything. She just stared at him in puzzlement. Now that he had carried out his plan and was stood in front of her, he was no longer so sure that his decision that morning to leap into action had been such a good one after all. Too much thought and too little action may not have served him well in the past, but was action without much thought serving him any better? Belatedly, he was realising that he should have used the hour he'd spent sitting outside the café working out what he wanted to say to her.

Finally, he found some words to break the ice. "Do you speak English?"

She nodded imperceptibly.

"Because my French is not great so, if it's alright, I'll speak in English."

She nodded again. Her continued silence was unnerving him.

He held up his hands in supplication. "I want to start by reassuring you that I've not come here in anger. I'm not a violent man. You have no need to be scared. I'm not going to have a go at you. I've come to see you because I want to try and understand what happened to Julia." He hesitated. Mireille sat, frozen, transfixed by his words. "You see – I know about you and Julia," he continued. "About what was going on between the two of you – at least, I think I know. I just need to find out……"

As he tailed off, tongue-tied, Mireille found her voice. It was resolute, authoritative.

"I'm sorry but I can't speak to you about this. I know nothing about Julia's death. And what little I do know I have already told the police. I must ask you to leave."

Jeremy had been considering whether to sit down in the cane chair at the side of the desk but now he stood hovering, uncertain what to do.

He decided to ignore what she'd said and soldier on. "You see, the police think that I murdered Julia – which, of course, I didn't. I only found out yesterday about the two of you – that you were having...So, I want to find out for myself what happened. If you could tell me......"

"I can't tell you anything." She had raised her voice. "There is nothing I can say to help you. I must ask you again to leave. If you do not, I will call the police." Her voice was calm, firm and growing in volume with each sentence.

The office door opened slowly and the two young shop assistants stood hesitantly looking in.

"Is everything alright, Mireille?" The girl from the window asked.

"Yes Sylvie. Monsieur Halliday was just leaving. If you could show him out please?"

Jeremy stared at Mireille trying to think of something else he could say and then turned towards the girls in the doorway. All three women were not much over five foot tall and he towered over them. Mireille Hafeez observed him with a look of unruffled authority. The younger women were visibly frightened, not understanding what was going on, and too nervous to ask. Their eyes were fixed on Jeremy, waiting apprehensively for his next move. Transfixed in the women's three-way stare, Jeremy pictured how he must look to them. Once he'd made his decision to act, he'd left the house in a hurry that morning before he could change his mind. He hadn't showered – he couldn't remember if he'd even washed or brushed his hair. He must look a mess – an intimidating, wild-eyed mess.

"I'm sorry. I guess I shouldn't have come." He walked towards the door. The girls sprang back in identical movements, as if choreographed, to let him pass. He felt his face reddening as he hurried across to the shop door and then fumbled for several seconds with the locks before opening it. Outside, he took several deep breaths and glanced up and down the street trying to remember in which direction he'd parked the car. As he headed off, he didn't look back at the shop, knowing the girls would be at the door watching him leave.

So much for his new dynamic self.

21

Mireille decided to abandon what she was going to do and go home early. She couldn't bear the anxious glances Sylvie and Sandrine directed at her every time she entered the shop even though she had assured them that she was fine. They were too polite and considerate to ask her directly what it had been about. When she told them that she was leaving – she'd decided to spend the rest of the afternoon working from home – the look of concern on their faces made her feel obliged to offer some explanation.

"It's nothing for you to worry about," she told them. "It was a misunderstanding. He was confused. He mistook me for someone else and then wouldn't believe that I wasn't the person he thought I was." She knew it sounded pathetic and wouldn't reassure them at all but any attempt to embellish her lie would only make it worse so she beat a hasty retreat.

Her mind had been in turmoil after her interview with Judge Bouchon. All she could think about on the drive back to Decazeville was how, and what, she was going to tell Mohammed. And then, on top of that, to be confronted by Julia's partner as soon as she got back. All the clichéd metaphors came to mind – lightning striking twice, kicking a woman when she's down, it never rains but it pours – but nothing could adequately sum up the day she had had. And it was a long way from over. She hadn't slept at all the previous night and, as she drove home, what she wanted to do more than anything was to curl up in bed, fall asleep and hope that she would wake up refreshed and with a clear head. But she knew that wasn't going to happen.

Why was this happening to her? It was so unfair. Until the affair with Julia, she'd lived a blameless life. She'd been the perfect, obedient child. Never even gone through the wayward rebellious teenager stage. Never taken drugs. She could recall just one occasion when she'd been mildly drunk. She'd only had one sexual partner before Mohammed and, except for Julia, she'd been faithful to her husband. Yes, she'd been a fool but, in the end, she had come to her senses and ended it. She should have been able to put it all behind her. Julia back in England, out of her life, and Mohammed none the wiser. Everything back to normal. All her frustrated energy redirected into making a success of her new business.

On her way home, she stopped at the hypermarket to get some food for the evening meal and, as soon as she arrived home, she set about preparing it. But the routine activities of chopping vegetables and mixing a pasta sauce couldn't take her mind off what was going to happen later that evening. What she needed more than anything was someone she could talk to: an empathetic friend who could offer her sage advice and a shoulder to cry on. But this was a problem that was much too big, too serious, to burden any of her friends with. In most circumstances, her mother was her first port of call when there were problems in her life but there was no way she could talk to her mother about this. The mere thought of her mother finding out gave her a hollow feeling in her stomach. No, she was on her own. However shattering the interview with Judge Bouchon had been, there was one sliver of comfort she could take from it. She would no longer have to cover things up. It would all have to come out in the open and, however awful the consequences might be for her and Mohammed, at least she wouldn't have to experience the continuing daily fear of being found out.

Standing outside the school waiting for Nathalie, she saw Marie Joubert staring intently at her from the other side of the playground. As their eyes met, they simultaneously turned away in embarrassment. Looking around, Mireille realised that she was the only mother standing on her own. All the others were chatting together in pairs or small groups. A sickening feeling came over her that she must be the prime subject of their gossip. She knew that Marie Joubert had been questioned by the gendarmes about collecting Nathalie from school that Tuesday afternoon. And now, she was avoiding Mireille. How much did she know, or suspect, about the reasons for that interrogation? And how many of these other mothers might also have been questioned? Rumours must be spreading like the flu. And then there was Sylvie and Sandrine at the shop. Of course, they had been questioned too. No wonder they had been staring at her with such suspicion.

It was a relief when Nathalie came running across the playground and leapt into her arms. Mireille hurried her out onto the street and into the sanctuary of the car. As they drove home, her daughter's stream of chatter about the events of her day put a stop for the time being to her growing paranoia that rumours about her affair with Julia Wainwright were spreading round the whole town.

Mireille was in the kitchen completing the final preparations for dinner when Mohammed arrived home earlier than usual. She could hear Nathalie's excited greetings coming from the living room before Mohammed appeared at the kitchen door.

"So, how did it go today?" He couldn't keep the anxiety out of his voice. Mireille stopped stirring the pasta sauce and turned to face him. He hadn't taken off his jacket and was still clutching his briefcase. "I was expecting you to phone me. I've been on tenterhooks all day," he continued. "Didn't you get my text messages?" Now the anxiety was replaced with a hint of irritation.

"No I didn't. I'm sorry. I've been up to my ears. As soon as the interview with Judge Bouchon was over, I had to rush back to the shop. There were loads of annoying little problems to sort out. I didn't get a second to check my phone."

It wasn't entirely a lie. She hadn't checked her phone, not through lack of time, but because she knew Mohammed would be calling and texting her.

"Well. Are you going to tell me what happened?"

"Papa, Papa. Come and look at my drawings." Nathalie tugged at her father's sleeve pulling him off balance. Mohammed gently extricated himself from her grip.

"Go back inside, cherie. I'll be there in a minute. I have to talk to your mother about something."

"Oh Papa." Nathalie pouted her lips in an exaggerated sulk.

"Go with her," Mireille said. "We haven't got time to talk about it now. Wait till she's gone to bed."

Mohammed opened his mouth, about to argue with her, but Nathalie was tugging at his sleeve again, this time pulling his jacket half off his shoulder. He tightened his lips, sighed and allowed his daughter to lead him away by the arm.

Dinner was tense. There was little conversation except for Nathalie's babbling stream of consciousness snippets. As soon as the meal was over, Mohammed volunteered to put Nathalie to bed and ushered her upstairs ignoring her protests that it was too early. Mireille stacked the dinner things in the dishwasher, poured herself another large glass of wine and took it through to the living room, placing it on a coaster on the marble-topped coffee table. She was about to sit on the sofa but then changed her mind and walked round the table to the white leather armchair. She didn't want to have Mohammed sitting next to her. She needed to be facing him, to observe his reactions.

"You're silence has got me worried," Mohammed said as he sat down opposite her. "I'm getting the feeling that things couldn't have gone well. Tell me what happened."

"Can I get you a glass of wine?"

"No," Mohammed said tetchily. "Stop piling on the suspense. This is not some television melodrama."

He was right. She couldn't prevaricate any longer, so she dived straight in. "Most of his questions were about my missing phone. He had a log of all the calls and messages sent from it. The last one was a text message sent to Julia on the morning of the day she died asking her to meet me in a café in Aurillac."

Mohammed interrupted. "I presume you told him you'd lost the phone so you couldn't have sent the text?"

"Yes."

"And what did he say to that?"

Mireille was staring intently at her husband, trying to gauge his reactions to everything she said. He was sprawled back on the sofa, his arms spread wide, appearing relaxed or, as it seemed to Mireille, trying to give the impression that he was relaxed.

"Naturally, he didn't believe me. You can't blame him. As he said to me – who else could have sent it?"

Mohammed said nothing at first, perhaps thinking of possible answers to the Judge's question. "I suppose he has a point," he said finally. "Maybe you're mistaken. Are you sure you didn't still have the phone then and lose it later? Perhaps you did send the message and you've forgotten about it?"

She gave him an exasperated look. "What do you take me for? A complete idiot? I......"

Mohammed held up his hand to stop her. "It's easy to forget things especially when you've been under so much stress recently. It's not easy starting your own business. I think you underestimated just how difficult it would be. I did warn you about working so hard. If you remember, I wanted to prescribe you some tranquillizers." He was talking to her as if she were one of his patients which annoyed Mireille even more.

"For God's sake, Mohammed. You know me better than that. I'm not some neurotic woman who collapses under pressure. Or maybe that is your image of me? Maybe that's the way you see all women?"

"Oh don't start throwing that sexism crap at me. It's nothing to do with you being a woman. Stress effects everybody. There's no need to be so defensive."

"Mohammed. I – did – not – send – that – text. My phone had gone missing." She enunciated each word slowly and volubly as if he was hard of hearing. "When the Judge saw that text message, he suspected me of murdering Julia."

"What? Are you joking? The man is obviously incompetent. Why on earth would you kill this woman? Because she was late delivering your orders?" He gave a forced laugh.

"Fortunately, I can account for my movements that day. I can prove I was nowhere near Aurillac." She paused and took a deep breath. "What about you? Where were you that Tuesday afternoon?"

Mohammed raised his eyebrows. "What's that got to do with anything? You think I might have murdered this English woman?" He produced a strangled chuckle. "What possible reason could I have to kill a woman I never even knew?"

She had been trying desperately to hold out, hold back the truth, hoping there was some way she could explain what happened in her interview without revealing her affair with Julia. But now she knew she had to bow to the inevitable.

"As I already said, for Judge Bouchon it all comes down to the fact that, if I didn't send that message to Julia, then someone else must have done. He suspects that someone could have been you."

There was no change in Mohammed's body language or expression. "That's ridiculous," he said in a calm voice.

"Well, he doesn't think so. That's why he's going to contact you tomorrow to call you in for questioning."

He laughed sardonically. "That'll be a waste of his time and mine."

Mireille drank the rest of her wine trying to steady herself while keeping her eyes on Mohammed as she spoke, although she had a powerful desire to look away.

"He has a good reason for wanting to question you. The other thing he found out was that I had been having an affair with Julia Wainwright. He thinks you found out about it and – voila – there's your motive."

There was still no change in Mohammed's expression. No sign of shock. It was obvious to Mireille that he already knew about it. He sat in silence, unmoving, as if turned to stone.

The tension was too much for Mireille. "Don't you have anything to say? You knew about us, didn't you?"

He lifted a hand to his brow and massaged his temples as if attempting to soothe a sudden headache.

"Of course I knew."

She waited for him to elaborate but he stayed silent.

"How did you find out? Why didn't you say anything?"

"Does it matter how I found out?" Now anger was creeping into his voice. "Let's just say that you weren't as discreet as you thought. Let's face it, things haven't been right between us for quite a while. At first, I put it down to your stress over the shop. But then my suspicions grew. Naturally, I suspected it was another man."

"So you just kept it bottled up? You didn't say anything? You didn't do anything about it?" She emphasised the word 'do'. She felt a huge sense of relief. There was no longer the icy feeling in her stomach. She'd feared an angry violent reaction but he remained in the same position, slumped on the sofa, emotionless.

"I took your phone that morning. I looked up the recent messages you'd sent each other. There was one from her sent that morning saying she was still in Aurillac but was about to head back to England so I sent her the text message arranging the meeting." He made it sound disconcertingly matter-of-fact. "When I first found out about the two of you, I was confused. I didn't want to believe it. Of course, I was very angry – disgusted, sickened. If it was a man, it might have been easier. But a woman. I couldn't understand it. It didn't make any sense. You weren't a lesbian. You couldn't be. Did I feel violent towards you? Of course I did. But I'm not a violent man. You know that. Once I'd calmed down and had time to think, I decided that I didn't want to have any more to do with you. I booked a flight to Morocco for myself and Nathalie. My plan was to wait until the day of the flight and then tell you it was all over between us. I wanted to keep any unpleasantness to a minimum. I didn't want a big scene, any lengthy arguments. I wanted to protect Nathalie as best as I could. It would be a fait accompli. Before we set off for the airport, I would tell you to pack your bags and be out of the house by the time we got back. My intention was that you would never see Nathalie again. But then, as the day drew nearer, I started to have second thoughts. Mainly thoughts about Nathalie. Could

I really stop her from ever seeing you again? Was there an alternative plan? Anyway, that's when I decided to try and speak with the English woman."

Mireille sat anaesthetised, struggling to take it all in. He was so low key, dispassionate. He may as well have been telling her about his day at the surgery or the people he'd met at the café at lunchtime. It was hard to believe that he was describing decisions that would change their lives. She found it less difficult to picture the emotional changes in himself that he was describing. It chimed in with what had first attracted her to him. Outwardly, he had been such a handsome, intelligent, powerful, masculine figure; a man who knew what he wanted from life and would make sure he got it. And yet, underneath, she could sense the remnants of an uncertain nervous boy who put on a domineering act to cover up his vulnerability. It was that consciousness of the hidden vulnerable Mohammed that had persuaded her to stay with him during those times when she'd found him disturbingly overbearing.

"So what did you say to her? What did you do?" She had to force the words out, both wanting and not wanting to hear his answer.

"I didn't say or do anything. I didn't go to meet her. I read the other messages on your phone. I saw that she was going back to England and it sounded like it might be all over between you. What I suppose I was going to tell her was to keep away from you. I would have tried to make her feel guilty – make her face up to the fact that, if your relationship carried on, she would be ruining your life and the life of our daughter. But then I thought that, if you didn't turn up to this meeting she thought you'd arranged, then that might send a more powerful message than anything I could say to her."

They sat in silence for a while. Night was falling and the

room was growing dark but neither of them made a move to switch on a light.

"And then you got the news about her death," he continued, "and that changed everything. It was like a message from God. A punishment for her sins. I still felt disgusted with you. Ashamed. But I started to think that maybe I should give it time. Perhaps I could overcome those feelings and keep our family together. I had to put Nathalie's future before my own feelings."

His implied accusation hit home. She felt the pain of it even as she was angered by how unfair it was. Yes, she had put her own feelings first when she started the relationship with Julia. She'd tried not to think about Nathalie and the possible consequences. But, in the end, it had been over between them because she had put Nathalie first, despite the pain and regret she had felt.

"Anyway, I booked a ticket for you on the flight to Morocco. I thought, if we could get away together for a while as a family, then it might be a start at getting everything back to normal."

He paused. Mireille waited to see if he was going to continue. She didn't know whether to believe him or not. What he said sounded heartfelt and honest but she found his tone unconvincing. Most of his story sounded plausible but she could detect holes that the Judge would surely expose.

"So what are you going to say to Judge Bouchon?" She said.

"Nothing. I didn't meet her. Like you, I wasn't anywhere near Aurillac." He put both hands up to rub his forehead as if massaging his brain into action. "I think it's best that I don't tell him anything. I just tell him that, until now, I didn't know anything about you and this English woman. That I don't know anything about your missing phone or the text message."

"Is that a good idea? If you're innocent – if what you have said is true – then wouldn't it be better to tell the truth? If he catches you out lying about it, then you will definitely look guilty."

"You don't believe me, do you? You think I killed her." For the first time, there was real anger in his voice. "We've been married for eight years and you still don't know me. You think I'm some barbarian Moroccan Muslim who thinks women are inferior and should be the slaves of men. Okay, I admit I was furious when I found out about you having sex with this woman. I was disgusted at the thought of it. Sure, I felt violent towards both of you. Just as violent as if you'd been having sex with another man. Any man would feel like that. But that doesn't mean that I could have killed anybody."

"Of course I don't think you murdered her." She tried to sound more confident than she felt. "I'm just trying to put myself in the Judge's position." She paused to consider the kind of questions he might be asked. "For example, if you didn't go to Aurillac that afternoon, where were you?"

He stifled his anger and took a deep breath to calm himself. She was right. He needed to think carefully about what he was going to tell the Judge. "I went for a long walk by the river. While I was there, I took the SIM card out of the phone and destroyed it and then I threw the phone in the river. I didn't need to go back to the surgery because I'd cancelled my appointments for the rest of the day, thinking that I'd be going to Aurillac. I can't remember exactly where I walked. I was doing a lot of thinking. My mind was in turmoil. All I remember is that, sometime later that afternoon, I went back to the surgery to sort out some paperwork and then I went home."

Mireille had that sinking feeling in her stomach again. "So what you're saying is that you don't have an alibi for that afternoon?"

"I don't know. I might have. It depends if Shamsun at reception remembers what time I returned." He paused, giving it more thought. "Whatever time it was, I doubt it would have been possible for me to drive to Aurillac, kill the English woman and then drive back." He paused and scratched the stubble on his head. "How do we know what time she died?"

"I assume it was sometime that afternoon. That's when the gendarmes were checking up on my whereabouts," she said.

They sat motionless in the growing gloom. Mireille could barely make out the expression on her husband's face. "I still think you should tell him the truth, especially if you have an alibi."

"No. I can't see how it would be a good idea to tell him about the phone and the text message. It was a stupid thing to do. If they know I arranged a meeting with her, pretending to be you, and then she's murdered a couple of hours later – well, they're bound to think I did it. I'd just be incriminating myself." He thrust his arms in the air and stretched, arching his back and yawning. "Anyway, I can't talk about this anymore. I'm exhausted. I'm going to bed."

Mireille's mind was focussed on trying to piece together the timeline of Mohammed's actions that day. "Have you checked with Shamsun if she remembers what time you got back to the surgery that afternoon?"

"Mireille. Are you listening to me? I don't want to talk about it anymore. I'm going to bed. Are you coming up?"

Mireille looked at him as if he was a stranger she'd met in a bar offering her a one-night stand.

"I'd prefer it if you slept in the spare room tonight," she said.

"I should sleep in the spare room?" It was too dark for her to see the angry incredulous look on his face. "You're

the one who's committed adultery – who's fucked this......
woman, but I'm the one who should be banished to the
spare room?"

"Alright. I'm sorry. I'll sleep in the spare room."

"No, no. Don't bother. I'll move in there."

He sprung off the sofa sending it screeching back on the
parquet floor and headed for the door.

He turned round as he got there. "It's a waste of time
talking to you. I don't know why I bothered. After all the
efforts I've been making to hold this family together. As
soon as I found out I should have thrown you out into the
gutter where you belong."

After he'd disappeared upstairs, Mireille remained
immobile in the darkness not wanting to move until he'd
taken his stuff from their room and was safely in bed. But
then a sudden feeling of nausea rose up from her stomach to
her throat. She rushed to the downstairs bathroom, arriving
just in time to kneel down and throw up into the toilet.

22

"What do you think? Is he telling the truth?" The Judge directed the question at Gilles Montfort who was returning to his seat beside the desk, having seen Mohameed Hafeez to the door at the end of their interview.

Gilles was flattered that Judge Bouchon seemed so eager for his opinion. "I don't know. He's an intelligent, well-educated man. A doctor. You threw everything you could at him but he didn't crack. He sounded quite convincing."

"Yes, but were you convinced?" The judge sounded impatient. He was fishing for a less guarded response.

"Not entirely. But if you're going to ask me why, I'll find it hard to explain. Just a gut feeling that it doesn't fit together. And you, Monsieur le Juge? What do you think?"

"I agree. I just wish he hadn't been so forewarned and prepared for what I was going to ask him. He might have cracked if I could have caught him on the hop. But, even though he sounded plausible, there are some things that don't make sense to me." He paused while he glanced down at his desk pad on which he'd been scribbling notes during the interview. "He said he cancelled his appointments that day because he was feeling unwell. So, he goes home but then he starts to feel better in the afternoon and goes back into work. Sounds strange to me. If you're a doctor, I would think you have to be really ill before you decide to cancel appointments. And, if you're that ill, how do you make such a speedy recovery? It's too convenient. If he did go to Aurillac to meet Julia Wainwright and murder her, then returning to the surgery that afternoon would be an attempt at providing himself with an alibi."

"The receptionist confirms that he came back that afternoon," interrupted Gilles, "but she can't say at exactly what time, only that it must have been before four-thirty because that's the time she leaves to collect her child."

"He could have gone to meet Julia Wainwright at midday, then…if she died at about two o'clock as the autopsy suggests, it's possible that he could have been back at the surgery by four-thirty," said the judge.

There was a moment's silence as they both pondered the timescale before Gilles changed the subject. "How convincing do you think he was when he said he didn't know about his wife's affair until yesterday? We'd need to prove that he already knew to give him a motive."

"I pushed him as hard as I could on it but he didn't budge. The key evidence would be his wife's mobile phone. There's only two possibilities that I can see. Either he took the phone and sent the message or she lied about losing it and sent it herself. Whichever one it is, there's your murderer," said the Judge.

"And if we're wrong and it's neither of those scenarios? Suppose it was some random maniac hitchhiker she picked up?"

Bouchon gave Gilles a disparaging look. "Very few murders are committed by strangers unless as part of a robbery or a rape or sexual assault. There was no evidence that anything had been stolen from the car nor anything in the autopsy to suggest a sexual assault."

The Judge took a deep breath and sat back, staring up at the ceiling. Gilles waited for him to continue but the Judge remained deep in thought.

Gilles decided to probe him further. "And Monsieur

Halliday? What did you make of his sudden discovery of the emails? Is he still a suspect?"

"We can't rule him out although I'm less sure than I was that he could have killed her. I'd put him in the same category as Doctor Hafeez. His motive for killing her is much stronger if he knew when she left him that she was having an affair with Mireille Hafeez."

"So you think he might be lying about only just having discovered the emails?"

"Quite possibly. Put yourself in his position. He knows we suspect him of the murder. He has no alibi. So, he hopes he can deflect suspicion from himself by drawing our attention to other suspects. He can't tell us that he already knew about his partner's affair because that just gives him a stronger motive to kill her so, instead, he pretends he's only just come across the emails."

"You think he's that Machiavellian?" Said Gilles. "He doesn't seem that clever to me."

"I tend to agree with you," said the Judge. "Between the two of them, I think Doctor Hafeez would be the more convincing liar."

"So where do we go from here?" Said Gilles. He asked the question with the rare confidence that Jules Bouchon was as much in the dark about the case as he was and seemed less inclined to adopt his usual tactic of blaming the lack of progress on his subordinates – namely Gilles himself.

"I'm not sure. I've asked the forensic team to go through all the evidence from the car again with as fine a toothcomb as possible. I doubt they'll turn up anything new but I'm desperate for anything we can find." He shrugged his shoulders. "Other than that, I thought I'd call Madame Hafeez in for further questioning. See if I can get her to contradict her husband on when he knew about her affair. Push her in general on whether he has given anything away now that it's all out in the open between them. He might have......"

He was interrupted by a muffled phone ringtone.

"I'm sorry, Monsieur le Juge." Gilles took his phone out of his jacket pocket and checked who the call was from. He looked up at the Judge. "Apologies, but I ought to take this. It's from the Aurillac gendarmerie."

The Judge signalled for him to go ahead.

"Hello. Ah, Jerome." He bent forward listening intently to the voice on the other end of the line. "Yes, that is good news," he said after a short while. "Does it show anything of interest?" Another pause. "Okay. That's excellent, Jerome. We'll have a look at it and I'll get straight back to you." He switched off the phone and looked at the Judge with a self-satisfied smile.

"Switch on your computer," he said to Bouchon. "It's possible we have some good news at last. Our colleagues in Aurillac have come across some new surveillance camera footage. A bank round the corner from the café in Aurillac has a camera focussed on its entrance and they've discovered some footage from that Tuesday lunchtime showing Julia Wainwright's car which was parked outside. They've transferred it through to us although he warned me that the quality isn't very good."

Minutes later, sitting side by side in front of the computer screen, they downloaded and started to run the video surveillance film. The Aurillac gendarmes were right – the picture quality was poor. Both men leaned closer to the screen, their brows furrowed, their eyes squinting in a vain attempt to transform the fuzzy images into state-of-the-art high definition. They had no trouble recognising Julia Wainwright's dark blue Golf on the left of the screen. Several people walked backwards and forwards along the pavement and then a blond-haired woman in a long-sleeved top and jeans stopped by the side of the car and opened the driver's door. Her back was to the camera so it wasn't possible to identify her positively as Julia Wainwright. Judge Bouchon pressed the pause button, rewound it and they both squinted even harder as they watched her enter on the right-hand side of the screen. They still couldn't get a clear sight of her face. The Judge let the video roll on. She tossed her shoulder bag across to the front passenger seat and started to climb into the car. As they watched what happened next, both men bent their heads even closer to the screen almost touching foreheads, desperate to get as good a view as possible of what was unfolding.

23

As the two gravediggers in their corporation blue overalls began to shovel earth on to the coffin, the handful of mourners shuffled past Jeremy shaking his hand and offering their condolences once again before wending their way down the central path to the cemetery gates. There were six of them; two distant cousins who Jeremy vaguely remembered having met at his mother's funeral, three of his father's ex-colleagues from work and the deputy manager of the care home. It was a pitiful send-off, Jeremy thought, but perhaps better than might have been expected for an old man who had lived alone for the past twenty years and spent the last five of those in a care home with Alzheimers.

On receiving the news of his father's death, he had asked the gendarmerie if they could return his passport so he could go to London for the funeral. He had anticipated a sympathetic refusal but the French police had, without delay, returned his passport and given him permission to go. To his surprise, Judge Bouchon made no stipulation about when, or even whether, he would be required to return to France. He accepted the passport's return with a mixture of gratitude and befuddlement. It was only once he was back in England that he considered that it might be a sign that he was no longer a suspect in Julia's murder. Such was his downbeat mood that the thought left him neither elated nor even relieved. Just numb. The news of his father's death hit him harder than he could have imagined. Having made up his mind when they moved to France that he would probably never see his father again, he would have expected his death to have little or no effect other than relief that it was one less burden on his finances. He even started to cry – something he hadn't done since he was a child; not even when he'd received the news of Julia's death.

Standing alone by the graveside with light summer raindrops peppering his face and rolling down the back of his neck, watching the earth engulfing the shiny oak coffin, he understood the reason for those tears. It wasn't grief for a father he'd never felt close to and who he'd been convinced had brought his mother's life to a premature end. It was grief for himself. As an only child brought up by a single parent from the age of twelve, he'd always been something of a loner. But now, with the death of his father following on so closely after Julia's, he was more alone than he'd ever been.

He'd closed up the house in Vendillac, turned off the water and electricity and left a set of keys with Guy so he could keep an eye on it. He told him he'd only be gone for a couple of weeks but now he wasn't so sure. He was at a loss to know where he really belonged. Although he'd heard nothing from Hattie about settling Julia's estate, it could only be a matter of time and then the house would have to be sold. He knew he should have sought some legal advice on any entitlements he might have to the proceeds from the sale but there had been too much else on his mind. Even if he could cobble together enough money to buy a small place for himself somewhere around Vendillac, did he want to carry on living in France? There was his gardening business which had been going well before Julia's death and which he was sure he could revive. But did he want to? He had considered the Merrigans and the other English families he'd done gardening work for as his friends but, since

Julia's death, even if he was no longer a suspect, he knew he wouldn't feel comfortable socialising with any of them. Apart from Guy, he had nobody else he could call a friend in France.

But what was there for him in London? He'd kept in desultory contact with some ex-colleagues and old friends, swapping the occasional emails and Christmas cards, but the only visitors they'd had at the house in Vendillac had been Julia's friends and he was sure he'd now be persona non grata with them. He'd considered contacting some ex-colleagues, such as Roger Worth, or other old school and university friends, on his return to London – he'd even composed a generic email to circulate – but it was still sitting in his 'drafts' mailbox. He couldn't imagine that any of them would be keen to meet up with him. They were now more acquaintances than friends. And if he were to meet them, he wouldn't want to go through the tedious awkwardness of having to tell them about Julia leaving him, her subsequent murder and the ensuing events.

So, he had no family left in London and hardly anybody he could call a friend. And, if he did come back, how would he earn a living? Did he want to go back to teaching? The answer was a firm 'no'. But what was the alternative? It was ridiculously expensive to live in London and, however much money he managed to squeeze out of the sale of the French property and its contents, it wouldn't be enough for him to survive on. He could try and start up a gardening business but that would be much harder than in France and he wouldn't have Julia's earnings to fall back on.

He held the small silver carriage clock up to the light and read the inscription on the back. It had been given to his father by his employers on his retirement. Such a depressing cliché. Just what you needed – something to record all those lonely empty hours, days, months, years stretching out in front of you. He placed it carefully in the large cardboard box on the bed and then wandered round his father's room gathering up the few remaining possessions. Seventy-eight years of life represented by one cardboard box of miscellaneous junk – mostly clothes.

Although his intention had been to pack everything up as quickly as possible and get out of this depressing place, he paused and sat down on the bed as if weighed down by these maudlin thoughts. Was this the way he was going to end up? The difference was that he wouldn't have a son to do this for him. For God's sake, he was only forty-two. He must stop thinking like this. But it was hard to know what else to think. Didn't everyone think this way when their parents died? He scrolled back through the major incidents in his life – everything that had gone wrong and led him to where he was now. If only his mother hadn't died. As the years passed, he'd found it harder and harder to remember what she was like. And when he did conjure up memories of her, he couldn't be sure that they were real. He was probably suffering from – what was that fancy name they gave it? False Memory Syndrome. But he was sure that, unlike his father, she'd been a positive person – optimistic, active, outgoing. If she had been there when he was growing into adulthood, he would have had somebody to talk to. She might have steered him away from the course that had led him to this present impasse in his life. You were supposed to inherit your character traits from your parents. Unfortunately for him, he seemed to have inherited everything from his father and nothing from his mother.

He didn't regret meeting and falling in love with Julia. Their early years together had been the best of his life. If only he hadn't become so stupidly and inappropriately embroiled with Susie Meredith and her problems. If he

303

could turn back time and expunge all that from his past, he and Julia would still be together in the house in Tooting, maybe with one or more of their own children. Or, if he couldn't erase the Susie Meredith debacle from his life story, maybe it was the move to France that never should have happened. If they'd stayed in London......if he'd stayed in teaching......had he even wanted to move to France? Wasn't it Julia who'd been the enthusiastic one? Hadn't she dragged him off to the middle of nowhere only to have an affair with that French woman and then abandon him? No. This wouldn't do. He must stop beating himself up by blaming everything on her.He must stop thinking about the past, full-stop. *Je Ne Regrette Rien* had never been one of his favourite songs and as for that awful *My Way*. He had a cornucopia of regrets, not least the fact that doing things 'his way' had mostly ended in calamity. He needed to get back to thinking about the future.

Until a week ago, he'd still been clinging to the fantasy of a burgeoning relationship with Ruth Gershon. Something had clicked between them. He was sure he hadn't imagined it. But circumstances had intervened and he'd had no chance to do anything about it. On the same day that he received the news of his father's death, she had knocked at the door.

She was bright-eyed and smiley. "Hi Jeremy. Hope I haven't disturbed you."

"Not at all. I was just pottering around. How can I help? No problems in the gîte, I hope?"

"No. Everything's fine." She hesitated, looking a bit shifty. "I've come to tell you that I've changed my mind. I'm not going to stay on in the gite after all. In fact, I've decided to head off back home tomorrow. Now that I've had some time to think about what's happened and it's started to sink in, I feel it's silly to put things off. I need to go back and start to sort my life out as soon as possible."

Jeremy could feel himself deflating. Now they'd got to know each other and shared intimate details of their lives, he'd hoped that, in the remaining three weeks of her stay, he'd have plenty of time to transform their budding friendship into something a smidgeon more romantic. He smiled inanely at her and said nothing. He would have needed all of those three weeks. He wasn't the sort of man who acted on the spur of the moment.

"I hope I haven't messed things up for you," she said. "You know...stopped you from taking other bookings. I'll pay for those extra two weeks you've booked me in for."

"Don't be daft. You don't need to do that. I haven't had any other enquiries. In fact, I can refund you for some of the time you've already paid for."

"Now you're being daft. I booked and paid for the two weeks. I don't need a refund."

"Okay. Well......I'm sorry to see you go." It was the closest he could get to the more intimate things he would have liked to say.

"I'm sorry to be leaving so soon. I've loved it here. Maybe I'll be back some day." Jeremy nodded. "Anyway, I'd better go back and start my packing."

The following morning, they'd swapped the briefest of goodbyes before she got in her car and crunched off up the driveway. No kiss. Just a cordial handshake. For Jeremy, it had been a much too conclusive goodbye. He kicked himself afterwards for not saying something, however trifling, to leave a channel open for future communication. Still, he had her email address and mobile phone number. If he did decide to stay in London, she was the one person he would definitely try to contact.

He circled the room for the final time checking the wardrobe and cupboard drawers to make sure he'd left nothing behind. The presiding colours in the room were beige and brown alleviated slightly by the powder-blue candlewick bedspread and the 1970s full-length floral curtains. Being in the room made him feel thirty years older. He picked the box up from the bed. It was heavier than he'd expected – and flimsier. It sagged in the middle and he had to thrust his arms underneath to support it.

He put it down on the floor in front of the reception desk.

"All finished Mr Halliday?" Said Mrs Eldridge, the care home manager as she emerged from the office behind the reception.

"Yes," he said, gesturing towards the cardboard box. "The room's all yours."

"Once again, Mr Halliday, please accept our sincerest condolences. Your father was a lovely man – a gentleman. He'll be very much missed by the staff and the other residents."

She sounded sincere but Jeremy assumed that it was one of a stock list of homilies that she was used to delivering considering the frequency with which her clients passed away. He was sure his father had been very little trouble but doubted he'd be missed. Even before his Alzheimers had worsened, when Jeremy had been a more frequent visitor to the home, he'd not been aware of his father having any particular friends.

"Thank you," he said and pointed down at the box again. "I hope you don't think I'm being cheeky but I was wondering if you could help me out. You see I'm living in temporary accommodation in London and I don't have any transport. It's going to be difficult to carry. I can't take it on the bus. I could call a taxi but, to be honest, there's nothing among my father's rather minimal possessions that I want to keep."

He paused, leaving space for her to second guess him and offer to help but all she said was, "surely there must be some keepsake to remind you of him?"

"No, honestly, there isn't. I hope you don't think I'm being presumptuous but could I possibly leave the box here? Maybe some of the residents might appreciate some of the things. To be honest, all I'd do with them is take them to a charity shop."

Mrs Eldridge stared down into the box with a dubious expression, like a pawnshop owner about to make a derisory offer. "If you're sure you don't want it, I suppose we might find a home for some of it."

Jeremy breathed in the diesel fumes of the heavy goods vehicles roaring past him as he walked down the Kingston Road towards the bus-stop. Unpleasant as it was, it was a relief from the smell of old-age and death.

EPILOGUE

Julia loved this café – L'Abside. It was like a charming carbuncle sprouting from the side of a beautiful medieval church in Aurillac. She was seated on a scuffed, sagging leather armchair in a far corner from where she had a clear view of the entrance as she waited for Mireille to arrive. She looked at her watch for what must have been the twentieth time. Twelve-thirty. She checked her phone again. Mireille's text had definitely specified twelve o'clock and there'd been no further message to say that she was running late. Julia was trying to leave off phoning her for as long as possible. She wanted to appear cool and detached. She'd accepted that it was all over between them and, despite the pain it had caused her, she had persuaded herself it was for the best. Nevertheless, she couldn't help feeling a shiver of excited apprehension when she'd received Mireille's text. There were only two possible reasons she could see for the meeting – either Mireille had changed her mind and wanted their relationship to continue or she wanted to say a final face to face goodbye. Julia thought the latter more likely and, so, didn't want to appear over-anxious about Mireille's lateness. She was trying, with limited success, to dampen down any hope that it was the former reason.

But how much longer should she wait before calling Mireille? Or maybe it was best not to phone her at all but just walk away, taking it as a sign that she'd changed her mind. Even if Mireille was coming to make a plea that they stay together, perhaps being older and wiser, she should be the mature sensible one who resists her inner passion and puts a firm end to the relationship. But then, if she had been mature and sensible, she would never have got involved in the first place. She'd had no such qualms about her previous affair with Marc Dessailly – and he was also married with young children. The thought of breaking up his marriage hadn't bothered her. When he ended their affair, she accepted it with barely a flicker of emotion, proving to herself what, deep down, she already knew – she didn't love him. With Mireille, it was because Julia loved her that she knew it had been right for it to end. Mireille was the one taking all the risks. Julia knew it was all over between her and Jeremy before they met. For Mireille, there was much more at stake. Julia was glad she'd never met her husband or daughter. Just seeing photos of them when she visited their house had made her feel queasy.

But it wasn't only Mireille and her family she was thinking about. If she was honest, she wasn't being entirely selfless in accepting the end of their relationship. Since leaving university, she'd bounced from one boyfriend to another. She'd never lived on her own for more than two or three months at a time. One failed relationship followed on swiftly from the last as if she was desperate at the thought of being alone. Once she'd made the decision to leave Jeremy, she felt liberated; determined, at last, to spend time on her own; give herself a lengthy breathing space in which to think seriously about what she wanted for the future. And then she'd met Mireille and all her plans were thrown up into the air. At first, she told herself it didn't matter. This time she wasn't repeating the past. Because it was with a woman, it was different from all those other relationships she'd jumped straight into. This would be an even bigger, more important, change in her life than her simple plan to live on her own.

Now she was no longer sure what she was feeling. If Mireille walked into the café in the next few minutes and announced she wanted them to spend the rest of their lives together, could she really turn her down? The more she thought about it the better she thought it would be if she walked out now before it was too late so that she was the one making the decision – putting temptation behind her. Another look at the watch. Twelve forty-five. This was stupid. She shouldn't go without talking to Mireille or at least leaving her a message. She dialled the number and hung on for over a minute as it rang waiting for it to go to voicemail, but nothing happened. She tried again. Same result.

Once she was outside, she paused to glance up and down the street for any sign of Mireille approaching. She waited for half a minute as if glued to the pavement before striding purposefully down the road, resisting the urge to glance backwards, and turned the corner heading for her parked car. She pressed the key fob to open it, placed her bag on the passenger seat and was about to walk round to the driver's door when two men in grey suits approached her. They looked to be in their thirties with identical dark skins and short black hair. She assumed they must be brothers. One of them had a thin close-cropped beard. He held out a laminated card with his photo on it.

"Julia Wainwright?" He said.

She took her eyes off the card and looked at him. "Yes."

"We're police," he continued, putting the card back in his jacket pocket. "Is this your car?"

"Yes it is." She looked at the other parked cars along the street. She'd checked the parking regulations when she arrived and bought a ticket from the machine but maybe her time had run out. She assumed it must be something to do with her being parked illegally.

"Can you open the back of the car for us?" It was still the one with the beard talking. His companion stared at Julia, expressionless.

"I'm sorry, but could you tell me what this is about? If I've gone over time on my parking ticket..."

"If you would just do as I ask, Madame Wainwright. Open the back of the car, please." He sounded impatient, officious.

She shrugged her shoulders, walked round to the back of the car and released the boot catch. The two policemen followed her and stood a metre back staring at the jam-packed contents.

"You have a very full load," the bearded one said with more than a hint of suspicion.

"I'm English," Julia said, starting to feel annoyed. "I've been living in France and I'm on my way back to England."

"So, you are saying that all these things belong to you?"

"Yes, of course they do." She could no longer hide her irritation.

"I have to inform you, Madame Wainwright, that we have received a report that this blue Volkswagen Golf, licence plate number LTO 4ZYN, contains stolen property." Both men continued to stare at her with blank expressions.

"What? That's ridiculous. This is my car and all of this is my property. Would you like to see my car registration document? I think I have it in the glove compartment." She started to move back towards the front of the car.

"That won't be necessary," said the bearded man. "We know it's your car."

Julia stood in silent confusion trying to organise her thoughts. Then it all became clear. "Who reported this stolen property to you?"

"I'm afraid we're not at liberty to say."

"It was Jeremy Halliday, wasn't it?" They continued to

stare inscrutably. "He's my partner – my ex-partner. I've split up with him. That's why I'm returning to England. He feels angry about it, obviously. But I can't believe he'd stoop as low as to do this. Surely you can see how stupid this is? He's just being vindictive."

There was still no change in their expressions. "As I have already said, Madame, we can't comment. We are going to need you to come to the gendarmerie with us for further questioning and to enable us to examine the contents of your car." The bearded man held his hand out towards her. "If you could give me your car keys, I will drive you and my colleague will follow in our car."

Julia stared at the outstretched hand and clutched her keys tightly. She was aware of passers-by slowing down and stopping to observe what was going on. She was fuming but she knew it wouldn't help to create a scene in the middle of the busy street. It was Jeremy she needed to be angry with. How could he do this to her? It was so out of character. But then maybe it showed how little she really knew him. She would never have thought of him as the revengeful type but how could she know how he would react after she'd hurt him so badly? She handed over her keys.

*

Jules Bouchon and Gilles Montfort sat transfixed in front of the screen until the man with the beard and the blond woman, who they could now identify as Julia Wainwright, climbed into the Golf and the car pulled away out of camera range. They sat back and exchanged satisfied smiles before the judge clicked on the mouse and re-ran the footage from the beginning, freeze framing it at several points to have a closer look at the faces of the two men. They were Arabic looking and about the right age but neither of them looked like Mohammed Hafeez. A pity, thought Bouchon, but it didn't matter. This was the breakthrough he'd so desperately needed. Now there was a good chance that he could solve the case and end his career on a high. He felt like raising his fist in a victory salute but, with Gilles Montfort watching him, he decided to maintain his decorum.

Lightning Source UK Ltd.
Milton Keynes UK
UKOW06f2100170216

268585UK00008B/91/P